D0001717

For Primo, who always pulls me up

PRAISE FOR

WARCROSS

A New York Times Bestseller

"[A]s visual, kinetic, and furiously paced as any video game."
—*The New York Times*

"A vibrant, action-packed shot of adrenaline."
—Leigh Bardugo, #1 *New York Times* bestselling author of *Six of Crows*

"All-consuming fantasy."
—*New York* magazine

"Electrifying."
—*Seventeen* magazine

★ "Think *The Hunger Games* meets World of Warcraft."
—*Publishers Weekly*, starred review

"Unlike anything I've ever read . . . It's absolutely fantastic."
—Sabaa Tahir, #1 *New York Times* bestselling author of *An Ember in the Ashes*

★ "A stellar cyberpunk series opener packed with simmering romance and cinematic thrills."
—*Kirkus Reviews*, starred review

"Addictive, fast-paced, and totally immersive . . . *Warcross* is Marie Lu's best book yet."
—Amie Kaufman, *New York Times* bestselling author of *Illuminae*

★ "A highly engaging and incredibly exciting science fiction novel for young adults."
—*School Library Journal*, starred review

"*Warcross* is pure genius. I'm ready for the sequel!"
—Kami Garcia, #1 *New York Times* bestselling coauthor of *Beautiful Creatures* and author of *The Lovely Reckless*

"A fast-paced, fun-filled adventure."
—*The Washington Post*

"A page-turner."
—*VOYA*

PRAISE FOR
WILDCARD

An Instant New York Times & USA Today Bestseller

Fall 2018 Kids' Indie Next List—Teen Pick

A Publishers Weekly Most Anticipated YA Book—Fall 2018

An Amazon Best Young Adult Book of the Month Pick
—September 2018

An Amazon Editors' Favorite Young Adult Book of Fall 2018

A Seventeen Magazine Best YA Book of 2018

A Kirkus Reviews Best YA Book of 2018

A BuzzFeed Best YA Book of 2018

★ "Lu's futuristic world, with its immersive technology, feels dangerously within reach in this action-packed escapade with a thoughtful, emotion-driven core." **—*Publishers Weekly*, starred review**

★ "The plotting is exquisite . . . A fast, intense, phenomenal read."
—*Kirkus Reviews*, starred review

"There's plenty of high-stakes double-crossing here, and this finale moves along at a breakneck clip. Series fans will be only too happy to zoom along for the ride." **—*Booklist***

"Fans of *Warcross* will enjoy even more time spent in the game, along with intrigue, action, and mystery." **—*School Library Journal***

WILDCARD

MARIE LU

PENGUIN BOOKS

Penguin Books
An imprint of Penguin Random House LLC, New York

First published in the United States of America by G. P. Putnam's Sons, 2018
Published by Penguin Books, an imprint of Penguin Random House LLC, 2019

Copyright © 2018 by Xiwei Lu

Penguin supports copyright. Copyright fuels creativity, encourages diverse voices, promotes free
speech, and creates a vibrant culture. Thank you for buying an authorized edition of this book
and for complying with copyright laws by not reproducing, scanning, or distributing any part of it
in any form without permission. You are supporting writers and allowing Penguin to continue to
publish books for every reader.

Visit us online at penguinrandomhouse.com

THE LIBRARY OF CONGRESS HAS CATALOGED THE G. P. PUTNAM'S SONS EDITION AS FOLLOWS:
Names: Lu, Marie, 1984– author.
Title: Wildcard / Marie Lu.
Description: New York, NY: G. P. Putnam's Sons, [2018] | Series: A Warcross novel; 2
Summary: "Teenage hacker Emika Chen embarks on a mission to unravel a sinister plot and is
forced to join forces with a shadowy organization known as the Blackcoats"
—Provided by publisher.
Identifiers: LCCN 2018011748 | ISBN 9780399547997 (hardback) | ISBN 9780399548017 (ebook)
Subjects: | CYAC: Internet games—Fiction. | Computer crimes—Fiction. | Hackers—Fiction. |
Spies—Fiction. | Bounty hunters—Fiction.
Classification: LCC PZ7.L96768 Wil 2018 | DDC [Fic]—dc23
LC record available at https://lccn.loc.gov/2018011748

Penguin Books ISBN 9780399548000

Printed in the United States of America

Design by Eileen Savage
Text set in FreightText Pro

This is a work of fiction. Names, characters, places, and incidents either are the product of the
author's imagination or are used fictitiously, and any resemblance to actual persons, living or
dead, businesses, companies, events, or locales is entirely coincidental.

5 7 9 10 8 6 4

In other top headlines, police headquarters around the world are entering a third day of overwhelming crowds outside their doors. Notorious crime boss Jacob "Ace" Kagan walked into a police station in Paris's 8th arrondissement this morning and surrendered himself to authorities in a startling move that has left many scratching their heads. In the United States, two fugitives on the FBI's Ten Most Wanted list have been found dead—both incidents have been ruled suicides. This has been your morning roundup.

—THE *TOKYO SUN* NEWSCAST,
MORNING ROUNDUP

In my dream, I'm with Hideo.

I know it's a dream because we are in a white bed at the top of a skyscraper I've never seen before, in a room made entirely of glass. If I stare down at the floor, I can see through it to the dozens and dozens of levels beneath us, ceiling–floor, ceiling–floor, until they vanish to a point somewhere far below, stretching deep into the earth.

Maybe there's no solid ground at all.

Even though the soft rays of dawn are streaking in, chasing away the dim blue of night to illuminate our skin with a buttery glow, an impossible blanket of stars can still be seen clearly against the sky, coating it in a film of gold-and-white glitter. Beyond the bedroom sprawls the landscape of a never-ending city, the lights a mirror of the stars above, continuing until it disappears into the cloud cover at the horizon.

It's too much. There is infinity in every direction. I don't know which way to fall.

Then Hideo's lips touch my collarbone, and my disorientation evaporates into warmth. *He's here.* I tilt my head back, my mouth parted, my hair rippling behind me, and turn my eyes toward the glass ceiling and the constellations up above.

I'm sorry, he's whispering, his voice echoing inside my mind.

I shake my head at him and frown. What he's apologizing for, I can't recall, and his eyes are so sad that I don't want to remember. *Something's not right. But what is it?* There's a nagging feeling in me that says I'm not supposed to be here.

Hideo pulls me closer. The feeling intensifies. I peer out at the city through the glass, wondering if maybe this dreamscape doesn't look as it should, or if it's the stars overhead that are giving me pause. *Something's not right . . .*

I stiffen against Hideo. His brow furrows, and he cups my face with a hand. I want to lean back into our kiss, but a stirring at the other end of the room distracts me.

Someone is standing there. It's a figure armored entirely in black, his features hidden behind a dark helmet.

I look at him. And everything made of glass shatters.

SHINJUKU DISTRICT

Tokyo, Japan

1

Someone is watching me.

I can feel it—the eerie sensation of being followed, an invisible gaze locked on my back. It prickles my skin, and as I make my way through Tokyo's rain-soaked streets to meet up with the Phoenix Riders, I keep looking over my shoulder. People hurry by in a steady stream of colorful umbrellas and business suits, heels and oversize coats. I can't stop imagining their downcast faces all turned in my direction, no matter which way I go.

Maybe it's the paranoia that comes with years of being a bounty hunter. *You're on a crowded street,* I tell myself. *No one's following you.*

It's been three days since Hideo's algorithm was triggered. Technically, the world should now be the safest it's ever been. Every single person who has used the new Henka Games contact lenses—even just once—should now be completely under Hideo's control, rendered unable to break the law or harm another person.

Only the few who still use the beta lenses, like me, are un-affected.

So, in theory, I shouldn't be worried about someone following me. The algorithm won't let them do anything to hurt me.

But even as I think this, I slow down to stare at the long line wrapping around a local police station. There must be hundreds of people. They're all turning themselves in to the authorities for anything and everything unlawful they've ever done, from unpaid parking tickets to petty theft—even murder. It's been like this for the past three days.

My attention shifts to a police barricade at the end of the street. They're directing us to detour down a different block. Ambulance lights flash against the walls, illuminating a covered gurney being lifted into the vehicle. I only need to catch a glimpse of officers pointing up at the roof of a nearby building before I fig-ure out what occurred here. Another criminal must have jumped to their death. Suicides like this have been peppering the news.

And I helped make all of this happen.

I swallow my unease and turn away. There's a subtle but sig-nificant blankness in everyone's eyes. They don't know an artifi-cial hand is inside their minds, bending their free will.

Hideo's hand.

The reminder is enough to make me pause in the middle of the street and close my eyes. My fists clench and unclench, even as my heart lurches at his name. *I'm such an idiot.*

How can the thought of him fill me with disgust and desire at the same time? How can I stare in horror at this line of people waiting in the rain outside a police station—but still blush at my dream of being in Hideo's bed, running my hands along his back?

We're over. Forget him. I open my eyes again and continue on, trying to contain the anger beating in my chest.

By the time I duck into the heated halls of a Shinjuku shopping center, rain is coming down in wavy sheets, smearing the reflections of neon lights against the slick pavement.

Not that the storm is stopping preparations for the upcoming Warcross closing ceremony, which will mark the end of this year's games. With my beta lenses on, I can see the roads and sidewalks color-coded in hues of scarlet and gold. Each Tokyo district is highlighted like this right now, the streets shaded the colors of the most popular team in that neighborhood. Overhead, a lavish display of virtual fireworks is going off, piercing the dark sky with bursts of colored light. Shinjuku district's favorite team is the Phoenix Riders, so the fireworks here are currently forming the shape of a rising phoenix, arching its flaming neck in a cry of victory.

Every day over the next week or so, the top ten players of this year's championships will be announced worldwide after a vote by all Warcross fans. Those ten players will compete in a final all-star tournament during the closing ceremony, and then spend a year as the biggest celebrities in the world before they play again next spring, in the opening ceremony's game. Like the one I once hacked into and disrupted, that upended my entire life and landed me here.

People on the streets are proudly dressed up as their top-ten vote this year. I see a few Asher lookalikes sporting his outfit from our championship game in the White World; someone's decked out as Jena, another as Roshan. Still others are arguing heatedly about the Final. There had obviously been a cheat—power-ups that shouldn't have been in play.

Of course, I had done that.

I adjust my face mask, letting my rainbow hair tumble out from underneath my red raincoat's hood. My rain boots squelch against the sidewalk. I have a randomized virtual face laid over my own, so at least people who are wearing their NeuroLink glasses or contacts will look at me and see a complete stranger. For the rare person who isn't, the face mask should cover enough to make me blend in with everyone else wearing masks on the street.

"*Sugoi!*" someone passing me exclaims, and when I turn, I see a pair of wide-eyed girls grinning at my hair. Their Japanese words translate into English in my view. "Wow! Good Emika Chen costume!"

They make a gesture like they want to take a photo of me, and I play along, putting up my hands in V-for-victory signs. *Are you both under Hideo's control, too?* I wonder.

The girls bob their heads in thanks and move along. I adjust my electric skateboard strapped over my shoulder. It's a good temporary disguise, pretending to be myself, but for someone used to stalking others, I still feel weirdly exposed.

> Emi! Almost here?

Hammie's message appears before me as translucent white text, cutting through my tension. I smile instinctively and quicken my steps.

> Almost.

> It would've been easier, you know,
> if you'd just come with us.

I cast a glance over my shoulder again. It would've definitely been easier—but the last time I stayed in the same space as my teammates, Zero nearly killed us in an explosion.

I'm not an official Rider anymore.
People would ask questions if they saw
us heading out as a group tonight.

But you'd be safer if you did.

It's safer if I didn't.

I can practically hear her sigh. She sends the address of the bar again.

See you soon.

I pass through the mall and out the other side. Here, the colorful blocks of Shinjuku shift into the seedy streets of Kabukichō, Tokyo's red-light district. I tense my shoulders. It's not an *unsafe* area—certainly not compared to where I came from in New York— but the walls are covered with glowing screens featuring the services of beautiful girls and handsome, spiky-haired boys, along with shadier banners I don't want to understand.

Virtual models dressed in scanty outfits stand outside bars, beckoning visitors to enter. They ignore me when they realize my profile marks me as a foreigner and turn their attention to the more lucrative Japanese locals navigating the streets.

Still, I pick up my pace. No red-light district in the world is safe.

I duck into a narrow street on the border of Kabukichō. *Piss Alley*, so this cluster of little walkways is called. The Riders picked it for tonight because it's closed to tourists during the Warcross championship season. Scowling bodyguards in suits stand at the entrances and exits of the alleys, shooing away curious passersby.

I take down my disguise for a second so they can see my real identity. One bodyguard bows his head and lets me in.

Both sides of the alleys are lined with tiny sake bars and yakitori stands. Through each of their fogged glass doors, I can see the backs of other teams huddled in front of smoking grills, arguing loudly at virtual projections on the walls showing interviews with players. The scent of fresh rain mixes with aromas of garlic, miso, and fried meat.

I pull off my raincoat, shake it out, and fold it inside out into my backpack. Then I head to the last stall. This bar is a little bigger than the others, facing a quiet alley blocked off on either side. Its doorway is lit by a row of cheery red lanterns, and men in suits stand in strategic positions around it. One of them notices me and moves aside, ushering me forward.

I walk under the lanterns and enter through the sliding glass door. A curtain of warm air envelops me.

Checked into Midnight Sense Bar!
+500 Points. Daily Score: +950
Level 36 | ₦120,064

I find myself standing in a cozy room with a handful of filled seats arranged around a bar, where a chef is busy putting out bowls of ramen. He pauses to call out my arrival.

A round of greetings hits me as everyone turns in my direction.

There's Hammie, our Thief, and Roshan, our Shield. Asher, our Captain, is sitting on one of the stools with his stylish wheelchair folded behind him. Even Tremaine, who technically plays for the Demon Brigade, is here. He keeps his elbows propped up on the bar as he nods at me through the steam rising from his bowl. He's sitting away from Roshan, who's fiddling with a bracelet of prayer beads on his wrist and making a point of ignoring his former boyfriend.

My team. My friends. The eerie feeling of being watched subsides as I take in their faces.

Hammie waves me over. I slide gratefully into the empty stool beside her. The chef puts down a bowl of ramen before me and steps out to give us privacy. "The whole city's celebrating," I mutter. "People have no idea what Hideo's done."

She starts pulling her curls tight into a thick pouf high on her head. Then she juts her chin at a virtual screen playing footage from the Final against the wall. "You're just in time," she replies. "Hideo's about to make his announcement."

We stare at the screen as Hammie pours me a cup of tea. It now shows a room of reporters with their faces turned toward a massive stage, all waiting impatiently for Hideo to arrive. Kenn, the Warcross creative director, and Mari Nakamura, Henka Games' chief operating officer, are already there, whispering to each other.

The room on the screen suddenly bursts into commotion as Hideo walks onstage. He straightens the lapels of his suit jacket once as he strides over to join his companions, shaking hands as he goes with his usual cool, careful grace.

Even the sight of him onscreen feels as overwhelming as if he'd walked right into this bar. All I see is the same boy I've watched my whole life, the face I'd stop to look for at newsstands and take in on TV. I dig my nails into the counter, trying not to show how embarrassingly weak it makes me feel.

Hammie notices. She casts me a sympathetic glance. "No one expects you to be over him already," she says. "I know he's trying to take over the world and all, but he still rocks a suit harder than a Balmain catwalk."

Asher scowls. "I'm right here."

"I didn't say I wanted to *date* him," Hammie replies, reaching over to pat Asher's cheek once.

I look on as Hideo and Kenn talk in low voices and wonder how much Kenn and Mari know about Hideo's plans. Has the entire company been in on this all along? Is it possible to keep such a thing secret? Would *that* many people take part in something so awful?

"As you all know," Hideo begins, "a cheat was activated during the Final of this year's championship that benefited one team—the Phoenix Riders—over the other—Team Andromeda. After reviewing the matter with our creative team"—he pauses to glance at Kenn—"it seems the cheat was activated not by one of the players, but by an outside party. We've decided the best way to resolve this, then, is to hold an official rematch between Team Andromeda and the Phoenix Riders, four days from today. This will be followed by the closing ceremony four days later."

An instant buzz of conversation fills the room at Hideo's words. Asher leans back and frowns at the screen. "Well, it's happening," he says to us all. "An official rematch. We've got three days to get ready."

Hammie slurps up a mouthful of noodles. "An official rematch," she echoes, although there's no enthusiasm in her voice. "Never happened in the history of the championships."

"Gonna be a lot of Phoenix Rider haters out there," Tremaine adds. Already, a few shouts of "Cheaters!" can be clearly heard from the other bars outside.

Asher shrugs. "Nothing we haven't faced before. Isn't that right, Blackbourne?"

Tremaine's expression is blank. The excitement of the new game is lost on all of us as we continue to stare at the screen. A rematch isn't the big news. If only those reporters knew what Hideo was really doing with the NeuroLink.

I'm tired of the horror in the world, he'd said to me. *So I will force it to end.*

"Well," Roshan begins, rubbing a hand across his face, "if Hideo's bothered by anything that's happened in the last few days, he's not showing it."

Tremaine's concentrating on something invisible in his view and tapping rapidly against the bar. A few weeks ago, I would've bristled at being in the same room as him. He still isn't my favorite person, and I keep waiting for him to sneer and call me Princess Peach again, but for now he's on our side. And we can use all the help we can get.

"Find anything?" I ask him.

"I dug up some solid numbers on how many people have the new lenses." Tremaine sits back and huffs out a sigh. "Ninety-eight percent."

I could cut the silence in here like a cake. Ninety-eight percent of all users are now controlled by Hideo's algorithm. I think of the long lines, the police tape. The sheer scale of it makes me dizzy.

"And the other two percent?" Asher manages to ask.

"Is made up of anybody still using the beta test lenses," Tremaine replies, "and who haven't switched over yet. Those folks are safe for now." He peers around the bar. "Us, of course, and a number of the official players, since we got the beta lenses before the full version went out. A lot of people in the Dark World, I bet. And the tiny number of people worldwide who don't use the NeuroLink at all. That's it. Everybody else is locked in."

No one wants to add anything to that. I don't say it out loud, but I know we can't stay on the beta lenses forever. Word on the street is that those lenses will download a patch that converts them into algorithm lenses on the day of the Warcross closing ceremony.

That's happening in eight days.

"Seven days of freedom left," Asher finally says, voicing what we're all thinking. "If you want to rob a bank, now's your chance."

I glance at Tremaine. "Any luck digging up more info about the algorithm itself?"

He shakes his head and pulls up a screen for all of us to see. It's a maze of glowing letters. "I can't even find the faintest trace of it. See this?" He stops to point at a block of code. "The main log-on sequence? Something should be here."

"You're saying it's impossible that there's an algorithm here," I reply.

"I'm saying it's impossible, yes. It's like watching a chair float in midair without any wires."

It's the same conclusion I came up with over the past few sleepless nights. I'd spent them searching every crevice of the NeuroLink. Nothing. However Hideo is implementing his algorithm, I can't find it.

I sigh. "The only way to access it might be through Hideo himself."

On the screen, Hideo is answering questions from the press now. His face is serious, his stance easy, and his hair perfectly tousled. As put together as ever. How does he stay so calm? I lean forward, as if the few moments we'd had together in our brief relationship were enough for me to see what he's thinking.

My dream from last night flashes through my mind again, and I can almost feel his hands running down my bare arms, his expression undone. *I'm sorry,* he'd whispered. Then, the dark silhouette watching me from the corner of the room. The glass all around us shattering.

"And what about you?" Tremaine says, snapping me out of my reverie. "Heard anything new from Zero? Have you contacted Hideo?"

I take a deep breath and shake my head. "I haven't reached out to anyone. Not yet, anyway."

"You're not still seriously thinking about Zero's offer, are you?" Asher has his head propped against one hand, and he's looking warily at me. It's the same expression he used to give me as a Captain, whenever he thought I wasn't going to listen to his commands. "Don't do it. It's obviously a trap."

"Hideo was a trap, too, Ash," Hammie says. "And none of us saw that coming."

"Yeah, well, Hideo never tried to blow up our dorm," Asher mutters. "Look—even if Zero is serious about wanting Emi to join him in stopping Hideo, there's got to be some strings attached. He's not exactly a model citizen. His help might come with more problems than it's worth."

Tremaine rests his elbows against the counter. I'm still not used to seeing genuine concern on his face, but it's comforting. A reminder that I'm not alone. "If you and I work together, Em, we can try to avoid Zero's help. There have got to be hints about Sasuke Tanaka out there somewhere."

"Sasuke Tanaka vanished without a trace," Roshan says. His quiet voice is cool and cutting as he wraps a length of noodle around his chopsticks.

Tremaine glances at him. "There is *always* a trace," he replies.

Asher speaks up before things turn more awkward between Roshan and Tremaine. "What if you contact Hideo first? Tell him you found out that his brother's alive. You said he created all of this—Warcross, the algorithm—because of his brother, right? Wouldn't he do anything for him?"

In my mind, I see Hideo look at me. Everything *I do is because of him.* He'd said that to me only a couple of weeks ago, in the steam of a hot spring, as we watched the stars wink into existence.

Even then, he'd been planning his algorithm. His words take on new meaning now, and I shrink inward, the warmth of that memory hardening into ice.

"*If* Zero really is his brother," I reply.

"Are you saying he isn't? We all saw it."

"I'm saying I can't be sure." I stir the noodles around my bowl, unable to work up an appetite.

Hammie tilts her head thoughtfully, and I can see the cogs of her chess mind working. "It could be someone who stole Sasuke's identity. It could be someone trying to throw people off his trail by using a dead boy's name."

"Ghosting," I murmur in agreement. I know the term for it because I've done it before.

"Emi can't tell Hideo something this big if it might not even be true," Hammie continues. "It could make him do something unpredictable. We need proof first."

Roshan suddenly gets up. His chair scoots back with a grating clatter against the floor. I glance abruptly up to see him turning his back to us and heading out of the bar through the sliding door.

"Hey," Hammie calls out. "You okay?"

He pauses to look back at us. "Okay with what? That we're all sitting here, talking about the technicalities of how Emi should throw herself into a situation that might kill her?"

The rest of us halt in our conversation, words hanging unspoken in the air. I've never heard real anger in Roshan's voice before, and the sound seems wrong.

He looks around at his teammates before letting his eyes

settle on me. "You don't owe Hideo anything," he says softly. "You did what you were hired to do. It's not your responsibility to dig deeper into this—into Zero's past or what happened between him and Hideo or even what he plans on doing to Hideo."

"Emi's the only one who—" Asher begins.

"Like you've always looked out for what she needs," Roshan snaps back. My eyebrow raises in surprise.

"Roshan," Asher says, watching him carefully.

But Roshan tightens his lips. "Look—if Zero's team is still set on stopping Hideo, then let *him* do it. Let the two of them go at each other. Step back and remove yourself from this. You don't have to do it. And none of us should be convincing you of anything different."

Before I can respond, Roshan turns away and heads out into the night air. The door slides shut behind him with a sharp bang. Around me, the others let out an inaudible breath.

Hammie shakes her head when I look at her. "It's because he's here," she mutters, nodding to Tremaine. "He throws Roshan off."

Tremaine clears his throat uncomfortably. "He's not wrong," he finally says. "About the danger, I mean."

I stare at the space where Roshan had been and picture his prayer beads sliding against his wrist. In my view, I can still see the last message from Zero sitting in my archives, the letters small and white and waiting.

My offer to you still stands.

Hammie sits back and crosses her arms. "Why *are* you going on with this?" she asks me.

"Is the fate of the world not enough of a reason?"

"No, there's more to it than that."

Irritation rises in my chest. "This is all happening because of me—I was directly involved."

Hammie doesn't back down from the edge in my words. "But you know it's not your fault. Tell me—*why?*"

I hesitate, not wanting to say it. In the corner of my view, I see Hideo's profile haloed in green. He's awake and online. It's enough to make me want to reach out and Link with him.

I hate that he still has this pull on me. After all, everyone has had that one person they can't help but obsess over. It's not like I haven't enjoyed flings that came and went in the span of a few weeks. And yet . . .

He's more than a fling or a bounty or a mark. He's forever bound to my history. The Hideo who has stolen the world's free will is still the same Hideo who grieved his brother so deeply that it left a permanent thread of silver in his dark hair. The same Hideo who loves his mother and father. The same Hideo who once lifted me out of my darkness and dared me to dream of better things.

I refuse to believe that he's nothing more than a monster. I can't watch him sink like this. I keep going because I need to find that boy again, the beating heart buried underneath his lie. I have to stop him in order to save him.

He was once the hand that pulled me up. Now I have to be his.

• • • • •

BY THE TIME we leave the bar, it's well past midnight, and the pouring rain has dwindled to a fine mist. Some people still dot the streets. The first two all-star players have just been announced, and virtual figures of them now hover under every streetlight in the city.

Hammie barely glances at the images of her best in-game moves now dancing below the light posts. "You should head back with us," she says, eyeing the neighborhood.

"I'll be fine," I reassure her. If someone really is following me, best not to make it so that they're following my teammates, too.

"It's Kabukichō, Em."

I give her a wry smile. "So? Hideo's algorithm is running on most of these people now. What's there to be afraid of?"

"Very funny," Hammie responds with an exasperated lift of her eyebrow.

"Look, we shouldn't all be traveling together. You know that makes us too tempting a target, regardless of the algorithm. I'll call you when I'm in back in my hotel."

Hammie hears the note of finality in my voice. Her lips twist in frustration, but then she nods and starts to walk away. "Yeah, you better," she says over her shoulder, waving her hand at me as she hurries off.

I watch her join the others as they head toward the subway station, where a private car waits for them. I try to picture each of them before they were famous, the first times they arrived in Tokyo, whether or not they felt invisible enough to take the subway. Whether they felt alone.

When my teammates disappear into the haze of rain, I turn away.

I'm used to traveling by myself. Still, my solitude feels sharper now, and the space around me seems emptier without my teammates. I shove my hands back into my pockets and try to ignore the virtual male model that now saunters up to me with a smile, inviting me in English into one of the host clubs that line the street.

"Nope," I reply to him. He vanishes immediately, then resets at the entrance of the club and looks for another potential customer.

I tuck the rest of my hair completely under my hood and keep going. Just a week ago, I probably would've been walking with Hideo beside me. His arm wrapped around my waist, his coat over my shoulders. He might've been laughing at something I said.

But I'm on my own here, listening to the lonely splash of my boots in the dirty street puddles. The echo of water dripping from signs and overhangs keeps distracting me. It sounds like someone else's footsteps. The feeling of being watched has returned.

A static buzz vibrates in my ears. I pause for a moment at an intersection, tilting my head this way and that until it stops.

I glance again at Hideo's green-haloed icon in my view. Where is he now, and what is he doing? I imagine contacting him, his virtual form appearing before me, as Asher's question rings in my ears. What if I *did* tell him about Zero's connection to his brother? Would it be so bad to see what happens, even without being entirely sure?

I clench my teeth, annoyed with myself for thinking of excuses to hear his voice. If I just give myself enough distance from him and focus on this whole thing like it's a job, then maybe I'll stop wanting to be near him so much.

The static buzzes in my ear again. This time I halt and listen carefully. Nothing. Only a few people are on the street with me now, each a nondescript silhouette. *Maybe someone's trying to hack me.* I start an inspection of my NeuroLink system to make sure everything's in order. Green text floats past my view, the scan looking normal.

Until it skips over running a diagnostic on my messages.

I frown, but before I can examine it closer, all the text vanishes from my view. It's replaced by a single sentence.

I'm still waiting, Emika.

Every hair on the back of my neck rises. It's Zero.

2

I whirl in place on the sidewalk, my eyes darting to each silhouette on the street. The colorful reflections on the road blur in the wet night. Lampposts suddenly look like people, and every distant footstep sounds like it's headed toward me.

Is he here? Has he been the one watching me? I half expect to see a familiar figure walking behind me, his body encased in fitted armor, his face hidden underneath that opaque black helmet.

But no one's there.

"It's only been a few nights," I whisper under my breath, my words transcribing into a reply text. "Ever heard of giving someone time to think?"

I did give you time.

Irritation flashes hot under my fear. I grit my teeth and start walking faster. "Maybe this is my way of telling you I'm not interested."

> **And are you not interested?**

"Not interested at all."

> **Why not?**

"Maybe because you tried to kill me."

> **If I still wanted you dead, you would be.**

Another shiver down my spine. "Are you trying to get me to take your offer? Because you're not doing a very good job of it."

> **I'm here to tell you that you're in danger.**

He's toying with me, like he always does. But something about his tone makes me freeze. I realize that maybe he's hacking through my shields right now, digging through my files, digging through *me*. He once stole my father's Memories from me. He could do it again.

"The only danger I've ever faced was from *you*."

> **Then you haven't been in the Dark World lately.**

A view of the Pirate's Den suddenly appears all around me. I jerk backward at the abrupt shift. Just a second ago, I was standing on a city street; now I'm belowdecks on a pirate ship.

Tremaine was right—a good number of people in the Dark World must still be using beta lenses, because Hideo's algorithm would never let them go down under. The ship looks crowded with virtual people, all of them gathered around the glass cylinder in the den's center. The screen that displays the assassination lottery.

Always the first pick, aren't you?

My gaze runs up the list. Some names are familiar ones—gang lords and mob bosses, politicians and a few celebrities. But then—

There I am. Emika Chen. I'm at the top, and beside my name is a reward sum for five million notes.

Five million notes for my death.

"You've got to be kidding me," I manage to say.

The Pirate's Den vanishes as quickly as it appeared, leaving me standing in Kabukichō again.

Zero's messages come rapidly now.

Two assassins are making their way up this street. They're going to reach you before you can get to a train station.

Every muscle in me tenses at once. I've seen what happens to others who end up on that list—and for a price that high, the assassinations almost always go through.

For a split second, I find myself wishing that Hideo's algorithm already affected everyone. But I quickly shake the thought away.

"How do I know that you didn't send them yourself?" I whisper.

> You're wasting time. Turn right at the next intersection. Head into the mall and go down to the basement floor. There's a car waiting for you on the opposite street.

A car? Maybe I wasn't just being paranoid, after all. He had been watching me, maybe had calculated what routes I'd take once I left the Riders.

I look around frantically. Maybe Zero's lying to me, playing one of his games. I pull up my directory and start to place a call to Asher. If the others are still somewhere close by, they can come get me. They—

I never finish my thought. A shot rings out behind me, whizzing narrowly past my neck to chip the wall at an angle.

A bullet. *A gunshot.* A sudden wave of terror sweeps over me.

I throw myself to the ground. Down the street, a random passerby screams and runs, leaving me the only person that I can see. I glance over my shoulder—searching for my followers—and this time, I see a shadow moving against a building, rippling in the night. Another movement on the other side of the street catches my eye. I start scrambling to my feet.

A second gunshot rings out.

Panic hovers at the edges of my senses, threatening to crowd out everything. The sounds come to me like I'm underwater. As a bounty hunter, I've heard gunshots before, the *ping* of police bullets against walls and glass—but the sheer intensity of this moment is new. I was never the target.

Did Zero send them? But he'd warned me to run. He'd told me that I was in danger. Why would he do that, if he's the one attacking me?

You have to think.

I flatten myself against the wall, throw my board to the ground, and jump on it. My heel slams down and the board surges forward with a high-pitched *whoosh*. Zero had said a car was waiting for me around the next turn. I crouch low on my board so that my hands can grip either side of it, then aim for the end of the street.

But another gunshot streaks past my leg—too close—and hits the board. Another knocks a wheel loose.

I jump off as the board veers sharply into the wall, roll, and push myself back to my feet—but my sneaker catches against a crack in the pavement. I stumble. Behind me come footsteps. My eyes squeeze shut, even as I struggle back up to my feet again. This is it; any second now, I will feel the searing pain of a bullet ripping through me.

"Around the corner. Go."

I jerk my head to one side at the voice.

Crouched beside me in the darkness is a girl with a black cap pulled low on her head. Her lipstick is black, her eyes gray and hard as steel and fixated on the shadowed silhouettes on the street. A gun's in her hand, and clipped around her wrist is a black cuff. I think the cuff is real for a moment before a virtual ripple of blue shines across it. She's balanced so lightly on her feet that she looks ready to fly away, and her expression is completely still, without even the tiniest ripple of unease.

No one was beside me a second ago. It's like she materialized out of thin air.

Her eyes flicker to me. "*Move.*" The word cracks like a whip.

This time, I don't hesitate. I bolt down the street.

As I do, she rises from her crouch and moves toward one of my hooded assassins. The girl walks with a sense of calm that borders on eerie—even as the attacker shifts his arm to shoot at her, she is shifting, too. By the time the attacker fires at the girl, she has twisted her body to one side, dodging the bullet as she raises her gun. She shoots at the attacker in a blur of fluid motion. I reach the bend in the street and look back at the same time her bullet hits my assassin hard in the shoulder. It knocks him backward, clear off his feet.

Who the hell is this girl?

Zero hadn't said anything about someone else working with him—maybe she's not connected to him at all. She could even be one of my attackers and is trying to throw me off track by pretending to be my rescuer.

I've already reached the mall complex. I'm rushing past crowds of startled people as I make my way down the first flight of stairs. *Basement level,* the words repeat in my mind. In the distance, I hear police sirens wailing down the last street I was on. How'd they know to come here so quickly?

Then I remember the passerby who'd screamed and fled at the first gunshot. If she was using the new, algorithm-affected lenses, then her reaction could have triggered the NeuroLink to contact the police. Could that be possible? It seems like a feature Hideo would have added.

It isn't until I reach the bottom of the stairs and burst through an emergency exit that I realize the gray-eyed girl is already here, somehow, rushing alongside me. She shakes her head when she sees me opening my mouth to ask her a question.

"No time. Hurry up," she orders in a terse voice. I numbly do as she says.

As we go, I quietly analyze what information I can about her. There's precious little. Like me, she seems to be operating behind a false identity, the various profile accounts hovering around her empty and misleading. She moves with single-minded focus, so intense and so sure in her gestures that I know she's done things like this before.

Like what? Like helping a hunted target get to safety? Or tricking one into following her to their demise?

I wince at the thought. That's not a gamble I can afford to lose. If she's trying to isolate me from her other rival hunters or something, then I need to find a good chance to bolt away.

This basement floor of the shopping center is laid out like cosmetics counters in a New York mall, except all of the kiosks here display an array of decadently decorated desserts. Cakes, mousses, chocolates—all so delicately packaged that they look less like food and more like jewelry. The lights are dimmed, the floor long closed for the night.

I race along the darkened aisles behind the girl. She edges close to one of the cake displays and brings an elbow down hard on the glass. It shatters.

An alarm starts to wail overhead.

Satisfied, the girl reaches into the broken display counter to grab a miniature mochi cake adorned with gold flakes. She shakes off bits of glass before popping it in her mouth.

"What are you doing?" I shout at her above the noise.

"Clearing our path," she replies through her mouthful of dessert. She waves her arm impatiently at the ceiling. "Alarm should scare some of them away." She tightens her grip on her gun and raises her other hand to make a subtle series of gestures in midair. An invite pops up in my view.

Connect with [null]?

I waver for a heartbeat before accepting. Neon-gold lines appear in my view, directing us along a path that she has set for us. "Follow it if you lose me," she says over her shoulder.

"What do I call you?" I ask.

"Is that really important right now?"

"If someone attacks me and we're separated, I'll know what name to scream for help."

At that, she turns around to face me and gifts me with a smile. "Jax," she replies.

A scarlet shape appears in our view, hiding behind a pillar at the other end of the floor.

Jax turns her head in its direction without slowing down. She lifts her gun. "Duck," she warns. Then she fires.

I jerk down to the floor as Jax's gun sparks. The other person returns fire immediately, the bullets lighting up against the pillars and shattering another glass counter. My ears ring. Jax continues moving with the same exacting motions as before, stepping out of the line of fire each time, cocking her gun, bracing her shoulder, and firing back. I race near her with my head hunched down.

As a bullet zings past her, forcing her to shift sideways, she tosses her gun effortlessly from one hand into the other. She fires back.

Her bullet makes contact this time. We hear a yelp of agony—when I glance up past the counters, I see the shape outlined in red collapse. The gold line dictating our path turns right, but before we take it, Jax strides over to the figure on the floor.

She points her gun straight down at the person and fires one efficient shot.

The assassin convulses once, violently, before going limp.

It's over in an instant, but the sound of the shot echoes in my mind like ripples disturbing a pond, the memory overlapping repeatedly over itself. I can see blood sprayed against the wall and the scarlet pool spreading under the body. The gaping wound in his head.

My stomach gives a violent lurch. It's too late to stop it, so I just fall to my knees and spill the contents of dinner on the floor.

Jax yanks me hard to my feet. "Calm down. Follow me." She tilts her head and signals for me to keep moving.

The blood on the wall splatters over and over again in my mind. *She killed him far too easily. She's used to this.* I think about bolting away—but Jax *had* defended me and hadn't tried to kill me herself. Is there a higher ransom on my head if I'm taken alive?

A thousand questions crowd the tip of my tongue, but I force myself to stumble dizzily after her. There is no sound now except for the echo of our boots against the ground. Police sirens and ambulances must still be at the scene of the shooting upstairs, and maybe someone has already discovered the dead body Jax has left behind.

The seconds drag on like hours before we finally reach our destination—where the gold line ends in front of a narrow utility closet.

Jax types in a code on the door's security lock. It glows green, lets out a single beep, and opens for us. She ushers me inside.

The room looks like a standard utility closet, filled with wooden crates and cardboard boxes stacked up to the ceiling. Jax leans against a counter and starts to reload her gun.

"Can't take you through the regular exit," she mutters as she goes. "There's a police barricade up there blocking the car. We'll go this way."

The car. Maybe she really is with Zero.

I huddle in a corner and squeeze my eyes shut. My throat still feels coated with acid. The killing shot echoes in my mind. I let out a long, shaky breath and attempt to compose myself, fixing my eyes on the girl's gun, but my hands keep quivering, no matter how hard I clench my fists. I can't seem to gather my thoughts properly. Every time I try, they scatter apart.

Jax sees me struggling to steady myself. She pauses, takes a step toward me, and holds my chin with one gloved hand. Blood stains the leather. I hold still for a moment, wondering how she can be this firm and calm after she just shot someone in the head. Wondering if this is when she'll snap my neck like a twig.

"Hey." She locks her stare on me. "You're okay."

I pull away from her grip. "I know that." A quaver lingers in my voice.

"Good." At my reply, she reaches behind her back and pulls another gun from her belt. She throws it at me without warning.

I fumble the weapon. "For chrissakes," I blurt out, holding the gun in front of me with two fingers. "What the hell am I supposed to do with this?"

"Fire when needed?" she suggests.

My blank stare continues until she rolls her eyes at me and snatches the weapon back. She replaces it on her belt before picking up her own gun and clicking the old cartridge out of its magazine. "What, you've never shot a gun before?"

"Not a real one."

"Seen someone die?"

I shake my head numbly.

"I thought you were a bounty hunter."

"I am."

"Don't you do that kind of stuff?"

"What, kill people?"

"Yeah. That."

"My job's to catch my marks *alive*, not to put holes in their heads." I watch her snap a new cartridge into her gun. "Is this my cue to ask you what's going on? Did Zero send you?"

Jax tucks the freshly loaded gun back into her holster. The look she gives me is almost pitying. "Listen. Emika Chen, isn't it? You clearly have no idea what you're getting yourself into." Without missing a beat, she pulls a knife out from the inside of one of her boots and continues. "You were having dinner with the Phoenix Riders tonight, weren't you?"

"You've been spying on me?"

"I was *observing* you." Jax walks over to the other side of the closet, where she pushes one of the stacks of crates aside. Behind it is an inconspicuous door, visible only as a thin rectangle against the wall. She takes her knife and jams it carefully into the subtle cracks. "Tell me I don't have to explain everything."

"Look, let's start with you telling me what the hell just happened, and we'll go from there." I cross my arms. It's an easier way to disguise my trembling, and the feeling of my arms crossed protectively over my chest gives me a small hint of comfort. Showing this girl weakness seems like a dangerous thing.

"I just saved you from your would-be assassins," Jax says, pointing her knife at me. "Zero warned you about them."

Hearing this confirmation from her sends another wave of dizzying fear through me. I steady myself against the wall. "So he sent you to fetch me?"

She nods. "I'm willing to bet that some of those hunters were working together, from the way they placed themselves on either side of the street and covered the basement floor of this place. They won't be the last, either. Plenty will be targeting you as long as that fat jackpot stays up in the Pirate's Den."

She walks over to me and drops a metal fragment into my hand. "Hold this." Then she heads back to the door and continues working on wedging her knife into the outline.

I look on, frozen in shock. "Why do people want me dead?"

"Is your connection to Hideo Tanaka not enough?" She grunts once as her knife's blade becomes stuck. "People think everything that's gone wrong in the games this year is because of your hack of the opening ceremony game and your fling with Hideo. Rumor's that you're also the one responsible for installing the cheat in the Final, as a rebellion against being kicked off your team." She shrugs. "I mean, they're not wrong."

Anger slices through my surprise. "People want me *dead* for that?"

"There are a lot of gamblers out there who probably lost big money on that Final. Doesn't matter. You're going to have assassins on your trail for a while, so I suggest you stick close to me." She yanks the knife out and presses it into a different spot in the crack, then pushes her weight against it.

Zero. This is the first time I've heard someone other than Hideo acknowledge his existence. "Why'd he send you?"

She pulls off her black cap, revealing short silver hair, and looks up at me. "Why else? To save you from being pumped full of bullets. And you're welcome."

A tingle runs through my limbs. Zero had been genuine about warning me, after all. Hadn't he? "No—I mean, what do you *do*?"

She pauses to glance at me. "Takes an assassin to stop one, doesn't it?"

An assassin. It shouldn't shock me, not after what I just witnessed her do, but suddenly I think back to the Pirate's Den in the Dark World, where I'd seen potential assassins watching the lottery rankings, their figures as patient and quiet as death. Maybe Jax was one of them.

I swallow hard. "You work for Zero, then? Are you part of his crew that was trying to sabotage Warcross?"

She considers this question thoughtfully before answering. "You could say that. We're both Blackcoats."

Blackcoats.

I frown, thinking through all the shadow groups I've come across in the Dark World. There are the bigger names, of course—the Wrecking Crew hackers; Anonymous—that the public knows, and smaller gangs who aspire to be notorious.

But the Blackcoats aren't a name I'm familiar with at all. I have no concept of how big or small they are, what they do, or what their purpose is. In my world, that's even more dangerous. They're not here to pull publicity stunts. They're here to do serious damage.

"I've never heard of them," I reply.

She shrugs again. "Didn't expect you to. If you had, I'd be more suspicious."

"And what if I don't want to?"

"Don't want to what?"

"What if I don't want to know more? What if I don't want to go with you?"

This time, a small smile creeps onto Jax's lips that changes her entire expression into something sinister. It suddenly occurs to me that I'm trapped in the same room as a professional killer.

"Then leave," she says, cocking her head once toward the door.

She's taunting me now, testing the resolve of my words. Out of sheer stubbornness, I lunge toward the door and seize the handle, ready to throw it open and rush out the way I came. I half expect to feel the searing pain of a bullet in my back, ripping through me to drop me on the spot.

"If you're fine with dying tonight," she adds casually behind me.

As much as I hate myself for it, her words stop me cold.

"Zero's going to be disappointed to lose you," she goes on, "but he's also never forced anyone to work with us against their will. Step out that door, and you'll be both free and dead. Your choice."

There are hunters on the other side of this door, waiting for me to come fleeing out into the dim basement level . . . and there's an assassin in here, one who claims to want to help me escape.

My hand tightens against the door handle. Jax is right. I'll last two seconds out there by myself, facing off against who knows how many unknown hunters all eager to claim my jackpot. Or, I can take my chances in here, with a so-called Blackcoat who nevertheless saved me and—so far—seems interested in keeping me alive.

I clench my jaw and force my hand to release the handle. Then I turn to glare at her. "This isn't a choice," I say. "And you know it."

She shrugs and goes back to her work. "Just doing my job. Zero's expecting you, and he'd prefer you in one piece." A subtle click finally sounds from the door, and she waves one hand at me. "Give me that thing."

I toss her the metal fragment she'd handed me a moment ago, then look on as she jams it back in the crack where her knife had triggered the click. It glows a soft green. The door makes a faint popping sound—then slides open to reveal a dusty underground walkway that looks like it hasn't been used in a long time. Some unfinished and long-abandoned subway tunnel. There are stairs at the end of it, leading up to a faint ray of light. The car Zero had mentioned must be waiting there for us.

I stay where I am. "Where are you taking me?"

Jax pulls out her gun again and rests its handle against her shoulder. I stare warily at it. "Do you trust me?"

"Not really."

"Well, that answers my next question." Then Jax points her gun straight at me and shoots.

3

I experience what happens next in fragments.

The searing pain near my neck from Jax's shot. The world around me blurring, the distant thud I hear as I collapse against the wall. A jolt of panic that cuts through the sudden numbing of my limbs.

I've been drugged.

The thought struggles up through the molasses drowning my mind. I turn my eyes up at Jax as she approaches. *What did you do to me?* I try to demand an explanation. But my entire body feels like it's made of rubber now, and even as I stay awake, I find myself sliding sideways until I'm lying on the floor, focusing on Jax's boots. My heart beats rapidly, the sound drumming in my ears.

Am I dreaming?

No, I'm awake. I can see what's happening around me, even

though it seems to be happening inside a dim tunnel, and the edges of my vision are dark.

The next thing I remember is the feeling of my arm draped around Jax's shoulders. Of her dragging me down the tunnel and toward a black taxi. I try to focus on the four-leaf-clover symbol on its glowing cab light. The faint smell of new leather permeates the space. Jax looks down at me. From my view, her face is swimming in a haze.

"You'll be fine," she says calmly to me. "You just won't remember this tomorrow morning."

My head lolls weakly to one side as the car begins to move, rumbling over the unfinished tracks in the tunnel. Slivers of weak light illuminate parts of the dark passage, and I remember the flash of gray against black against gray on the fabric seats. I struggle to remember our route. My heartbeat is irregular, fluttering frantically.

Can I record a Memory? I try to bring up the menu, try to send an invite to connect to Hammie or Roshan—to anyone—but my mind is far too numb to make it happen. *Help me.* I try in vain to send a message out. *Help.* I want to scream Jax's name as I stare at her, but I feel like I'm still wading through the air, and my tongue feels thick and immobile.

My level changes as we emerge from the tunnel into the night, and suddenly we're surrounded by office buildings that rise up along either side of the street like woods bordering a path. They stretch up ominously like living things.

Welcome to Ōmotesando District!
+150 Pts. Daily Score: +150
You Leveled Up!
Level 85

My determination momentarily shifts as I notice the change in the sky's colors. Unlike Shinjuku, where the Phoenix Riders' scarlet and gold coat everything, Omotesando's favorite team is the Winter Dragons—so the sky here is covered instead with a sheet of undulating blue and orange-gold. The light posts are draped in vibrant banners, and over them hover virtual versions of the Dragons' players.

Jax leans over briefly to check on me. She barely glances at the passing celebrations, and when she does, she watches them stoically, without much interest. I fight to keep looking at her, but my thoughts fade into darkness.

My nightmares are full of faces. There is Jax's grim look as she points her gun down at a human and puts a bullet through his skull. There is Hideo, his voice whispering my name close to my ear, his furrowed brow cutting dark lines over his eyes, his hair brushing against me as he leans in.

Then, there is Zero. A mystery. I can only see him in the form I've known, his black armor reflecting red light surrounding him, his features completely hidden behind a black helmet as he sits across from me and laces his fingers together. He's telling me to run.

I don't know how long we ride in the taxi before it finally comes to a stop behind a building.

Jax opens my door and helps me out. I turn weakly toward her, trying to move my limbs, but all I can feel is the faint sensation of pavement beneath my dragging feet. Jax has her arm around my waist, keeping me up, and she's saying something to people standing at the building's sliding glass doors. It looks like a hotel.

"Out partying too hard," she explains in a singsong voice to the attendee at the entrance. I want to blurt out that she's lying, but it takes all my strength just to stay upright. The world spins.

Remember this. Remember this. But even the thought itself flitters out of my mind the instant I think it. My vision blurs more, and the more I fight it, the more it fades. I end up focusing on Jax. She runs a hand through her hair and casts me an unconcerned glance.

There's the inside of an elevator, then a hallway. As I start to fade away again, all I can hear is Jax announce our arrival.

"Tell Zero she's here."

4

Five Days until the Warcross
Closing Ceremony

Darkness. Two voices.

"She should have been up by noon. You shot her with too strong a dose."

"I thought she could handle it."

"Let her sleep, then."

Weak light slanting across my face makes me squint.

I roll over in bed and curl into a ball. Where am I? A swirl of images rotates through my mind—dreams, maybe, but brighter, hazier in a way that I can't explain. I furrow my brow.

Was there a taxi? *A black car. An unfinished subway tunnel. A district of colors.* My heart pounds furiously. I lie still for a while, willing it to slow down until I'm able to breathe at a normal rate again. Then I open my eyes. The orange light of early morning streaks across my bedsheets, coming gradually into focus as my vision adjusts.

No, wait—this isn't morning light at all. It's sunset.

I blink, disoriented. I'm lying in a bed in a luxuriously stark hotel room, adorned with gray-and-white-striped wallpaper and a series of plain wall paintings.

Waves of memories rush back at me now. The assassins. The subway tunnel. The image of Jax standing over my pursuer. The gunshot.

The Blackcoats.

And then . . . what? The last thing I remember is Jax pointing her gun straight at me.

She drugged me. I'm sure of it. Maybe it was to make sure I didn't remember anything about where we were going or what path we took to get here—but now here I am, lying in an unfamiliar room with holes in my memory.

I bolt upright. I'm still dressed in the same clothes I'd been wearing that night. I check myself gingerly for any injuries, but besides some bruises and a sore spot on my neck, I'm unharmed. My moment of panic pools gradually into a sense of foreboding that invades my chest. I watch the faint light filtering in through my window.

It takes me a moment to realize that I have a dozen unread messages from the Riders, each one more frantic than the last. I frown. How long have I been missing if they're this worried? Had they heard about the gunshots fired near where we had dinner? It must be on the news, unless Hideo can somehow control that, too. I hesitate, wondering whether I should tell my teammates what really happened, before sending out some quick replies of reassurance.

> I'm ok, don't worry.

> Lost reception for a bit. Talk soon.

Then I freeze when I reach the last unread message. It's an incoming invite, accompanied by a profile image haloed in soft, blinking green.

Hideo is calling me. Asking me to Link with him.

My heart jumps into my throat.

What does he want? Is it possible he knows what's happened to me, even though I'm using beta lenses? I glance quickly around the room, looking for any sign that I'm being recorded. But there aren't any cameras in the ceilings.

Don't answer it.

I know I shouldn't.

But I still find myself lifting my hand, reaching up, and tapping on the invite hovering in my view. I regret it immediately. Maybe the drug Jax used on me has lowered my inhibitions and hijacked my common sense. But it's too late now. I don't see him appear right away, but through our newly formed Link, I can feel a trickle of his emotions.

They're a knot of urgency and fear.

Emika.

I startle again. Hideo's voice is speaking in my mind, his telepathic messaging invention. I should be used to it by now, but even after a mere couple of weeks, his voice hits me just like it did the first time we spoke on the phone. I narrow my eyes, more annoyed at myself than at him.

Why are you calling me? I say to him.

You called me.

This brings me up short. I did? It must have happened while I was drugged—maybe an unconscious reaction. Now I have a faint recollection of trying desperately to call for help. Apparently, I'd decided to call Hideo.

I wince. Couldn't I have called Hammie or Roshan instead? *Any* of the Riders? Did my instinct have to be Hideo?

Well, it was an accident, I counter.

Where are you? I felt nothing but panic coming from you. You asked for help. Then you disconnected.

Hearing Hideo's voice in my mind is so overwhelming that I almost want to sever our Link right away. Then I remember that he can sense my emotions. In return, a stab of concern from him hits me, followed by a ripple of unease. His brother's name teeters at the edge of my mind, ready for me to tell him—the thought is so strong that I almost send it. With a huge effort, I pull it back.

I'm fine.

You're fine. He sounds doubtful as he echoes my words back at me.

There's another pause on his end, and an instant later, my surroundings shift. I find myself sitting on a white couch across from an open terrace, staring out at a twilight of glittering city lights beyond a balcony lit by a circular, stone fire pit. Wherever he is, it's not his home that I'm familiar with, nor is it Henka Games. It's an estate more lavish than anything I've ever seen in my life, overlooking a city I don't recognize. Baroque columns tower up to the sky, and gossamer curtains drift on either side of the entrance leading out to the balcony. Neatly trimmed bushes dot the space. Somewhere in the distance come the buzz of voices and the clinking of glasses, the sounds of a party.

Hideo's shadowed silhouette stands against the open terrace, leaning against the railing of stone pillars. Dim light outlines the edges of his body.

My dream. His hands on me. His lips on my skin.

I try in vain to stop my cheeks from heating up.

It takes me another moment to notice a young woman at his

side. I don't recognize her, but in the darkness, I can tell that she's in a slender, glittery dress, her long hair falling in waves past her shoulders. She leans close to Hideo, her hand running along his arm, and whispers something in his ear with a smile.

Bitterness shoots hot through my veins before I can rein it in. Who the hell is this, and why is she cozying up to Hideo?

And why the hell do I care? I'd broken things off between us, anyway. Is it such a surprise that someone is already trying to catch his attention?

Hideo doesn't lean back toward her. Instead, he gives her his polite smile that I've come to know so well, then murmurs something to her that makes her remove her hand from his arm. She tilts her head at him, flashing him another smile, and then strides off the balcony. Her stilettos click rhythmically against the floor tiles.

Hideo turns his attention to me without watching her go. He doesn't look like someone capable of controlling the minds of almost everyone in the world. He doesn't seem like the reason why we might all lose our freedom of thought. Right now, he's the person I fell for, flesh and blood and painfully human, looking at me like he's seeing me for the first time.

A jolt of jealousy from him surges through our Link, and I realize that, from his view, it looks like I could be in someone else's bed. I allow myself a petty moment of satisfaction.

"Where are you now?" I mutter.

He glances briefly over his shoulder at the sparkling city behind him. "Singapore," he replies. "I have some financial business to take care of here."

Financial business, billionaire dealings. He's probably expecting me to comment on what kind of party he's at or the identity of the woman who just left, but I'm not about to give him that.

"Well," I say archly. "I guess you seem fine."

"What happened to you?" Hideo says.

His words are cold and distant, but a torrent of his emotions crowds my mind. Joy, at seeing me again. Anger. Frustration. Fear, for my safety.

For an instant, I want to tell him that I miss him. That I keep dreaming about him every night. That I can't bear to turn my back on him, even now.

But then the reality of our situation returns, and my own temper flares. "Nothing. I was just about to leave this Link."

He steps toward me until it's as if he were standing barely a few inches away. "Then why are you still here?" he says.

It's been a long time since I've heard the ice in his voice—the tone he uses for strangers. The realization hits me harder than I thought it would. "You have no right to be upset with me."

"I'm not. I just don't want to see you. Isn't that what you want?"

"More than you know," I snap.

"You're hunting me, aren't you?" he murmurs. His emotions suddenly shift into doubt, the reminder that we have a wall separating us. He looks sidelong at me. "That's why you reached out to me, isn't it? This is all a setup. You were lying about needing help. This is part of your hunt."

"*You're* suspicious of *me*?" I scowl at him. "Do I need to remind you of what you're doing?"

"Enlighten me," he says coldly.

"Are you serious? You must've heard about the long lines at police stations—you've seen footage of people committing suicide. None of that chills you?"

"Of *convicted sex traffickers* committing suicide. Of *untried murderers* turning themselves in. Meanwhile, reported crimes over the past week have plummeted." Hideo's eyes are hard and unmoving. "Now, what are you trying to convince me of?"

He's confusing me, and it only angers me more. "You shouldn't have this power."

"The algorithm is unbiased."

"You *betrayed* me. You made me think I was working with you to do something good."

"That's what you're most angry about. Not the algorithm. *This*." Hideo lowers his head, closes his eyes for a heartbeat, and opens them again. "You're right. I wish I'd told you sooner, and I'm sorry for that. But you know why I'm doing this, Emika. I opened my heart to you."

"Your choice to, not mine," I fire back. "It's as if you believe I owe you something for it."

"That's what you think?" An edge comes into his voice. A warning. "That I'd use my past to bait you? Because I wanted something from you?"

"Didn't you?" I say. My words are hoarse. "Why *did* you open up to me, anyway? I was just another bounty hunter on your payroll. Just another girl passing through your life."

"I've never told anyone about my past," he snaps back. "You know that."

"How can I believe anything you say now? Maybe what happened to your brother is something you tell every girl you want to get into your hot spring."

I can tell I've gone too far the instant the words escape my lips. Hideo flinches away. I swallow, telling myself not to feel bad for spitting my retort out at him. "We're done here," he says in a low voice. "I suggest you not waste our time by contacting me again."

He disconnects our Link before I can respond.

The suite, the glittering city lights, and Hideo's blue-black silhouette vanish abruptly, and the white couch I'd been lying on shifts back into the silk sheets of my bed. I realize that I'm trembling all over, my forehead hot and damp with a light sheen of sweat.

My burst of fury is over as quickly as it came. My shoulders droop.

I shouldn't have said it. But all I want to do when I'm angry is stab the deepest wound I can find. And it shouldn't matter anymore, should it? If the distance in his tone hurts, it's just because I'm not used to it. Because I'm exhausted. Too much has happened over the course of the day, and with Hideo's brief presence, I'm suddenly so worn-out that all I want to do is sink into my bed until I disappear.

I shake my head, then head to the bathroom. In the mirror, I see a dark bruise on one side of my throat. It must be from where Jax shot me with that drug. I rub carefully at the sore spot before I turn away and step into the shower.

The steam from the hot water clears my head a bit. Maybe I was fool to think I could ever pull Hideo off his current path. If anything, my conversation with him has only confirmed how unwilling he is to compromise. He's unfazed by what's happening around the world, and that means he's moving full steam ahead to make sure the last two percent of the population is hooked into the algorithm, too.

Soon, that'll include me.

I have to stop Hideo. Before it's too late to pull him back. I repeat this to myself, trying to feel convinced, until the water has wrinkled my fingertips.

By the time I step out, the aftereffects of the drug seem to have worn off, and I feel a sense of alert wariness instead of the fog of panic. I walk out into the bedroom with a towel wrapped around me and bring up my menu. I know I'm in a hotel in Omotesando, but that's about all I can find. Nothing about my suite or this building tells me anything about the Blackcoats. Not that I'd expect it to.

An hour has passed when I finally get an invite to connect from someone I don't have in my contacts.

I'm about to accept it, but it goes through before I can. I freeze, clutching my towel closer. Has someone hacked into my NeuroLink?

"You're awake."

I recognize Jax's voice. I feel a curious mix of relief and unease at her words. "Are you watching me?"

"I just saw your status blink green." She sounds as clipped as I remember.

"And where am I, exactly?"

"A hotel, of course. You should probably stay here for a while, at least until you're no longer at the top of the lottery."

"Why'd you drug me yesterday?"

"Two days ago. You've been asleep for an entire day."

I'd lost a *day*? I blink. So this isn't the sunset after the night Jax had come for me. No wonder all the Riders sounded so worried.

"Why'd you do it, Jax?" I ask again. After my argument with Hideo, I'm in no mood to play around.

"Relax. I needed to get you here without you causing a scene. You said you didn't trust me entirely, so I couldn't trust you not to attack me in the car. I could've thrown a sack over your head, but I didn't want to freak you out."

I make an incredulous face. "Because I totally didn't freak out when you *shot me* instead."

She responds with a bored sigh. "You're fine. Now go get dressed."

"Why?"

"Because Zero is heading upstairs to see you."

That brings my sarcastic comments to a halt. The thought of Zero coming into my suite sends a trill of fear through me, and I find myself stepping toward the bathroom before Jax can say another word.

"I'll be ready," I mutter.

I pull on a fresh change of clothes that I find folded neatly in my room's closet. They're crisp in their newness and fit a little loosely. The sight of myself in the mirror, dressed fully in black, only reminds me of how foreign everything feels right now, how deeply I've gone into a hive and how likely it is that I might never come out of it, and I look quickly away, wishing my old clothes hadn't been ruined by blood and smoke.

I'm smoothing down my new shirt when I hear a soft knock on my door, followed by silence. I hesitate.

"Come in," I say, feeling strange giving someone permission while I'm the one here against her will.

The door of my suite opens and closes, followed by the soft sound of footsteps against the carpet. He's here. I take one more deep breath. My heart won't stop racing, but at least I don't see it spelled out on my face.

Then I step out to see someone already seated in a chair by the window, waiting for me.

5

There are three of them, actually.

Jax stands beside a chair, her hand resting casually on the handle of her gun. She looks relaxed, but her gray eyes follow me without blinking, and I know that if she wanted to, she could whip out that gun and kill me before I could even open my mouth.

Sitting in the chair next to her is an older woman with glasses, her silver-streaked hair tied back into a neat bun that matches her neat clothes. A faint, pleasant perfume hangs in the air around her. She has the sort of face that belongs to a scholar—careful eyes, a controlled mouth, a stare that analyzes me for the unspoken things. Her hands are folded neatly in her lap. She gives me a sympathetic smile when she sees me looking her way.

But it's the third person, the one whose presence owns the room, who stops me in my tracks.

He leans back against the wall, his arms crossed casually over his chest, one of his legs propped against the other. His face is no longer hidden behind a black helmet, and instead of his armor, he's wearing a simple black sweater and dark pants, his shoes polished to a shine. But his mannerisms are unmistakable to me.

One side of his mouth tilts up in a smile. "Well, Emika," says Zero. "Welcome."

The first time I ever crossed paths with Zero, he was nothing more than a snippet of code, a glitch in Hideo's matrix that runs all of Warcross. And the first time I ever saw a virtual version of him, he was standing in the middle of the Dark World's Pirate Den, surrounded by people all hiding behind fake names and exaggerated avatar monsters.

Even then, he'd stood out. Against a backdrop of monsters, he was a lean, dark, armored shadow, as silent and unapologetic as the night. I can still remember the chill he'd sent through me at the mere sight of his virtual figure—the way my hands clenched and my nails cut into my palms.

Now I gape at his exposed face.

It's like looking at Hideo through a dream.

He's younger by a couple of years, his features harsher and fiercer. Still, I can immediately see the resemblance between the two—the liquid dark eyes and hair—and I can easily recognize in him the small boy from Hideo's reconstructed Memory.

In a more normal setting, after a more normal day, he'd probably seem like a handsome stranger anyone might meet on the street, the kind of boy who's never had trouble getting a date or making a friend, the sort who doesn't talk much but grips everyone's attention when he does. But here, there's something unsettling about him that I can't quite put my finger on. While Hideo has a piercing stare, there's a wildness in Sasuke's eyes, something deep and unfeeling. Something less human. I don't know how to describe its unusual light. It draws me in at the same time it repels me.

The older woman speaks. Her eyes are soft, sweeping over me from head to toe. "This is the girl, then?" she says to Zero in an accent I can't quite place.

"Emika Chen," Zero replies.

"Emika Chen." The woman rests her chin against her hand and frowns. "She looks exhausted. We should have given her an extra day to rest."

"We don't have that kind of luxury," Zero says. "She was the only one of Hideo's bounty hunters who managed to stay on my trail. She can handle a long day."

At that, the woman gives me a helpless look. "I'm sorry," she addresses me directly. "Everything will make more sense once we explain."

Zero tips his head subtly in her direction. "This is Dr. Dana Taylor," he says. "And you already know who I am." He studies my face. "Jax tells me you gave her a little trouble."

I finally find my voice. "Well, it's not like she killed anyone in front of me or anything."

"Come on," Jax mutters to Zero. "She's completely inexperienced. Did you know she's never even fired a gun before?"

"I've fired stun guns," I say.

Jax holds a hand out in my direction. "See?"

"With you around, she doesn't need a gun," Zero replies.

Jax makes an annoyed sound, but doesn't counter that.

Zero observes me in the same way he'd done in the Dark World. My heart beats a rapid rhythm at his gaze. For all I know, he's doing a scan of all my data, checking to make sure I'm not signaling anyone to follow me here.

Does he remember his brother? How could he possibly forget—or, worse, not care?

"I sent her to save your life, you know," he says.

I turn my head up to meet his gaze as my anger flares again. "You forced me here under threat of death."

Zero's eyes swivel to the black door I'd entered through before settling back on me. "You accepted my invitation."

"And how do I know you didn't send those other assassins after me, too, just to set this entire thing up?"

"You think I have nothing better to do with my time than mess with you."

"I think you play more games with me than you should."

Dr. Taylor frowns at Zero before she takes a deep breath and looks at me. "We're glad you're safe, Emika," she continues in a soft tone. "You may not have heard of Jax before, but she's well-known in our circles. The sight of her defending you will send a clear message to every hunter watching the assassination lottery to stay away from you."

I look over my shoulder toward the door, feeling no safer at this knowledge. If I dared to turn my back on Zero and leave this place, would Jax put a bullet through my head?

Zero points at my eyes. "I'm assuming you use the beta lenses."

"Yes," I reply. "Why?"

"You're going to need some extra protection on your account." Zero flicks his hand subtly, and a menu pops up between us, asking me to accept his invite.

I hesitate.

Zero gives me a wry smile. "It's not a virus," he says.

I'm not in much of a position to argue with him, so I accept it.

A download bar appears.

55 %

It completes and vanishes as quickly as it'd arrived.

Zero takes a step toward me. He holds out one of his palms.

As I stare at it, a black virtual cuff materializes to hover over his hand. Then he places that hand over my arm, and the cuff snaps into place around my wrist with a clean click. Like a shackle. A coat of black armor identical to Zero's virtual gear clips all over my body in a ripple of movement, and for a brief moment, I look like I once did in that red virtual cavern, when Zero first approached me during the championships.

The armor disappears again, as if it had faded away right into my skin. The cuff glows a soft blue before it vanishes. It reappears only when I stare long enough at my wrist. I'd seen the same thing on Jax when she first showed up during my attack.

"It's a Blackcoat mark," he says. "You are now under our watch. No one else will touch you."

He's officially claimed me for the Blackcoats. I'm theirs now.

I rub at my new cuff. Even though it's a virtual object, I can almost feel it burning into me.

"So, what are you all? Vigilantes or something?"

Zero returns to where he'd been leaning against the wall. "That term's a little sensational. But I guess it applies."

Taylor turns her steady gaze on me. "We believe that too much power in the hands of a single entity is always a dangerous thing. So we fight that, whenever and wherever we can. We have wealthy patrons who support our cause."

I wait for her to tell me who those patrons are, but she doesn't. My eyes flicker uneasily to Zero. "How many of you are there?"

"Our numbers shift, depending on what we're doing," he replies. "We bring on those we need and part ways when we're done—but there are, of course, a handful of us who are always involved. And as you know, our current target of interest is Hideo Tanaka and his NeuroLink."

So, I wasn't wrong. I've known since Hideo first hired me that someone was lurking in the shadows, trying to undo his work and threaten his life—but it's one thing to be investigating those clues and another thing to hear it confirmed.

My gaze returns to Jax. "The assassination attempt on Hideo," I say, my voice suddenly tight. "Right after the first Warcross game. Was that—"

Jax fixes me with her cool gray eyes before I can even finish my sentence. She shrugs. "Would've succeeded had his security detail not been so tight," she replies. "Anyway, it doesn't matter anymore. Killing him now won't disable his algorithm."

Jax had been the one who tried to kill Hideo. My eyes dart to Zero, searching for a reaction from him that's as horrified as how I feel. But his face stays calm and collected. It's as if Hideo were nothing but a name to him.

"Let's talk about our common goals, Emika," Zero says. "Because they're one and the same, aren't they?"

I stare at him, trying to sound calm. "To take down the NeuroLink's algorithm."

Zero nods once in approval. "And do you know what we need to do that?"

The words come out of me, cold and calculating. "To get into Hideo's account."

"Yes. Through someone who's capable of winning that kind of trust. You."

They need someone to get into Hideo's systems, and in order to do that, they need to get under his skin. But after my talk with him, I'm going to be the last person he'll be willing to confide in.

What about Zero himself? Surely Sasuke is a better option to use than me?

A million questions threaten to spill out of my mouth. In the light, Zero's eyes are a very dark brown, and if I look closely, I can see thread-thin slashes of gold in them. The vision of him as a small boy, his high-pitched laugh as he ran through the park with his brother, flashes through my mind. I think of him grinning as Hideo looped the blue scarf around his neck, and him calling over his shoulder as he went to retrieve the plastic egg that Hideo had thrown too far.

Sasuke should be the only connection to Hideo that the Blackcoats would ever need. If Sasuke were to approach Hideo, he would give up the world for his lost brother, would move heaven and earth if Sasuke asked him to.

Would Sasuke do the same in return? Why is there no hint of emotion for his brother in his eyes?

I push down the rising tide of questions in my mind. There's too little that they're revealing about the Blackcoats, and something about the tension in the air tells me that I shouldn't be openly asking about Zero's connection to Hideo yet. I need to wait for a moment alone with him.

"So, you're trying to stop Hideo out of the goodness of your hearts?" I ask.

"Why else would we be doing it?"

I throw my hands up. "*I don't know.* You haven't told me much of anything about your shadow group. Why'd you try to kill me when you blew up the Riders' dorms? Was that out of your good-will, too?"

Zero seems completely unsurprised by my remark. "Sometimes, doing the right thing means making hard decisions along the way."

"And how do I know you won't make another hard decision with me?"

"You don't believe me."

"No, I don't believe that you're telling me everything I need to know."

Taylor suddenly straightens. "You went to prison for a while, didn't you?" she says. "Earned a red mark on your record because you saw an injustice done to some girl you barely knew?"

My jaw tightens at her words. "You've been snooping around in my files."

She ignores my tone, her eyes bright. "Why did *you* do it, Emika? What did *you* get out of it, aside from years of hardship? What took *you* down that path? You used your talents to break into the private files of all your fellow students. You released that data onto the Internet. That was a crime, wasn't it? And yet, you did it anyway—because you were standing up for a girl who had been wronged."

The memory rushes back—my arrest, my trial, the sentencing.

"You're still so young," she goes on. "Is it so hard for you to believe that someone else might want to do the same? Try to remember how you felt at that time, then take that and expand it into something bigger than yourself, a group of people, all of whom might believe in a higher cause?"

I don't say anything.

Taylor leans toward me. "I know you're hesitant," she says gently. "I can see it on your face, your distrust of everything I'm telling you, and I understand why. We didn't get off on the best foot." She glances at Zero with a lifted eyebrow. "But you're now aware of what Hideo's true plans are. And no matter how little you know about us or we know about you, we're both on the same side. We have no intention of harming an ally. No one's going to force your hand." Her voice hardens now, a tone that doesn't seem to match her face. "Nothing I've ever seen has frightened me quite as much as what Hideo Tanaka is doing with the NeuroLink's algorithm. Isn't that why you cut ties with him, in spite of everything he could give you?"

She says this in a way that hints at my brief relationship with Hideo, and to my annoyance, my cheeks warm. I wonder exactly how much she knows about me. My eyes flicker again to Zero.

A sudden surge of rage grips me. All I can remember in this moment is the way Zero had stood there in the dark hall, hidden behind his virtual armor, mocking me as I discovered all my files had been emptied. All I can feel is the same skin-crawling sensation of Zero being inside my mind, his theft of my most precious Memories.

This is someone who has betrayed me before. And now here he is, asking me to help him.

"Why should I trust you?" I ask. "After everything you've done?"

Zero regards me with a penetrating look. "It doesn't matter if you trust me or not. Hideo's moving forward, regardless, and we're running out of time. We're going to stop him from abusing his NeuroLink, and we can do it faster with your help. That's all I can tell you."

I think of the colorful maps of minds that Hideo had shown me, then the ability he had to stop someone dead in his tracks by doing nothing more than shifting that map. I think of the eerie blankness on people's faces.

"So." Zero laces his fingers together. "Are you in?"

I'm ready to refuse him. He had taken my soul out of my chest and done something obscene with it; even now, he is messing with my emotions. I want to turn my back on Zero and step out of this room, do what Roshan said and return to New York and never think about any of this again.

Instead, I scowl at Zero. "What do you have in mind?"

6

Zero smiles. He exchanges a stare with Taylor, then with Jax, and as he does, Taylor rises from her seat. She gives me an encouraging nod before she turns away.

"Glad to have you on board," she says over her shoulder, and then heads out of the room.

Jax lingers a second longer, locked in a silent exchange with Zero that feels like something shared between familiar partners. She doesn't bother looking my way before she leaves, too. "I'll be next door," she calls out as she goes. I can't tell if it's meant to reassure or threaten me that she'll be on guard so close by.

The door closes behind her without a sound, leaving me completely alone with Zero.

He moves closer to me, looking amused at my fascination and unease. "You've always worked on your own, haven't you?" he says. "It's uncomfortable for you, being marked with a group."

Somehow, his physical appearance seems even more

intimidating than his virtual one. I realize I'm clenching my fists and force myself to relax my hands. "I was doing fine with the Phoenix Riders," I reply.

He nods. "And that's why you've already told them everything you're doing, right? That you're here now?"

I narrow my eyes at his mocking tone. "And what about you?"

"What about me?"

"How long have you been with the Blackcoats? Were you the one who formed them? Or have you never been a loner?"

He puts his hands in his pockets in a gesture so reminiscent of Hideo that, for an instant, I feel like he's the one here instead. "As long as I can remember," he answers.

Now's my chance. All the questions swirling in my mind sit on the edge of my tongue. My breath is suddenly short as the words pour out. "You're Sasuke Tanaka. Aren't you?"

My statement is greeted only by silence.

"You're Hideo's younger brother," I urge him, as if he didn't hear me the first time.

His eyes are absolutely devoid of any emotion. "I know," he says.

I blink, thinking I'd misheard him. "You *know*?"

There's something unusual about his eyes again, that empty stare. It's as if what I've said means *nothing*. It seems irrelevant to him, like I'd revealed he was related to some faraway stranger he knows absolutely nothing about . . . and not the brother he'd grown up with, the brother who had destroyed his own life and mind out of grief for him. The brother he is now trying to stop.

"You—" My words falter, my voice turning incredulous as I look at him. "You're Hideo's brother. How can you know that and still talk like this?"

Again, no response. He looks completely unaffected by my

words. Instead, he steps closer to me until we're separated by a mere foot. "A blood relation is meaningless," he finally replies. "Hideo's my brother, but more importantly, he's my mark."

My mark. The words are harsh and cutting. I think back to the grin on young Sasuke's face in Hideo's Memory, when they were both at the park. I puzzle over the deep wounds that Sasuke left behind in Hideo and his family when he disappeared. This is a boy who had been loved deeply. Now he doesn't seem to care at all.

"But—" I say, faltering, "what *happened* to you? You vanished when you were a little boy. Where did you go? Why are you called Zero?"

"Jax didn't warn me about how curious you are," he replies. "I guess this is what makes you a good bounty hunter."

The way he's responding reminds me of code stuck in an infinite loop, going round and round in useless circles, or politicians who know exactly how to evade a question they don't want to answer. People who can turn a question on you to take the heat off themselves.

Maybe Zero doesn't want to answer me. Maybe he doesn't even *know.* Whatever the reason, I won't be getting anything out of him voluntarily—nothing more than these piecemeal replies. I shove down the urge to keep pressing him. If he won't tell me himself, then I'll have to gather info on my own.

So I try a different kind of question. "What are you planning?" I force myself to say.

"We're going to insert a virus into Hideo's algorithm," Zero says. He holds his hand out, and a glowing data packet appears over his palm. "The instant it's in, it will trigger a chain reaction that deletes the algorithm entirely and cripples the NeuroLink itself. But to do this successfully, we have to launch it from inside Hideo's own account, his actual mind. And we have to do this on the day of the closing ceremony, at the very moment when the beta lenses finally connect to the algorithm."

I guess the rumor about when the beta lenses would convert to algorithm lenses is true, after all. It makes sense—theoretically, there'll be a split-second delay when the beta lenses are hooked into the algorithm but not yet influenced by it. When it's setting itself up. That's the only chance they'll get to insert a virus.

"And when, exactly, are the beta lenses connecting to the algorithm?" I ask.

"Right at the start of the closing ceremony's game."

I look sidelong at him. How does he know so much about Hideo's plans? "So, I'm going to have to get into his mind," I repeat. "Literally."

"As literal as it gets," Zero replies. "And the only way into the algorithm—into his mind—is for Hideo himself to allow it. That's where you come in."

"You want me to warm up to Hideo."

"I want you to do whatever it takes."

"He'll never go for it," I reply. "After our last encounter, I doubt he'll ever want to see me again. He already suspects I'm out to stop him."

"I think you underestimate his feelings for you." He waves his hand once.

The world around us disappears, then wraps us both inside news footage of Hideo leaving an event while being swarmed on all sides by anxious reporters and fans. This is from two nights ago, after Hideo had announced the rematch between the Phoenix Riders and Team Andromeda.

His bodyguards shout and push, cutting a path for him, and a good many paces behind him walks Kenn, who looks pale and distraught. I've never seen the two of them like this, walking so far apart. As the security team forms a stern line in front of the crowds, one of the reporters shouts a question at Hideo.

Are you still dating Emika Chen? Are you two an item?

Hideo doesn't react to the question—at least, not obviously. But I can see the tightening of his shoulders, the tension in his jaw. His eyes stay turned down, focused intensely on the path before him.

I look away from Hideo's haunted expression, but it remains seared into my mind. "But *you're* his real weakness," I insist, forcing myself to concentrate. "You must know that! Hideo would do anything for you."

"We have discussed Hideo's potential responses to me," Zero says casually, as if he were telling me about the weather. "He hasn't seen me in a decade—his reaction to me won't be directed at me, but at the Blackcoats. And it will be revenge he's seeking. So, we need someone with one degree of separation. You."

He speaks of Hideo as if his brother were nothing more than target practice—when I search his gaze, all I see is darkness, something impenetrable and unfeeling. It's like looking at a person who isn't a person at all.

I lean against the desk and bow my head. "Fine," I mumble. "How do you suggest I do this?"

Zero finally smiles. "You're going to break into Hideo's mind. And I'm going to show you how."

7

"Come join me in the Dark World," Zero says. He waves his hand once again, and a screen appears between us, asking me if I want to Link with him for a session.

A direct connection with Zero. What kind of thoughts and emotions would I get from him? I hesitate for another moment, then reach out and accept our Link. The hotel room around me darkens at the edges until I can't make out Zero's face anymore. A few seconds later, I've sunken into a pitch-black abyss.

I hold my breath at the familiar, drowning sensation that always settles over me right before I go down under to the Dark World.

Then, slowly, it materializes.

At first, I recognize it. Water drips into potholes dotting the streets, forming miniature reflecting pools of the red neon signs that line the building walls. They display a constant stream of personal data stolen from unprotected accounts that dared to wander down here. Stalls line the road itself, each one lit with strings of lights, hawking all the things I'm used to seeing—drugs, illegal weapons, cryptocurrency exchanges, discontinued Warcross virtual items, and unreleased avatar clothing.

This is a location I should be familiar with, and yet none of these buildings are what I remember, nor are the streets or signs recognizable. All the sidewalks are empty.

"Looks strange, doesn't it?"

Zero's sudden presence beside me makes me jump. When I face him, he's hidden behind armor again; black metal plates covering him from head to toe gleam under crimson lights. He moves like a shadow. While the few people passing us are anonymous, no one appears to notice him. In fact, if I didn't know better, I'd say they were giving him a wide berth without even realizing he's there. It's not clear to me if they can even see his figure, but they definitely notice the black cuffs we both wear. No one wants anything to do with us.

Tentatively, I reach out through our Link to see if I can catch any emotions coming from Zero. But he feels calm, his temperament smooth as glass. Then, a ripple of amusement.

"Poking around already? Too curious for your own good," he says, and I remember that he can sense me, too. I quickly lean away.

"Where is everyone?" I ask him.

"After Hideo activated his algorithm, any user who had already switched to the new NeuroLink lenses became restricted from logging on to the Dark World. It took out a good number of the people who used to wander down here. Others have been compelled to go to the authorities with what information they know about this place. There have been dozens of raids in the past couple of days. Those who can still access the Dark World have gone deeper underground, rebuilding as they went. Many of the spots you're familiar with won't be here."

I wander down the road, trying to get my bearings. On a normal day, a market like this would be swarming with anonymous avatars. Today, it's a trickle, and many look too uneasy to stop at the illegal stands.

This is a good thing, I tell myself. I should be happy about it, and Hideo is right to do this to the Dark World. Haven't I spent years hunting people down here? This isn't a good place. There are pockets of the Dark World so disturbing that they ought to be permanently wiped out, people so perverse and evil that they deserve to rot in jail. They *should* be afraid.

But . . . the idea of one person having that kind of reach down here, to put his hand inside someone's mind and *compel* them to leave this place . . .

"What's going on over there?" I ask when we walk past a stand in a night market. Even though it's a small shop, there must be a crowd of well over two hundred people gathered around it. When I look long enough at the stand, a number appears over it.

50,000

The sheer volume of visitors keeps causing the shop to crash, and from here, it looks like the stand is collapsing into a pile and resetting itself over and over.

"They're auctioning off cases of beta lenses," Zero replies. "Rare commodities, as you can guess."

I realize that the number over the stand is the price that the beta lenses are currently going for. Fifty thousand notes for a single pair.

The bidders obviously have their own beta lenses to even be

in the Dark World, so my guess is that they're here on behalf of others. There's a desperation in the space that makes it feel dangerous. Already, arguments are breaking out, and overhead, I can see users being doxed by angry competitors, their private info thrown up on the neon-red signs spanning the sides of the building walls. I quicken my pace until we've left the stand behind us.

We're somewhere close to where the Pirate's Den was the last time I saw it, although the roads have shifted since then. When the black lake comes into view, there's no ship floating on the water.

I turn to Zero, startled. The Pirate's Den has never been successfully shut down. "Is it gone?" I ask him.

He looks skyward. I tilt my head to follow his gaze.

High above the Dark World's nonsensical buildings and Escher-like stairways, under a smoky brown night sky, is a pirate ship suspended in midair. Rope ladders dangle from it, far out of reach. Its masts are lit up with cascading neon colors that highlight the clouds with electric shades of pink and blue and gold.

"After Hideo activated his algorithm," Zero says, "one Dark World user afflicted by the new lenses went to authorities and ratted out where the Pirate's Den was. There was a raid down here. But cockroaches are hard to eliminate."

I give him a humorless smile at that. The Dark World won't go down without a fight. The pirates just move out of the water and into the skies.

Zero cocks his head slightly to one side. He must already have the entrance code to the new Pirate's Den figured out, because a second later, one of the ship's rope ladders starts descending toward us. It stops right in front of us, at the perfect height.

Zero holds a hand out at the ladder and turns to me. "After you."

I walk past him and grab one of the ladder's rungs tightly. He steps on it after me, his gloved hands clasping the rope on either side of me. As we rise, I look over his arm and down at the city. I've never seen the Dark World from the sky before. It looks even less logical than it does from the ground. Some of the buildings resemble spiral staircases that disappear into the clouds, with dozens of window lights that shift colors in gradients. Dark, anonymous avatars walk sideways along other walls, as if the people were held up by strings. Other buildings are painted all in black, with no windows at all—only thin neon lines that run vertically along its walls. Who knows what the hell goes on inside there. There are spheres that hover in midair, supported by nothing, with no obvious way of getting inside. As we rise as high as the clouds, I can look down and see some of the towers forming circular patterns on the ground, as if they were alien crop circles.

We finally reach the floating ramp leading into the Pirate's Den. Now that we're close enough, I can see how enormous this new ship's masts are, stretching up like screens on the sides of skyscrapers. What I'd seen as gradients of neon colors on the masts are actually advertisements showcasing that day's matches, as well as the current bets on the Phoenix Riders and Team Andromeda rematch.

Zero steps off first. He walks onto the ramp and gestures for me to follow. My eyes shift from the broadcasts to the ship's entrance, where dozens of avatars are walking in underneath the Pirate's Den slogan.

INFORMATION WANTS TO BE FREE

We step inside. I can hear the pulsing rhythm of my heart in my ears, the blood pumping in time to the soundtrack playing around me, no doubt some stolen track from an unreleased album. Fog hugs the ground. The avatars here are as twisted and strange as ever, a weird mix of people with random, forgettable faces, and users who have remade themselves with monstrous features.

But what makes me freeze is the sight of the glass cylinder looming in the center of the cavernous space. The assassination lottery looks like it always does, with its list of names in scarlet letters and the current bid beside each one. Up on the higher deck and looking down at the list are assassins and hunters carefully analyzing the list.

What looks different is the name at the top of that list.

Emika Chen | Current Offer: ₦5,625,000

No wonder everyone's after me: 5,625,000 notes for my assassination.

"They can't see you," Zero says, cutting through my paralyzing terror. When I glance at him, he gives me a simple nod. I can't see any part of his expression behind his dark helmet, of course, but his body is turned vaguely toward me, giving me the sense that he's protecting me.

In spite of everything, I feel oddly safe beside him. It's hard to believe that, not long ago, I'd first seen Zero in this very same space as my enemy, the bounty I was hired to hunt down by Hideo. Now the bounty has reversed.

Betting on the Final rematch is happening in another corner of the space, while others are clustered in a large crowd around the current Darkcross game, throwing amounts of money around at an increasingly frantic pace. Over the onlookers is a banner showing the match, followed by how much is at stake.

MIDNIGHT RAIDERS vs. HELLDOGS
Current Odds 1:4

"New game!" a voice calls out. An automated announcer is speaking now, its androgynous voice echoing around us. "Match ends when a player takes their opponent's Artifact. Bets may be placed two minutes before the game's opening call and can continue until the official start."

I look at the chaotic audience. All of the patrons of the official Warcross teams are public figures with deep pockets, each one well-known. But the identities of the patrons of the Dark World teams are a mystery. Rumor has it that they are mafia bosses, gang leaders, and drug lords. None of them are stupid enough to publicly sponsor a team—but one Dark World team can earn double the profits of the Phoenix Riders. No wonder the teams down here can recruit such talented players. Some of them are even ex-Warcross professionals, those whose reflexes can't keep up with the younger, upcoming stars. If you don't mind playing an illegal game that could get you arrested at any time, then you'll be showered with riches far beyond that of a legit, official Warcross player in the real world.

Of course, as with everything else down here, playing Darkcross comes with its own unique risks. Unlike Warcross played legally, where the only consequence of losing a game is your money and your ego . . . the patrons of Dark World teams are a dangerous crowd to disappoint. If you lose enough Darkcross games, you might see your own name up on the assassination lottery list. I remember one Darkcross player who was found hanging in his garage, his body bloodied and broken, and another who was pushed in front of a train.

"Several teams lost their players after the algorithm triggered," Zero goes on as we move to a different part of the den. Here, the room is darker and emptier, some distance away from the others and partially separated by a film of light that acts like a curtain. "Of course, this has just made the betting all the more exciting and unpredictable."

"Is that what we're down here for? The games?" I look at him. "I thought you were going to show me how to break into Hideo's mind."

"We are." Zero nods. "And I am."

"How?"

"We recently uncovered a glitch in Hideo's Link system. The same system that allows two people to communicate through their thoughts. The glitch only appears if you and I are Linked during a game of Warcross."

I suck in my breath. "What kind of glitch?"

"During a regular Link session, you have to get permission from the other person in order to access any of their thoughts. But during Warcross, with the right hack, this glitch allows you into that person's mind and memories without their consent."

A glitch that lets you into your Linked partner's mind. I imagine a stranger's cold claws piercing my thoughts and memories, me powerless to stop it. How in the world did Zero find a glitch this huge?

Zero smiles at my confusion. "Even the biggest companies in the world aren't that secure," he reminds me.

No wonder we're here. And no wonder Zero has wanted to Link with me. I stare up into his black helmet, suddenly feeling very exposed.

Zero brought me here to play a game of Warcross while Linked.

A slight buzzing tickles my ears. It's the same sound I'd heard back during the Warcross championships, when Zero first interrupted my underwater game with the Phoenix Riders. A clicking sound makes me look down. I'm now encased in dark armor of my own, crimson-red plates in contrast to Zero's black. No doubt that if I were looking at myself, I would see my face hidden behind a helmet.

Then the Pirate's Den vanishes, and I find myself standing in a Warcross world.

I'm going to play against Zero, one on one.

8

A one-on-one game of Warcross is called a Duel. It's the same game as Warcross itself, except without a team to back you up—and without a team, everything falls onto your shoulders. You are the Captain, Architect, and Thief. You are the Fighter and Healer.

I've watched Duels in the Dark World before, but I've never played in one. And down here, where screwing up in a game could endanger my life, I'm not feeling good about my chances.

Already, a crowd of gamblers has gathered around, and an announcer has started to take bets for and against each of us. I find myself wondering if anything will happen to me if I lose this game. Just how much do I trust Zero to demonstrate getting into my mind? What if he damages my account permanently? It seems like a lot of trouble to bring me here just for that . . . but it's hard to be sure of anything with him.

Our Duel's virtual world is a night setting. Sheets of stars sweep the skies, while streaks of pink and purple linger at the horizon, an image of the minutes right after sunset. Hundreds of giant glass archways curve through the air, each of them reflecting the light. When I look down at my feet, I realize with a start that I'm not standing on solid ground at all—but on the back of a creature. A moving creature.

A *dragon*. As long as a whale.

Its scales are illuminated with glowing neon stripes, and its wings are haloed in gold light, as if it were a robot. And when I look closer, I realize that the scales beneath my feet aren't organic, but metallic.

I fall to my knees as the beast arches its enormous neck and lets out a column of fire from its mechanical jaws, outlining the clouds below us. Its shriek echoes across the world.

"Welcome to the Dragon's Nest." A voice reverberates overhead. Familiar, glowing power-ups materialize in the air, lighting up the evening with their colors—and at the same time, a selection of weapons appears in front of me.

Rope. Knives. Dynamite. Gun. Bow and arrows. Shield.

It's a selection of the weapons that each Warcross team player would have, and I'm allowed to choose three of them to hang on my belt. A timer counts down above it. I have ten seconds. My mind whirls, and I grab for what's familiar to me. The rope. The dynamite. Then I remember that I can't just be an Architect—this isn't a game where Roshan can protect me. So I put back the dynamite and grab for the shield and the bow and arrows right before the selection vanishes.

I clip on the silver shield armguards, then swing the arrows over my back and loop the bow across my chest. The gun might be useful, but if I'm on a dragon, then Zero probably will be, too, and I might need a way to swing up onto his. Rope and a bow will be my best bet.

My dragon swoops toward the closest glass arch to us. I look around for Zero, but see him nowhere. Even as a chant goes up from the Blackcoat spectators, indicating the start of the game, I'm still gliding alone through the air. Reflections from the arches throw me off. I whirl, thinking Zero's behind me, but there are only more clouds.

"Game! Set! *Fight!*"

Suddenly, an enormous shadow lands on top of the arch right over us. A web of cracks jolts across the glass with a deafening splinter.

My head jerks up—and I see him there, Zero, on the back of a dragon with scales as black as a rain-soaked raven, its metal spikes shining with edges of dark silver light. His dragon hisses at me, then brings its wings down in one mighty swoop. The glass arch shatters into a thousand pieces.

I throw myself against my dragon's shoulders and cross my forearms to activate my shield. The circular blue field bursts out from my armguards as glass shards pour down on me. The impact nearly knocks me flat. I flinch as if the weight were real.

[Player B] | Life: -20%

||||||||||||||||||||

If it weren't for my shield, a hit like that would have easily slashed my life bar in half. And in a real Warcross game, giving my opponent the advantage of a surprise attack like that before the starting call would be impossible. But here, cheats are commonly written in, sometimes as a game progresses live.

When is Zero going to show me the hack?

A roar from the onlookers fills my ears. I peer up through my shield in time to see Zero leap from the back of his dragon to hurtle down toward mine. He lands on one of its wings, then yanks a sword from his side. He slashes hard into the wing, puncturing the fold, and cuts a deep gash.

My dragon screams—it pitches to one side. The sudden lurch sends me tumbling, forcing me to break my armguard pose. My shield deactivates as I instead grab the edge of one of the beast's scales and hang on. Below us, other dragons glide in and out between the glass arches, black silhouettes against the evening. A series of glowing power-ups hover above them, golden speed bursts and ice marbles, a sphere of green vines and a fireball.

My mind whirls, gauging the distance between me and each of them. That fireball is a Flamethrower power-up, strong enough to swallow an opponent whole. The sphere wrapped with vines is a Vine Trap, capable of entangling a player for five seconds, immobilizing them on the spot.

I haul myself up along the dragon's scales. Zero lunges for me—I roll to one side before he can seize the glowing Artifact hanging over my head. He misses it by a bare inch. I roll over and over as he lunges for me again. My hands fumble for the rope at my waist, but then I feel Zero's hand clamp down on my arm. He pulls me toward him.

I grit my teeth and kick—my metal boots hit him in the chest, and I push off as hard as I can. He loses his grip on me. I fling myself free of both Zero and my dragon, then plummet through the air. Wind screams against my ears.

As I go, I activate my shield again and turn it at an angle. It catches the air, letting me steer myself slightly sideways. I manage to navigate myself toward the fireball and the vine power-ups. I throw both arms wide, grabbing the two power-ups simultaneously.

I look up to see Zero jump from the dragon and follow me down. I pocket the vine power-up, then take the fireball and unleash it, swinging it straight at him.

It explodes with a thunderous roar. Flames engulf both Zero and my injured dragon in a giant blaze.

[Player A] | Life: -100%
[Player B] STRIKES OUT [Player A]

I ignore the cheers and boos from the audience. Zero's going to regenerate in no time, and with the way this game's structured, he might have an unfair advantage again. As the wind whistles past my ears, I yank out an arrow strapped to my back holster and frantically knot the rope at my waist to it. I tie the rope's other end around my chest. Then I fit the arrow to my bow right as I fall like a stone past the entire herd of dragons. I twist, point my bow up at the nearest dragon to me, and shoot.

The arrow hits true, lodging in between two scales on a dragon's chest. Sparks fly from the burn of the arrowhead's metal against the scales. The beast lets out a roar of annoyance as the rope pulls taut, yanking me to an abrupt halt with it. I pull myself up as quickly as I can as the dragon veers sharply to one side, narrowly avoiding colliding with a glass arch.

Above me, Zero reappears on the back of his black dragon. Its ice-colored eyes fix on me, and it plunges in my direction just as I swing myself up onto my new dragon's back. This time, I point my dragon toward the arches.

"Higher," I snap, urging it up. It obeys, turning its mechanical head where I want it to.

Zero's dragon hurls toward me, its jaws open. It lets out a column of fire. I pull my dragon to one side, just missing it, but some of the flame catches my dragon's wing, scorching the metal black. I force it into a tight spiral around the arch's columns.

"What the hell is she doing?" I can hear a couple of the spectators shouting, their words almost drowned out by the cheers.

Zero gives chase. He steers his dragon to fly sidelong against mine, avoiding the spiraling pattern that I'm doing. He looks ready to pull in close again and jump onto my dragon's back.

I aim for the gently curving top of the glass arch. As I reach it, Zero nears me. I grab my vine power-up in my inventory. If I can lure Zero closer and set it off on him at the right time, it'll ensnare him in its tangle of thick vines and freeze him there, hanging from the top of the arch. I can leap off my dragon and slide down the tangle of vines to grab his Artifact.

I glance over my shoulder. He's drawing closer now, taking the bait. A small smile threatens to creep onto my face. I turn to stare down at the top of the arch. Time to strike—

Then a flash of light hits me. The world washes out into blinding white. Did the game end? Then I realize a split second later that Zero has used his own power-up on me. A lightning strike. I see the top of the glass arch rushing at me as I fall toward it. I hit it full force, without a chance to even pull up my shield.

[Player B] | Life: -60%
WARNING

▌▌▌▌▌▌▌▌▐▐▐▐▐▐▐▐▐

I struggle to my feet as Zero walks to me on top of the arch. Hastily, I bring up my vine power-up and point it at him.

The world around me flickers, like static cutting through the air.

I blink, frowning. Could everyone see that? Was it just me?

Zero's focus is trained on me. As he approaches, he waves his hand in a subtle gesture. The static flickers again. It reminds me of when he took over my view during one of the Phoenix Riders' championship games, how we both ended up in that dark-red cavern.

I hold a hand out at him, as if that could possibly stop him. "Wait—" I start to say. "What are you doing—"

Time for us to stop playing around, Zero says. His words echo in my mind through our Link.

And in the blink of an eye, the virtual world around us shifts into something else.

I gasp. It's my old foster home.

I'm standing back in those familiar halls, surrounded by peeling yellow wallpaper and slants of gray light. There's a storm raging, the lights outside stuttering with every streak of lightning, the ground trembling with every roll of thunder. Nearby, one of the doors in the hallway—the girls' room, *my* old room—is ajar from where I'd just crept through.

This is the night when I escaped from the foster home.

That's impossible. If I wasn't sitting in a chair in real life, I'm sure my knees would've buckled. My breath comes up shallow.

How did Zero create this? How did he know? How did he get inside my head, find this memory, and populate this virtual world around me?

The glitch.

But when? Did he get in right after I accepted his Link invite, just before we headed into our Duel?

I can't hear the roar of the audience anymore, so I can't tell if they're also seeing what I'm seeing. Just like the championship game and the red cavern, I'm probably the only one who knows what's happening to me right now.

I tremble at the sight of the hall, at the familiarity of this night. Everything looks the same, except somehow exaggerated, like it might appear in a nightmare. The walls are so much taller than they should be, stretching so high that I can barely see the ceiling, and the patterns on the wallpaper ripple in the light, like it's in motion. When I look down at myself, I realize I'm even wearing the same clothes I'd worn that evening as I made my escape—my worn sneakers, my torn jeans, my faded sweater.

The same fear from that evening thrums through my veins. The same thoughts race through me. I'd planned every detail of tonight's escape. Counted down from when I saw the light go out in Mrs. Devitt's room. Stashed all I could fit into my backpack. The Dragon's Nest Duel has all but vanished from my mind. Gone are the thoughts of winning our game.

It's as if Zero had opened a gate into my soul.

"Every locked door has a key."

I whirl to see Zero standing there in the dark corridor, his armor making him nearly invisible in the midnight shadows of the hall, his face hidden from view behind the opaque helmet. "That's what you're telling yourself right now, isn't it?"

"Get out of my head," I growl at him.

He approaches me, opening one of his hands palm up to reveal a hovering cube, crimson and glossy. "This is the hack—the key to this glitch," he says. He hands the cube to me.

"I can't be here," I whisper. The sight of the foster home is making it hard for me to catch my breath. "Get me out."

Zero shakes his head. "Not until you can do the same to me," he replies.

I clench my fists as my fear boils over into anger. "I won't say it again."

"Neither will I." He stands before me, cold and impassable. "Look in your Memory. Open the cube."

Everything around me seems like it's blurring, spinning in a dizzying circle. I try to concentrate—but then, the old grandfather clock at the end of the hall starts to chime, and the sound of a muffled voice in the kitchen catches my attention.

My heartbeat quickens. I'm back in that awful place again. I'm fourteen, the clock is chiming two in the morning, and I'm out in the hall, sneakers and backpack on, quivering at the sound.

I forget that I'm learning a hack. Instead, I bolt away from Zero and run as fast as I can. My shoes catch against the carpet, making me stumble in the same way I'd stumbled that night. Then I'm out of the hall and in the front room of the home, where the main entrance is staring back at me.

"*Hey!*"

A shout behind me makes me look over my shoulder. It's Chloe, one of my older roommates. Her eyes are focused on my backpack and my shoes as she points a finger at me.

"Mrs. Devitt!" she yells, raising her voice so that it seems to drown the whole house. "Emika's running away!"

I don't know if it's because I'm inside my own Memory, but my body does exactly the same thing I did that night. I dart past the kitchen, my eyes on the front door. My legs feel like they're dragging through mud.

Then comes Zero's voice again, but I don't care what he wants from me anymore. All I need to do is get out of here. If they catch me, I'm dead. As I reach the door, I start to sprint.

A force tackles me from behind. It's Chloe, and suddenly her hands are grabbing for my hair and my throat. We both fall to the floor. I kick blindly out at her, as violently as I can. The lights in the farthest bedroom turn on. We've woken up the others.

My shoe connects hard with Chloe's face. She lets out a yelp and releases me. "Little *bitch*!" she spits as she grabs for me again.

I manage to slip out of her grasp, scramble to my feet, and burst through the door out into a stormy night.

The grass is so slick that I nearly slip, but I regain my footing in time. The chain-link gate is right in front of me. I slam into it, just as I realize that it's held shut with a heavy padlock. Panic ripples through me. My hands hook on to the wiring of the chain-link fence and I haul myself up, not caring when a sharp edge on the metal slashes a red line across one of my fingers.

I crumple in a heap on the other side of the fence, off the property of the foster home. *Get up. You can't be here—they'll catch you.* Behind me, someone emerges from inside the house. They sweep a flashlight beam across the porch. Faint shouts drift to me in the wet air.

I drag myself up to my feet again and dash down the street. I'm not sure if I'm crying in real life or if this is another figment of the memory. All I know is that eventually I huddle in a doorway, almost able to feel the texture of wet wood grain against my hands as I push against either side of the door in an attempt to steady myself. My fingers curl—my nails dig into the chipping paint on the wood.

Zero appears on the sidewalk in front of me. Before I can even start thinking about what to do next, he rushes at me with impossible speed.

Every single instinct I have as a hunter kicks into high gear. I spin out of the way, my arms up in self-defense to protect my face as he lunges at me. He seizes me by my collar before I can run, then yanks me up onto my feet. He brings his face close to me.

"Calm down and think," he says angrily.

The vividness of the Memory shudders, and his words cut through my panic. This isn't real; you're not really back here. *You're playing in the Dark World, inside a ghost from your past.*

How dare you. A surge of anger hits me, forcing me to focus only on Zero. He has broken into my mind, has violated my privacy yet again. *The cube. His hack.* I stare up at his figure towering over me and bring up the code again. This time, I look inside my Memory.

There. I can even *see* what he's done—there is an extra file in my account that shouldn't be there, an access file that the cube had somehow planted.

I open the access file he's downloaded into me to see a hidden Link between us, the gateway he'd opened up that led me right back to him. Then I open the cube of data and run it on him.

A ring of files appears around Zero, each one a gaping, door-like void with a view of another world on the other side. Windows into Zero's mind. I'm in.

I don't wait for him to react. I just pick the closest door to me—and suck my breath in as his mind suddenly envelops everything around us.

The stormy night vanishes; so do the familiar midnight street and the foster home behind chain-link fencing on the other side of the road. New York disappears.

Instead, I'm now on a carpeted floor, in a strange place. When I look up, I see what appears to be a bedroom. A figure is crouched in one corner, huddled tightly against the wall. *I'm in Zero's memories.*

The figure crouching in the corner of the bedroom now stirs.

It's a young boy, with his arms wrapped around his knees. His wrists are bony, protruding from a baggy white sweater, and when I look closer, I notice a symbol embroidered on his upper left sleeve. It's not a mark I've yet seen associated with Zero or the Blackcoats, nor is it anything else I recognize. I can't make out his face in the darkness—but my eyes hitch on a thick scarf wrapped around his neck. A blue scarf.

The same scarf Hideo had given Sasuke the day he disappeared.

The sight startles me so much that I stop short, frozen in place. I pause long enough that, when I blink again, the figure in the corner is gone, and Zero is standing before me again. He reaches out to seize my arm before I can turn away. His hand closes around my wrist, and suddenly I feel like I'm falling, paralyzed. I try to pull my virtual self back up onto my feet, but it's like I've completely stopped responding. All I can see is Zero standing over my figure, dark armor reflecting the dim light in the boy's bedroom, before it all disappears into darkness.

The Pirate's Den comes back into view. The onlookers around us are riotous, shouting over one another as payouts fly, the transparent numbers over their heads changing wildly. I blink, confused and lost. On a hovering screen, I see a playback of the last moments of the Duel. I see the moment when Zero struck me with a Lightning power-up, causing me to collapse on top of the glass arch. Zero walks up to me. I run from him along the arch and I recognize my frantic gestures from when I was running down the hallway in the memory of my foster home. I see myself fight back against Zero—the moments when I'd actually hacked into his Memory—only to have Zero paralyze me with a grip of my wrist, another power-up.

He takes my Artifact.

No one in the audience saw my Memory or Zero's. No one has any idea what happened, that Zero had hacked into my mind or that I had hacked into his. All they witnessed were the same actions playing out in the Duel world. They heard none of the things Zero said to me. It had only been through our Link, as were my words to him.

Some of the onlookers snicker at me, but others seem impressed with the way I played. I nod back at them as if still in a trance. Zero stands beside me. When he looks at me, the black brace around my wrist reappears.

"Well done," Zero says.

Then the ship fades away, and abruptly I find myself back in the real world, sitting exhausted in my hotel suite before Zero. He's back in his black outfit and his real body, his cool eyes still studying me like I'm some sort of sculpture.

Our Duel is done.

I can barely remember the dragons and our brief fight. All I can think about is that Zero had dragged one of my worst moments back up to the surface. Forced me to relive every awful second. He'd used my greatest weakness—my past—against me. Suddenly a wild anger sears me to the bone. I feel careless. All I want to do is hurt him back.

I lunge across the room at him.

Zero sidesteps me like a shadow. I stumble past him, clawing at the air, and fall to my knees. Again, I push myself up and go for him, but he dodges again, as smoothly as if he were toying with me.

"I wouldn't," he warns, his eyes flashing.

I lean against the room's writing desk and meet his eyes warily. "Your Memory," I mutter as I try to steady my breathing. "What was going on in there? Was that when you first disappeared? The symbol on your sleeve—"

"—is a Memory I didn't intend you to access," he answers, his voice still eerily detached. He puts his hands in his pockets. "What matters is that you were able to get in through the vulnerability exposed by our Link, in the same way I used the cube to get into your mind." He gives me a serious look. "That's your ticket in. But be careful in how you use it. Being inside a mind that's not your own means the other's defense will constantly be on the lookout for you. When I seized your wrist, that was my mind realizing you weren't supposed to be in there and pushing you out. It means you won't be able to get back in again."

"But what was that room? Where were you?" I press.

"And where were *you* trying to run away to?" he interjects, a sharpness suddenly entering his voice. He gives me a small smile. "You ran from me like you could see nothing through the terror in your Memory. Like you didn't want to spend another second in that house."

I close my eyes and fight the massive tide of resistance rising in my chest. "Fine, fine," I snap, crossing my arms over my chest. "Point taken. You don't ask me, and I won't ask you."

He studies me with a curious gaze but decides to let his own questions drop. He brings up the glowing cube between us, the key to this hack. "For you," he says.

I take it and store it away in my files. My palms feel clammy.

"You'll have every freedom you had before you met us," Zero continues. "If you need any equipment, let me know. Jax mentioned you lost your board during your escape. I'll have a new one sent for you. Keep me updated on how things are going between you and Hideo."

I nod without saying a word. The thought of me invading Hideo's memories the way Zero just did mine makes me feel sick.

It's nothing that he isn't doing with the NeuroLink, I remind myself, and in much worse ways than that.

Zero pauses at my door for a moment. When he glances at me over his shoulder, there's something else in his gaze—something stiff, as if I'd struck a nerve. "I didn't know which Memory of yours would appear," he says.

It's almost an apology. I don't know what to make of it. All I can do is stand here quietly, fishing for the right words, trying not to let my mind linger on the night of my escape and the terror of crouching alone in that doorway.

It's strange, this moment. It's almost as if he'd let down his guard to reveal a hint of his opaque interior. But it lasts only for a second. Then he steps out of my room, leaving me alone with my endless questions.

I think of Sasuke's small figure, huddled in a corner. His blue scarf, given to him by the brother he doesn't seem to remember loving, wrapped desperately around his neck, the way he clung to it as if it were all he had in the world. Most of all, I linger on the glimpse of the mystery symbol embroidered on his sweater. I pull the image up again now and let it hover before me.

Why did he let me see such a personal Memory? Why was it so easy for me to access? It could be that it was just a random mistake, just like I never meant for him to see mine. But Zero is one of the most powerful hackers I've ever met. How could he be careless enough to expose this sensitive moment from his past to me? I stand there quietly, struggling to figure him out.

Why does Hideo's name mean nothing to you? Who took you? What does that symbol mean?

What happened to you?

9

True to his word, Zero has a new board sent up for me within hours. This one is all black, from surface to wheels to bolts. I test it out tentatively, letting myself adjust to its weight and traction. It should be good for traveling at night.

I stay in the hotel room until it's fully dark outside, inspecting the corners of the walls, searching for signs of hidden cameras or some other surveillance. Then I run a careful check on my account, in case Zero had indeed installed some kind of tracker on my system in addition to my black cuff.

To my surprise, I find nothing. Maybe Zero and Taylor are serious about giving me my privacy.

From the balcony, I can see the silver and blue overlays on the streets below, showcasing the area's loyalty to Team Winter Dragons. The hotel is somewhere in the middle of Omotesando, a glittering, upscale district full of luxury shops housed inside grand architecture. Silver and blue lights wrap around every tree. Purses and shoes on display in store windows sport bejeweled crests from the Phoenix Riders and Team Andromeda, celebrating the Final. Since I first arrived, another two top players have been announced for the closing ceremony, and now their images are being broadcast against the windows of Prada and Dior.

SHAHIRA BOULOUS of TURKEY | ANDROMEDA
ROSHAN AHMADI of UK | PHOENIX RIDERS

It occurs to me that Jax had brought me here in a state of unconsciousness. Now the Blackcoats are letting me step out the door unattended and fully alert.

I don't quite believe it. I could easily go back on my word to them. But there's not much I could do to them at this point—I don't know where they are or anything incriminating about them.

Get into Hideo's mind. That's what the Blackcoats are asking of me. I look in the direction of Tokyo Dome, where enormous virtual symbols for the Phoenix Riders and Team Andromeda are already hovering in the night sky above the stadium, with a timer counting down the next twenty-four hours until the game happens. Hideo will be at the Final rematch tomorrow.

My thoughts wander back to Zero. I'd spent a moment running searches on the symbol on Sasuke's sleeve, but no matches turned up. It doesn't belong to any corporation I've ever heard of, nor does it resemble anything that might hint at what it is. It's simply a series of polygons overlapping each other, as abstract as anything can be.

I quietly put a call out to Tremaine.

He answers almost immediately. "Hey!" he exclaims in my ear so loudly that I wince. An instant later, his virtual figure appears, and I see him walking on a crowded, brightly lit street, his hands buried in his pockets.

"A little quieter," I reply. "I can hear you fine."

"Where the hell are you?" Tremaine squints at me, trying to make sense of my surroundings. "Are you okay? The Riders are freaking out about you. Roshan even called me to see if I knew what was going on."

"Where are you?" I ask.

"Someplace in Roppongi. Where are *you*? I've been trying to track you down."

His hurried voice makes my mind whirl. "Omotesando. Don't track me. It's too dangerous. I'll come find you."

"What do you mean, it's too dangerous? I heard about gunfire in Shinjuku a couple of days ago. It was all over the news—they said some kind of madman opened fire. It's unheard of in Japan, even in Kabukichō. Two people were killed. I thought one of them could have been you. What happened?"

It already seems like years since I last talked to them in the bar. I bite my lip. "I'm okay," I reply. "It's a long story. I'll explain when I see you." I keep my voice low. "But first, I need you to look at something for me."

Before Tremaine can answer, I send him the screenshot of young Sasuke in the room.

His bewildered voice now turns curious. "Who's this?"

"Sasuke Tanaka, apparently, when he was young. See that symbol on his sleeve?"

"Yeah. What is it?"

"I have no idea. That's what I need your help with."

"You run a search on it yet?"

"Yeah. I turned up nothing."

Tremaine pauses, and I imagine him studying the symbol

with a frown, trying to match it up with something. "Hmm," he finally murmurs under his breath. "I'm not finding anything on it, either, not on a first try. But I think I know someone who can help. Where'd you get this screenshot?"

"That's part of the long story." I glance out my balcony, looking on as icons blink on across Tokyo's landscape wherever my eyes sweep. "Tomorrow night, after the Final rematch. Let's meet up with the others, and I'll tell you what I know."

"Hopefully I'll have something for you by then." He nods at me, and we disconnect.

The paranoia hits me instantly. What if Zero had overheard my conversation with Tremaine? I haven't forgotten what happened to me the last time I was out in public alone just a few short days ago. Now I'm sitting safely in a hotel room, but I still can't ignore the feeling that someone might burst in at any moment.

Concentrate.

I am about to place another call, this time to the Phoenix Riders—when a movement out near my balcony makes me freeze. I crane my neck, eyes searching for a moment, until I see that someone has emerged onto the balcony of Jax's suite next to mine.

It's Zero.

The glow from the city sprawl below outlines his shape in dim light. He stares out at the landscape for a moment, his eyes sweeping slowly toward my room. I want to turn my gaze away, in case he can see me watching him.

A voice says his name, and Zero turns as Jax joins him on the balcony. I hold my breath, looking on as she stops before him. She's fiddling with her gun again, just as she'd done when she was with me, taking out its cartridge and clicking a new one into place, her movements subtle and efficient. It's as if the habit comforts her.

As I look on, Jax takes a step closer to Zero so that she is nearly touching him, and then she says something to him that I can't hear.

Something softens in his expression. He leans toward her and closes his eyes, then murmurs something into her ear. Whatever it is, it makes her shift slightly in his direction. They don't touch. All they do is stay that way, locked in a subtle embrace, sharing something that makes me think of the way Hideo used to pull me to him.

He follows her back inside, and then the two are gone.

I find myself breathing again, my cheeks flushing slightly at the scene. There's an undeniable familiarity between them.

Moments later, her front door clicks shut. I don't know where she's going, but the fact that she's gone makes my shoulders sag a little in relief. Maybe Zero's gone with her. Or maybe she's alone now and watching *me*. After all, Zero had told me that she would be looking out for my well-being.

I take a deep breath, then send out a joint invite to the Phoenix Riders.

Asher connects first, and before long, so do all the others. They're back in Asher's home, no doubt prepping for tomorrow's game. He lets out a long breath at the sight of me, while Hammie spits out a curse and crosses her arms.

"About time," she snaps at me.

"We were about to report you missing to the police," Asher adds, one of his hands tapping on his wheelchair's armrest, "except that would alert Hideo that something was wrong with you."

"I'll explain everything," I say in a low voice. "But first, I need a favor."

"What is it?" Roshan asks.

"When do you all head out to Tokyo Dome tomorrow?"

"Right around sundown. Henka Games is sending cars for us. Why?"

"I need to be in the dome with you," I say, "in the restricted areas, where only the players are allowed. I need access to Hideo."

"What's going on?" Hammie asks. "It's Zero, isn't it?"

I glance toward the balcony again, lingering on the empty spot where Zero and Jax had just been moments earlier. "Yeah."

At that, Hammie uncrosses her arms, blinking rapidly. "Okay, I didn't think you seriously contacted him."

"I didn't. He contacted me." I hesitate. "He saved me from a few Dark World assassins who were out for a bounty on my head."

"*What?*" Hammie's eyes widen even more at that, while Roshan leans forward, muttering a rare curse under his breath.

"You should've told us," he says.

I decide not to mention my accidental call to Hideo yet. "I'm okay," I reply. "And, yes, he did make me an offer. It's too much to explain like this. But, listen—if they're serious about what they want me to do, I'm going to need your help."

10

In the history of the Warcross championships, there has never been a rematch of any kind—and what that means this afternoon, hours before the game starts, is that no one really knows how to celebrate it.

The districts of Tokyo, previously lit up in the colors of each neighborhood's favorite professional team, are now lit again in either red and gold or blue and silver. Footage from the first Final replays along the entire sides of skyscrapers. I pass a line of tricked-out supercars on display down one street: Lamborghinis, Bugattis, Porsches, Luminatii Xs (the fastest electric car currently on the market), each of them sporting neon blue or red lights installed along the bottoms of their doors, and rims decorated in the colors of the rival teams. With the NeuroLink, they transform into vehicles that look impossible: cars with virtual wings; cars that look like jets with trails of flames behind them. They'd been out during the first Final; now, with the rematch, they're at it again, the drivers arguing in the streets.

Vendors selling merchandise—hats and shirts, figurines and key chains—have pulled out their leftover wares from the first Final. Their faces look haggard and stressed as they run out of supply and try to bring in more. I glimpse a few figurines of myself among those being sold, my rainbow hair painted onto the toys in globs of gradient colors. It's a surreal sight.

Eight streaks of laser light suddenly zip past overhead at blistering speed, leaving rainbow-hued lines in the air and causing the crowds on the ground to let out surprised cheers. *Drone racing*, I think. Like street racing with cars, it's strictly illegal; these participants must all still be on beta lenses. I've even hunted a few drone racers down in the Dark World before and released their info to police. Racers must be feeling pretty bold tonight, but with the cops preoccupied with security for the rematch and breaking up scuffles between rival fans, tonight's their chance to show off.

People I pass on the streets argue heatedly in favor of either team; entire groups of fans dressed as the teams are actually facing off on street corners, some of them shouting. A few yells come in my direction from clusters of Andromeda cosplayers.

"Why are you dressed as the cheater?" one shouts.

He's almost immediately answered by calls from Phoenix Riders supporters. "Emika Chen for life!"

I just keep my head lowered and focus on riding my board down the street. At least there are three other girls dressed up in some variation of Emika Chen, and no one seems interested in looking my way for long. Besides—if what Zero said is true, it means I'm now no longer a mark to all the hunters and assassins who had been trying to get to me. Maybe Jax is guarding me from somewhere, but I don't see her.

By the time I near Tokyo Dome's amusement park, some of my nerves have faded, and I feel more like myself as I make a smooth turn onto the sidewalk.

A message comes in from Hammie, asking me to accept. I do, and a private virtual image of her appears next to me, looking as real as reality. Her hair is in dozens of braids tonight, with gold and crimson woven into them, and her dark eyelids are coated with glitter. After two days with the Blackcoats, I'm so happy to see her that I almost try to hug her projection.

"You look ready," I say to her.

Hammie rolls her eyes at me. "If one more person touches my hair, I'm gonna knock their head off." She points toward the back of the dome. "It's the tunnel they take us through," she says, "except there won't be any guards or fans. Watch for me."

A golden line appears in my view, guiding me along the path she wants me to take. I nod once, then steer myself in the right direction.

Soon, I've made my way close enough to the dome's sprawling entertainment complex to see the enormous team portraits of each of tonight's players hovering over each lamppost. The surrounding complex itself—Tokyo Dome City—is teeming with people, just as it had been during the regular championship season. The amusement park's rides are lit up in different colors, and through my lenses, I can see an entire carousel of landscape options for me to choose from. When I select a *Fantasy* option, the entire park transforms into a medieval-looking kingdom with the dome as an enormous castle before me. When I select a *Space* option, the park shifts yet again into a futuristic station on an alien planet with giant rings arching across the night sky.

I hop off my ride and walk into the complex to join the masses. At least it's easy to get lost in the crowd. People gather around rides and shops, their attention focused away from me. I slip through the throngs without a trace.

Lines of people are gathered near the entrance, waiting to check into the stadium. The gold line veers sharply around them. I follow it until I've passed the main entrance gates, bustling with fans. Before long, the back gates come into view, heavily barricaded and swarming with guards. Rows of black cars wait in anticipation of the match's end. Even though tonight's game is just between the Phoenix Riders and the Andromedans, all the other teams are here to watch. Crowds of fans linger at the edges of the barricades, hoping to be one of the first to peek at the teams when they leave.

"Here," I murmur to Hammie in a message.

"I see you," she replies. "When I say *go*, climb over the left barricade closest to the gate." Then she goes dark.

A few minutes later, a riotous commotion suddenly starts at the barricades closest to the back gate. Asher appears, with Hammie and Roshan flanking him on each side, their professional grins on and their hands waving in the air. Behind them come Jackie Nguyen and Brennar Lyons, the replacements for Ren and me. Hammie's already dressed in Phoenix Rider scarlet, the outfit hugging her curves, and her familiar little smirk is prominent on her face. Asher's sitting in a new black-and-gold designer wheelchair, and Roshan looks sleek with his head of dark curls carefully combed and his outfit spotless.

The fans burst into shouts and screams; a wave of flashing lights engulfs the team. People rush the barriers closest to them, forcing all the security to hurry to contain them.

I smile at their surprise appearance. Perfect. Over the crowds, Hammie sends me a quick message. "Go."

As security struggles with the concentration of fans on one

side, I swing myself quietly over the other and dart in toward the gate. A few others try to follow me—which is when Hammie raises the alarm, pointing exaggeratedly at the few fans now trying to come over the barrier. A couple of guards rush to intercept them, and I disappear into the dark recesses of the entryway.

All I can see here are the dim blue outlines of silhouettes. The corridor brings a wave of nostalgia, and I think back to being led out into the arena by a team of bodyguards, my heart pounding in anticipation of the Wardraft. That wasn't so long ago, but it feels like an eternity.

"Ash," I message him as I make my way down the familiar halls. "Can you make sure the security cams in the Phoenix Riders' waiting room are off?" Before every game, the Riders wait in an elegant suite overlooking the expansive arena.

"Already done. Careful of the hall leading to our room, though. They installed some new cams there, and we couldn't gain access to any outside our suite."

I shrink further underneath my hoodie. "Got it."

"Meet us afterward." He sends me an address. "We'll talk then."

Finally, I reach the Riders' empty waiting room and slide the door shut behind me. The silence in here is punctuated by the muffled noise coming from down below, where fifty thousand fans are cheering as the latest track from BTS thunders from the speakers. I stand before the window, feeling for a second like I've gone back in time to when I was still a player. The stadium is completely packed, with more people streaming in to their seats with each passing second. An announcer is recapping the original Final game as footage plays in the enormous 3-D holograms.

A glowing light is already flashing over the suite's door, calling for the players to head down to the center of the arena. Analysts sitting in the top rows broadcast their debates, predicting which team has the best chance of winning.

My attention turns to the private glass box on the other side of the arena. In there, I can see several figures moving around that I identify as Hideo, Mari, and Kenn.

On the ground level, the first members of Team Andromeda have started emerging into the center of the arena. The crowd's screams rise a deafening octave.

"Good luck," I murmur to my team as they start appearing, too. My gaze lingers awhile longer on their sleek outfits. Even after everything, the energy in this space fills every inch of me, and I want nothing more than to be down there with them, soaking in the world's applause and wondering what new, fantastical realm I'd be dropped into next. I want to be excited again with my whole heart, before everything became so complicated.

I shake my head, take a seat, and pull up a grid of the entire dome's security cams.

There's more surveillance in this dome than I've seen anywhere else—at least two or three cams in each room. It seems they've added layers of security since the breach that nearly killed Hideo. *When* Jax *nearly killed Hideo*, I remind myself as a shiver runs through me.

The announcer finishes introducing each of the players. The lights in the stadium dim, leaving only the teams illuminated, and in the center of the arena, a hologram appears to show the world that everyone will be immersed in. It's somewhere high in the sky, shrouded by clouds in every direction, and piercing through the cloudbank are hundreds of narrow mountain peaks with towers on top, each connected to the others around it with narrow rope bridges.

"Welcome to the Sky Kingdom," a familiar, omniscient voice

rings out across the stadium. The audience lets out a deafening roar of approval.

I look away from the arena and scroll quietly through the various security cams until I reach the ones that are inside Hideo's private box. The shields on the cams are tight, and I can already tell I won't be able to alter any of their footage. If security notices me in here and realizes that I'm not one of the Phoenix Riders, they're going to start asking questions.

But nothing's stopping me from zooming in on the surveillance cams in Hideo's box, to follow the feeds that the security guard manning the cameras can see. I find his profile, then make my way in.

Footage from every security cam in the dome fills the space around me. I rotate through them until I find the ones in Hideo's box, and then zoom in on the most central one.

Suddenly, it's as if I'm hovering on their ceiling, watching them like a ghost.

And I find myself listening in on a conversation that makes me recoil in horror.

11

Kenn's arms are crossed tightly, and he has a frown on his face as he addresses Hideo. "But there's no proof of that," he argues.

Mari lets out an exasperated sigh. "Kenn, we're not here to rush out a subpar product." Her Japanese translates rapidly into English in my view. "We need to check if this is caused by the algorithm."

I suck in my breath sharply. So Hideo hadn't kept it all to himself; Mari and Kenn are aware of the algorithm. Not only that—they sound like they were actively involved in putting it into effect.

But what is Mari talking about? What does she think the algorithm is doing?

"Suicides can be caused by anything," Kenn says with a wave of his hand. "Have you become just like those stuck-up legislators? They think they can prevent progress by banning new technology in their cities—"

"They're not always wrong to do it," Mari replies. "This is serious. If this is our mistake, we need to fix it immediately."

Suicides? I think of the police tape fencing off that block in Kabukichō. They must be talking about the criminals who have been killing themselves around the world. The ones Hideo mentioned in our last argument. *Convicted sex traffickers committing suicide*, he'd said. But that had sounded like something the algorithm was always supposed to allow.

"Just wait a few months," Kenn says. "Everything will smooth out."

My gaze goes to Hideo, who hasn't said a word yet. He looks composed as he leans back in his seat and regards each of his colleagues. A closer look at his face, though, tells me he's in a dark mood.

"The entire purpose of the algorithm is to protect people, make them safer," Mari insists. "It's not supposed to be responsible for users taking their lives."

"This is crazy!" Kenn puts his hands up with a laugh. "There's *no* evidence. You're really trying to suggest that the algorithm is making regular people—people who are innocent—kill themselves?"

My blood chills at his words. I steady myself against my chair. The algorithm may be causing the deaths of innocent people now.

"Look at these numbers!" Mari waves a hand, bringing up a graph to hover before the three of them. I stare at it in horror. The graph's curve looks exponential, sweeping ominously up. "The number of suicides worldwide started trending up the day after the algorithm's deployment. These aren't all people with criminal backgrounds."

"You're reaching," Kenn says with a dismissive shrug. "Why in the world would innocent suicides be connected to us? I'm sure if any of those *are* related to the algorithm, it's because those folks were guilty of something." Kenn says this with a careless shrug.

It's the same easy gesture he'd once used when I was first introduced to him and the team—except this time he's not reassuring me about Hideo's distant politeness. Now he's shrugging off dire consequences of the algorithm.

I stare at Kenn's face, remembering the way his eyes would twinkle with good cheer every time I spoke to him. Is this the same man who used to text me, worrying about Hideo's well-being or harping on his stubbornness? Who had once asked me to keep an eye on Hideo?

I hold that warm smile in my memory while I take in the man before me. He's lit by top-down light from the ceiling, casting that same face in ominous shadows. I can't make out his expression.

Mari brings up another chart. "Past studies have shown a connection between purpose being removed from people's lives and a higher risk of death. If people have nothing to strive for, if their motivations are tampered with, suicides rise." She leans forward to meet Kenn's gaze. "It's *possible*. We have to investigate."

"Oh, come *on*. The algorithm isn't taking away people's drive for *life*," Kenn complains. "Just the drive to commit crimes."

"We might have a bug on our hands that triggers the same reaction," Mari snaps. She looks to her side. "Hideo, *please*."

Hideo's expression is a tired one, the dark shadows under his eyes only accentuated by the room's lighting. After a pause, he finally speaks up. "We'll investigate," he says. "Immediately."

Mari smiles in satisfaction at his words, while Kenn starts to argue. Hideo holds up a hand, cutting him off. "I can't tolerate a potential flaw in the algorithm," he says, shooting Kenn a disapproving look. His gaze swivels to Mari. "But the algorithm will stay running. We're not going to pause it."

"Hideo—" Mari starts.

"The algorithm *stays running*," Hideo snaps. His steely reply stills both Mari and Kenn. "Until we have evidence proving Mari's theory. That's final."

I want to scream at him. *What are you doing, Hideo?*

Kenn's the first to break the silence. "Norway was on the phone asking what you'd like in exchange for loosening certain restrictions on the algorithm. And the Emirates wants a different set of guidelines for what's considered illegal there. So, what—now are you going to tell them we're investigating this rumor?"

"I'm not doing this for favors," Hideo replies.

I freeze. Hideo's scheduling meetings with various leaders around the world. The public doesn't seem to know about the algorithm—or perhaps they are willed not to know—but these presidents and diplomats sure seem to. Morality shifts over country lines. Everyone's going to want something different from Hideo.

"And you realize the Americans landed on the tarmac this morning, don't you?" Kenn finishes, glowering at Hideo.

"The Americans can wait."

"*You* tell that to their president."

"He's a fool," Hideo replies coolly, cutting him short. "He will do exactly what I tell him to do."

There's a breath of hesitation from both Mari and Kenn. Hideo hadn't even raised his voice with those words—but the power in them is clear. If he wanted to, he could control the US president with a single command from the algorithm. He could give orders to every head of state of every developed nation, of every country in the world. Anyone who has used the NeuroLink.

Anyone—including Kenn. Including Mari. Are they also using beta lenses? They must be; Kenn would probably be more worried about the suicides if he were at risk of being affected. But if Hideo had *chosen* to give them the privilege of wearing only the beta lenses, then he's already picking favorites.

Down in the stadium, an enormous cheer explodes from the audience. Shahira, the Andromedan Captain, has just sent Hammie spinning out of control below the clouds, forcing her to spill a rare, precious power-up she'd nabbed. The analysts are talking rapidly, their voices echoing around the stadium.

I look away from the game.

The algorithm is supposed to be neutral. Free from human imperfection, more efficient and thorough than current law enforcement. But that's always been Hideo's ridiculous pipe dream. It's barely been a couple of weeks since he triggered the algorithm, and already, the inefficiencies and tangled webs of human behavior are complicating and corrupting it. What if he *does* agree to certain favors for certain countries? Special guidelines? Exclusive permissions for wealthy people or political figures? Would he ever go down that path?

Is it even possible for him *not* to?

"I'll talk to the Americans," Mari says. "I'll take them on a tour of the headquarters and show them some of our new work. They're distracted easily enough, especially if only for a few days."

"A few days." Kenn snorts. "Enough of a delay to set off all kinds of chain reactions."

Hideo gives his friend a penetrating look. "Why are you in such a hurry?"

"I'm not in a hurry," Kenn says defensively. "I'm trying to help you run a business on time. By all means—knock yourself out investigating these unfounded rumors."

"We're not here to run a system that's dysfunctional. If Mari finds something substantial, we're going to halt the algorithm."

Kenn shakes his head and sighs in exasperation at Hideo. "This is about Emika, isn't it?"

I blink. Me? What do I have to do with this?

Hideo seems to have the same reaction, because he lifts an eyebrow at his friend and frowns. "How so?"

"Do I need to lay it out for you? Let's see." Kenn holds up a finger. "You walked out in the middle of an interview because a reporter asked you about Emika." He holds up another. "Your knuckles have been a bloody mess—literally—since you talked to her." He holds up a third. "Has there been a single day when you haven't brought her up?"

My face is hot now. Hideo has brought me up every day?

"I'm not in the mood, Kenn," Hideo mutters.

Kenn shoves his hands in his pockets and leans toward Hideo. "You were going to agree with me on this, remember? That this whole suicide thing was a rumor. Then you have one conversation with Emika, you tell me you're not interested in seeing her again—and now you're having Mari start a whole investigation."

Hideo's frown deepens, but he doesn't deny it. "This isn't about her."

"Isn't it?" Kenn replies. "For a girl that you claim you don't care about, that little wild card sure has a grip on you."

"That's enough." Hideo's words cut the tension between them like a pair of shears, and Kenn halts immediately, his unspoken words practically dangling in midair.

Hideo glares at him. "I expect us to do this right. Up until now, I thought you had the same standards." He nods once at the door.

At that, Kenn turns slightly pale. "You're dismissing me?"

"Well, I'm certainly not asking you to dance, am I?"

Kenn scoffs and pushes up from his chair. "You used to get these insufferable airs in uni, too," he mutters. "Guess nothing's changed." He waves a flippant hand. "Do whatever you want. I just never took you for an idiot."

They watch as Kenn steps out of the room. Down below, another burst of excitement comes from the crowd. Jackie Nguyen, the Phoenix Riders' new Fighter, has managed to seal the Andromedan Fighter in a crevice on a mountainside. Asher targets Shahira with a purple-gold Toxin power-up and slows her movements to a lurch.

With Kenn gone, Hideo lets his shoulders relax for a moment. He stares down at the arena with a grave expression.

"He's too eager," Mari says to Hideo as she glances at the sliding glass door. "He wants to see the positive impact in our bottom line already."

"He's always been eager," Hideo replies in a low voice. He leans his arms against his knees and watches the game halfheartedly.

"It will be fine," Mari says gently. "We'll get to the bottom of this. I want Kenn to be right, that the suicides don't have anything to do with the algorithm."

"And if it does?"

Mari doesn't answer. She clears her throat. "I'll field the calls today," she finally says.

"No. Let me deal with the Americans. You get back to me with results on this investigation as soon as you can."

"Of course," Mari replies with a bow of her head.

There's a brief silence between them. Then Hideo gets up and walks over to the glass window. He rests his hands in his pockets. On the holograms, Roshan and Hammie are in a heated battle with two of the Andromedans, each team protecting their Captain's Artifact while trying to break through to grab the enemy's.

"Any other news for me?" Hideo says after a while, turning his head slightly without taking his eyes off the game.

Mari seems to know exactly what he's talking about. "I'm sorry," she replies. "But we still have many other potential suspects left in Japan."

Hideo's expression is bleak, his eyes lit by dark anger. It's the same fury I'd seen in him when I'd once hacked into his Memory, when I saw him training with the ferocity of a beast. I recognize it as the look he gets when he's thinking about his brother.

"Dozens of predators that had previously escaped the justice system have already turned themselves in," Mari adds. "Did you hear about the two men responsible for running illegal sex shops in Kabukichō?"

Hideo glances at her. His shoulders are stiff now.

"Well, they showed up at a police station this morning, sobbing. Confessed everything. Tried to stab themselves before they were brought into custody. You've taken a lot of dangerous people off the streets."

"Good," Hideo murmurs and turns back to the game. "But they're not the ones, are they?"

Mari tightens her lips. "No," she admits. "Nothing in their mind palettes generated by the algorithm matches Sasuke's time and location of disappearance."

Of course. Now I understand why Hideo refuses to let the algorithm stop running.

He's using it to hunt for his brother's kidnapper, probably scanning through millions of minds in search of a memory, a spark of recognition, an emotion that hints at someone being responsible for what happened to Sasuke.

Perhaps this was always his goal, the entire reason why he created the NeuroLink in the first place.

"Maybe Emika was right," Hideo says quietly. His voice is so soft that I barely catch it. But I do, and my heart tightens. "That we're not here to bring the world peace."

"You're doing your best," Mari answers.

Hideo just stares down at the game. Then, he turns to face her. "Keep searching."

Down in the arena, Asher seizes Shahira's Artifact. The rematch is over—the Phoenix Riders win again, officially. Everyone in the stadium jumps to their feet, screaming loud enough to shake the dome. The analysts join in the shouts.

Hideo raises his glass stoically, nodding once down at the ecstatic crowds. His distant, controlled smile plays on the giant screens around the dome. And even though he is already breaking his promise—his vow that he and the algorithm would be two separate things—even now, my heart cracks for him. It's hard not to feel drawn to Hideo's relentless drive, not to ache for his determination.

What would he do, if I told him his brother is alive?

What will he do, once he figures out who took his brother?

Maybe Emika was right.

I clench my hands into fists. It's not too late. If Hideo is having doubts, if he's truly worried about what his algorithm might be doing . . . maybe, maybe there's still time to pull him back from the abyss. Before he goes too far. Before I'm forced to turn away from him for good.

And the only way I can do that is to uncover what happened to Sasuke.

I'm walking a tightrope between Hideo and Zero, the algorithm and the Blackcoats. And I have to be very careful not to slip.

I stand up and pull my hoodie over my head. There isn't much time left. The algorithm is supposed to make the world a safer place—but if Mari's right about the algorithm, then safety's exactly what we'll need to worry about.

An incoming message from Tremaine snaps me out of my whirling thoughts. His voice fills my ears.

"Em," he says. "I've made contact, and they have info on that symbol you sent me, the one from Sasuke Tanaka's sleeve."

I swallow hard at Tremaine's words as red and gold confetti rains down from the arena's ceiling. "What is it?"

"They won't share it with you over a message." He pauses. "You're going to want to hear this in person."

12

I have no trouble exiting the arena, not with all the rowdy, dressed-up fans flooding out around me. Phoenix Rider supporters are screaming at the top of their lungs. Andromedans look sullen but satisfied. A crowd has already lined up near the back entrance to watch the black cars take the players away. Others are making a beeline down to the overstuffed subways. The cool night wind whips my hair over my shoulders as I hop on my board and turn myself in the direction of Akihabara.

Some of Tokyo's districts always close down a few of their main streets once a week, turning them into *hokoten*, giant pedestrian walkways. Since it's a game night tonight, almost every district in Tokyo has done so, and none more grandly than Akihabara, temporarily earning it the nickname *Hokoku*, or a mash-up of "Pedestrian District." The entire area looks like a light show, populated by masses of people swarming up and down eight-lane roads usually crammed with cars. Each towering building has the smiling face of a Phoenix Rider playing against its walls, accompanied by their best moves from the rematch.

In spite of everything that's going on, I still feel a swell of team pride at the images of Asher, Hammie, and Roshan. Right now, all I want is to celebrate with them and collapse into their arms, their uncomplicated friendship.

Dozens of neon streaks linger in the air, the trails from racing drones that the police are too overworked to deal with. Music blares in the streets, where a DJ has set up temporary camp in the middle of the road and is currently surrounded by jumping fans. The ground is lit up with virtual red lava flowing in grids, and virtual phoenix feathers glitter, hovering, in the bushes, on the ground, or in front of buildings, each worth twenty points if you can grab it.

Welcome to Akihabara!
Double points during Hokoku Night!
You leveled up!

By the time I arrive in front of a massive entertainment complex draped on every side with my teammates' faces, the black cars carrying the teams have already parked in a line in front of the building, blocking off access to this part of the street from the masses. One of the guards catches sight of me. When I approach the lineup, he shakes his head, unwilling to let me pass. He can't tell who I am, not with my randomized identity hovering over me.

I send a quick message to Asher.

> Here now. Your boys are
> blocking me out.

Asher doesn't reply. But a beat later, the guard gives me a slight bow of his head, then steps aside so that I can squeeze between the black cars. I duck into the complex and through the entrance's sliding doors.

The first floor of the building is crammed with Warcross merchandise, hats and figurines and claw machines where you can try your luck at winning plush versions of team mascots. I make my way down the corridor until I reach the stairs, then hop up them to the second floor.

Here, I step into a surreal realm.

It's a gaming hall, with a high ceiling probably built by knocking down one floor to combine it with another. There's fog everywhere, creeping down from a stage where a virtual pop star is performing. Neon lights sweep from the ceiling, lighting up the smoke with streaks of color. Crowds of people are dancing near the front of the stage, while the rest of the room is full of tables with games projected on them, where people are playing each other at a variety of games. I see several tables of checkers, while others play card games or board games enhanced with virtual images. Service drones zip from one table to the next, serving drinks with animated colors hovering over them and skewers of tender, grilled meat.

I recognize members from several other teams: Max Martin's in a corner with Jena MacNeil, hunched over a table game of some sort and laughing his head off at something his Captain has just said. Shahira Boulous is gesturing wildly with a drink as she explains a game technique to Ziggy Frost, who just listens quietly with wide eyes. Pretty much everyone in here is either some current team member or a former one. I pass invisibly through their ranks, feeling a strange mixture of belonging and not belonging, while I search for the Riders.

They're gathered near the stage, where the tables end and the dancing begins. As I draw nearer, I realize they're almost hidden from view behind a crowd of spectators, all shouting and cheering over something.

Then I see Hammie appear over the crowd as she hops onto a chair. She raises both her fists up with a whoop. Her knot of braids has loosened a bit, and a light sheen of sweat beads on her dark skin, catching neon outlines from the ceiling lights. She has a huge grin on her face.

"*Checkmate!*" she calls out.

They're playing speed chess. She's sitting across from Roshan, who knocks his king flat with a defeated grimace. As the crowd shouts out new challenges and exchanges bets, Roshan gets out of his seat so that someone else can play Hammie, then heads over to wrap an arm around the waist of Kento Park.

They exchange some intimate words I can't hear. I look around, wondering whether Tremaine's here to see them.

"Move over, move over." Asher's voice comes from the crowd, and some people part to let him through. He shoves the chair Roshan was sitting in out of his way and wheels himself into its place, then smirks at Hammie and leans against the table. "You can't win two rounds against me in the same night," he says. The crowd roars with approval at the challenge.

"Oh? Can't I?" Hammie cocks her head at him and hops down from her chair. Her eyes are still bright from her win.

As I watch, the chess game before them resets. Virtual fire engulfs the edges of the chessboard, and a magnified version of the game appears over their heads for everyone to see. It's no static chessboard, either—the knights are real knights, the rooks real castle towers, the bishops replaced with fire-breathing dragons that now lunge their necks forward.

A new timer appears to float over the table. I glance at it. Each player gets one second to make a move.

The game starts. Everyone cheers.

Hammie's playful banter silences, replaced by a look I know well from our training days. Smug, wicked confidence. I shake my head, lost for a moment in awe as I watch her move. Pawn. Knight. Queen. Each play sends a column of fire racing around the hovering chessboard. Hammie's eyes dart from position to position—her hand flies out without the slightest hesitation each time her turn comes up. Over her head, the virtual, animated chessboard is aflame, each position waging an epic war. Hammie's knight clashes with one of Asher's bishops, skewering the character with her lance; the opponent's queen walks right into a trap she set up with several pawns and her rook.

The crowd around Hammie screams at each move. Asher's brow furrows deeper as he fights a losing battle, but Hammie ignores him blissfully, singing along to the music at the top of her lungs, even dancing in place in between moves.

I smile along. I've never seen Hammie play in person. She's even better than I thought; it's like watching a game already preset and planned out, and she's merely executing the moves. If I could only be as sure of my next steps as she is.

"*Checkmate, son!*"

The crowd around her bursts into a mass of cheers as Hammie corners Asher's king. She slaps her hands down hard on the table, hops onto her chair in one nimble move, and lifts an arm up high in a V-for-victory sign. Her level bumps up by one, and her notes tick frantically upward. Asher throws his head back with a loud groan as Hammie does a little dance on the chair.

When the crowd settles and some move on to watch another nearby game, I finally walk up to their table. Roshan notices me first. He blinks in surprise—and then steps away from Kento, breaks into a grin, and claps his hands loudly at Asher and Hammie.

"Team reunion?" I manage to shout at them over the music, unable to stop myself from returning Roshan's smile.

Asher lets out an exclamation at the same time Hammie hops down from her chair and makes a beeline for me. And before I can say anything more, I'm swept off my feet by a hug from both her and Roshan.

For a moment, I forget why I'm here. I forget about the Blackcoats and Hideo and the mess I've somehow gotten myself into. Right now, I'm with my friends, indulging in their messy, jostling greeting.

Asher looks bright-eyed, his cheeks flushed, his hair as rumpled as his clothing. He joins us as Hammie and Roshan finally let go of me. "You scared the hell out of us when you went MIA, you know that?" he exclaims.

"Captain," I reply with a forced wink, trying to keep myself looking lighthearted here.

Hammie's bright, glittering eyes turn serious. "Tremaine's been waiting for you," she says to me. "He says he has something to show us."

At her words, I glimpse someone standing in the crowds nearby. It's Tremaine, leaning against a wall with an uncertain look on his face. My momentary happiness wavers at the sight of him.

You're going to want to hear this in person.

"Come on." Hammie gestures up at the ceiling. "The next floor is full of private karaoke rooms. You can fill us in up there."

I nod wordlessly back, and together, we all cut our way through the throngs until we make our way into the elevator.

A private suite is already waiting for us in the karaoke hall.

Muffled music thuds around us from parties raging in the other rooms. I notice immediately that someone's already in here, a barely perceptible figure sitting in the dark corner of the sofas. Then Roshan shuts the door behind us, sealing us in, and the shouts and music outside suddenly turn into a muffled din. My ears ring in the silence.

Tremaine speaks first. "This is the contact I told you about," he says to me, nodding at the stranger now sitting beside us. "Jesse. Prefers they."

At that, Jesse leans back against the sofa and studies me without acknowledging the others. I study them back. They have strikingly pale green eyes set against light brown skin, and a lean physique that gives off a false impression of fragility—but I see their slender fingers tapping with precision against the sofa. I recognize gestures like that. They're the signs of a racer.

"I owe Tremaine a debt," they finally say, skipping any formal greetings and instead fixing their green eyes on me. "He went into my records once and deleted a citation from the police."

"They'd gotten caught drone racing," Tremaine explains. "Jesse's one of the best in London's underground scene."

"I remember you," Roshan says, eyeing Jesse with his arms crossed.

"Same," Jesse replies, returning the look. "You'd earned quite the name for yourself in the underground, Ahmadi."

Asher lifts an eyebrow at him. "You never told us you used to race drones."

"Why would I tell my Captain I was doing something illegal?" Roshan replies. "I wanted you to pick me for the Riders."

"No wonder I never had a chance against you at *Mario Kart*," Hammie adds. "You know I used to bet on drone racing? Maybe I've put my money on you before without even knowing it."

Asher massages his temples. "Would anyone else like to share their illegal activities with their Captain?" he says.

Hammie ignores him and nods at Jesse. "You owed Tremaine a debt?"

Jesse cracks a subtle smile. "Well, now Tremaine tells me he's calling in his debt to me for this one's sake." They tilt their head at me. "Emika Chen, isn't it? Yeah, I know you. You're the bounty hunter who first reported me to the police a couple of years ago, for drone racing."

I flush. So, this is one of the people I'd tracked down in the Dark World during my past hunts. Now I remember this specific target from several years back, when I'd broken into a drone racing name directory. I'd won a thousand-dollar bounty for that. "Sorry," I reply.

Jesse shrugs. "Don't say stuff you don't mean. It's fine. Because of Tremaine's request, I'll call the beef between us settled. Lucky you."

Roshan makes an irritated sound. "Way to make this situation even more uncomfortable, Blackbourne," he mutters at Tremaine. "But that's always been your specialty."

Tremaine holds his hands up. "You think you can do better, you go ahead."

I shift awkwardly in my seat, but under the table, I touch Roshan's hand once. "I'm okay," I reply before I turn back to Jesse. "Tremaine tells us you have some info we could use."

Jesse nods, then waves a hand in front of them and brings up the symbol from Sasuke Tanaka's sleeve. "You want to know where this is from, right?" It hovers over the table before us. "But, first," they say, "you're going to tell me why you need this info."

I hesitate. Being at the mercy of a former mark isn't exactly ideal. Beside me, Tremaine offers a helpless look.

"Fine," I reply, nodding once at Jesse. "Then we're even."

Jesse folds their arms. "After you."

Asher pushes himself out of his chair and onto the sofa, then turns his full attention onto me. "All right, spill. Are you okay? What really happened to you out there?"

I take a deep breath. "I'm okay. Mostly. I got into some trouble."

"How bad?"

"An assassin saved my life from some other assassins."

There's a heavy pause from everyone. "O-*kay*," Asher replies warily. "What, like the Yakuza or something?"

"Don't be silly," Hammie says with a snort, even as she instinctively drops her voice. "The Yakuza has too much political cred. They're not gonna be so crass as to run around shooting people in the middle of the street."

"No, not the mafia or anything," I say, shaking my head. "At least, not a mafia I knew existed." I meet my friends' concerned gazes. A part of me still wants to turn inward, to keep what I know from them. But it won't make them any safer to keep them out of the loop—I'd learned that the hard way when Zero first attacked our dorms.

So instead, I tell them everything that's happened since the last time we saw each other. I explain in a low voice about the assassination lottery and the hunters who came after me. About Jax. About Zero, and Taylor. About the Blackcoats. Finally, I tell them about what I'd overheard between Hideo, Kenn, and Mari.

An ominous silence falls on the room. Roshan's face looks drained of color, while Asher runs a hand through his hair and stares out toward the door.

"Damn," Hammie finally whispers as she tosses a loose braid

behind her shoulder. In the dim light, her eyes are wide and liquid-dark, full of all the same uncertainty churning inside me. "Innocent suicides. This is unraveling fast."

"The Blackcoats are actively working to stop Hideo's algorithm," I add. "They seem like vigilantes, although I don't know enough about them to agree."

"And Zero hasn't said anything about his past to you?" Roshan asks.

I shake my head. "He refuses to answer any questions I've asked him. But I was able to gain access to one of his old memories. I shouldn't have been able to get it so easily." My attention goes to Jesse, who has been listening quietly the entire time. This must be news to the newcomer, but if it's stunned them, they don't show it.

Jesse whistles once. "You got yourself into one mess of a situation, girl."

"I'm hoping you'll be able to tell me something that can get me out of it," I reply. "That's all I know. Your turn."

Jesse straightens, swipes two fingers casually in an upward gesture, and displays a screenshot of the symbol on Sasuke's sleeve.

"I was asking around about it down under because I thought it might be some obscure illegal racing group logo," Jesse says. "You know, maybe just some shirt that was merchandise for a Dark World team we hadn't heard of."

Jesse pauses to spin the symbol in midair. "But then, someone anonymous responded. They showed me a work badge with this same symbol on it. I don't know how they got their hands on it, but I forwarded that badge to Tremaine."

Now Jesse pulls up a virtual image of the work badge. It's a plain white card, with a name and a sixteen-digit code printed on it. Sure enough, right beside that is the symbol I'd seen on Sasuke's sleeve. It's a logo.

"I did some digging, then went out to see for myself where that badge came from," Tremaine goes on. "Ready?"

"Ready," I say.

Tremaine loads another screenshot. The new image shows the exact same symbol, except this time it looks like it's printed as a small sign next to a door in some sort of nondescript hallway.

"I unearthed these from private servers." Tremaine brings up a second image. This time, the symbol is tiny and subtle on a pair of sliding white doors.

"Where is this?" I ask Tremaine, my eyes darting from the symbols to him.

He takes the original screenshot, spreads his arms wide, and brings his hands together. The screenshot zooms out until it looks like a hallway, then a network of hallways inside an enormous complex. I frown as he keeps going, until the entire campus has zoomed out, and we are now looking at a large sign made of stone in front of a campus's gates.

I stare at the title engraved on the complex's entrance. JAPAN INNOVATION INSTITUTE OF TECHNOLOGY. "It's a company?"

"Yes. A biotech company. My guess is that the symbol you found belongs to some project being done at this institute."

I slump back in my seat. "You're saying that when I saw the glimpse of young Sasuke in a room, wearing that symbol on his sleeve—he was here? How did he even find himself in a place like this?"

"That's not even the surprising part," Tremaine replies. He brings up a third screenshot. It shows a young Japanese woman standing with her small team of colleagues, all of them wearing matching white lab coats and posing in front of the institute.

My eyes lock on to the woman's face at the same time Tremaine points to her.

"Before she quit twelve years ago, she used to work at the Innovation Institute," Tremaine says. "That's neuroscientist Dr. Mina Tanaka. Hideo and Sasuke's mother."

13

I squeeze my eyes shut. "No," I snap. "Back up. That doesn't make any sense!"

Tremaine's face doesn't change. "I know. I thought maybe you had an explanation for it."

Jesse must have made a mistake. Tremaine too. Because if any of it's true, it means that the mother of Hideo and Sasuke also used to work at the company that apparently held Sasuke captive. The memory of meeting her flashes back to me—her small figure, now delicate from grief, her large glasses and her warm smile. The way Hideo had hugged her protectively.

"It doesn't add up," I insist. "Are you saying that Hideo's mother had something to do with Sasuke vanishing like that? She was permanently traumatized by his disappearance—she and Hideo's dad searched madly for Sasuke. She was so distraught, she could no longer work. What happened destroyed her mind.

She forgets things constantly now. I *saw* her with my own eyes. I *met* her. Hideo showed me his Memory of it."

Tremaine leans forward and raps his fingers against the table. "Maybe she didn't know," he replies. "And Hideo probably knew nothing about it—he was so little at the time. Memories aren't always accurate. I mean, is there any public information about *why* she quit working for the company? Was it because of the trauma of losing her son? Or was it because of something that had happened at the company?"

More questions are piling onto the ones I already have. I sigh and rub my hands across my face. If Sasuke was a part of this institute, how did he get there?

"Hey."

I look through my hands at Hammie, who's squinting at the photo of Hideo's mother with her colleagues. She holds a finger up at the list of tiny names running across the photo's bottom. "Dana Taylor, PhD. Isn't this *your* Dana Taylor, Em? The one who works for Zero?"

I search the photo until my gaze rests on a familiar face. "That's her," I blurt out. She looks much younger here, and her hair isn't streaked with gray, but her thoughtful look is the same.

Taylor used to work with Hideo's mother—with *Sasuke's* mother. What did that mean, then, for how Sasuke became Zero? What do the Blackcoats have to do with the company where Mina Tanaka used to work?

In his corner, Tremaine folds his arms against the table and furrows his brow. There's fear in his eyes, an unusual sight. "This feels all wrong," he mutters to himself.

"Are you going to tell Hideo?" Asher asks in the silence that follows.

I stare grimly at the symbol still rotating slowly before us. I've met Zero, I've heard him speak—and now this is more confirmation that what had happened to Sasuke was real. "The Blackcoats expect me to make contact with Hideo soon, anyway," I finally say. "He deserves to know."

Asher snaps his fingers. "Hideo invited a few of us to a formal party at an art hall," he says. "It's supposed to be both a congratulations for our win and an apology for all the chaos around this year's championships. If you go, you could have a conversation with him that's somewhat private and probably in a setting where he wouldn't want to do something extreme."

A private meeting. A formal banquet. "When's the meeting? Where?"

"Tomorrow night, at the Museum of Contemporary Art."

"But how do I get in? Hideo's guaranteed to have me on some sort of watch list, and his guards will be on alert for me."

"Not if you're in the Phoenix Riders' car. Even if it's you instead of us, it'll clear you through the entrance gates. Once you're in, though, you're on your own."

The thought of seeing Hideo in person tomorrow night sends a surge of fear and anticipation through me. It's risky, but it should work. "Okay," I say with a nod. "Let's do it."

Jesse grimaces at me. "If you're as smart as Tremaine says, you'll get out of this right now. You're wedging yourself in a tight spot, between two very powerful forces." They hold both hands up as they slide out from the sofa. "I'm washing my hands of this either way. You never heard it from me." They point at Tremaine. "And we're even from here." Without another word, they swing a backpack over their shoulders and step out of the karaoke room. A momentary blast of noise—cheers, singing, laughter—comes from outside. Then the door slides shut again, sealing us back in our muted silence.

Tremaine shifts uncomfortably. His eyes dart to Roshan for a second before he looks back at me. "Look, Em," he says. "Jesse's got a point. These waters are getting pretty murky. Are you sure you want to keep digging?"

The only sound comes from the party still pounding from all around us. "You're saying I should step away from this. Leave the Blackcoats behind. Forget about the algorithm."

"I'm saying that something tells me Sasuke's story is a whole lot uglier than we could ever imagine," Tremaine replies. "I don't know how it all connects, but I can feel it. Can't you? It's like that instinct on a bounty hunt when you just *know* things are about to get worse. Hell, you've already been targeted—and shot at."

"Jax is the one who saved me from those hunters," I reply, even though the memory settles over me like a dark cloud.

"And what's going to happen if she finds out what you're really after? The Blackcoats don't sound like the forgiving type."

"You're on this hunt, too," I say. "And you're the one who went digging."

"No one's after *me*." He shrugs. "It's safer for me to poke around."

When I first accepted Hideo's bounty job, the biggest risk I thought I was taking was getting my identity stolen, or maybe having to face off against a hacker inside Warcross. Now, somehow, I've become tangled in a web of secrets and lies, and the wrong step in any direction could cost me my life.

"It's too late to back away from this." I lean back against the sofa and stare at the glass door. "The only way out is through."

"We're all taking the same way out." I turn to see Roshan

looking straight at me. "You're not a lone wolf, Em. If they're going to come for you, they'd better save themselves some time and come for us, too. You're a Phoenix Rider. We're a team for a reason."

Right now, I wish we weren't. I wish I were still a lone wolf, and that the only life on the line in all of this is mine. But those words don't make it past my lips. Maybe it's because I don't believe them, and that if I'm going to be staring down this barrel, I'd rather have a fighting chance with others by my side. Even so, all I can do is give Roshan a weak smile. I lean my shoulder into his.

"For better or worse," I reply.

Tremaine's lips tighten, but he doesn't look surprised. "Well, I'm not a Rider. So I guess this is when I leave." He gets up without looking at the others and heads out the door.

● ● ● ● ●

By THE TIME I step out into the back alley of the complex, a steady rain has started to fall, leaving the streets slick and shiny. Bright lights pour from the entrance directly across from me, a building filled with pink claw machines dispensing Warcross merchandise. Parties thud from its higher floors, but otherwise, the alley— blocked off on both ends by security—is almost peaceful.

Tremaine's out here, his back against the wall, waiting out the rain under the canopy. He barely turns his head at the sight of me before going back to staring at the entrance across from us. In the neon light, his pale white skin looks blue.

"Off to report to the Blackcoats?" he says. "You're on so many teams, I can't even keep track anymore."

I don't comment on the edge in his voice. There's a brief silence between us before I speak again. "I wanted to thank you for finding what you did," I say.

"It's what hunters do."

I shake my head. "You didn't have to. It's dangerous enough as it is, with just one of us on this."

"You've got enough problems. Don't worry about me." He holds his hands together and blows warm air between them. "I didn't do it for you, anyway."

"Then why? It's not like you're getting paid for this job."

His gaze sweeps along the street. "Roshan's worried about you," he finally says. "He's been afraid of how deep in you're getting, and it sounds like his suspicions were right. So I promised him I'd watch your back."

My teammate's concern is a balm on the stress of the past few days. It's all I can do to not turn around right now and return to them, instead of heading back into the arms of the Blackcoats. "You helped me because of Roshan?"

"He says you have a tendency to be a loner about everything. You won't ask for help, even if you need it." He holds his hands up when he sees me about to interrupt. "Hey, no judgment from me. I'm a hunter, too; I get it." He smiles a little. "Besides. We also get into this sort of stuff for the thrill of it, don't we? I don't think I'll ever get a shot at this big of a conspiracy again."

I find myself smiling back. "It sounds to me like you're still fond of Roshan. Even after you left the Riders."

Tremaine shrugs, trying not to look concerned. "Nah. I saw him with Kento. It's fine."

We wait in silence, both of us staring at the steady stream of rain.

After a while, he glances at me. "Did he ever tell you why we don't talk anymore?"

I hesitate. "He told me you left the Phoenix Riders because you wanted to be on a winning team, and that was what triggered the breakup between you two."

Tremaine laughs. When he looks back up at me and sees the confused frown on my face, he ruffles his hair. "Typical Roshan," he mutters, almost to himself. "That's just his way of telling you he doesn't want to talk about it."

"Then what happened?"

Tremaine leans his head back against the wall and focuses on the spot where water is gushing down from the canopy. "Do you know anything about Roshan's family?"

I shake my head. "It's not something he's ever brought up."

Tremaine nods, as if he expected this, too. "His mum is a prominent member of Britain's parliament. Roshan's father owns one of the world's largest shipping companies. His brother married some kind of duchess, and his sister is a surgeon. His cousin's related to royalty. As for Roshan—he's the youngest, so everyone dotes on him the most."

Of all the things I would've expected from Roshan, being the son of a prominent family wasn't one of them. "He doesn't act like it at all. He doesn't even talk like it. He's a champion gamer . . ."

"It's possible to be both, isn't it?" Tremaine gives me a humorless smile.

Back during the opening ceremony party, hadn't Max Martin taunted Roshan about his "pedigree"? I'd assumed it was an insult about Roshan being on the Phoenix Riders, or maybe because he came from a poor background—but I guess it was the opposite kind of put-down, a challenge flung from one wealthy son to another. "Fancy," I say. It's all I can muster.

"Know what my pedigree is?" Tremaine replies. "When I was in primary, my dad got shut away for shooting a store clerk over fifty pounds in a register. My mum tried selling me once, when she was high and ran out of money for another hit. The only reason I could afford to get into Warcross was because a local team was recruiting trainees, offering to pay food and lodging to kids with the most potential. I squeaked in."

I picture Tremaine as a little boy, on his own as much as I'd been at that age. "I'm sorry," I say.

"Oh, don't give me that pitiful face. I'm not telling you this for sympathy points. I just figured you'd understand." He taps his foot unconsciously against the ground. "It's fine. I still love my mum, she's doing well in rehab, and I'm a Warcross champion now with millions in my account. But you try explaining that kind of upbringing to Roshan's family. That their beloved boy is dating someone like me."

Tremaine lowers his head and stares blankly at the wet pavement. "I'm not saying Roshan's always had it easy. But he's smart as hell, you know? He mastered Warcross within a year of playing it. By his second year, he was in the Wardraft. People like him immediately, are drawn to that quicksilver mind of his."

"You're smart, too."

Tremaine grimaces. "No. I'm . . . that guy who needs all year to study for something that Roshan could ace just by skimming the same material an hour before the big final. I couldn't read until the sixth grade." His cheeks flush in the night at this admission. "Roshan was the first pick in our year's Wardraft, back when we were both wild cards. Two teams fought over him, did you know that? That was the cause of the original rift between the Riders and the Demon Brigade. And that was back when he barely practiced. I was just a straggler who lucked out because Asher saw something in me. I resented Roshan for being the one who always stayed up late to help me out. I fell for him for the same reason."

"So you started seeing him."

Tremaine hesitates. "And I started taking pills to keep up with everyone."

I blink. "Drugs?"

"I started with half a pill a day, and I don't really remember when I got up to seven or eight."

I recall the abrupt leave Tremaine had taken from Warcross, right before he left the Phoenix Riders. How gaunt he'd looked that year. Had that entire episode been because of pills? "How long did that go on for?" I ask.

"About a year."

"Did Roshan know?"

"Everyone knew, especially after I passed out during a practice session. They tried forcing me to quit. Asher threatened to cut me from the team if I didn't stop. But it wasn't until I overheard Roshan's father talking to him before a game that I realized Roshan was out of my league. His father patted his shoulder and said, 'I'm sorry, son. But what did you expect? It was only a matter of time before he followed his mother's example.' I ended up getting in a fistfight with another player during that game, and the Riders were temporarily suspended."

"I remember," I murmur.

"I didn't sleep that night," Tremaine says. "I knew I was single-handedly crippling my team. The next day, I packed my things and left without telling Asher or saying good-bye to my mates. Roshan came running after me, asking where the hell I was going." He shakes his head. "I was so mad and ashamed that I told him I was sleeping with someone else behind his back, that we were done. Coincidentally, the Demons were on the hunt for a new Architect, and they were only too happy to stick it to the Riders."

I listen quietly. Roshan had never mentioned any of this.

"Look, I'm not proud of it, yeah?" Tremaine mutters. "It doesn't mean I think I was right. It's just what happened."

"And you never cleared the air with Roshan?" I ask.

"Couldn't bring myself to. And now it feels too late."

I can't help but think back to how I'd clutched my head in my hands the night I'd glitched myself into the Warcross Opening Ceremony, completely unaware that my world was about to change forever. Everything became amazing; then, everything turned awful. Life is always like that—you don't know when you'll suddenly claw your way out of your circumstances, or when you'll go crashing back down into them.

"I'm not going to tell you it's never too late," I reply. "But, in my experience, it's always the *not doing* that I regret more."

The rain has stopped now, and the puddles in the alleyway have turned into undisturbed mirrors. Tremaine's the first to push away from the wall. He shoves his hands into his pockets, then glances at me over his shoulder. Whatever vulnerabilities he'd shown a second ago have vanished behind his cool exterior.

"So," he says, his bravado back. "No chance you're quitting, huh?"

I shake my head. "Afraid not."

"Well." He lingers for a moment, nodding out toward the main streets. "Then we'll need to stop fooling around in virtual reality and head to the institute for ourselves."

I look quickly at him. "What do you mean, *we*? I thought you were out, either way."

He sends me a message, and a map appears in my view with a blinking red cursor hovering over a place somewhere beyond the northern fringes of Tokyo. Japan Innovation Institute of Technology, the cursor says. Saitama-ken, Japan.

"If you're going to continue, then I guess I'll stick it out with you." He points to the map. "When I went, all I could do was observe the campus from the outside. But I'm sure there's plenty more going on behind those closed doors than what I could glean from their servers or their front gates. We'll need to head in at night, when there aren't so many guards."

I stare at the map, my fingers tingling. This is where Hideo's mother had worked, and where Sasuke may have spent his childhood. From the map, it doesn't look like much—a building of glass and steel, a single structure in a sea of thousands. How can one place hold so many secrets?

"So, tomorrow night?" he says.

I give him a half smile. "Done."

He heads out into the alley. His emotions are packed away again, but his usual sneer is now replaced with something more open. "See you soon, Princess Peach," he replies. This time, the nickname sounds affectionate. "And keep yourself safe until then."

• • • • •

THE HOTEL WHERE the Blackcoats are staying is quiet tonight, and I'm the only one walking down its halls. I sigh as the door identifies me and lets me in. My mind is a whirlwind of clues and questions. What if the institute has covered its tracks? What if I can't find anything? There's not much time before the closing ceremony, and I still know so little about Zero.

Where is he tonight, anyway?

The instant I close the door to my room, I know something is off. There's the faint scent of perfume in the air, and a lamp on the far end of the room is turned on.

"Out late?" someone says.

I whirl around to see Taylor waiting for me.

14

I freeze at the sight of her silhouette sitting casually in my chair, one of her legs crossed over the other. Weak light from the windows cuts a striped pattern against her. Even from the other side of the room, I can see her eyes in the shadows, studying me. She's perfectly groomed, her hair combed neatly back, and her outfit is sleek and monochromatic, blacks and grays. I find myself unconsciously comparing her to the photo I'd seen earlier, of her in front of the institute.

"We heard you were out celebrating with the Phoenix Riders tonight," she says. "Congratulations to your former team."

Jax had trailed me, after all. I fight the urge to look around to see if she's standing in here right now, somewhere I hadn't noticed. "I don't need you guys to chaperone me all over the city."

Taylor uncrosses her legs, the sole of her shoe hitting the carpet with a soft thud, and leans forward to rest her elbows against her knees. Her eyes meet mine and lock me in. "Where were you?"

So, she doesn't trust me. "I was out on the mission that you and Zero assigned to me," I reply evenly. "Find a way to get in touch with Hideo. That's what you want, isn't it?"

She frowns. "And did you accomplish anything?"

I take a deep breath. "The Riders are going to let me use their private meeting with Hideo tomorrow."

"Is that so?" At that, Taylor's eyebrows lift in mild surprise. "Well. Maybe you are as good as Zero says."

"I always earn my keep."

"And is that all you did tonight?"

Here's the real question she'd wanted to ask me, and why she was waiting for me here in my room. *Be careful out there.* Tremaine's warning reappears in my mind. I narrow my eyes at her. "What are you saying?"

"I'm saying that someone accessed the Blackcoats' image databases today, and it wasn't any of us." She studies me. "The timing makes me wonder if you know something about it."

Image databases. *Japan Innovation Institute of Technology.* My heart leaps into my throat. Tremaine had been poking around in the corporation's database earlier. I think of the maps he'd shown me, the interiors of the building. Is Taylor talking about him? What if he'd accidentally left a trail? Does she know what he took?

Stay calm, I tell myself. "It couldn't have been me," I reply. "I didn't do anything except meet the Phoenix Riders after tonight's game and have a conversation with them. No downloading, no hacking."

She stares at me, but I don't dare add more. The crow's feet at the corners of her eyes crinkle as she studies me thoughtfully. A few long minutes pass.

Then, her stare softens, and she relaxes her shoulders. She glances toward the windows. "If Zero suspected you of breaking into our files, he would be here himself, interrogating you. And he wouldn't be this civil about it."

The thought sends a chill through me. "Then why are you here instead?"

"I'm here to warn you," she replies, giving me a concerned look. "You don't want to get in over your head."

"But I didn't do anything."

She looks doubtful. There's a pause, and then she clears her throat. "How old were you when you first started bounty hunting?" she finally asks.

"Sixteen."

She shakes her head. "I was young, too, when I started my first job. Back then, we lived in Estonia, and my father laundered money using the pharmacy he ran as a front. Drugs, you know."

I watch her carefully. It shouldn't surprise me that she had early ties to something illegal, given that she's working for the Blackcoats—but I must look startled by her answer, because she gives me a small laugh.

"Ah, that surprises you. I don't seem like the type, do I?" She looks down. "I was sharp for my age, and I could repeat things back, word for word, so my father had me run messages for him." She makes a casual gesture with her arm, miming a back-and-forth action. "You don't want digital messages lying around on phones to incriminate you. I could say what I was told to say and then forget it the second I said it. He told me I had a good memory. That it's useful for lies." She shrugs. "But he wasn't as good at it as I was."

I clear my throat. "What makes you say that?"

"I came home one day to see him sprawled on the floor, his throat cut and his blood soaked into our rugs. That copper smell still lingers with me." The curve of her lips straightens, like she bit into something bitter. I shudder. "Later, I learned that a client of his had come looking for him, and he'd tried to lie his way out of it. The client hadn't believed him."

I swallow hard. Taylor doesn't look at me as she continues. "After that, all I ever did was wonder about how the wires in my brain were hooked up. How those wires stop working the instant your body shuts down. I'd wake up in the middle of the night in a cold sweat, dreaming of being alive one moment and then dead the next."

She sounds like I imagine a neuroscientist would, someone fascinated with the inner workings of the mind. Had she moved to Japan to work at the institute? I try to picture her as a child with wide eyes and those straight, innocent brows. The thought of her getting away with lies so often seems pretty possible. "Why are you telling me this?" I ask.

"I could convince myself of a lie so well that I'd sincerely think it was true. Do you know what that's called? Self-deception, Emika. Lies are told more easily when you don't see them as lies. My father said he wished he had my ability to believe wholeheartedly in something untrue, because if you're able to believe anything, then you can believe your way into happiness. That's why I'm alive, and he's dead. Because my brain could connect that wire, and his couldn't." She leans forward, looking earnestly at me. "Maybe you're good at it, too. I imagine it's a useful skill for a bounty hunter."

Stay calm. "I'm not lying to you," I tell her in a firm voice this time. "I didn't hack into any Blackcoat databases—I wouldn't even know where to look."

"Then you have nothing to worry about," Taylor agrees.

Her voice *sounds* genuine, and her expression *looks* genuine, but I stay wary, waiting for her to make some unexpected move.

What did you work on at the institute? And what, exactly, do you do
for the Blackcoats?

"I hope you understand how important your role is." Taylor gives me a nod before she rises from my chair and straightens her blouse. She nods toward the streetlights outside the window. "Look."

Two new virtual figures appear to hover underneath each light, followed by a wave of cheers and boos from the revelers on the street. I recognize my own rainbow hair instantly.

IVO ERIKKSON of SWEDEN | ANDROMEDA
EMIKA CHEN of USA | PHOENIX RIDERS

At the same time, a message pops up front and center in my view.

Congratulations, Emika Chen!
You have been chosen as a
TOP TEN PLAYER
of the
WARCROSS CHAMPIONSHIPS VIII

Taylor smiles at my stunned expression. "You're the only one chosen so far by write-in votes alone," she says. "Very impressive." As she walks past me, she says something in a voice just loud enough for me to hear. "I won't tell Zero about our conversation, but let this be the last time we need to have one. I think you owe it to all your fans to perform well at the closing ceremony."

Then she's gone, leaving me standing in the middle of my room alone with all my questions.

15

The few hours of sleep that I manage to get are plagued by nightmares, visions of myself standing in an arena, a woman sitting in my chair, a girl with short silver hair training her gun on me, Hideo pulling me close in a bedroom made of glass. I dream of Tremaine leaning against the wall at the Innovation Institute and watching the rain.

That's what finally shakes me awake—the image of him standing there, unaware of someone watching him in the shadows. I jerk upright in bed mumbling his name, trying in vain to warn him.

By the time I meet the Riders at Asher's place, I'm an exhausted mess, with dark circles prominent under my eyes. Secretly, I count my blessings that at least the event I'm attending requires makeup and formal wear, so that I don't show up looking like a ghost.

Asher answers the door. "You look terrible," he says, leaning one elbow against his chair.

"You too," I reply.

He flashes me a grin before ushering me inside. "Well, Hammie's going to do something about that."

Hammie's already here and waiting for me. She takes my hand and leads me to Asher's bedroom, where she shuts the two of us in and pulls me over to the closet. I find myself staring at a small rack of dresses.

"I did a little shopping," she says, holding one of the dresses up against me. She squints an eye shut. "These look about your size."

I'm quiet as I change out of my clothes and slip on the first dress. It's Givenchy, a shimmering sea of midnight fabrics that hugs my hips.

Hammie studies me with a thoughtful frown. "It fits a little weird up here," she says, tapping my shoulder. She turns to grab another dress. "Let's try a Giambattista Valli. Give you some volume."

She holds up a beautiful, fluffy pouf of a gown in pale champagne pink. I stare at myself, drowning behind layers of tulle, and imagine what it will be like to see Hideo in person again. "Maybe this is a bad idea," I start to say.

"Mm, you're right," Hammie ponders out loud, hanging the dress back on the rack. "Too much pouf. How about a Dior?"

"No, I mean—" I take a deep breath and close my eyes. "Hideo. This isn't going to go well."

Hammie pauses to look at me as she holds up a new ball gown with a bold black-and-white print. "You're afraid to see him, aren't you?"

My eyes meet Hammie's in the mirror. "You didn't see the look in his eyes when we last talked. He's not going to hear me out. More likely, he'll have his bodyguards on me the instant he knows I'm at the party."

Hammie doesn't deny it, and I'm almost grateful she doesn't

try to console me with any lies. "Listen," she replies instead. "One time, my mom and dad had an argument before New Year's. I don't remember what it was over. Walking our dog? Something dumb. Anyway, they both decided, regardless, to go separately to their friends' New Year's Eve party. I went with my dad. When we got there, my dad saw my mom, sparkling in the most gorgeous silver gown you've ever seen in your life. Know what he did? He walked right up to her, said he was sorry, and then they kissed over and over and over. It was disgusting."

I give Hammie a withering look. "That's different. Your parents are in love. And they weren't fighting over the fact that your dad wants to control the world."

Hammie waves a flippant hand. "Details. I'm just saying. You think *you're* not over Hideo? He's mad about you. You heard Kenn say it. Even Zero knows. And now the girl he can't get out of his head is going to show up right in front of him, without warning, in a stunning dress? You're going to knock his socks off with a battering ram."

"Well, I'm glad one of us thinks so." I pull on a new dress and adjust the straps. This one fits like a glove, with a plunging back and a full skirt ending perfectly at my feet. "I don't think being unpredictable is a good thing with Hideo," I say.

"Everything about you has been unpredictable since the moment you hacked into his game." Hammie steps back, admiring the dress's clean lines. "If he doesn't at least give you the time of day when he sees you like this, he really has no soul. Then you can kick his ass."

We pause at a knock on the door. Hammie calls out that we're done, and it opens to reveal Roshan leaning against the doorway. He glances over at me with an approving look.

"Car's here," he says.

"Give us a sec," Hammie replies. "While I do her hair and makeup."

The world is hanging by a thread, and yet here the Riders still are, acting like this is nothing more than getting me ready for a party. I feel an overwhelming rush of gratitude for them.

"Hideo's going to know you all helped me," I say to Roshan.

"You don't need to worry about us right now," Roshan replies. He meets my gaze with his steady one. "Just be careful."

I close my eyes as Hammie starts dusting glittering shadow on my eyelids. It's just as well. Tremaine's story about their past is still fresh in my mind, and looking at Roshan's unsuspecting face sends an ache through my chest.

Finally, I'm ready. As I head out of the house, I hear Hammie call out one last *"Good luck!"* in my direction. Then I'm getting into the car, and the door seals me in.

I spend the entire ride with my hands clasped tightly in my lap, lost in the silken folds of my dress's skirt. Beyond the window, high-rises blur by with little shrines squeezed between them, followed by garden walls and an expansive park. The sun is already setting, and more neon lights are starting to turn on. As we drive alongside a river that reflects the subways running on the opposite side of the banks, I can see the interior of the train cars packed with people, many of them decked out in their Warcross virtual outfits.

Too anxious already, I force myself to look away, then concentrate on overlaying a randomly generated face on my own. My rainbow hair turns into sleek dark brown, and my eyes change to a pale hazel. When I see my reflection again in the car's rearview mirrors, I look unrecognizable.

I don't need to tell him much tonight, I remind myself. Right now, I just need to convince the Blackcoats that I'm making progress in getting closer to Hideo. I need Hideo to agree to meet me again in private, so that I can talk to him safely.

He's mad about you. I try to repeat Hammie's reassurances to myself. But it's harder to believe without her beside me.

The drive feels both like it took forever and no time at all. The Tokyo Museum of Contemporary Art's main entrance is entirely blocked off today, thick with security, but my car takes a turn into a smaller side entrance that brings us through the surrounding park grounds. We go up the winding path a brief distance before stopping on the side of the building. Here, it's quieter, a few other black cars ahead of us. I hold my breath as we reach the front of the line. Here, the car comes to a full stop at the entrance, and its door slides open.

"Have a wonderful evening," the car says. "Congratulations again on your team's win."

"Thank you," I mutter at it before I exit, fanning out my dress.

Everyone else inside the building is decked out in elaborate attire. Some of them are wearing half masks adorned with jewel-encrusted feathers, while others hold delicate, porcelain-colored fans across their faces. I stand there for a moment, feeling at once vulnerable and invisible. Thank goodness Hammie forced me to choose such an elegant dress. Anything less would have made me stand out in this crowd.

The main entrance hall of the museum is a soaring corridor of glass and metal, enormous triangles cut through with a steel mesh of circles. The giant glass panels are actually screens, and as I walk, the NeuroLink simulates scenes on each panel from this year's championship worlds. I recognize the rematch's world of cloud plains and cliffs, then the ice world of my first official game. I pause for a moment in front of a panel showcasing the eerie underwater ruins that we'd played in the Riders' third round.

This was the world where Zero had broken into my account and made me his offer.

All around me, groups of social elites cluster and laugh politely over conversations I can't understand. I see women drenched in jewels, men in sharply tailored suits and tuxedos. Asher had said these people would be the upper crust of society, billionaires and philanthropists, the kind of people Hideo must constantly cross paths with.

Then, finally, I reach the end of the hall, where I spot who I've been searching for.

Every muscle in my body tenses at the same time. Hideo's standing there with a small circle of his bodyguards, each of them dressed in matching black suits, and he's deep in conversation with several other well-dressed people. Kenn. Mari is here, too, in a long-sleeved, silver dress with a sheer tulle train. There's a young woman about my age who's leaning into Hideo, laughing at something he's just said. I try not to pay attention to how beautiful she is. A few others, women and businessmen alike, wait on the sidelines for their chance to talk to him.

At least Asher was right about this setting—if Hideo sees me here, he's not going to want to cause a scene. There have been enough disruptions during this year's championships, and too many elite folks are here. But if he doesn't want *me* to cause a scene, he'll have to agree to talk to me.

As I watch him politely field the girl's questions, I gradually start to dissolve the anonymous virtual face I've overlaid over my own, erasing it so that only Hideo will be able to see behind it. Then I step forward until there's no one before me except him and the girl.

He glances in my direction. Then he freezes. His distant expression vanishes, and for an instant, all I can see beneath it is a look of shock.

Beside him, the girl touching his arm looks in my direction and gives me a confused scowl. To her, I still look like some stranger, someone she doesn't know, and she lets out a nervous laugh. "Who's this, Hideo?" she says.

One of the bodyguards must sense Hideo's sudden change in demeanor, too, because I see his hand fly to his gun. I instinctively brace myself. I've made a mistake, I've misjudged this event—Hideo's going to let his guard take me down, he doesn't care about making a scene here, no matter how many powerful people are at this party.

But then Hideo holds up a warning hand at the guard. He meets the man's eyes and shakes his head once. "Excuse me," he says to the girl at his side, then takes a few steps toward me. He gives me a polite bow of his head, and I return the gesture.

"It's been a long time since I've seen you," he says. He takes my hand and presses it once to his lips. Behind him, the girl he'd been with sucks in her breath and exchanges a quick look with a friend. The conversation around us turns quiet.

His mind must be spinning right now. He must be wondering how I got in here, whether the Phoenix Riders are in on whatever my plans are.

On the surface, though, I just smile back and play along, as if everything were fine. "Well, is that my fault, or yours?"

He turns briefly to his other guests, all of whom are staring at us with obvious interest. "My apologies," he says. His eyes go to his bodyguards. "Stay here. I won't be long." Without waiting to hear their responses, he turns to me and places one hand at the small of my back. I try to ignore the sensation, that the only thing separating us is the silky fabric of this dress.

His expression is tired, and I wonder if he's learned anything new about the bug in the algorithm since I eavesdropped on his conversation. He doesn't seem like he trusts me, but for some reason, he still nods and steers us through the hall until it branches into the museum's interior, where one corridor leads out into a vast courtyard.

There's a slight chill in the night air, and the grounds are sparsely populated with only a few people here and there. Trees line the sides of a towering structure that curves up to the evening sky. Other art installations look like they're dedicated specifically to Warcross. One series of 3-D sculptures forms the Warcross logo from certain angles, and from other angles looks like an Artifact, or a popular virtual item, or the outfit of an official player. Another piece of art is a stylized interpretation of the various worlds used in this year's championships, a series of white polygons in a row, representing the ice columns from the White World I'd played in or modern art ruins of a city encased behind a giant glass cube tinted an underwater green color. Yet another looks like a real-life ode to Warcross's virtual-reality realms: dozens of giant, round lights installed in the ground, so that each shoots a colored beam up toward the sky. Orchestral music plays softly, changing whenever we step onto one of the light columns, matching each color to a different musical cue. As we walk through them, we cast shadows haloed in the color of that column of light.

The mood would feel almost peaceful, if it weren't for the reason we're out here.

Now Hideo leads us close to the light installation. Blue and yellow beams cast their colors against his skin.

"Where are we going?" I say.

Hideo's gaze turns dark. "I'm escorting you out," he says in a low voice.

I'm not surprised by his words, but they still hit me hard. He doesn't speculate about the fact that I'd clearly gotten help from the Riders or that I might be here to hurt him. He just looks at me like I'm nothing more than some distant associate that he'd already forgotten. I can feel my cheeks warming, my heartbeat beginning to race. It's stupid of me to still be bothered by him, but I can't force the sting down. It makes me think that maybe I'd always read him wrong.

Unless he's afraid of me being here. Maybe he's afraid that I've been sent here after him. And he'd be right.

"Please," I respond before I can think through my words. "Just hear me out. I'm not here to argue with you. Neither of us has the time for that."

"What *are* you doing here, Emika?" Hideo says with a sigh. He glances briefly toward the bright museum hall, the impatience obvious in his glare.

I swallow hard, and then take a step onto one of the light columns. Yellow light illuminates everything around me, and the music shifts to an active orchestral piece. Hideo follows me. "I've found something you need to know," I say, my words shielded from any prying ears by the music. From a distance, it looks like we're just two people enjoying the art installation.

I hold my breath, ready for Hideo to call for his guards. He doesn't. He studies my expression, as if searching for what I might say next. "Tell me," he says.

I take another step onto a different light column. This time, I'm bathed in blue, and the music shifts to a deeper track. The words sit at the tip of my tongue. *Your brother is Zero. The same hacker we'd been tracking throughout the championships.*

Once he knows, there's no turning back.

"I'll show you instead," I reply.

Then I bring up an image of Zero without his armor, his face exposed and unmistakable. The image hovers between us.

It's as if I'd struck Hideo straight in the chest. He doesn't move, doesn't breathe, doesn't blink. The color drains from his face. In the blue light, his skin takes on an ominous glow from below, and his eyes look like black marbles. His lips tighten. His hands move slightly, and when I look down at them, he's balled both into fists so tightly that his scarred knuckles have turned white.

His stare never leaves Sasuke's face, one that looks so similar to his own. He scrutinizes everything—the way his eyes turn sideways, the thoughtful tilt of his head, the hardness of his smile. Maybe he's making a mental list of all the ways the two of them are alike, or maybe he's matching up these features with what he remembers of Sasuke as a child, as if he'd drawn a new image in his head with these two pictures combined.

Then his eyes shutter. Whatever he thinks of the photo disappears behind a cloud of disbelief. He turns to me. "This has to be fake. You're lying to me."

"I've never been more truthful." I keep my words steady and the image unwavering.

He straightens and takes a step away from me, so that half of him is in a red column of light. "This photo isn't real. That isn't him."

"It's real. I swear it on my life."

The anger on his face is growing every second, a wall bricking in the part of him that had believed me. Still, I stay where I am, digging my nails into the palms of my hands. "I've met your brother." Then I join him on the red light as I continue, slower and more forcefully this time. "I don't know everything about him yet, and I can't tell you everything here. But I saw him with my own eyes—I've spoken with him directly. Zero is your brother."

"You're baiting me."

There in his voice. I hear it, the tiniest hint of doubt, a delay long enough to tell me that I may be getting through to him.

"I'm not." I shake my head. "Didn't you originally hire me to hunt for people you're searching for? This is what I do."

"Except you don't work for me anymore." He narrows his eyes at me. There's fire in his gaze, but beyond that, I can see fear. "There's nothing holding us together that would make you do this, unless you want something from me. So what is it, Emika? What do you *really* want?"

He's reading me better than I thought, assuming that because of what he'd done to me, I'm doing the same to him. I'd told him once that I was coming for him, and he hasn't forgotten it.

"I'm not hunting you," I say. "I'm trying to tell you the truth."

"Who are you working for?" He draws closer now, his eyes focused on me with that familiar, searing intensity. "Is it Zero? Did someone put you up to this?"

He's leaping ahead now, guessing too much. For a moment, I think I've gone back in time to when I'd first met him, when I had to stare him down to prove my worth.

"It's not safe to tell you more here," I reply. My voice does not falter under his scrutiny, and I don't look away. "I need to talk to you in private. Just the two of us. I can't give you anything more than that."

Hideo's face looks completely closed off. I wonder if he's replaying in his mind every detail from the day that Sasuke went missing, every excruciating moment he lived through afterward. Or maybe he's trying to break this scenario down, puzzling over whether I'm setting a trap for him or not.

"I'm not the one who broke our trust," I go on, more softly now. "I always told you the truth. I worked faithfully for you. And you lied to me."

"You know exactly why I had to do it."

My anger now flares at his stubbornness. "Why'd you lead

me on, then?" I snap, growing angrier with each word. "You could've just stayed away or hired someone else. You could've left me alone instead of pulling me in."

"Believe me, I regret nothing more," Hideo snaps back.

His answer startles me, and I forget the retort I already had prepared. He doesn't look like he was ready to say it, either, and he turns away from me, looking back toward the museum hall. Peals of laughter come from inside. The sounds echo down to us.

I try one more time. "Do you care enough about your brother to believe that maybe, just *maybe*, I'm telling you the truth?" I finally reply. "Do you still love Sasuke or not?"

I've never said his brother's name out loud before. It's this that finally seems to crack through his shield. He winces at my words. For a moment, all I can see is Hideo as a small boy, his terror as he realized his brother was no longer in the park. He's spent so many years building up his defenses, and now here I am, ripping right through them with a simple question. Forcing Sasuke back into the present.

For a while, I think he might refuse me again. I've miscalculated everything in my plans against him and the Blackcoats—I've sorely overestimated how well I could control this situation. This is too big a hurdle for me to cross.

Then Hideo turns back to me. He leans down slightly, so that our two silhouettes nearly touch.

"Tomorrow," he says in a low voice. "Midnight."

16

By the time I get back to the hotel, a masquerade parade has broken out in the neighboring district, and cosplayers have spilled over from Harajuku's Takeshita Street onto the sidewalks of Omotesando. People dressed in their most elaborate getups—both real and virtual—are walking around while crowds gather along the shop entrances to gawk and admire. The streets themselves are lit up in virtual neon colors, fading gradually from one team's hues to the next, and each time they shift, a burst of cheers comes from the fans. A closer look tells me that most of the cosplayers are dressed in some variation of the teams' outfits from this year's championships.

I catch glimpses of their vibrant costumes from my window as I hurry around, changing out of my dress and throwing on my black jeans and sweater. Black gloves go on my hands, fresh socks and sneakers on my feet. My pair of slim knives is tucked inside my boots, while my backpack is filled with my usual supplies—my grappling hook, handcuffs, and stun gun. Finally, I download a randomly generated face to set over my features and pull a new mask over the lower half of my face.

I may be running with a fancier crew now, but the familiar ritual and the weight of my old tools feel right, convincing me that I actually know what the hell I'm doing, even as Hideo's words from the banquet earlier whirl around in my head.

He looked like I had ripped his heart right out of his chest.

Believe me, I regret nothing more.

I scowl and yank harder on my shoelaces. None of this was ever my fault, and he knows it. But my encounter with him has still left me spinning, my mind crowded with all the different emotions that he brings.

An incoming message from Zero cuts through my train of thoughts. I startle in the darkness and glance up, half expecting to see him standing there in the middle of my room.

> How was your meeting
> with Hideo?

"I managed to get a second one with him," I whisper back, my words transcribing in midair before being sent back to him.

> When?

"Tomorrow night. It'll be private—no public settings."

There's a pause, and I wonder whether he or Jax had somehow spied on my earlier conversation already, and whether he's just testing me now to see if I'll tell him the truth.

> **Make sure it counts.**

Outside, a huge roar goes up as the streets shift to red and gold, the Phoenix Riders' colors. Cars honk in enthusiasm as they drive by.

"It will," I say.

No more replies come from him.

I wait a little longer, then sigh and bring up Tremaine's map of the Innovation Institute. I tap on Tremaine's profile to send him a message.

"Hey," I murmur, watching my words appear in my view. "You still in for tonight?"

I wait for a while. There's a bit of static on his end, but nothing more, and when he doesn't respond, I take a look at his profile. He's still online, and his profile is haloed in green.

> **Hey.**

I message again.

> **Blackbourne. Wake up.**

Maybe his connection's bad. Or maybe he really doesn't want to talk to me anymore, not after everything he spilled to me last night. I unplug my board from its charger, trying not to dwell on what other reasons he might have for being silent.

When he still doesn't answer me after a few more messages, I get up and grab my board. Heading to the institute without Tremaine is probably a bad idea, especially after Taylor's talk with me. At least I'd given something to the Blackcoats, enough to keep them satisfied that I'm doing my job for them—but if I'm going to be meeting Hideo tomorrow, any extra info I find on Sasuke will need to happen tonight.

I'm running out of time.

● ● ● ● ●

I DON'T LEAVE my hotel through the front door. If Jax is watching me tonight, she'll expect me to go through main entrance. So instead, I pull out my old cable launcher from my backpack, hook the end onto the balcony railing, then climb over the ledge and leap off.

Wind whips my hair up in a stream, but from the outside, no one can see more than a rippling shadow moving along the side of the complex. I squint, shivering in the cold as the cable launcher carries me down, jerking to a halt less than a story from the ground.

I release the cable and let myself fall with a soft thud. Then I toss down my board and head in the direction of the institute.

For the first time in a while, I head down into the first subway train I can find. They're still congested at this hour of the night. Salarymen exasperated with all the festivities slowing down their travels jostle past me without sparing so much as a glance, while groups of eager fans clog the trains, each trying to get to some party or Warcross street game happening in the city. Ramen stalls and bakeries lining the station interiors are all still packed, while high-end stores bustle with customers, everyone looking for limited-edition championship purses and belts and shoes that will all go away once the Warcross season ends. Alongside the advertisements covering the walls of the station are the virtual figures of two more top players chosen for the closing ceremony.

ABENI LEA of KENYA | TITANS
TREY KAILEO of USA | WINTER DRAGONS

I hold my breath and let myself get lost in the fray, hoping that no one recognizes me through my disguises when we're all pressed together in the trains. I ride a few different subway lines until I feel like I can't even find myself in the midst of all the bodies. If Jax still manages to catch up with me, it'll hopefully take her long enough to give me some time to check out the institute on my own.

Half an hour later, I emerge into the darker, quieter residential streets beyond the outskirts of Tokyo. Here, the virtual overlays diminish into little more than building names in subtle white letters—Curry House, Bakery, Laundry—and the block number I'm currently on, then rows and rows of nondescript house labels. Apartments 14-5-3. Apartments 16-6-2.

My board streaks silently through the roads until the homes come to an abrupt end. A solid stone wall wraps around the next block, ending in a security window and a lowered barrier gate. I pull to a stop in front of it. There, looming past an expanse of lawn and fountains, is a large office complex, its main atrium made entirely of glass.

My gaze stops on the words engraved into the slab of stone just beyond the barrier gate, the same one that Tremaine had shown me in his photo.

JAPAN INNOVATION INSTITUTE OF TECHNOLOGY

The parking lot isn't empty. I see a few black cars here, parked in one corner.

My hackles rise at the sight. It's entirely possible that some people are just working late—but something about the cars reminds me of the one I'd ridden in with Jax when she'd first taken me to the Blackcoats. Maybe Tremaine is here, too. At the thought of him, I do another quick scan of my messages. He's still online, but he hasn't answered me yet.

I hesitate for another second before I finally pull my hood on tighter, switch my randomized facial features to a new set, and squeeze past the car barrier.

The main entrance is locked, of course. From the outside, it's hard to make out exactly what's past the all-glass front atrium— but it soars at least three to four floors high, and some kind of dim gradient of colored light is sweeping around inside, from top to bottom. The entire building looks shut down for the night. I glance back at the cars, considering, and then wander away from the main entrance to follow the building's wall.

I make my way around the entire complex, looking for a good way in, but everything seems locked down, with no security faults anywhere. I huddle down near a clump of bushes on the side of the main building and bring up Tremaine's maps again, hoping to see some security vulnerability I might have missed. Then I run a search on whether the complex has any online system that I can worm into. Once, I'd broken into a closed Manhattan boutique by getting past its security cameras' simplistic passwords. But here, I find no weaknesses.

What good was coming here if I can't even get inside? I sigh, then poke around the perimeter of the building a second time, looking for what clues I can gather. There are several different buildings connected here: a physics wing, a neuroinformatics wing, a research resources tech center, and several cafés. None of this is new info—I'd seen all of this in my online research on the institute.

I'm about to call it a night when I suddenly hear the faint sound of footsteps.

Ahead of me, one of the side entrance's glass doors slides open—and Jax steps out. She glances over her shoulder for an instant, and her gaze sweeps over the campus.

I duck below the bushes surrounding the building. My mind stumbles frantically from one possibility to another, each thought as rapid as my heartbeat. What the hell is she doing in here? Who is she with?

Jax probably didn't travel here alone. She's a bodyguard and an assassin, which means she's either here guarding Zero or Taylor, or she's here on a mission to cop someone. I count to three under my breath, then dare to peek around the side of the bushes.

Several guards have emerged from the building to join her. They're dressed in black, too, and I wonder for a moment if any of them are the same people who'd watched me duel Zero in the Dark World. Maybe they're the type of low-level goons you'd hire out of the Kabukichō area in Shinjuku.

Jax exchanges a few terse words with them, then heads off toward the far side of the complex at a brisk pace. A couple of the guards follow her, while two others start heading back into the door.

I move before I can think everything through. Shoulders hunched; eyes forward. I sneak along the bushes like a shadow, as quickly and silently as I can toward the open door. As the last guard disappears inside the door and it starts to close, I dart forward. I slide into the building's dark interior without a sound, right as the door slides closed.

Immediately, I slip into the closest hidden crevice I can find—a row of tall recycle bins. But the guards have already disappeared down the hall. I squeeze my eyes shut for a moment and lean my head back against the wall, then pull down my mask so I can take in some deep gasps of air. A sheen of cold sweat covers my entire body.

In my next life, I'm going to be an accountant.

Farther down the hall, the guards' footsteps grow steadily fainter. I wait until it's completely silent before I pick myself up and move forward.

The building is dark, and no one seems to be on duty. I go until the ceiling starts to get higher and the sound of my footsteps changes. Then I emerge into the main atrium, and I freeze, my mouth open.

The institute's main lobby could be a museum in itself. The ceiling soars many stories above me, and in the vast space is suspended what I can only call an enormous art sculpture that resembles the electric pulses of a brain—except on a massive scale, extending all the way from the ceiling down to a few feet above the floor. Hundreds of lines of light connect colorful orbs, and as I watch, the lines flash and fade, glow and darken. It's hypnotizing.

Other displays are encased behind glass boxes—human-like machines with metal limbs and legs, structures made of thousands of cylinders and circles all moving in a rhythmic pattern, curtains of light that look like a neon waterfall.

For a moment, I forget myself and wander from display to display, awed by the eerie beauty of it. I stop at a large timeline projected against the entirety of one wall. It shows the origins of the institute, old black-and-white photos progressing until the timeline ends on a modern-day image of the current building. Then everything shifts, the photos expanding so that they fill the wall, details printed over each image in white letters before scrolling to the next.

Headlines appear filled with praise for the institute—a center devoted to giving its clients cutting-edge technology, to conducting experiments decades ahead of their time, to the constant advancement of science.

The muffled sound of some distant sob cuts through my thoughts. I crouch against the wall on instinct, pushing myself deeper into the shadows. The cry has come from somewhere farther down one of the halls. Something about it seems familiar.

I wait. When I don't hear anything else, I leave behind the main atrium and hurry down the hall closest to me.

It's too dark in here to see the ceiling now, although the sound of my footsteps tells me how high the space is. Two thin purple neon lines highlight the edges of the floor. Several long minutes drag on, occasional sounds and voices ringing out. Somewhere ahead of me comes another muffled thud, then voices I don't recognize.

The hall ends abruptly, leading into another enormous space—this time with several brightly lit rooms covered on all sides with thick glass walls.

Inside one room is Zero.

I frown. No, it's not Zero—just something that looks like him, a black metal suit, tall and lean, its head and body completely encased in armor. A robot? Standing outside the glass room is Zero himself, deep in conversation with Taylor. She has several screens hovering in front of her, all of them only blank white, from my view. As Zero talks, she pushes her glasses up on her nose and types onto a screen in midair. Her shoulders look fragile in their hunched position.

Zero steps away from Taylor toward the glass. She nods at him. And, as I look on, *he steps right through the glass wall and into the room with his armor.*

I blink. He's not here in person—he's a virtual simulation. Then where is he?

Zero walks around the robot version of himself, inspecting it carefully. A loud *beep* sounds out from the glass room—and suddenly, the robot moves. Zero holds out his hand; the robot moves its limb in the exact same motion. Zero turns his head; the robot turns its head, too. Taylor pushes the door open and joins him in the room. She tosses a metal object at the robot, and Zero's hand whips out. The robot does the exact same gesture, catching the object in a perfect grip.

I gape. Whatever this robot is for, it's entirely hooked up to Zero's mind, with a level of accuracy that frightens me.

The muffled sob I'd heard earlier now comes to me again. This time, I turn to see Jax emerge from the shadows of another hall at the other end of the space, shoving a figure forward until they're both standing before the glass room. As Taylor and Zero step out, Jax forces the figure onto his knees.

In an instant, I forget all about the robot. I forget about Zero's virtual self controlling the robot with his mind, and Taylor peering at her screens through her glasses. All that matters is the crouched, trembling figure, his skin washed white from the lights, his hair hanging in sweaty strings, his mouth gagged with a cloth.

Tremaine.

Jax's words drift to me, her voice echoing in the space. "Found him messing with the security cams," she says. "He tried making a run for the panic room when he realized I was on to him. Somehow, he knew the panic room's system is off the main grid."

Zero folds his hands behind his back and observes Tremaine's bowed figure. "Sounds like someone has been studying the institute's blueprints," he replies.

"Sounds like someone was laying a path out for someone else," Jax adds. "He's not here alone."

Tremaine shakes his head vigorously. His cheeks gleam wet under the light.

I can't swallow. Any sound around me has now faded completely away behind the roar of blood in my ears, and the edges of my vision blur. No wonder Tremaine hadn't responded to any of my messages tonight. He came here after all—and they'd known, maybe had even been waiting for him.

Taylor's words rush back at me. *And is that all you did tonight? I'm trying to warn you.* I half expect her to step in and help him out, protect him from Jax and Zero. But she stays where she stands, screens still hovering around her.

They must have found out Tremaine was the one behind the hack into the institute's files, that he had passed along the information—maybe even that he'd given it to me. How did they find out?

Through me. Maybe they were spying on our conversations; they've hacked into my accounts. Or they might have traced something Tremaine accidentally left behind.

Suddenly I feel a tidal wave of nausea—it's the same feeling I have when I know danger is creeping forward, and all I want to do is push everyone else away from me so it can't hook into any of them.

Tremaine has turned his face up to Zero now. Even in his terror, I can see the recognition registering on him—he's never met Zero before, but he knows who he is. Jax leans down and removes Tremaine's gag. Zero asks him something, but Tremaine's lips don't move to respond. All he does is stay silent. Jax's shoulders shift as she sighs. Zero takes a step forward, but Jax shakes her head and holds a hand up.

Let me, she seems to be saying.

She takes her hands off Tremaine's shoulder and stands back. The terror in me reaches a fever pitch. Everything around me seems to fade away as Jax pulls her gun from her holster and pulls it back with a click.

This should be the part when I scream something out, where one word from me makes everyone stop and look in my direction.

But instead, I can't utter a sound. Jax points the gun straight down at Tremaine's forehead. She fires a single shot.

Tremaine's body jerks. He crumples to the floor.

My hands clamp over my mouth to keep me from letting out a cry. The shot rings in my ears.

The kill I'd once seen Jax make now comes back to me in a wave, and I double over, hunching against the wall as I try to brace myself against the onslaught of the memory.

We believe that there are too many people in the world who go unpunished for committing terrible crimes.

Those were Taylor's words that had ultimately persuaded me to join the Blackcoats. She had told me they fought for causes they believed in. Their actions were justified because she—they all—feared what Hideo was capable of.

But in a single moment, every positive thing I ever thought about the Blackcoats, every word they'd plied me with, vanishes. Tremaine was alive just a second ago and now he's dead, and it's because of me.

Breathe.

Breathe.

But I can't think straight. I can't function in this moment except to crouch like some kind of coward, trembling uncontrollably against the wall. The glass room in front of me blurs and straightens. I think I see Taylor stepping back as two guards drag the body away, another lingers behind to clean up the floor. Zero leans toward Jax to speak in a low voice, while Taylor tucks something into the hands of the other guards. No one looks concerned. It suddenly occurs to me that the guards here were paid to wait around and bring Tremaine's body outside, so that they could drive it off somewhere. They were prepared to execute him.

My panic is cutting my breath short. I feel faint. The edges of my view are darkening, fading out, and I fight against it, the logical part of my mind telling me that if I collapse now, *here*, they'll find me. And if they know I've seen all this, they won't hesitate to do the exact same thing to me that they just did to Tremaine.

Jax looks bored—*exasperated* with that person who took up her time—she hadn't even looked back at Tremaine's body, which she'd left on the floor. How many has she killed this way?

The Blackcoats are murderers. Tremaine had warned me to stay away from them from the start—he'd only been here because he was looking out for *me*. And I'd gone ahead anyway. Now he's dead. What if the Blackcoats are already out looking for me, having learned the connection between Tremaine and my work?

What have I done?

I can't do this. I can't stay here. I close my eyes and count, forcing myself to focus on the train of numbers in my head until they're all I see. Hideo needs to know this. But what do I tell him? I don't even understand everything I just saw. What is that robot that Zero had been commanding? And if he's not here in person, where is he?

Get up, Emi.

I whisper the words over and over, until finally I unfreeze myself. I push my body off from the wall, rise from my crouch, and stumble back the way I came. Feverishly, I pull up my menus and set my maps for the hotel. I make my way far enough so that I've left the horrible room behind me and have reentered the soaring main lobby of the complex.

I swing my new board down toward the floor, ready to hop on it—but my hands are shaking so badly that I drop it with a clatter. I lunge in vain to catch it.

A click makes me whirl around. Jax is standing there, her pale skin stark against the black walls, her gun pointed directly at my head. Her gray eyes pierce through me.

"You're not supposed to be here," she says.

17

I don't dare answer. I just stay where I am and lift my hands over my head.

She waves her gun once at me. "Up."

I do as she says. There are a few flecks of blood on her glove, *Tremaine's* blood, and my eyes lock on to the sight. She's going to kill me for being here, and there's nowhere for me to hide. I'm going to die on the floor of this building, just like Tremaine did.

"Why the hell did you come here?" she snaps at me in a whisper.

"I was looking for Zero," I say, not even believing my own bad excuse. My words come out haltingly, and I can hear the tremor in them. "I'm meeting Hideo tomorrow night. I—"

Jax observes me carefully. She knows I'm lying—but instead, she says, "You saw, didn't you?"

I shake my head vigorously. "I heard." Usually, I can lie better than this—but right now, the panic in my eyes gives me away. "It was too dark. All I got were voices down the hall."

Jax sighs; she almost looks like she feels sorry for me, and I wonder if she recognizes the same look on my face from when she'd killed my assassin. "It's impressive that I didn't catch you on your way into the building. But here we are now."

The echo of Tremaine's killing shot still rings in my head, bursting over and over again, and my hands yearn to reach up and cover my ears.

Jax tightens her grip on her gun. *This is it.* My limbs are frozen in place.

"Walk."

What? My feet feel rooted to the floor.

Jax seizes my arm and shoves me once. Her nails dig hard into my skin. "If they know you're here, you're dead," she growls in my ear, shoving me forward. "*Go.*"

Her words register through my chaotic mind, and I manage to shoot her a confused glance as she starts pulling me along the shadowed wall of the main lobby. "Where are you taking me?" I whisper.

Jax leads me down another dark hall on the opposite end of the lobby. "Less talking, more walking," she replies.

Whatever shred of silence I'd managed to hold on to now breaks, and my words come spilling out. "And then what? Will you take me out, too? A shot to the head, just like Tremaine? Where are you taking his body?"

She turns those pale gray eyes on me again. "So, you did see."

I shake my head repeatedly, trying in vain to get Tremaine's crumpled body out of my mind. "What are you all doing here?" I say over and over again. "What is that robot Zero was controlling? Where is he?"

Jax doesn't answer me. We reach the end of the hall and a

small side entrance that opens into the back of the building, where a few cars are parked.

Here, Jax suddenly shoves me up against the wall and presses a gloved hand over my mouth. She looks as cold as ever, but there's tension in her eyes now, and she keeps glancing around to make sure we're alone. "In a minute, I'm going to tell you to go outside and get in the car farthest to your left. It'll take you back to the hotel. The guards out front are busy with Tremaine's body. Keep your head down and don't try to come back here. Do you understand me?"

I struggle out of her grip. "But you—"

She shoves me again hard and puts her gun right against my head. Ice-cold metal. I hear it click at my temple. "But I hit your stupid friend Tremaine with a grazing shot to his head. I'll direct his car to a hospital. Don't you dare visit him tonight, unless you want Taylor to find out that you somehow knew he'd be there the instant he arrived. Wait until tomorrow morning."

None of this makes sense at all. "What? Taylor?" My whisper turns hoarse. "*You* shot Tremaine. *Zero's* the head of—"

Jax lets out a quiet, surprised laugh and lowers her gun. "You think Taylor works for Zero, don't you?"

A note of hesitation enters my voice. "She tried to warn me. Zero—"

Jax's smile is cold. "Zero doesn't run things. Taylor does. We follow *her* command."

Taylor leads the Blackcoats. I blink. That can't be right—she's far too quiet and uncertain for that. Her soft voice, her delicate shoulders, and thoughtful look . . . Hadn't she deferred to Zero the first time I met them? Hadn't she let him talk?

Let him talk. Like he worked for her.

"But," I try to say, "Taylor doesn't seem like . . ."

My voice trails off at Jax's expression. She is dead serious, and in her eyes, I see an emotion I've never seen before on her face. Real fear. Fear of *Taylor*.

Jax, the girl who can eat a snack and then shoot someone in the head, who doesn't bat an eye at the sight of blood . . . is terrified of Taylor.

Now I'm truly frightened.

Jax tears her gaze away and leans close. "Once you get back to the hotel," she murmurs against my ear, "I'm going to send you an invite to the Dark World. You're going to meet me in there, and then I can tell you more."

"Why should I believe you?" I spit each word out, relying on my anger to keep my tears at bay.

"Because you're still alive," she replies, "and not bleeding out on the floor."

There are so many things I want to say back to her. That I saw her standing on the balcony with Zero; that I don't know why she's sparing me right now, or why she's going behind Taylor's back on Tremaine. But this is no time to press her. All I can do is follow her instructions—even though nothing's stopping her from hunting down my car the instant I get inside it.

Maybe this is her strategy for killing me tonight, too. She'll talk me into getting into the car and then run it right off the road. Call it an accident.

Faint footsteps come from the other side of the main lobby. Jax turns her head sharply in their direction, then looks back at me. "You get one warning from me. If you ever come back here again, I'll put a bullet in you before I can even think it through. Now, shut up and go."

●●●●●

MY NUMB LEGS somehow carry me to the car. I sit in silent shock as it starts up, then takes me back to the hotel. I want to scream at the car to bring me to Tremaine instead. I want to figure out wherever he's been taken to. Tell him I'm sorry and beg him to forgive me.

He's lying in a hospital somewhere, fighting for his life, because of me. If he dies, my hands will be dipped in his blood.

Jax's last words to me ring in my head. Part of me expects my car windows to shatter from gunfire—that she's set me up and is just waiting for me to turn my back.

But everything outside my window looks exactly as I'd left it; the cosplay parade is still in full swing, the streets still neon-colored. Some are cheering the final two top-player announcements as excitement for the closing ceremony builds to a fever pitch.

OLIVER ANDERSON of AUSTRALIA | CLOUD KNIGHTS
KARLA CASTILLO of COSTA RICA | STORMCHASERS

Others whistle as a group of their friends goes by in spot-on Phoenix Riders gear from one of our championship games.

For them, no time has passed at all. They haven't just witnessed someone they know get shot, smelled the blood on the ground. They don't feel like they'd just seen a slice of truth that changes everything about what they're doing. As far as they're concerned, the world is still intact. They're not responsible for putting their friend in fatal danger.

When I arrive, the car door opens for me and I step out, as if everything were fine. The elevator dings like it's supposed to. The bed in my hotel is still there, freshly made, and a plate of fruit—

lychee, starfruit, pears—sits on my writing desk, wrapped in a clean film of plastic wrap. I stand for a moment in the shadows of my curtains, watching the colors and the outfits go by on the street below. Everyone is laughing and waving, blissfully unaware of the dark world around them.

I wash my hands in the sink. A few flecks of blood dot my clothes, and for an instant, I think they're Tremaine's until I see the gash in my sleeve. I must've cut myself in my rush. I strip off my clothes, step into the shower, and let the water scald me until my skin turns pink. Then I wrap myself in a robe and sit down on the bed, the sounds of festivities still ringing from the street.

I notice the earlier messages I'd tried to send to Tremaine, still unread and unanswered.

What tears couldn't come earlier now emerge in a rush. I cry deep, choking sobs that echo in my chest, barely able to catch my breath before I let it out again. My hands clench at the bedsheets. Has it only been hours since I stood beside Hideo and told him about his brother? Has it been only a heartbeat since I watched Tremaine crumple to the floor?

I can still picture his silhouette against the rain, his faraway look, and that careless shrug. Right now, Tremaine's out there in some hospital, lying on a gurney while they probably rush him into the emergency room. He'd gotten too close, and he'd taken the hit that should have been mine. Now I'm alone, lost in this battle between Hideo's algorithm and the Blackcoats' secrets. How will Roshan react when he finds out what has happened? Are the other Phoenix Riders going to be in danger, too, if I keep them involved?

Every locked door has a key. But maybe that's not true at all. What key is there now? I no longer know which way to turn. I don't know which way is right, or even which way is out.

The image of Tremaine on a gurney is abruptly replaced by old memories of hospital corridors, that familiar, awful smell of disinfectant seared permanently into my memories. For a moment, I'm eleven years old again, walking through the door of my father's hospital room with an armful of peonies and a dinner tray. I'd put the flowers in a vase and sat cross-legged on the end of his bed as we ate our hospital food together. Dad's once-thick, bright-blue hair was patchy and gray, falling out daily in chunks. His hospital gown crinkled against his gaunt shoulders in a weird way. He would spear each piece of soggy broccoli individually and pop it into his mouth, cut each piece of meatloaf carefully with his fork. But he avoided the little square of chocolate cake.

Sugar might as well be poison, he'd told me when I asked him why he left it on his plate.

And all I could think about at the time was the space shuttle *Challenger,* which I'd just learned about in school that morning. The government likes the official story to be that the shuttle's explosion killed the entire crew instantly—but the truth is that the cabin was intact after the *Challenger*'s rocket blew. They went sailing three more miles into the sky and then plummeted for two and a half minutes until they hit the Atlantic Ocean at full speed, fully conscious and aware the whole time. And in spite of staring directly into the face of death, they'd still pulled on their oxygen masks, had their seat belts clipped in.

We fight for survival with everything we've got, as if the oxygen mask and the seat belt and avoidance of a square of chocolate cake might be the thing that saves us. That's the difference between the real and the virtual. Reality is where you can lose the ones you love. Reality is the place where you can feel the cracks in your heart.

When the world is murky, guide yourself with your own steady light.

My father's old words are a low, steady undercurrent in my mind. I can see him smile wearily at me over our dinner trays, his fingers first tapping his temple, then his chest over his heart.

Hold steady, Emi. Keep going.

I sit in the darkness until my tears have dried and my breathing has turned even again. It's two o'clock in the morning now. The parade outside has finally quieted, and people start heading home. I sit until I can think straight again. Tremaine had chosen this path. If I back out now, his sacrifices would have been for nothing.

I sit until a new message blinks in my view. It's from an anonymous account, asking me to Link with this person in the Dark World. It's Jax. Jax, who's right in the middle of this murky nightmare, with nothing for me to trust about her except the fact that I should be dead by her hand right now.

Are you ready? she asks.

I look up at the hovering invitation through my blur of tears. *Why are you doing this?*

Who do you think gave Jesse info in the first place?

The anonymous contact who'd shown Jesse the institute badge. That had been Jax.

She's been watching me after all, has known I was working with Tremaine, had noticed Jesse asking around in the Dark World about Sasuke's symbol.

We don't have all night, Emika.

I stare at the prompt, steadying myself. Then I reach up and accept it.

18

Two Days until the Warcross Closing Ceremony

The room around me vanishes into darkness. A moment later, I find myself standing in the middle of a nondescript, black street illuminated by highlights of blue and red neon; a small but steady trickle of encrypted passersby bustle back and forth behind me.

Next to me stands an anonymous girl with a face I don't recognize. I don't need to, though. When she rests her hand unconsciously on her belt and drums rhythmically against it, itching for a gun handle, I know right away that it's Jax.

She doesn't introduce herself. She just turns her face toward the closest corner and nods for me to follow her. I do without saying a word. As we walk, a giant STOP sign—painted yellow instead of red—appears at the intersection of two streets, and when Jax leads us to the other side of the road, another STOP sign appears. They keep popping up until the signs line both sides of the street, and the closer we walk, the more appear. The optical illusion is an eerie one, and the way it shifts makes me dizzy.

"Close your eyes," Jax says when she sees my expression. "After Hideo's algorithm triggered, the keepers of this place put this in as a deterrent to any past visitors who might now be compelled to rat it out. If you keep looking at it, it'll make you violently ill—unless you know the new password. So close your eyes, then follow my instructions."

Again, I do as she says. In the darkness, Jax calls out the number of steps for me to take and when to turn. I fight the constant sensation that I might trip over something and force myself to keep moving.

Finally, we stop.

"You're good now," Jax says. I open my eyes.

"Ever heard of this place?" she asks, nodding at the block before us.

All I can do is shake my head and stare. Towering in front of us is an enormous, impossible building that looks like a giant glass dome reaching higher than the Empire State Building, taking up the entire block. Thin black bridges extend from the dome like toothpicks in a bubble, connecting it with giant, floating glass circles suspended in the air. The entire structure looks like a grand model of the sun and planets. Black metal lattices crisscross the glass, as if needed to hold it all up, and around its base are a series of spotlights shining against it, casting beams of crimson color into the air and onto the ground. Fountains as tall as waterfalls line the perimeter of the dome in a lavish display, a dozen times grander than any physical fountain could possibly be.

"It's the Dark World's Fair," Jax continues, motioning me forward with her toward the huge, arched entrance, where a stream of people are entering and leaving the place. "It's like the World's Fairs in real life—except here, the exhibitions for sale are a bit more illegal."

I crane my neck in awe as we walk underneath the towering dome. The first time I'd ever heard of World's Fairs was in school, and I can still remember staring down at my laptop at an article about them. The Eiffel Tower was originally built for the Paris World's Fair in 1889. So was the original Ferris wheel, invented for the Chicago World's Fair back in 1893. Dad was a fan of researching these grand exhibitions because he found them incredibly romantic, each one a creator's dreamscape. I remember sitting up at night, listening to him describe one famous World's Fair after another.

I wonder what he'd say if he could've seen this place.

Now we step through the entrance with other avatars and emerge inside a space that takes my breath away. Underneath the soaring glass ceiling is a vast area full of displays, each one roped off and surrounded by clusters of admirers and potential buyers. Strings of lights hang in elegant arcs from the glass ceiling, adding to how surreal the place looks. Tiny mechanical birds flit by, as if in an aviary. When I look closely, I notice them carrying blank notes strapped to their wiry legs.

"Those birds are encrypted packets. For secure messaging between the visitors here." Jax nods at a couple of the exhibitions we pass. "These are funded by secret patrons, developed illegally at the Innovation Institute," she says in a quiet voice. "By Taylor."

One of these exhibits is a cloud of data, a million tiny specks that swarm and separate from each other, then swarm close again. Another is a display of weapons with glowing blue ovals running along their edges, sensors for your specific fingerprints. A third is a demonstration of invisibility done through the NeuroLink; instead of downloading a randomly generated face over your own as a disguise, it maps your surroundings and combines them into a lattice that covers your body, making you vanish from view.

I look at her. "And Taylor . . . is selling these technologies?"

She nods. "Quite a few of them. For the right price."

I shake my head and stop right underneath a grand, rotating display of armored suits. "How is Taylor developing all these illegal devices from a proper science institute? And how are the Blackcoats connected?"

"What do you know about Taylor?"

"Not much. Just what she's told me. She said her father was killed because of his illicit activities."

Jax's lips tighten. "Dana Taylor grew up during a rough time, around when the Soviet Union collapsed. Her father laundered money for a living. As a child, Taylor saw more than her share of death. She ended up studying neuroscience because she was always interested in how the mind works—the way it manufactures every aspect of our world. The mind can make you believe whatever it wants you to believe. It can bring dictators to power. It can crumble nations. *You can do anything, if you put your mind to it.* You know the saying. Well, she truly takes that to heart. If the mind weren't dependent upon the rest of the body, it could operate forever."

I nod absently at Jax's words. They echo what Taylor had said to me.

"When she got a job at the Innovation Institute as a junior researcher and moved to Japan, that became her obsession—learning how to disconnect the mind from the body. Separating its strength from its ultimate weakness."

Her obsession. I think of what Taylor had told me. "Is it because of her father's murder?"

Jax pauses for a moment. "Everyone's afraid of death, but Taylor is absolutely *terrified* of it. The finality. Of seeing your father dead, gone forever without an explanation. The idea of her mind just . . . shutting off one day, without warning."

An uneasy feeling lurches in my stomach. In spite of myself, I can understand that fear. I can taste it in my mouth.

"And what about the Blackcoats?" I say.

"Taylor worked her way up the ladder at the institute rapidly until she became its executive director. But there were some studies she wanted to do that the institute simply wouldn't approve. As you know, she grew up around illegal dealings—the idea of her not being able to do what she wanted was unacceptable. Hence: the Blackcoats. She created the group as the shell for all the experiments she wanted to conduct that she didn't have permission for."

"I don't understand."

"Let's say, for example, that Taylor wanted to do something that she knew she couldn't get approved by the institute. She would go ahead and conduct that experiment anyway, under the guise of something else. Some innocuous study. And she would make sure every shred of paperwork and evidence of that experiment would get funneled toward the Blackcoats instead. If she sells the results of that experiment to someone—a foreign government, some other foundation—it would be traced only to the Blackcoats."

I narrow my eyes as I start to understand. "So the Blackcoats . . ."

"They're essentially a false business name," Jax finishes. "An empty shell, underneath which all of Taylor's secret projects are kept."

"None of the data would ever lead back to her," I say in realization.

"Right. Let's say that news got out about some illegal weapon Taylor was developing at the institute. Investigators would find the trails leading not to Taylor's name, but to some mystery group called the Blackcoats. Taylor could claim she was an innocent bystander, her identity stolen and used by the Blackcoats. The clients who bought the tech from her can also point their fingers at the Blackcoats. So, the news reports would all say something like, 'Who are the Blackcoats? *Mystery criminal ring in the business of illegal tech development.*' The Blackcoats get the blame and the reputation as some shadowy crew."

"What was all that about the Blackcoats being a group of vigilantes who fight for causes they believe in?" I say.

"Lies," Jax says with a shrug. "We're not vigilantes, Emika. We're mercenaries. We do what we get paid for."

"But how does Hideo's algorithm fit into all this? Why does Taylor care about destroying it? Is someone paying her for that?"

At that, Jax gives me a dark look. "Taylor doesn't want to destroy the algorithm. She wants to control it."

To control it.

The obvious truth of it hits me so hard that I can barely breathe.

Of course she would. Why would someone like Taylor, obsessed with the power of the mind, want to cripple the Neuro-Link by ripping out such an intricate system like the algorithm? Why hadn't I guessed that she might have other plans for it?

During our first encounter, Taylor had sat across from me and looked so sincere, *so* genuine, about what she wanted to do. She knew how to turn my own history against me, baiting me with what I had done for Annie that had gotten me the red on my record. She manipulated me into agreeing with her that what the Blackcoats were doing was noble.

The conversation tears through my mind. How timid and quiet she had seemed. How perfectly she had played that moment.

Jax watches me as these thoughts sink in. "I know," she says, breaking the silence. I nod numbly back.

Jax looks away from me and up at the bridges lining the main dome's ceiling. "The Blackcoats use the Dark World's Fair as storage for their archives. Every experiment they've conducted, every mission they've run, everything they do is locked away here in a blockchain, one secured packet after another."

A *blockchain*. An encrypted ledger of records, nearly impossible to trace or change.

Jax stops at the very edge of the dome's glass, in an empty corner. "This is what I wanted you to see—the story behind Sasuke. It's what you've been after, isn't it?"

My heart squeezes when I hear her words, and again I see the Memory I'd glimpsed in Zero's mind, the image of Sasuke's small figure crouched in a room, the strange symbol on his sleeve.

I bring up the image now for Jax. Her eyes immediately jump to Sasuke, and her face softens for a moment. *What is* your *story?* I find myself thinking. *How did you cross paths with Sasuke?*

She finally touches my arm and motions me forward. As she does, she slides her other hand once against the glass. A panel shifts with her movement, like an invisible door in the dome, with stairs curling downward into darkness.

"Only Taylor and I have access to these archives." Jax suddenly hesitates, and in her silence I understand that if word got out that Jax had shown this place to me, Taylor would kill her, too.

"Just you and Taylor?" I ask. "Not Zero?"

"You'll see why in a second." She gestures for me to follow her in. "Careful you leave no traces behind."

I watch as Jax steps in through the door, then glances around to see whether anyone else might be watching. But no one seems able to see us or the entrance that Jax opened up. It's as if we'd existed in an entirely different virtual dimension from the others here. I look back to see Jax's figure disappear into the shadows of the stairs. I take a deep breath and follow her in.

The stairs vanish rapidly into pitch-black, and even though I know I'm in a virtual world, I still instinctively put my hand out, searching for the wall beside me. Moving in the darkness here, where nothing's real, makes me feel like I'm not moving at all. The only hint I get that we're making progress are the sounds of Jax's footsteps, still moving steadily downward ahead of me.

Gradually, the ground before us lightens, and when we reach the bottom of the stairs, everything is illuminated in a soft, dim blue glow. We step out into a vast chamber that takes my breath away.

"Welcome to the library," Jax tells me over her shoulder.

It looks like all the books in the universe, shelved in an endless, circular room framed by ladders that stretch in both directions. I imagine every book is a file that the Blackcoats have stored—archives upon archives of research, data on specific people, records of missions. This is their central directory. We stand on a platform, looking up and down into the endless space, and I have to close my eyes to fight off the vertigo.

Jax motions me onto one of the ladders. We click right into place against it, so that it's impossible to fall, but I still feel a wave of dizziness. "We store every iteration of a Memory, and duplicates of every file." She opens a search directory, and in front of us, types in "Sasuke Tanaka."

The world around us blurs, and an instant later, we're on the ladder against a new section of the library, where certain books are now glowing with a blue halo. Jax pulls them out with a wave of her hand. They form a ring around us, and when I stare at any one of them long enough, it starts to play the first few frames of the recording.

There are records from the Blackcoats' security cams, from Sasuke's Memories, from white-coated technicians, and from what look like actual tests and trials. There are police reports, files about his disappearance, and data on his parents. There are also files about young Hideo.

I remember the first time I sat in Hideo's office, studying Zero's hacks, wondering who my bounty was. I remember the way Hideo tilted his head up to the sky at the *onsen*, the endless versions of his constructed Memory of how Sasuke had disappeared.

These files will show me what really happened to Sasuke all those years ago.

Jax looks at me, then gestures at the files. "We can't stay in here forever," she reminds me. "If you want to know something, find it now."

I hesitate for only a second. Then I scroll through, sorting the files by date so that I can look at the oldest ones first. I find one dated ten years ago, the year Sasuke disappeared, and tap it.

It's a recording from a security cam. And it starts to play.

19

We're standing in a room with two dozen young children, probably no older than ten, each one wearing a yellow band around their wrist. They're sitting at white desks arranged in neat rows, as if in some sort of classroom. The bare walls are decorated with cheerful drawings of rainbows and trees. Posters that say READ and LEARN SOMETHING NEW TODAY! and DIFFERENT IS SPECIAL.

In fact, the only part that doesn't look like a classroom are the technicians in white coats at the front, watching the children.

A long window runs along the room's back wall. A bunch of adults are clustered there, looking on with craned necks, their faces curious and worried. Some are wringing their hands or talking to each other in low voices. Their expressions tell me, without a doubt, that they're parents.

I look at the timestamp of the recording. This was before Sasuke was kidnapped.

My gaze returns to the kids. I study each of their faces—until

I find one that I recognize. I spot Sasuke, sitting near the center of the room.

Jax stands next to me, looking on at the scene, too. She smiles a little at the sight of young Sasuke, then nods toward a girl at the front of the room, her brown hair in two low pigtails.

"Is that you?" I ask.

"I was seven," Jax replies. "Just like everyone else in the room. It was a requirement of this particular study conducted by the institute—specifically, by Taylor. This is where I first met Sasuke."

I glance toward the parents at the window. "Are your parents over there?"

She shakes her head. "No. Taylor adopted me."

Now I look at her in surprise. "Taylor's your mother?"

"I wouldn't call how she raised me motherly," Jax mutters. "But yes. She found me in the hospital wing of an orphanage. Later on, I learned she adopted me to put me in this study. "

Jax points out two of the adults at the far-left side of the window. It takes me a moment to recognize them as Hideo and Sasuke's parents—the same elderly couple I'd once met.

"They look completely different," I murmur.

Decades younger, as if it hadn't only been ten years since their son went missing. The mother, Mina Tanaka, is sharply dressed in a suit and a white lab coat with the institute's logo on its pocket, her face young and her hair glossy black. The father seems nothing like the frail, sickly man I'd seen at Hideo's home, but like a slightly older version of Hideo now, with his handsome features and tall stature. I glance back at Jax. "What kind of study is this? Why are you and Sasuke in it?"

"Every child you see in here is dying," Jax replies. "Of a disease, of an autoimmune disorder, of something terminal that medicine has deemed incurable."

Dying? Hideo had never mentioned that. My gaze returns to Sasuke, his large liquid eyes dark against a small, pale face. I'd assumed it was the lighting. "Did . . . did you know? Did Sasuke's parents know?" I stammer. "What about Hideo?"

"I have no idea if his parents ever told Hideo," Jax says. "If he's never mentioned it to you, it probably means his parents kept that from him. I certainly was too young to grasp how sick I was. I didn't know that the reason no one wanted me was because, well, who would want to adopt a dying child? Sasuke himself didn't even know. All he thought at the time was that he got sick much more easily than other kids." She shrugs. "You don't really question things when you're that small. You believe everything is normal."

I think of Hideo calling out for Sasuke to slow down at the park, the way he'd scolded his little brother as he wrapped the blue scarf snugly around Sasuke's neck.

"And this study focused only on terminally ill children?"

"The study was a trial for an experimental drug that was supposed to be revolutionary," Jax says. "Something that could cure various childhood diseases by taking advantage of the child's young cells to turn their own bodies into collections of supercells. So, you can imagine that parents who were running out of options would jump to sign their children up for this radical study. What was there to lose?"

I look back at the room, lingering on each of the parents' faces pressed against the glass. They seem hopeful, watching every move their children make. Mina Tanaka clutches her husband's hand tightly to her chest. Her eyes never leave Sasuke.

A deep nausea settles into my stomach. The scene reminds me of the false hope every new drug gave me and my father. *This is the one. This might save you.* "There's always more to lose," I whisper.

We look on as a researcher adjusts the wristband on one

child. "Of course, the study was a cover," Jax continues. "While the study's small team was working earnestly on a real drug, Taylor was also conducting her own research. The *real* study."

"So what was her actual experiment?"

"The third requirement of this study was each child's mind. A minimum IQ of at least one sixty was necessary for the trial. They had to show remarkable self-discipline. They needed to demonstrate unusually high drive and motivation. Their brains had to light up in a very specific way during a series of exams Taylor gave them." She looks at me. "You know how smart Hideo Tanaka is. Sasuke was even more so. He tested effortlessly into every single academy he qualified for. The way Taylor found me at the orphanage in the first place was because she'd heard about my high IQ score. She found out about Sasuke's through Mina herself, since the two of them worked in the institute. We both passed her exams."

I swallow hard. Hideo had told me this about Sasuke, that his little brother had sat for many tests measuring his intelligence. "What was Taylor looking for?" I ask.

"A candidate whose mind was strong enough to withstand an experiment to separate the mind from the body."

Suddenly, I make a connection so horrible that it makes me dizzy . "So that's why Taylor had wanted each child to have a terminal illness," I breathe.

Jax's eyes are stone-cold, bleak with truth. "If they died during the study, it could easily be blamed on their original illness. Covered up. Their parents had already signed consent forms. This way they wouldn't get suspicious and start asking questions."

As we look on, the recording finishes, then automatically goes to the next. We watch at least a dozen of them. Some of the kids in the study change as the recordings continue; the number of parents standing at the window start to dwindle, too. I don't want to ask Jax where they went, whether those were the children who couldn't make it all the way through.

We shift to a recording with a room empty of kids, with the sun setting through the windows. Taylor is speaking Japanese with another researcher, in a voice low enough that translations start appearing in English at the bottom of my view. I blink—the researcher is Mina.

"This is the third time your son has tested top of his group," Taylor says. She's giving Mina the same sympathetic, encouraging look she's always given me. "In fact, Sasuke tested at a margin so high, we had to rework our categories."

Mina frowns and lowers her head in an apologetic bow. "I don't like how it's making him act at home. He has so many nightmares and can't seem to concentrate on anything. His doctor tells me his blood counts haven't improved enough. And he's lost more weight."

"Don't do this, Tanaka-*san*," Taylor says gently. "We might be so close to a breakthrough."

Mina hesitates as she looks into her colleague's eyes. I don't know what she sees there, but she manages a smile. "I'm so sorry, Director," she finally says, and in her words is a deep exhaustion. "I would still like to withdraw Sasuke from the trial."

Then Taylor gives her a sorrowful, pitying look—the same one that had made me want to trust her. "This might be your only chance to save your son."

The guilt in Mina's eyes twists like a knife in my chest. She shakes her head again. "We want him resting at home. Where he can be happy, at least for a little while."

Taylor says nothing to that. Instead, the two women just bow to each other. Taylor stares at the door long after Mina leaves through it.

The next recording skips ahead, but this one starts with Taylor seated in what looks like her office, across from another researcher. "You told me you had this well-organized," Taylor says to him in a soft voice.

The man bows his head in apology. "Mrs. Tanaka has already filed paperwork with the institute. She doesn't want to keep her son in the program. You know she has a good relationship with the CEO. We have to let them go."

"Does Mina suspect what we're doing?"

The researcher shakes his head. "No," he replies.

Taylor sighs, as if all of this genuinely pains her. She flips through a stack of papers on her desk. "Very well. Do we have any other participants in the program who might work?"

"Your girl. Jackson Taylor." The researcher slides another stack of papers toward her. Taylor studies them in silence.

"Her numbers are good," she replies, pushing up her glasses. "But her exam reactions are far less ideal. She's too unpredictable to be a reliable candidate."

Taylor's indifferent tone takes me aback. I glance at Jax to see what she might be thinking, but she only drums her fingers idly against her belt.

Taylor closes her eyes, her brow furrowed in frustration. "Show me Sasuke's files again."

The researcher does as she says, handing over a stack of papers and pointing out several lines on the top page. The two sit quietly for a moment, flipping the pages, occasionally nodding.

"Far more consistent." Taylor's voice is clipped and efficient in a way that sends a chill down my spine. She closes the folder and begins to rub her temples anxiously. "It's too significant a difference. He would have been perfect. And now he'll just die at home, withering away to nothing in a couple of years. What a shame. What a *waste*."

"You won't be able to continue on with him," the researcher says. Then his voice lowers. "At least, not with his parents as willing participants."

Taylor pauses to look sharply up at him. "What are you suggesting?"

"I'm just stating the facts." But I can hear an unspoken suggestion in his words.

She puts her hands down and studies his face. She doesn't speak for a long moment. "We're not in the business of kidnapping children," she says.

"You want to save his life. How is that any worse than what will already happen to him? It's like you said. He'll be dead soon."

Taylor sits with her fingers laced together, lost in thought. I wonder if she's thinking about the murder of her father, if she's dwelling on her loss, her fear of death. Whatever's going through her mind, it leaves a calm resolve on her face. Something *righteous*.

"Those poor children," she finally whispers, almost to herself. "What a shame."

I can see it in her eyes. She thinks what she's doing is noble.

The realization makes me shrink back in horror. It reminds me of the determination on Hideo's face when he first told me about the algorithm.

The image lingers in my mind as I consider both of them, willing to do terrible things to save the world.

"If this experiment succeeds," the researcher goes on, "you are going to have on your hands one of the most lucrative technologies in the world. The amount someone would pay for it would be astronomical. And think of all the lives you'd save." He leans closer. "We are never going to find another patient better matched for this trial. I can promise you that."

Taylor rests her chin against one hand as she stares out into space. The light in the room has shifted before she speaks again. "Make it quick. Make it discreet."

"Of course. I'll start putting together a plan."

"Good." Taylor takes a deep breath and straightens in her chair. "Then I recommend we move forward with Sasuke Tanaka for our Project Zero."

20

Project Zero.

My heart seizes. I'd thought—*Hideo* had thought—that this nickname was just a hacker name, his marker. And it was. But what it really referred to was what Taylor called him. Project Zero. *Study* Zero. Their first experiment.

Taylor lets out a deep sigh before closing the folder in her hand and sliding the papers back toward the researcher. "Sasuke's time is limited. We can't afford to wait around."

Before I can fully process what I'd just witnessed, the scene shifts to a small boy crouched in one corner of a room. Immediately, I recognize this as the same room I'd seen Sasuke in during our Duel.

So Taylor had taken him. She was the one responsible for that day in the park, when a young Hideo called for his brother and never heard him answer. She unknowingly triggered the start of the NeuroLink itself, the result of Hideo's overwhelming grief. The reason Tremaine's lying unconscious in a hospital bed.

She's the reason why I'm even here, ensnared in this madness.

The scene now seems like dawn, with the barest hint of light from the windows, but Sasuke's bed looks untouched, like he's been sitting in the same spot all night. Instead, he stays in the corner with his knees tucked up to his chin, still wearing that white, long-sleeve sweater with the symbol embroidered on one sleeve. His fingers worry endlessly at the blue scarf around his neck.

The same scarf that Hideo had wrapped around him on their last day together.

The door finally opens, casting a slanted rectangle of golden light onto the crouched boy. Instead of scrambling to his feet, he just shrinks farther against the wall and tightens his grip on the scarf. In the entryway stands a tall woman I recognize as Taylor.

"How do you feel today, Sasuke?" she says in a gentle voice.

"Dr. Taylor, you said if I stayed quiet, you would let me go home today."

Sasuke replies in English, and his young voice sounds so innocent it pierces my chest. This was when he was still fully himself.

Taylor sighs softly and leans against the door. Her kind face seems so sincere that, if I didn't know better, I'd genuinely believe that she loved him as a mother would. "And I meant that, sweetie, with my whole heart. You've been so good. We just have a little bit more to learn about you, and then we'll take you home. Can you do that for me?"

Sasuke tilts his head at the woman. "Then I want to call my mom first," he says, "to tell her that I'll be coming home today."

He's only seven, but he's already trying to negotiate. In this moment, I'm fiercely proud of him for not falling for Taylor's trusting voice as easily as I had.

Taylor must have had the same thought as me, because Sasuke's words bring a smile to her face. "You're such a smart boy," she says, a note of admiration in her tone. She walks over to him and crouches down to lean on her knees. "But today, we just need to do a quick scan of your brain. If you talk to your mother on the phone, it might upset you, and your mind won't be as calm as we need it to be. But I promise, it's so easy—you'll blink and it'll be done. Then you'll be on your way. Doesn't that sound nice, Sasuke-*kun*?"

Sasuke ignores her attempt at an affectionate honorific. "No."

Taylor smiles again at his reply, but this time she just looks on as a researcher steps in. Sasuke starts shaking his head as the man reaches him and tugs on his arm. "I'm not going," he says, his voice turning more urgent.

"Now, Sasuke-*kun*," Taylor says. "If you don't, you'll force me to take away your scarf." She reaches out and taps the scarf's fabric once, teasingly. "And I know that would make you very sad."

At that, Sasuke freezes. He turns his large eyes up at her.

"I'm only trying to help you, you know," she says softly to him, reaching out to pat his cheek. "That's what your mom and dad were hoping for, when they signed you up. They wanted this for you, do you know that? That's why you're here."

His small fingers close so tightly around the tail of his scarf that, even in the recording, I can see his knuckles turning white. Sasuke casts a reluctant glance back at the room before he follows Taylor and the researcher out. The door shuts again, returning the space to darkness.

My hand comes up to cover my mouth. While Hideo's parents searched frantically for him, while Hideo lost his own childhood fixated on his brother's disappearance, Sasuke was being held here against his own will.

The next scene opens back in the testing room. This time, Sasuke is sitting alone at one of the desks with his head resting on his arms. He's staring blankly off into space. When he shifts, I notice a telltale pinprick in the bend of his left arm. A thin stripe of hair has been shaved off the side of his head, and there, near his temple, I see another pinprick.

The door opens. A girl steps in, whom I now recognize as young Jax. She sees him, hesitates, and then twirls one of her pigtails around her finger. She takes a seat next to him.

"Hey," she says.

He doesn't say a word. He doesn't even seem to notice her in the same room.

When he stays silent, Jax bites her lip and nudges his arm. Sasuke lifts his head to glare at her. "What do you want?" he mutters.

Jax blinks at him. "I'm Jackson Taylor."

"Oh. You're the daughter." Sasuke looks away again and puts his head down. "I remember you from the study."

Jax scowls and puts her hands on her waist. "Mom said you might like some company your own age, for a change."

"Tell your mom I'm not interested in whatever she's thinking up." He pauses to give her a skeptical look. "You don't look all that sick."

She smiles at him. "The drug study they were doing on us? It's been working really well on me. Mom says it's a miracle."

Sasuke stares at her for a second longer before turning away again. "Good for you."

"Hey, it's slowed down your disease, too. Maybe you're turning into a bunch of supercells. That's what my mom said. She said the study helped ten percent of us." She hesitates. Her eyes wander to the shaved stripe along the side of his head. "What are they injecting you for?"

Sasuke rests his head against his arms and closes his eyes. "Why don't you ask your mom?" he mutters.

Jax doesn't say anything. Her cheeks flush in apology.

When she still doesn't reply, Sasuke looks up and sees her expression. He sighs. After a moment, he seems to take pity on her. "Trackers," he explains. "They need it in my bloodstream. That was the injection. They said it's preparation, for my procedures."

"Oh." She studies his face. "You don't look so good."

He goes back to closing his eyes. "Go away. My stomach hurts, and I feel sick."

Jax stares at him as he breathes evenly in and out. After a while, she straightens to leave. "I was going to ask if you wanted to check out this hidden nook I found, up near the institute's ceiling. And my mom *doesn't* know about that." She starts to walk away. "There's a metal grate that's open to the fresh air. It might make you feel better."

As she goes, Sasuke lifts his head to look at her retreating figure. "Hang on," he says. When she turns back around, he clears his throat, suddenly shy. "Where is it?"

Jax smiles and tilts her head. "I'll show you."

"I'm not supposed to leave the room."

Jax winks at him. "No one tied you down, did they? Now, come on." She steps out the door, and a second later, he scoots his chair back and follows her.

There are several scenes like this one, each showing the two of them hanging out in the empty study room, or in the hallways, or in the back shelves of the institute's library. One scene is from Jax's point of view—she's kneeling on the tiles of a bathroom floor, gently patting Sasuke's back as he throws up over and over again into a toilet. Another is of Sasuke making funny faces at her until she bursts out giggling.

Yet another is of them crammed into a tiny wedge of space together, over which a metal grate exposes a square of the night sky. Jax seems lost in thought, absently pointing out one constellation after another. She stops talking long enough to glance over at Sasuke, only to see him staring at her instead of the stars. He turns his head hurriedly away, but not before she catches the blush on his cheeks. She grins. Then she gets serious.

"Hey—do you know what a kiss is?" she asks him.

He shakes his head. "You mean, like a kiss from my mom?"

"No, silly, gross." Jax laughs before steeling herself. "I mean the kind you give to someone you like," she murmurs. "In *that* way." Then she leans over and presses her lips quickly and quietly to his cheek before jerking away.

Sasuke stares wide-eyed at her, his face pink in the night. "Oh," he says hoarsely.

"I saw it on TV," Jax replies. She laughs nervously, a little too loud, and it makes Sasuke laugh in return. He kisses her cheek back. It makes her giggle even harder. Soon the two have dissolved into quiet laughter.

I look away to the Jax standing beside me. She nods toward her younger self. "These are my Memories," she says to me as we continue to look on. "Taylor had them recorded and archived after the NeuroLink came out."

In a third one, both of them look a little older. They're sitting in front of a TV—an older model that probably dates back at least seven or eight years—and on the screen, a thirteen-year-old Hideo is walking out onto a press stage to be greeted by an avalanche of flashing lights. He looks so unsure of himself at that age, lanky and shy-eyed, his clothes baggy and ill-fitting, his demeanor little more than a passing resemblance to the man he would become. He greets the reporters with a nervous wave.

Sasuke grips Jax's arm. For an instant, the smile on his face is a genuine one. "That's my brother, Jax!" he exclaims, pointing at the screen. "There! He's on TV! You see him? Look at him! He's so much taller!" His eyes are wide-open, shiny with new tears, fixated on the TV as if terrified the broadcast will stop. "Don't I look like him? Do you think he's looking for me? Do you think he's thinking about me?"

He still cared for his brother then. I tear my gaze away. It's too hard to watch.

Beside me, Jax watches with a grim calmness. "It was part of Taylor's study, you know, letting him watch the TV," she says.

"Why?" I ask.

Jax only nods as the scene ends and another starts to play. "You'll see."

Sasuke is crouching back in the same dark bedroom in the next scene. He's thinner this time, alarmingly so, his arms whittled down to sharp limbs and his eyes hauntingly large in his small face. How many years has it been? His illness must be eating away at him.

This time, when the door opens, he sits up straight and stares sidelong at Taylor.

"How do you feel today, Sasuke?" Taylor asks him.

Sasuke is quiet, his child eyes regarding her with a look of suspicion beyond his years. His hands are still clutching the blue scarf. Then, he says, "I'll make a deal with you."

These stern words coming from such a small boy makes Taylor laugh.

"Let me skip today, and I'll eat my dinner."

Now the woman laughs in earnest. When she finally stops, she shakes her head at Sasuke. "I'm afraid not. You can't skip a day. You know that."

Sasuke gives her a thoughtful look. "Let me skip, and I'll give you my scarf."

At that, Taylor regards him with a curious smile. "You love that scarf," she says in a coaxing voice. "We can't even pry it from you in your sleep. Surely you can't be serious, giving it up just for a day off."

"I'm serious," Sasuke says.

I lean forward, unable to tear my attention away from the exchange.

Taylor walks over to Sasuke, stares down at him for a moment, and then holds out a hand. "The scarf," she says.

"My free day," Sasuke replies, his hands still tight around the cloth.

"You have my word. You won't be at the labs today. We won't bother you. Take your time and rest here. Tomorrow, we'll start again."

Sasuke stares at her. Finally, his fingers loosen on the scarf. When she takes it, I can see Sasuke's hands visibly tremble, as if it took all of his strength not to lunge for the scarf right then and there. But he hands it over, without making so much as a sound.

Taylor looks at the scarf, then tightens her hands around it and turns to leave the room. "We'll see you the day after tomorrow, Sasuke-*kun*," she says over her shoulder. "I'm proud of you."

Sasuke doesn't reply, and he doesn't cry. He doesn't crouch like he did in the first video I saw of him, either. He just stares calmly, carefully, as Taylor leaves the room, closing the door softly behind her. When it clicks shut, Sasuke's shoulders droop. His hands clutch instinctively for the scarf that is no longer around his neck. When I look closer, I realize that he's wiping tears away. Then he jumps to his feet, walks up to the security cam, and breaks it.

I startle. The tape buzzes with static. When it plays again, I see Sasuke struggling wildly in bonds, in a coldly lit room. Nearby is Taylor, watching him with a calm, cool expression. "And who helped you try to escape, Sasuke-*kun*?" Taylor asks.

Sasuke doesn't look at her. His eyes are fixed instead on the door leading out of the room, like he might be able to will himself out of the lab. When Taylor walks over to him, standing purposely between him and the door, his eyes finally shift up to the woman.

"Who helped you try to escape, Sasuke?" she repeats.

Sasuke stays quiet.

When he still doesn't answer, Taylor shakes her head and motions for one of her researchers to bring a young girl forward. My eyes widen. She has shorter hair here, but she is unmistakably Jax. She follows the researcher obediently to stand beside her mother, and the sight of Jax in such a frightened state is so odd that I can hardly believe it's her.

"Did Jackson help you?" Taylor asks, still in that cool, calm tone.

Sasuke shakes his head again, although now his eyes are on Jax. I walk invisibly around in the recording, noticing how Sasuke's leather bonds are stretched tight now, his arms so tense that I can see a vein standing out against his skin. He still doesn't answer.

Taylor nods once at the others. As I look on, they loosen Sasuke's bonds, so that his wrists and ankles are suddenly free.

Sasuke doesn't even hesitate. He bolts upright and leaps off the table, his eyes narrowed at the door. But the others are already moving, too. Taylor reaches for young Jax's wrist, drags her forward, and pulls her toward the same bench that Sasuke had been strapped to only moments earlier.

"Come here, my love," Taylor says to her.

This movement is the only thing that makes Sasuke freeze near the door. Jax whimpers, too afraid to run as her mother ushers her up onto the bench.

"You want to leave so badly, don't you, Sasuke?" Taylor says soothingly to him as a researcher begins to wipe Jax's temples with a damp cloth.

Sasuke watches with a frozen expression. It takes me a moment to recognize that expression as fear. Temptation. Guilt.

"Then go. Die out there instead of letting us save you," Taylor says, turning her back on Sasuke and focusing her attention now on Jax. "You aren't the only patient we have in our ranks, and your progress has been slower than I would have expected. If you're unwilling to cooperate, then I'll simply have to replace you with someone else. Jax has always been the alternative for our study."

The girl stares at Sasuke with a desperate expression, but doesn't plead. Instead, she shakes her head. *Go*, she seems to be insisting.

Taylor turns around to meet Sasuke's paralyzed gaze. "Well? The doors are unlocked. What are you waiting for?"

And for a moment, it really does look like Sasuke will make a run for it. There are no guards stopping him, no one looking his way. Taylor is too far away to catch him. No one will come for him, not if he runs now.

But he stands there and doesn't move. His hands clench and unclench, his eyes darting from the woman to Jax, his expression tight.

Taylor sighs. "You're making me impatient," she says, turning back toward Jax.

Sasuke takes a step toward them. The movement is enough to make Taylor pause. Sasuke meets Jax's eyes, then takes another step forward. When he speaks, he tries to keep his voice steady, but I can hear the trembling in it. "She's not a part of the program."

Taylor doesn't move to release her. "You have so much potential, Sasuke," she says. "But I need you to choose, and choose decisively. If you want to leave, then leave. We won't come after you. But you know you are the only one this entire experiment hinges on, and what you do could change everything. The results of your study could save millions of lives. It could save *your* life. We've all worked so hard for you. And here you are, ready to throw it all away." She gives Sasuke a disappointed look.

Even though Sasuke still seems afraid to step forward, I can also see hints of guilt on his face, Taylor's manipulation wrapping around him like a vise. As if he'd suddenly *owed* this operation something, like he'd felt obligated to her—but most of all, like whatever happens to Jax will be his fault if he leaves. He meets her gaze now, and I can see traces of that unspoken bond between them, the accumulation of their days spent together and their nights huddled away in a nook.

I find myself wishing silently for Sasuke to turn and run away, to leave it all behind. Of course, he doesn't. Instead, I see his shoulders droop again, his head lower ever so slightly, and him take the first steps away from the door and back toward the lab table.

"Let her go now," he says to Taylor about Jax. On the table, Jax shoots a bewildered look at him, some panicked expression telling him not to do it.

Taylor smiles. "And you're not going to run."

"I'm not going to run."

"And you're going to commit to this."

Sasuke hesitates, briefly meeting the woman's eyes. "I will," he replies.

The recording ends. I realize that my heart is beating so fast now that I've had to sit down on the floor of my room.

The next scene is dated only a month later, but Sasuke is a little taller, his limbs longer and his body ganglier. The most noticeable change on him is a single, thin strip of black metal now running along the side of his head, where part of his hair has been newly buzzed again. He's back in the same laboratory, and answering a series of questions from the same technician who had been working with Taylor before.

"State your name."

"Sasuke Tanaka."

"Your age."

"Twelve."

I do the quick calculation. By this point, Hideo was fourteen, I was eleven, and Warcross had already become an international phenomenon, the NeuroLink welcomed into millions of households.

"Your city of birth."

"London."

"What is the name of your brother?"

"Hideo Tanaka."

"Your mother?"

"Mina Tanaka."

The questions go on for a while, a long list of simple facts and details about his life. I watch Sasuke's face as he mentions the names of his loved ones—and for the first time, I notice that he doesn't seem to react to the names. No flinch. No wince. There is recognition that sparks in his eyes, but it is as if he were saying the names of acquaintances instead of his family members.

"Show him the TV," Taylor says.

The technician pauses to switch on the screen. As we look on, the TV plays an interview with Hideo, now gradually growing into his newfound fame. I glance back at Sasuke. Not long ago, he had grabbed Jax's arm and cried at the sight of his brother. Now he watches the interview with some notable interest, although he doesn't seem truly affected by it. It's as if he were fascinated by a celebrity instead of missing his brother.

The questions start again.

"Who is this?"

"Hideo Tanaka."

"And is he your older brother?"

"Yes."

"Do you miss him?"

A hesitation, then a shrug.

As he answers each question, the technician observes a series of data appearing on a screen beside him and taps down notes on a pad he's holding. As he goes, he reads out some of his reactions. "Zero's signs of recognition still holding steady at eighty-four percent. Overall response times have improved by thirty-three percent." The man drones on as Sasuke answers each question.

Whatever it is that they've been doing to him, they've taken away *something*—something real and human, an intonation in his voice and a light in his eyes—something that defines him as Sasuke. There's no sign of struggle now, and Sasuke seems perfectly willing—if not eager—to do as he's told.

"Zero's cognitive skills are all wholly intact," the technician finally concludes, as the final question happens. Someone injects Sasuke in the arm with a needle, and as I look on, his eyes roll back, his body going limp against the platform.

"Good," Taylor says with her arms crossed. "And what about his reactions to mentions of his family? He's still responding to them with a degree of emotion. That should be tracking down faster than this."

"He's holding on harder than I expected. Don't worry. He'll be yours before long and believe he has always worked for you. We should be all caught up in the next few weeks. He'll be fully downloaded well before he expires."

Before he dies.

As the tech talks, I pick up on something else in the recording. Now that the system has been switched to the NeuroLink, I'm able to wander around the recording, and I notice something on one of the screens in the room that catches my eye. At the top of it is the same symbol I'd seen on Sasuke's sleeve, and below it is written the following in large letters: PROJECT ZERO.

I head over to it, suddenly afraid of what I might see. Beside me, Jax does the same, talking softly as we go.

"Project Zero is an artificial intelligence program," she tells me. "Over the past few years, artificial intelligence has improved everything from search engines to face recognition, to the ability for a computer to defeat a human at complicated mind games like Go. But Project Zero is building on that, to install the advances of AI into the human mind and the human mind into AI, to blend the two so that we can have all the benefits of a computer's mind—logic, speed, accuracy—and the computer mind can have the benefits of a human's—gut reactions, imagination, instinct, spontaneity."

Taylor is literally separating his mind from his body. Downloading his mind into data. She is transferring his mind into a machine. A machine that she can control.

I sit back, my world spinning, my mind flooding with questions. Why not just stick to the artificial, to installing human instinct into machines? Why destroy a human like this?

"What's the end goal of this technology?" I whisper to Jax.

"Immortality," Jax replies as we go on to a final recording. "You know how Taylor fears death. She wants the mind to live on beyond the body. With this technology, she can."

In this one, Sasuke no longer looks like Sasuke, but like the Zero I recognize, standing in the middle of the lab room with his cold, unfeeling gaze.

"But what did they do to him?" I finally ask as I stare at Zero, still puzzled. "He's gone this far, he's being experimented on in this artificial intelligence program—but what's the end result? What can he do now, that he was unable to do before?"

At that, Jax fixes me with a hollow stare. "The end goal is to transform him into nothing but data."

I blink. "Data?"

"Emika, Zero isn't real."

Right as she says it, I see a technician walk straight *through* Zero, like he's nothing more than a virtual simulation. A hologram. Just like what I'd seen at the lab earlier tonight, when I witnessed him walk right through the glass wall.

Blood rushes to my head. That can't be true. "What do you mean, he isn't real? I've *seen* him. He's physically been in my room, in the same space as us, plenty of times. He's—"

"Has he?" Jax interrupts me, her eyes distant and bleak. "Zero isn't real. He's an illusion. Sasuke Tanaka's real body died years ago on a lab gurney. What you've seen standing before you is a virtual projection. Emika, Zero is Sasuke's human mind successfully transmitted into data. He *is* an artificial intelligence program."

21

Zero isn't real.

All this time, I thought he was flesh and blood. But he is an illusion, a projection, a virtual image so realistic that I couldn't even tell the difference.

That's impossible.

The thought bubbles up in my mind, and I feel a desperate urge to laugh at Jax. I must not have understood her.

But then my memories come back to me, faster and faster. The first time I'd ever seen him was in the Pirate's Den, a virtual space. The second time, inside a game of Warcross. The third time, he had been standing in my dorm room, only to vanish when everything exploded. When I arrived at the hotel to meet with him and the Blackcoats, Jax and Taylor had been with him, and he'd been leaning against the wall, not touching anyone.

But no! When I saw him standing on the balcony with Jax, hadn't he pressed his hand to her back, pulling her to him? My mind whirls frantically, remembering that moment and searching for a sign that would make this conclusion false.

No, Jax had only stood *close* to him, and he had only bent down near her to whisper something in her ear.

I have never touched Zero, and he has never touched me. We have only ever been close to each other—never making physical contact. That cold, artificial look in his eyes is because he *is* artificial.

The realization sends me spinning, and I put a hand out, steadying myself against my desk.

Zero isn't real. He is an illusion.

Sasuke Tanaka died a long time ago.

Jax watches me as the information hits me in waves. There is a haunted expression on her face now. "Living eternally inside a machine is something we've always talked about, isn't it? Only now, Taylor has actually done it. Zero's mind is as accurate and agile as a human mind—in an intellectual capacity, he's every bit the same as he was when he was Sasuke. Only now, Zero can exist anywhere and everywhere. He has no physical form. He does not age. And so long as there is an Internet, so long as there are machines, he'll exist forever."

"What—" My voice catches, and I have to try again. "What about his memory? His recognition of his family?"

"Taylor can't have him going off to see them, can she? Reporting to the authorities?" Jax replies. "She gave him immortality. In exchange, she took away his memory, linking his mind to hers. He does what she wants. He believes what she believes. And when she dies, he'll shut down."

Jax has scrolled us onto another file, and I stare numbly as this one shows a detailed list of names. Clients.

The military. The medical-industrial complex. The one percent. Tech companies. Government officials.

My mind aches. There are plenty of people eager to benefit from the results of this research—maybe to make obedient super-soldiers or as a cure for the terminally ill or whatever it was they needed. Maybe just to live forever.

"It's ironic, isn't it?" Jax says in a resigned voice. "In a way, Taylor did keep her promise to Mina Tanaka. She saved Sasuke's life by making him permanent. The only price was to kill him."

I think back to institute, how I watched Zero move in tandem with that armored figure, how his gestures manipulated the machine. "What about the robot in the lab?" I ask. "The one Zero was controlling?"

"A physical form for him," she replies. "He can sync with that machine, as surely as if that were his own body. He can control one of them; he can control multiple ones if he wants to."

Supersoldiers.

"Now, imagine this hooked up to the NeuroLink. How easily Taylor could replicate this, on a massive scale."

"But," I say hoarsely, clearing my throat, "do all these clients—patrons—know how she did this experiment? What it took?"

"Would it matter now, if they knew?" She shrugs at me. "If the end results are this remarkable, would you throw away the research just because the process was unethical? Immoral human experimentation has been around forever, has been performed by your country, by mine, by everyone. You think people don't want the results of this kind of research, regardless of how it's obtained? People ultimately don't care about the journey, if the end is worth it. And what was the price tag here, in exchange for immortality?"

One life.

She's right. If the experiment is exposed, it can be blamed on the Blackcoats, and all of these clients can just point the finger at them, denouncing it as heinous and illegal while being absolved of any blame for funding the research. But no one would throw away these findings just because Sasuke had died for it.

"His parents," I whisper. "Sasuke's mom. Did she . . . ?"

"She never knew what happened to him. She knows he disappeared several months after she withdrew him from the program, and I know she nearly killed herself trying to find out what happened to him—but what could she do? People disappear frequently in Japan. There isn't even a national registry that catalogues the missing. Taylor was the director of the institute. She had the power to hide whatever needed to be hidden, and an accusation this wild would've just made Mina look like a grieving mother gone mad."

"And what about you?" I ask softly.

"Taylor often hired people as needed for her projects. Most who worked with us weren't exactly upstanding citizens. So as her ambitions grew, she wanted someone like me to enforce her control and protect her. I may not have gone Sasuke's route, but I tested very well for my reflexes. So she had me trained." Jax smiles bitterly. There's the fear in her eyes again. "Nothing commands authority like a professional killer, and no killer surprises someone more than a young girl."

Even though Jax doesn't say it, I know she still thinks of Taylor as her mother. A cruel one, one who doesn't care about her. But family, nevertheless. It's hard to sever the mind's ties, no matter how painful they are.

Taylor had made me believe that she was a force of good, that her mission was still fundamentally moral, the need to rid the world of regimes and technology like Hideo's that sought to control others.

But sometimes, the need to protect the world from being controlled translates to seizing control for yourself.

Jax pulls us out of the recordings. I glimpse the vast library again, the repository of the Blackcoats' secrets, then at the Dark World's Fair, and then the streets of the Dark World itself. Then, we leave the virtual space, and I return to my room, lit only by slices of moonlight and streetlamps. The virtual image of Jax is still here, standing beside me as I lean against my bed for support.

"Why are you telling me all this?" I say to her. "You're risking your own life."

Her expression, as always, doesn't waver. "Because I don't believe Sasuke's completely gone."

She pauses, but her eyes go straight to me. My thoughts are already racing. The specific memory that Zero had shown me when he'd taught me how to break into Hideo's mind. Zero had said that he didn't mean for me to see it. But what if *Sasuke* had, from some corner deep in Zero's mind?

"The symbol," I whisper to Jax. "The memory of Sasuke in that room."

She only nods back. "I don't think it was an accident that Zero let you into that memory. I think Sasuke did it."

The hopeful way she says his name is a sharp contrast to her usual curt tone. To her, Sasuke is still alive. No wonder she will never try to kill Taylor—not while Sasuke might still be trapped inside Zero's mind.

Jax suddenly looks to her side, her expression focused again. She listens for a while. I tense, wondering what it is she's hearing and where she is in reality right now. Then she leans close to me.

"Listen carefully," she says at a rapid clip. "Zero is fully under Taylor's control. By nature of his programming, he must listen to her commands and obey whatever she says. You need to get access to Hideo's algorithm. But once you do, you can't let Taylor get hold of it. If you can use the algorithm to force Taylor to give up control of Zero's mind, you can free Zero from her."

I study Jax's face as she talks. The abrupt urgency and uncertainty in her voice jar me. Right now, she doesn't sound like a ruthless assassin, but a small girl, terrified of her keeper. "Like the rest of us, Taylor's wearing beta lenses. They aren't connected to the algorithm." She reaches into her pocket and pulls out a small box. "But they *will* be, for a moment, right after you get access to Hideo's algorithm during the closing ceremony."

She's right. In the split second after Taylor's beta lenses hook into the algorithm—and before her code installs *her* as the algorithm's master—she'll be vulnerable to Hideo seizing control over her mind.

"We're going to have just one second to do this," I tell her. Then I add to myself, *And only if I can persuade Hideo to cooperate.*

Jax nods. "It'll be the most important second in history."

If this goes wrong, my own beta lenses will be hooked up into the algorithm, too. I'll be under *Taylor's* control instead of Hideo's. All of us will. I try not to think about what Taylor would do with that level of power. What she would turn us into.

"What happens after we free Zero from her?" I say after a while.

"That library I showed you. It contains everything, remember? Every study and experiment that Taylor has ever done. It also contains every iteration of Sasuke Tanaka's mind, during every stage of his trial."

At that, she holds out a compressed set of data to hover between us. I don't need to say a word to know that this contains those records. "You need a way straight into Zero's mind. Download all of Sasuke's Memories back into Zero. Zero has no desire to go against Taylor . . . but *Sasuke* might."

Use the algorithm to save Hideo's brother. It's a plan that will almost certainly go wrong.

But I still nod at Jax. "We'll do it."

Jax jerks her head away from me again, as if she's heard something. In a flash, any trace of weakness vanishes from her face. "I have to go," she whispers to me. She meets my gaze one final time. Then she disconnects, and I'm suddenly alone again in my room.

It's dead quiet in here now. The contrast is startling.

I remain leaning against my bed in the silence. The recordings I'd seen run through my head repeatedly, refusing to disappear. I bring them up again, one by one, each file that Jax had given me. The images of Sasuke, all his Memories, circle me in a halo.

This is the key I've been looking for.

Slowly, a plan begins to take shape.

22

I barely sleep that night. Every time I close my eyes, all I see is Sasuke as a young boy in that room, tears running down his face. I see him kissing Jax. Screaming as he's strapped down for his procedures. The memories fuse with each other, creating new, twisted ones. There's Jax standing with Zero on her balcony, her face turned up to him, him leaning down to kiss her neck. Jax turns into me, Zero into Hideo. We're back in that glass tower, lying in his bed. His head snaps back as Taylor shoots him. He transforms into Tremaine as he crumples to the floor.

Then I jolt awake crying, my body damp with sweat.

I'm too scared to go back to sleep, so instead, I sit awake in bed and fiddle with the glowing cube that Zero had given me, the hack that will get me into Hideo's mind.

Use the algorithm to force Taylor to give up control of Zero.

Will Hideo go along with this? To allow someone else access

into his algorithm? Even Zero had refused to reveal himself to his brother, knowing how unpredictable his reaction might be. There's no guarantee that Hideo will even believe me.

But Sasuke is buried somewhere inside the monster that Taylor has created. If there's even the slightest chance that we can rescue him . . . I have to believe that Hideo will hear me out.

And if he doesn't . . . if he doesn't, I'll have to hack into his mind. Force him.

I study the data until dawn streams into my room. The instant the light shifts from blue to gold, an incoming call pings in my view. I jump, thinking it might be from Zero himself—that he or Taylor has figured out what Jax has done.

But it's from Roshan. I accept the call, and his hoarse voice fills my ears, telling me what I already know.

"Tremaine's in the hospital," he says. "He's hurt pretty bad." His words falter a little. "Em, he'd listed me as his emergency contact. That's why the doctor called me. I—I can't—"

I can hardly bear the pain in his voice. My hands shake in my lap as he gives me the name of the hospital. "On my way," I whisper, and dart out of my bed before he responds.

A half hour later, I arrive at the hospital to find Roshan and a doctor locked in conversation, the latter trying in vain to explain to Roshan that he can't visit Tremaine yet.

"We've been out here for hours!" Roshan's voice echoes down the hall. "You said we'd be able to see him over an hour ago!" He's shouting in Japanese at a doctor, his translated words appearing in a mad dash in my view. Beside him, Hammie and Asher stay unnaturally quiet, not bothering to stop him. He must have lost his temper already earlier.

"I'm sorry, Mr. Ahmadi," the doctor explains, giving him a small bow of apology. "But you are not Mr. Blackbourne's legal spouse; unless you have an official certificate, you will need to wait with your friends until we can allow you to visit—"

"We're a *couple*," Roshan snaps, forgetting in the heat of the moment that that's no longer true. "Didn't you all pass a same-sex marriage law last year?"

"But you are not currently married," the doctor counters. "Are you? Do you have papers?"

Roshan throws his hands up and storms back toward the waiting room where I stand. Behind him, Asher and Hammie exchange a quick glance. Roshan catches sight of me as he walks, then gives me a quick nod.

My heart sits in my throat as I reach them. Roshan looks pale and haggard, and his eyes are bloodshot. "Why weren't you with him?" he snaps at me. "They said he was dropped off at the hospital alone."

Roshan's anger stabs me hard through the chest. I start to offer excuses—that I couldn't reach him, that the Blackcoats had figured out Tremaine hacked their databases. But this isn't what Roshan needs to hear. "I should have been there," I manage to choke out. "It's my fault this happened to him. He should never have—"

Roshan glances over his shoulder toward Tremaine's room, then closes his eyes and lowers his head. "I'm sorry," he says. "I'm glad you weren't there."

"Can you see him through the window?"

Roshan nods. "His bandages are bloody. The doctors say they're waiting for the swelling to go down, but they don't know when that'll be. They said he's incredibly lucky the bullet hit the way it did. A tiny bit to the left or right, and he would've arrived dead on the scene."

I think of Jax's promise that she'd shot Tremaine with a glancing blow. She'd kept her word, after all.

"What happened?" Asher asks as he wheels over to us, followed by Hammie.

Other players—the Demon Brigade, a smattering of other teams—have shown up, too, filling the waiting area with an awkward gaggle of rivals. So I keep my voice down and tell my teammates as much as I can. That Tremaine and I had gone to the institute, and that everything went completely wrong.

But I don't tell them about Sasuke. I can't handle the thought of bringing them any closer to real danger.

"You have to stop," Hammie says to me as I finish. "That could be you in there too—it could be so much worse."

I want to listen to her, but tonight I'm seeing Hideo. The closing ceremony happens in two days. We're out of options. There's simply no time to stop anymore. All I can do is nod weakly at her. She can see the lie in my eyes, but she doesn't press me.

As we settle into our chairs in the waiting room, I find myself staring at the date in my view. When the closing ceremony game starts, everything will either end or become a living nightmare.

●●●●●

HIDEO ISN'T AT his home tonight—at least, not the one I remember. Instead, the car he sends for me takes me across the bridge spanning Tokyo Bay, where the ocean meets the city and the reflections of skyscrapers trembles against the water. Tonight, the bridge is entirely lit with the colors of the Phoenix Riders, and through my lenses, cruise ships and tourist ferries dotting the harbor have a smattering of hearts and stars hovering over them.

The scarlet Phoenix Rider lights reflected against the ocean look like blood spreading across the water, and the cityscape like millions of shards of glass. I focus down at my lap instead, where I'm pressing my hands tightly against each other.

We travel along the waterfront until we leave most of the boats behind and enter a quiet stretch of luxury high-rises. Here, a team of security guards waves the car through a gate, and when it finally stops at the end of a dock, more bodyguards in suits come to open the door for me.

I step out of the car and stand facing the water, breathing in the salty air, my lips parted at the sight.

Floating serenely before me is the largest yacht I've ever seen. The entire ship is matte black, blending in with the night, save for the lines of soft silver lights running along each deck and the trails of fairy bulbs strung across the top.

"Mister Tanaka has been waiting for you," one of the bodyguards says to me. He holds a gloved hand out, gesturing for me to step onto the ramp leading up to the yacht. I nod wordlessly, suddenly queasy with anticipation and dread, then head up to the ship's lower deck and into its interior.

The space opens up into a two-floor-high ceiling, where a chandelier dripping with crystals hangs. Floor-to-ceiling glass walls, tinted for privacy, line the chamber, and at the far end is a set of double doors already open, inviting me in. I walk to them, stopping hesitantly at the entryway to peer into the vast suite beyond.

The lighting is dim, the walls made of more tinted glass that reveals the outline of the city against the water. Thick white rugs and plush divans dot the space. Sheer, pearlescent curtains glide idly in a sea breeze from an ajar window, under which lies a low, luxurious bed.

The space is as immaculate as I remember Hideo's main home being—at least, until I see the broken porcelain on the floor.

"Watch your step."

Hideo's familiar voice drifts from across the room, where

he's heading in from the balcony with a dark jacket slung over his shoulder. He tosses it unceremoniously onto a nearby chair. In the low light, all I can see of him is his tall silhouette and the silver of his hair, but I can still tell that his shirt is uncharacteristically rumpled, his sleeves rolled up haphazardly, and his collar pushed up. The shadows cover his expression entirely.

"What happened?" I ask.

He straightens and walks toward the long couches, coming slightly into the light as he goes. "I'll sweep it up in a bit," he replies, his classic habit of answering without answering.

My eyes dart straight to his hands. His knuckles are an angry red, cut up, and crusted over with blood. Dark circles rim his eyes.

Has he been here since that night at the art museum, agonizing over all I'd told him? I've never seen him so weary, like his whole heart is struggling underneath a great weight.

I take a seat across from him, then wait until he leans forward and regards me with a piercing stare.

"You brought us here," he says quietly. "So, tell me. What do you know about my brother?"

No need for small talk tonight. In his voice is an anger I remember only from the night Jax had attempted to assassinate him, when he'd leaned over his injured bodyguard and ordered the rest of his men to find the culprit. Even that night is nothing compared to now. I feel like I'm staring into a void that has opened up inside him, threatening to swallow him whole.

I don't answer right away. There are no words I can say to ease us into this conversation. Instead, I Link with him and bring up a screen to show him a Memory I'd saved of my first encounter with Zero, of him in my hotel room.

Hideo just stares at his brother's face. There is a whirlwind of emotion in his eyes. First disbelief, that this person could possibly be him. Then recognition, because there is no question that this young man is the same little boy who disappeared so many years ago.

"How did you find out?" he finally asks.

"I figured it out after the final game, after I left your suite," I go on, wanting to fill the heavy silence. "The hack I pulled at the end to stop him also exposed his identity, and that was when I saw his name."

"It's not him."

I bring up a second video of Zero, this time of us walking side by side as he escorts me to my room. "It's him," I insist in a quiet voice.

Hideo stares at him for a long time. He stares until it seems he may have frozen solid.

"What—" His voice breaks for a moment, and I feel my own heart crack at the sound. I don't think I've ever heard him falter like this. "What happened to him?"

I sigh, running a hand through my hair. "I shouldn't be the one to tell you this," I reply. "But your brother . . . when he disappeared, he was very ill. Your mother had, in desperation, entered him into an experimental trial that had a chance of curing him."

Hideo shakes his head at me. "No," he replies. "My parents would have told me. Sasuke was playing in the park with me on the day he vanished."

"I'm only telling you what I know." As Hideo looks on, I show him each recording I'd duplicated, in chronological succession. The testing room in the Innovation Institute, with a child at every desk. The hopeful, worried faces of Hideo's parents peering in from the window. The private meeting between Dana Taylor and Mina Tanaka. The small silhouette of Sasuke, cowering in the corner of a room, of him begging to go home to his family. The bright blue scarf wrapped around his neck. His friendship with Jax, and all the moments they spent huddled together. The way he tried to negotiate with Taylor for his freedom, paid the price of his scarf, and then failed to escape. The slow, gradual, crippling disappearance of his identity with each new procedure done to him, of Sasuke becoming less of a person and more a series of data.

The truth behind Project Zero.

I expect Hideo to tear his eyes away at some point, but he doesn't. He watches all of it in silence, his stare never shifting away from his brother as Sasuke ages a little in each video and loses more of himself. As Taylor takes away Sasuke's scarf. As Sasuke watches his brother's first public announcement. Each scene rips a gash in Hideo's heart.

When the recordings finish, Hideo doesn't say a word. I fixate on the dried blood on his knuckles. The silence roars in our ears like a living thing.

"Sasuke died years ago," Hideo finally whispers into the dark, echoing the words Jax had said to me. "He's gone from this world, then."

"I'm so sorry," I whisper back.

The heavy weight that has been crushing his heart—the polite, stiff distance, all the careful shields he'd always put up one by one—gives way. His shoulders sag. He lowers his head into his hands, and suddenly, he starts to weep.

That weight was the burden of not knowing, of years and years of anguish, of imagining the thousands of things that could have happened, of wondering whether his brother might ever walk back through the door. Of all those countless iterations he'd made of his Memory, trying to figure out how Sasuke could have disappeared. It was the silver strand of an unfinished story.

There's nothing I can say to comfort him. All I can do is listen to his heart break over and over again.

When there are no more tears left, Hideo sits in silence and stares out the windows. He looks lost in a fog, and for the very first time, I see uncertainty in his eyes.

I lean forward and find my voice. "Even though Sasuke is gone from this world," I murmur softly, "he's still alive in another."

Hideo doesn't answer, but his lashes lower as his gaze turns toward me.

"Zero is Taylor's creation," I go on. My voice sounds deafening. "He's tethered to her in every sense of the word. Just as your algorithm controls those who wear the new NeuroLink lenses, Taylor controls Zero's data. His mind. But Sasuke isn't gone. I think he reached out to me through Zero because he's trapped somewhere in that darkness, crying for help."

Hideo winces visibly. He still says nothing.

I put a hand on his arm hesitantly. "Hideo, Taylor's after your NeuroLink. Her people are behind every recent attack against it."

"Let them come." Hideo's words are a quiet and clear threat. He rises from the couch, turns away from me, and walks toward the window. There, he puts his hands in his pockets and stares out at the city on the water.

My words fade away. After a while, I push myself off the couch and go to stand beside him at the windows.

When I glance at him, I can see the tears on his cheeks, his red eyes.

Finally, after a long moment, he turns his head slightly toward me, his gaze still directed outward at the city. "Does he remember anything?" he asks in a low voice.

I can hear the real question he's asking. *Does he remember me?*

Does he remember our parents? "He knows who you are," I reply softly. "But only in the way that a stranger might know you. I'm sorry, Hideo. I wish I could tell you something better than that."

Hideo continues to stare blankly out at the city. I find myself wondering what he's thinking, if maybe he wishes he could use the NeuroLink to will away what happened in the past.

"Jax told me that the only way to help Sasuke is if we use your algorithm to turn Zero against Taylor."

This breaks through his trance. Hideo looks sidelong at me. "You want me to link the algorithm to her."

"Exactly. If you open the algorithm and connect Taylor to it, you'll be able to control Taylor and free Zero from her."

"What about Sasuke?" Hideo's jaw tightens at his brother's name.

"Taylor has archives of Sasuke's past mind. All the iterations of him. If we can combine those versions with who he is now, we can make his mind whole again." I pause. "I know he can never be *real* . . . but you'll be able to have him back in some sense."

"You're asking me to give you access to my algorithm."

I hesitate. "Yes."

He's still struggling to trust me, but with his guard down, I can once again see his beating heart behind the armor. All the thousands of possibilities of what could have happened to Sasuke are wiped from his gaze and replaced by clarity—a path forward. He has a chance to talk to his brother again, bring him back in some small way.

For this, I know he's willing to tear the world's order to shreds. He's willing to risk anything.

Hideo looks back out at the water. A long beat passes before he finally says, "I'll do it."

Without thinking, I take a step closer to him until we're nearly touching. My hand comes up to rest on his arm. I don't say anything. He stirs anyway, sensing my own mix of emotions—the wavering trust I'm putting in him, the pull I always feel when I'm near him. My fear of letting him in again. Beneath his shirt, his skin is warm. I can't bring myself to move away.

He turns to face me. "You're risking your life, telling me this," he says. "You could have returned to New York and left all of this behind. But you're still here, Emika."

For a moment, I imagine myself back at the little bar with Hammie and the other Riders. I see Hammie leaning forward and fixing me with her steady gaze. *Why are you doing this?*

Then I do something I never thought I would. I think back on the morning I'd crouched, thin and hollow and hopeless, in my foster-home bed and heard his story on the radio. I let the Memory form, crystallizing into a clear image, and then I send it to him, every last thing I saw and felt and heard that day. I let him see the broken side of me that had stirred at the knowledge of him, the pieces that somehow found each other again.

I don't know how much of it he can see and understand. It's a jumble of thoughts and emotions, not a real recorded Memory. Suddenly, I'm afraid that he won't get what I'm trying to say at all. That this vulnerable, naked moment might mean nothing to him.

I turn away in embarassment. But when I glance back at him, his eyes are locked on me, taking me in as if I am all that matters. As if he understands everything I tried to share.

It's almost more than I can bear. I swallow hard and force myself to look away. My cheeks burn hot. "Hideo . . . I'm never going to agree with what you're doing. I'll never feel right about the deaths connected to your algorithm or your reasons justifying them. But that day, when you were just a boy being interviewed on the radio, hiding your broken heart, you reached a girl searching for something to hold on to. She found *you*, and you helped her pull herself up."

Hideo stares at me, his gaze searing me to my core. "I didn't know," he whispered.

"You are forever a piece of my story. I couldn't turn my back on you without turning my back on myself. I had to try." My quiet words hang in the air. "I had to hold out my hand to you."

He's so close now. I'm on dangerous ground—I never should have come here. But I stay still and don't move away.

"You're afraid," I murmur, noticing the emotions pulsing from him.

"I'm terrified," he whispers back. "Of what you're capable of. Because you're here, walking on a razor-thin line. I've been afraid ever since I met you, when you looked me straight in the eye and broke down my system in a matter of minutes. I spent hours afterward studying what you did. I remember everything you've ever said to me." An ache enters his voice. "I'm afraid that every time I see you might be the last."

I think back to the piercing gaze he'd given me during our last meeting. Underneath that had been fear, all along. "You told me you never wanted to see me again," I manage to say.

His voice is low and raw. "Because every time I see you, it takes everything in me to turn away."

I realize that I'm leaning toward him now, yearning for something more. He must be able to sense it through our connection, and as if in answer, I feel the need coming from him, shadows of what he wishes he could do, fleeting thoughts of his hand at my waist, pulling me in. The space between us feels alive, sparking with a searing desire to close.

He hesitates. With his heart exposed and vulnerable, I can

now see the fear in his expression. "What do you want, Emika?" he whispers.

I close my eyes, take a breath, and open them again. "I want to stay."

It is the last trembling rope holding him back. He closes the inches between us, takes my face in his hands, and leans down toward me. His lips touch mine.

Any sense of control I'd felt now shatters. He's warm, his body familiar, and I fall into him. There is none of the gentle hesitation of our first kiss—this is deeper, more intense—both of us are making up for lost time.

My arms wrap around his neck. His hand pushes against the small of my back, pressing my body to his. My fingers run through his hair. He breaks our kiss only to touch his lips to my neck, and I exhale, shuddering at his warm breath against my skin. Glimpses and fantasies and sensations spark from his mind to mine, mine to his, leaving me tingling down to my toes.

I vaguely register him lifting me effortlessly into his arms. He's carrying me toward the bed.

Don't do this, I warn myself. *You're on thin ice. You need to keep a clear head.*

But when we fall against the bedsheets, all I focus on is the cut of his jaw in the shadows. I admire the slant of deep blue light against his skin as I fumble with the buttons of his shirt and tug his belt loose. His hands are yanking my shirt up over my head, sliding along my skin. The cool air in the room hits my bare chest, and I'm struck with a sudden instinct to cover myself in front of him. But he stares down at me, his eyes dark with desire. A shy smile touches his lips. The city's glow outside catches on his long lashes.

When I reach for him, he kisses me on the cheek, then trails his lips along my neck and my collar. His breathing is heavy and uneven, his hands warm and gentle. I tremble against him, and after a heartbeat I realize that he is shaking, too. I run a finger along the muscles of his chest down to his stomach, blushing at the way this simple touch makes him shiver. His mouth brushes against mine, asking me in a whisper what I want, and I tell him, and he gives it to me, and in this moment, I don't think about anything else, not the Blackcoats, not Zero, not the dangers waiting for us. I just think about now. Just my body entwined with his. Just his sharp intake of breath, my name feverish on his lips, the cool sheets beneath us, the heat of him moving against me, my fingers clinging desperately to his back.

Just me.

Him.

And the gentle lapping of the ocean outside, ink under a midnight sky, separating us from the glittering city that awaits us.

23

One Day until the Warcross Closing Ceremony

I don't stir until the first rays of dawn enter the room, casting a weak palette of light against the tangled sheets. For a moment, I can't remember where I am—an unfamiliar room, in an unfamiliar bed. The space next to me is empty. The room is rocking ever so slightly. A boat?

Slowly, the memories from the night before come back to me.

I frown, gathering the blankets around my chest and pulling myself up into a sitting position. Did Hideo leave? I look around the room until my eyes finally settle on a sliding glass door left ajar, beyond which the silhouette of a man stands bathed in gold, leaning against the ship's railing and looking out at the city.

I let myself watch him for a moment. Then I reach for my clothes, pull them on, and slip out of his bed.

The air outside is still cool, smelling of salt and sea, and my skin prickles as I stop to lean against the open door. Two steaming mugs sit on a small table beside where Hideo's standing. Morning dew lingers on the doors' glass. I run an idle finger along it, noting the feel of the moisture, and remind myself that I'm in the real world now, not in a virtual one.

Hideo looks to his side so that I can see the profile of his face. "You're up early," he says.

"You knew I'd be," I reply, nodding at the two mugs of coffee. "Or you wouldn't have poured me that."

He glances briefly at me, a small smile on his lips, and takes a sip of his own coffee. He looks pale this morning, dark circles still under his eyes, but other than that, I wouldn't be able to tell what he's going through. Every vulnerability that he had exposed to me the night before has been neatly stored away again, and for a moment I'm afraid he's gone back to not trusting me again. Thinking this was all a huge mistake.

Then I meet his gaze, and in it, I see something open. No, he hasn't retreated entirely. The real Hideo I've been searching for is here.

When I still linger by the door, he nods for me to come join him, handing me my mug of coffee as I reach him. "Taylor expects you here," he says quietly, his eyes going out to the stirring city.

I nod. My mind returns briefly to Zero. They might be watching us right now from some unknown place on shore. "They want me close to you," I reply as I put my mug back down on the table.

Hideo's eyes flicker, and I know he's thinking about his brother. Whatever it is, though, he doesn't say it out loud. Instead, he reaches for me and pulls me to him. His hands are warm from the coffee mug. I suck in my breath as he turns me around so that my back is against the balcony, and his arms are pressed against the ledge on either side of me, pinning me in.

"This is what they expect to see, isn't it?" he murmurs, his face tilted toward my ear.

"Yes." My skin tingles at his closeness, and all I can think of is what happened last night. He's right, of course, and if the Blackcoats *are* watching, it'll help my case for them to see me with Hideo. Again, I find myself thinking of my dream of shattered glass, where Zero was watching us from the other side of the bedroom. It's enough to make me glance to my side, half expecting him to be here on the yacht.

But it's just us.

Hideo gives me a half smile, leans close, and presses his lips against my neck. "Kiss me, then," he murmurs, and pulls me toward him.

I close my eyes at his touch, shivering, and turn my face toward his. I kiss him slowly, savoring the moment. If only things could stay this simple between us.

Finally, I force myself to push away. "We won't have much time to act during the closing ceremony tomorrow," I murmur to him. "We'll need to do it right as your beta lenses update."

He watches me carefully from the corner of his eye. The fire in his gaze is dark, a seething hate. "Good," he says. There is a note in his voice that unsettles me. "I'll be ready for Taylor. I want to see her face."

The memory of the lines of the guilt-ridden outside the police stations come back to me, all those suicides by criminals compelled by the algorithm. The suicides of some who weren't criminals at all.

"And what happens if we succeed?"

"What do you mean?"

"If you get your brother back, even an echo of him . . . what then? What happens to the algorithm? Will you keep it going?"

He's silent. Everything he's ever done has been to find the person responsible for taking his brother from him and to prevent the same thing from ever happening again to anyone else. Now he knows who did it. He'll be confronting her in a day.

"You always said that the algorithm is meant to be unbiased," I say. "But that's never going to be true, is it? Not when it's controlled by a human. I uncovered everything I could about Sasuke because I cared about what had happened to him. Because I care about *you*. But the bigger reason I did it was to give you a reason to stop using your algorithm."

I don't add that I'd overheard what he'd said to Mari and Kenn, or that I know he's been using the algorithm to try to hunt down Sasuke's kidnapper. But I don't need to. Hideo knows what I'm talking about.

"Please, Hideo," I add softly to him. "This is your chance to do what's right. End the algorithm."

For the first time since he told me about his plans, I can see him wrestling with the choices he's made. But he doesn't reply. He straightens and moves to stand at my side, where he rests his elbows against the railing. Out across the ocean, Tokyo's skyline is rimmed in light.

I do the same—turn myself toward the city and study the day as it grows brighter. Hideo doesn't answer me, not directly, but his eyes are heavy. He looks away from the light and toward the shadows that still stretch across the docks, casting the streets in blue and gray.

What will *I* do, if we succeed and Hideo continues ahead with the algorithm? What if I've been wrong about him all along?

The thought stirs in me, dark and troubling. In my files, I quietly bring up the cube that Zero had given me. It rotates before me in midair, invisible to Hideo.

If Hideo doesn't change his mind, I know what I need to do. And this time, there will be no forgiving. No second chances.

If he won't give up the algorithm willingly, then I'll have to take it from him.

24

The Day of the Warcross
Closing Ceremony

Late afternoon on the day of the closing ceremony is muted with clouds. Even though I have my lenses on, I know that underneath the bright hues of the official teams coloring the sky, Tokyo is covered in shades of gray, turning steadily darker.

How appropriate. The timer in my vision tells me that I have one hour until the beta lenses patch.

A black auto-car picks me up at my hotel in Omotesando, and once I'm inside, it steers itself in the direction of the Tokyo Dome. Outside my window, the city's celebrations have taken on the heat of a fever, and everyone is cheering at our line of black cars cutting through the city. As if today were another typical Warcross tournament day.

I turn away from their eager faces and stare down at my hands in my lap. What will this city be like after everything goes down?

A message from Zero cuts through my thoughts.

> When the closing ceremony starts, you'll
> be in the center of the arena with the other
> all-star players. Hideo will greet each of
> you in turn.

Zero has the inside workings of the tournament today down to every fine detail. I imagine his virtual self, hacking into the Henka Games schedules and downloading everything. Then I picture Sasuke, the *real* Zero, curled in a ball in a corner of that mind. *If* he's there at all. And even if he is, how much of all this is he aware of? Would he know what's about to happen?

I send a reply.

> When will I see you and Taylor?

> When Hideo finishes greeting you, the new
> Warcross world for the closing ceremony will
> open. Hideo will personally announce it to
> the audience. For a moment, you, the other
> players, and Hideo will all be inside this world
> at the same time. That's the moment right
> before the beta lenses get patched, and the
> moment you will be able to hack into his mind.

Zero pauses.

> Be prepared. We'll see you on the floor of
> the arena.

> I will.

Our conversation ends. I bring up the cube in my hand again, letting Zero's hack hover in my palms. I know Hideo will seize the chance to trap Taylor in the algorithm, hopefully freeing his brother. But the algorithm itself . . . I think back to the image of Hideo's uncertain face as he stood with me on the deck of his yacht.

I break open the cube to stare at the code, letting the glowing blue rows of text fill the interior of the car, and then close it back up again. I have to believe that he'll do what he knows is right. End it.

But if he doesn't, I'll be ready for him.

I take a deep breath. Then I reach out to Hideo, asking him to Link with me. For a while, I stare at the glowing green halo around his profile, suddenly wondering if he's changed his mind.

Then, a pleasant *ding* sounds. I feel the familiar trickle of his emotions into my mind. He's tense and uneasy. But most of all, he feels *ready*, surrounded in a dark, sure aura. Neither of us says a word.

I close my eyes at his presence, letting myself stay immersed a while longer in nothing but this glimmer of his feelings and thoughts. Then we reach the grounds of the Tokyo Dome, and I open my eyes to the roar of crowds gathered outside the stadium.

Thirty minutes until the beta lenses patch.

Giant projections of today's players broadcast against building walls and holograms of our championship highlights looming along the stadium's perimeters. As the sight of my own footage comes into view, I hear the broadcast paired with it.

"—in the move to allow controversial wild card Emika Chen, originally of the Phoenix Riders, to play in the closing ceremony following her dismissal from the team. Chen, this year's number one draft pick, had so many write-in votes that—"

For a brief moment, I feel that thrill again of being escorted to the dome for another game of Warcross, of standing with teammates and fidgeting, eager to be the ones to win.

Now I'm heading back into the arena for a different reason altogether.

Soon, I join other black cars carrying official players until there is a caravan of us heading in the same direction. I find myself clenching and unclenching my fists in rapid succession. Stripes of all the teams' colors adorn the sides of the dome today, and suspended overhead is an enormous Warcross logo in silver chrome, rotating slowly.

I step out of the car in a daze and follow the bodyguards that are already waiting for me on the red carpet leading into the stadium. People crowd along either side, dressed up like their favorite players and waving their banners and posters. They let out a deafening cheer when they catch sight of me. All I can do is look back at them and smile desperately, unable to tell them any of what's really happening. Behind and ahead of me, I recognize a few of my fellow top-ten players who will play today. They're all here. More cheers shake the ground as each of them make their way past the throngs.

Then we're inside the dome, and I'm shrouded in the arena's darkness, illuminated only by a path of colored light leading out into the center of the stadium. The booming voices of analysts along the top floors echoes around the space.

"And here come another wave of players, folks! We've spotted Team Andromeda—Captain Shahira Boulous leading her players in, Ivo Erikkson, Penn Wachowski—"

"—followed by the Demon Brigade's Jena MacNeil and her crew—"

Their words are nearly drowned out by the audience. As I

reach the edge of the arena, the Phoenix Riders come into view. Hammie and Roshan are already here, waiting with the other players of today's match. Asher's out in the audience with the players who weren't chosen or who'd already been chosen last year.

Out of all the players, my teammates look the most tense. They know what's going to happen. The sight of them tugs at my heart, and I find myself unconsciously turning toward them.

Roshan sees me first, nudges Hammie, and waves to me. Overhead, the analysts say my name, while images play around the arena of footage from when I was still an official player.

Even in a stadium full of people, I feel vulnerable. The last time I was exposed in public like this, I'd almost died. My gaze sweeps the audience, searching in vain for Taylor and expecting to glimpse Zero in the shadows of the arena's halls. The back of my neck prickles as it once did on the rain-swept streets of Shinjuku. He could be anywhere. Everywhere. And even though I can't see him, I know he's watching me.

Still, I keep my smile plastered on, knowing that I'm currently being projected for everyone to see. *Jax.* If Zero is here, then that means she probably is too, looking out for me. The thought of her gives me some small comfort, and for a second, my smile is genuine.

Fifteen minutes until the beta lenses patch.

As the last of the players file into the arena's center, the sweeping lights dim and the overheads brighten. Everyone in the stadium disappears behind the glow that surrounds us. I stare out into the darkness as a voice starts to introduce each of us.

"Ladies and gentlemen, we've finally arrived at the end of this year's unexpected and truly epic Warcross championships!" The audience bursts into an excited roar that drowns out the announcer. She pauses, then lists each of us, followed by what position we play in our teams and what we'll be playing tonight. As she finishes, a 3-D view of today's environment hovers over our heads, rotating slowly for the benefit of the audience. The other players and I see a smaller version of it in front of us. It's a setting in outer space, with a planet's enormous rings slanted behind a series of small fighter pods.

"And, of course," the announcer continues, "behind the game itself is the one responsible for this entire revolution—Hideo Tanaka!"

As the stadium explodes into wild cheers and spotlights blaze on a passageway, I see him: Hideo, his head held high and hands in his pockets, walking toward us with his mob of bodyguards on either side. Audience members sitting in the seats near his path crane their necks and bodies forward in an unconscious attempt to be closer to him.

In spite of everything, Hideo seems as poised as ever, his trained, polite smile on. As he raises a hand to wave once at the crowds, they scream their approval back at him. He appears to have his attention fixated on the audience, but through the emotions coming from him in the Link, I can sense his focus on me, searing me even as he pretends not to notice. I stand still, careful to copy the other players, and keep my gaze turned up at the dome. I can hear the rhythmic roar of my heartbeat in my ears.

I find myself marveling for the hundredth time that he's able to control his emotions even after everything I've told him. Maybe it means he'll be the same way when he's forced to confront Taylor, or even when he sees Zero for himself—reacting with stone-cold calm.

Hideo greets each of the players in turn, giving his customary thanks to us for the championship season. The stadium has reached a fever pitch now, and all eyes are on him, drinking in his every move. He edges closer to me. My palms are sweating, and I wipe them against my thighs repeatedly.

Ten minutes until the beta lenses patch.

Hideo greets my other teammates. He shakes Roshan's hand, congratulates Hammie.

And then he's here in front of me, gives me a tense smile, and holds his hand out to me. The audience is losing their minds. I reach out my hand to shake his—and as I do, I grip it hard for a moment longer than I should.

His eyes hold mine. Through his Link comes his voice, deep and strong.

We're still on the same page, he says. It's a question.

I don't blink or look away. *I am if you are.*

Our hands stay joined for a beat more, until we know that any longer will stir murmurs. Finally, he pulls away, and so do I. My breath rushes out of me.

He walks to the center of our ring of players, then turns his face up to address the audience. The lights start to sweep again across the rows of seats. As he starts to thank the crowd for their enthusiasm, I turn my attention to the rest of the stadium. High up, near the dome's ceiling, the countdown clock for the beginning of the game ticks.

Five minutes until the beta lenses patch.

Everything around me feels surreal. Maybe nothing will happen. The closing ceremony seems to be progressing like it normally would—Hideo greeting the players, him addressing the audience, the people cheering for the game to start. In some alternate universe, they'll watch the match without incident, they'll file out of the arena and head back home, hop into their flights or their trains or their cars. And everything will be fine.

"—to let the match begin!"

Hideo's final words jolt me back into the present. The game world loads all around us then, and we are enveloped in the sweeping blackness of space, the infinite sky dotted with stars. Giant planetary rings arc across my view in a gradient of silver.

For this one moment, I dare to think that we might actually start playing this final match. Maybe none of the events of the past few weeks have ever happened.

But as I finish this thought, the game world flickers. It goes out, returning us to the dome—just in time for me to see Zero step onto the floor of the arena. And he's not alone.

25

He and Jax are flanking Taylor. They take a few steps to the middle of the arena, then stop right in front of where Hideo stands near me.

One of Hideo's bodyguards makes a move toward them, but Hideo shakes his head once. "Stop."

His bodyguards freeze where they are, their eyes blinking but blank, as if in a trance. But they're not the only ones. All around us, everything halts: the analysts hush in mid-sentence; the audience ceases waving their arms, the cheers quiet. Most of the other players—anyone not on the beta lenses—stop moving.

Only Hammie and Roshan stay unaffected. Still, they gape at Zero, Hammie's lips slightly parted, Roshan looking like he's about to lunge forward to protect me.

Where just moments earlier the noise in here was deafening, the stadium instantly plunges into eerie silence. It's as if someone had simply pressed a button and paused the world, leaving only a few of us still running.

That's exactly what just happened.

Hideo is using the algorithm to control everyone in here. I start to shake. I haven't seen the sheer power of his abilities with my own eyes until now.

Hideo, I say, reaching out through our Link. But he doesn't respond. His attention is focused on Taylor.

Taylor stares at Hideo with a soft smile I've come to know all too well. When I look at her eyes, though, they are hard as stone. "I've been watching your career for a while," she finally says to him. "You're very impressive, as is this algorithm you've developed."

Hideo has gone so still that for an instant I think he's being controlled, too. He says nothing as he stares at the woman who kidnapped his brother and stole his life.

But his emotions—the dark, seething hatred churning across our Link—is a flood of barbs and thorns, a force so powerful that I can almost feel the edges of it clawing into my skin.

"Your creative director agreed to give us the way in," she says. "Among other details."

Kenn.

I gasp through the overwhelming wave of Hideo's emotions. My eyes dart up to meet Taylor's. Kenn had let them into the dome. What else has he given them?

Hideo's eyes are hard and glittering. "How long?" he says quietly.

"Months." Taylor takes a step forward and folds her arms. "It's hard to find friends you can trust, isn't it? I suppose everyone has their price."

Everyone has their price. I realize they are the exact words Zero had once said to me, when he'd confronted me during the Warcross championships. *Months.* So Kenn has been working with her since before the championships began.

The argument I'd seen between Kenn and Hideo comes back to me in a flash. How eager he'd been to skip Mari's study on the NeuroLink's flaws.

But maybe his frustrations ran deeper than that. Deep enough for him to betray Hideo and let Taylor in.

And suddenly I understand how Zero always seemed to know so much. Every detail of the closing ceremony. Every piece of Hideo's plan to patch the beta lenses at the opening of today's game. The bug that allows a way into Hideo's mind. The existence of the algorithm in the first place.

Kenn had been the one feeding them information. Maybe this is why he used to ask me to watch out for Hideo's safety. It was never actually out of concern. It was to *keep tabs* on Hideo.

The truth of it hits me so hard I can barely breathe. My gaze flies from Taylor up to the glass box overlooking the arena, where Kenn now sits. His silhouette is angled down toward us.

Maybe he had even been the one who'd let Jax slip into Hideo's secured box in the stadium during the failed assassination attempt.

My breaths are coming in short gasps now. Had Taylor offered him a stake in this mission in exchange for his help? She must have. And he, frustrated and ambitious, had agreed.

Fifty-nine seconds until the beta lenses patch.

Hideo's attention is no longer on Taylor. He's staring at Zero, whose eyes—unmistakably that of Hideo's brother—stay cold and unfeeling.

Hideo's studying Zero as if everything I'd told him couldn't possibly be real.

"Sasuke," Hideo says hoarsely. The wave of his anger shifts into grief.

All semblance of practicality has vanished from him. There's a note of wild hope in his voice, like Zero might snap out of it if they could just talk to each other. And for a moment, even knowing that it's impossible, I think it might work.

But Zero doesn't react in any way. Watching him in front of his brother for the first time in years, I can't tell if he registers any emotion at all. Beside him, Jax's hand is wrapped tightly around the handle of her gun.

We are standing in the middle of a powder keg, and the fuse is about to blow.

Thirty seconds until the beta lenses patch.

"This is the deal, isn't it, Hideo?" Zero finally says. His voice sounds like it always does, and there's not even the slightest hint of recognition in it. "Or has Emika not told you what she should?"

Hideo looks at me. His eyes are black with anguish, filled with a deep feeling of loss, the realization that everything I told him was true, that Sasuke is looking at him, saying his name but not reacting to what it means. When he speaks again, his voice grates, harsh with desperation. "You're not a work of code," he says. "You're my *brother*. I know you're reluctant to hurt us. I can hear in your voice the memory of who you are. You know, don't you?"

"Of course I know," Zero replies, in that eerily calm way of his.

The words hit Hideo like bullets.

Taylor just smiles at him in that knowing, manipulative way. "Look at it this way, Hideo. You created your life's work because of your brother's disappearance," she says. "Everything happens for a reason."

"That's the most bullshit saying in the world," he snaps.

"Come on. Now your brother is here, when I could have just let him die of his illness. Is this not better?"

Hideo narrows his eyes at her. The pure hatred in his gaze—the rage that has surfaced at the sight of what Taylor did to his brother, that Taylor is now threatening my life—is boiling over now. The deep, soulless fury I've witnessed in him before, the scarred knuckles . . . it's nothing compared to this.

Taylor glances at me. She's expecting me to follow through on my promise now, that I will break into Hideo's mind.

Zero seconds.

An electric current rushes through my head. Nearby, Hammie and Roshan also flinch. The beta lenses start to patch, steadily downloading the algorithm onto them.

I pull out the cube that Zero had given me. The hack. And in the space of that moment, I hesitate.

I don't know what gives me away to Taylor. Something about the light in my eyes, the shift in my stance, the slight hesitation in my actions.

Does she know I have other plans?

She suddenly raises a gun and aims it directly at my head. She keeps her eyes on Hideo as her finger hovers over the trigger. "Open the algorithm, Hideo," she says calmly.

Hideo's lips curl into a snarl at her threat to me. His hatred pours over like oil across the ocean.

At the same time, Jax—who had been so still—suddenly draws her own gun and points it directly at Taylor. "Shoot her, and I shoot you." Her hand is clenched tightly enough around her gun's handle to wash her skin white.

Taylor looks sharply at her. This time, the woman is surprised. "What's this?" she murmurs. "You're in on this, too, Jackson?"

Jax winces at the use of her full name.

Taylor tightens her lips. Deep anger flashes across her face. I remember what Jax had said to me about Taylor's greatest fear. *Death.* Now her daughter is threatening her with it.

Panic floods Jax's eyes, that terror she'd had as a small girl cowering under the influence of someone supposed to be her mother. Her hand trembles. But this time, she doesn't back down. Everything building up inside her since the death of Sasuke has erupted to the surface, and its strength keeps her arm lifted.

She tears her eyes away from Taylor long enough to glance at me. "*Now,*" she hisses.

Hideo, I gasp through our Link.

Taylor looks back at him and tightens her finger on her gun's trigger.

Hideo moves.

He snaps his fingers once, pulling up his own small, rotating box to hover between us. Before I even have time to register that this is the key to opening his algorithm, he flicks his wrist and unlocks it.

A maze of colors bursts from the box, a million bright nodes connected to each other with lines of light, the way a brain's circuits link to one another. It's massive and intricate, extending far beyond our space on the floor to fill the entire arena. For one brief instant, I am looking into a web of commands that can control the minds of every single person in the world hooked up to the NeuroLink. If time could have stopped right now, I would stop to marvel at this frightening masterpiece.

Hideo homes in on Taylor's account, seizes it, and links it to the algorithm. Her mind's palette suddenly appears as a new node in the matrix, connected to Zero by a glowing thread.

Hideo flicks his wrist again. The thread snaps.

Taylor shudders violently as he rips away her control of Zero.

Now, Hideo, I cry out silently. The cube in my hand flickers in and out as I tremble. *Destroy the algorithm.*

But Hideo's eyes are still black with hate. And I realize, abruptly, that he isn't done yet—he's not satisfied with this part of our plan, to merely hook Taylor into the algorithm and force her to free Zero from her control. He's snapped loose from his measured self and allowed his rage to run free. He's going to unleash the full, unthinking force of his power on her.

"*No*—" I start to say. But it's too late.

In that same instant, Taylor's lips part in terror as she realizes what he's about to do. She holds out a hand instinctively in front of her.

Hideo narrows his eyes. Through our Link, I hear him send a quiet, unspoken command to Taylor.

Die.

26

I see it happen in slow motion.

Taylor doesn't even have time to utter a sound. She only gets a fraction of a second—and all she can do is turn her disbelieving expression to Hideo, her eyes dilated like a deer's at the end of the hunt, right after the predator's teeth sink in. Her lips part, but she never gets a chance to say a final word. Maybe she'd wanted to scream.

Then her face goes milk white. Her eyes roll back. Her legs give way like their bones have been crushed within her flesh.

She collapses hard on the floor, her head cracking with a horrifying sound. She lies there in a sickening, wrong way, and I'm reminded of the way I'd seen Tremaine fall to the ground, the spray of blood against the wall.

At the same time, the node that was her mind's palette flashes a brilliant, blinding white—then vanishes, deleted from the rest of the algorithm. The links to it snap back into place with other nodes, as if Taylor's mind were never there. The command had instantly forced her brain to shut itself down.

She's dead.

My mind is a blank slate, with only a single thought coming in through my shock.

Hideo killed her with a single command.

This is supposed to be the one thing that the algorithm was designed to protect against—it was supposed to cure humanity of impulsive violence, of inflicting pain and suffering on anyone else.

Yet in this single moment, in his rage, for everything she had done to his brother, everything she threatened to do to me . . . Hideo disproved everything he worked for.

Jax looks stunned. But Zero . . .

Zero turns to face Hideo. There is nothing on his face except for an icy smile. He isn't shocked at all. He nods his head, like everything just went according to his plans.

He lifts a hand, waves it once, and brings up a bit of code I've never seen before. This is not the virus he had shown me. Before Hideo can react, Zero installs it into the algorithm.

The web of nodes around us shakes—and then, right before my eyes, the colors change, the millions of nodes of blues and reds and greens shifting, one by one, into black. It sweeps across them in a tidal wave. It reaches Hideo and, in an instant, severs his control of the algorithm.

Zero's helmet folds back up, shielding his face from view once again. Then the algorithm shifts into place *with him*.

I realize what has happened before anyone can say it.

Zero had no plans to destroy the algorithm. He has instead

merged with it. I watch in horror as the new algorithm solidifies with Zero at the center of it.

His artificial mind had managed to evolve, to circumvent Taylor's control, and he had been developing it independently all along behind her back.

Hideo tries to wrestle his control back—but it's too late. He has been cut entirely from his creation.

One look at Jax's face tells me that Zero's plan had never been the same as Taylor's. He had never intended for her to take control of the algorithm or even to potentially destroy it, and his goal had never been to stop only Hideo from using the NeuroLink to control people.

He had done this solely to take control of the NeuroLink and the algorithm. He knew. He'd guessed that if Hideo saw Taylor, he would kill her himself. It's the whole reason why he let me reconnect with Hideo in the first place, why he concocted this plan for me to cozy up to Hideo and persuade him to show me his algorithm. It's probably why no one ever caught me doing what I was doing, because Zero knew and wanted me to go through with all my plans.

And that means, I realize, that Zero had always *wanted* Taylor dead. She had tortured his mind so severely that she had molded him into the same monster she became.

In one move, Zero has gotten rid of the person who took his life, has forced Hideo to show the folly of his algorithm, and has taken control. In one move, he has gained the most powerful instrument in the world.

My shock is reflected in the faces of Hideo and Jax. What have we done?

The cube. The virus I have. This is still the only moment when

I have a chance to break into Zero's mind. I could hack him. I lunge forward, aiming to sync the cube into his account. It flashes a blinding blue-white.

But I'm too late.

Zero turns to look at me. "Thank you, Emika," he says.

I don't know what happens next, because everything goes black.

27

Sounds and sensations around me flicker in and out: Jax shouting at me, a din of voices I don't recognize, and then the feeling of floating in midair. Maybe the shock is too much. Maybe Zero had uttered a command that killed me, and I just don't know that I'm dead.

My dreams—they must be dreams, because they make no sense—are sharp and strange, switching abruptly from one scene to the next. There's a small boy wearing a blue scarf, and I'm chasing after him, trying in vain to tell him to turn around. I'm a child again, holding Dad's hand as we walk together through Central Park. Today he looks sophisticated, his hair smoothed into a slick shine and his jeans and black shirt switched out for a well-tailored blazer and trousers. We've gotten out of an afternoon concert at Carnegie Hall, and he's in a bright mood, singing an off-key rendition of the concert piece as I twirl in a tulle dress. I want to lean into the familiarity of it, the loudness and the sheer joy.

He points out something in the distance, and I rise up on my toes to look at what it might be. There's a dark spot in front of us, right on the park's path, like a paint streak. When I stare at it longer, it starts to grow, expanding until it soaks the path and covers everything around us.

Dad pauses, afraid, his hand gripping mine tighter. When I look around me, the park is gone, and in its place is the Dark World, the towering nonsense skyscrapers reaching up into a black sky, the crooked dark streets and the neon red lights of exposed names hovering over us.

Wake up, Emika Chen.

An amused voice tugs me gradually out of the darkness.

When everything comes back into view, I'm in a dimly lit room with a white ceiling and floor. Tall glass windowpanes line every wall.

This is the room where I saw Jax shoot Tremaine.

We're back at the Innovation Institute, only now I'm on the other side of the glass. It takes me a moment to realize that I'm strapped down tightly to a chair, and another moment to notice the figure standing several feet away from me.

Of course the voice had belonged to Zero. He's shielded behind his armor, and when he glances casually over his shoulder at me, I see that his face is masked behind virtual steel and glass. His hands are tucked easily behind his back, his chin tilted in thoughtful curiosity. It's such a Hideo-like gesture.

A note of fear cuts through my foggy mind. *Hideo. Where is he? Is he here? Is he okay?*

"What happened?" I say. My words still sound a little out of place, slower than my thoughts are coming to me.

"Stay still," Zero says, his voice echoing in the space.

Nearby, a girl with short, silver-white hair has her back turned to me as she pulls containers of lenses off a shelf and places them on a counter.

Jax. The name floats up to the surface of my groggy mind. Jax, who had been working with me. I watch her, wanting to scream. What if she has been in on it all along? Has played me for a fool? Hadn't she shot Tremaine without a second thought? What made me think that she could possibly be trustworthy?

She turns around now, so that I can see her face, and takes a box of lenses to the sink. There's something off about the way she glides from one activity to the next, as if she were on autopilot rather than conscious.

Zero must be controlling her, using the palette of his mind to move Jax—the girl he'd once loved, the one he'd given up his freedom to protect—around like a puppeteer would his marionette.

An icy claw grips my heart.

That means Zero must now be in control of everyone in the world who'd been using Hideo's lenses, anyone who Hideo had originally connected to his algorithm.

Jax, I try to say, but my voice chokes, dry from hoarseness. Had I been screaming?

"I wiped your NeuroLink account clean and rebooted your connection," Zero calls back to me as he walks toward the other side of the room. "It's updating, and it will go more smoothly for you if you let yourself relax. This isn't something you'd want to glitch, Emika."

Central Park. My father. The boy with the blue scarf. What I thought were dreams were probably just a mash-up of all of my Memories and saved recordings, jumbled into a fray as they were deleted from my account.

And what I thought was me passing out—the darkness that had engulfed me—was actually Zero powering off my NeuroLink, so that all I could see in my view was a black field. Everything I had—my level, my Warcross account, everything in it—is all gone, downloaded into some external place I can't access.

This isn't something you'd want to glitch, Emika.

"What do you mean?" I finally croak out through my disorientation. "What kind of glitch? What are you doing to me?"

"I'm not going to hurt you," he replies. "Your lenses—and your connection to me—are just not as stable as I'd expect, given how much control I have over everyone else. I think you may have broken something when you launched the hack against me."

The cube I'd used. A vague recollection of the moment comes back to me now, splintered and blurry, the brilliant blue-white flash followed by suffocating darkness. It hadn't worked . . . I don't have a pathway into Zero's mind. Not that I can see.

But if I'm supposed to be completely under Zero's control . . . then I don't quite feel that, either. Something about the hack colliding with Zero's mind must have altered my lenses, preventing me from being properly connected to him.

That's what Jax must be doing right now—preparing new lenses to give me, replacing mine and finally, properly, connecting me to Zero and the algorithm so that he can have full control.

I struggle against my bonds, but they're strapped so tightly that I can't do anything more than wriggle my arms and legs by a fraction. *I have to get out of here.*

Zero pauses on the other side of the room beside a second raised gurney, to which someone else is tied tightly. I pause in my struggles at the sight of him.

It's Hideo.

He looks drugged and barely conscious, his head leaning against his headrest, and a light sheen of sweat gleams on his face. It's a sharp contrast to the last moment when we'd stood together.

When he'd lifted his hand, his eyes black with fury, and *willed* Taylor to die.

After all this time, no matter what the situation or his mood, I've only seen Hideo in control—in his office, in the arena, in his home. Even in despair, with his heart torn open, he never looked the way he does now. Helpless. His creation wrenched out of his control.

In spite of everything I've seen him do, I can't help but feel afraid now that he's no longer running the NeuroLink and the algorithm. It means that someone much, much worse is now in command.

Zero stands in front of the gurney. If he feels anything at the sight of his brother, he doesn't show it as he lifts a steel hand and grips Hideo's chin.

I suck in my breath sharply.

I'd thought Zero was walking around in here as a virtual simulation. But no, he's in the armored suit that I'd seen him testing with Taylor on the night that Tremaine had been shot. The robot that had moved its arm in sync with Zero's.

Zero's mind is operating from within a *real* metal suit, an artificial being that seems alive in every technical sense.

He forces Hideo to turn his face up to meet his. One brother versus another. Zero studies him curiously, like a specimen, before he releases Hideo again. He folds his hands behind his back and flexes his steel fingers in a smooth wave, stalking a slow circle around his bound brother.

I clench my teeth, the white-hot heat of anger rising in me in a wave. "Leave him alone," I growl.

Zero pauses to look at me. "You still care deeply for him," he says quietly.

"You think?" I snap.

"Tell me, Emika, what that's like?" Now he sounds fascinated.

"He's done terrible things. And yet I can still sense your connection to him."

I realize with a start that it's because Sasuke was never old enough to understand what love really means. Not even the early, innocent feelings he had for Jax could possibly compare to how complicated love actually is. He'd lost his humanity before he was ever able to experience that. My anger wavers as my heart breaks for him.

"Whatever it was that you did, Emika," Zero says, addressing me as he turns back to Hideo, "it seems you affected the lenses of those you've Linked with before, too. And that means his." He finishes a full circle around Hideo and leans close to him. "But don't worry. We'll fix that easily enough."

His words, mockingly soothing, bear an echo of Taylor's thought process. Even though she's dead, her influence over him must have been so complete and so extreme that it still lingers underneath those smooth plates of steel.

"But first," Zero continues, finally turning away from Hideo and heading back toward me. Every muscle in me tenses as he approaches. "Let's fix you."

I glare at him, wishing I could see some sign of Sasuke trapped inside, but the only thing staring back at me through his opaque mask is my own reflection.

By the sink, Jax has ripped open the box with the lenses and pulled out a set. I glance at her again. She still has that blankness on her face, going about her motions like she's not entirely here.

Then . . . her eyes flicker to me. I realize that Zero doesn't know I've Linked with her before. Her flint-gray irises gleam under the fluorescent light. In that instant, I see her familiar wit, her mind alert behind a carefully controlled expression. She's not under Zero's influence, no—but merely pretending to be.

She shakes her head once at me, then her eyes look toward the door. A red light illuminates it from above, suggesting that it's locked—but beside the door is the emergency box I remember from the first night I'd been in the institute. I look back at Jax, who goes back to preparing my new lenses at a counter closer to the door.

Hope cuts through my dread. Maybe Jax is still my ally, after all. If I can stall for more time, maybe she can help us get out of here before Zero forces the new lenses on me.

"You can't be real," I manage to choke out as I stare up at him. "I don't believe you. You're nothing but a simulation."

"Then see for yourself." Zero reaches over and presses a flat button near the top of my gurney. The metal cuff restraining my left wrist snaps open with a *clang*, freeing my hand.

I pull it immediately out of the binding, flexing my wrist in relief. My eyes return to him. Hesitantly, I reach out toward him. He doesn't move.

My hand touches his upper arm. I almost flinch. Cold, hard metal. There's nothing human about the steel plate my fingers brush against, nothing that suggests a soul might exist inside. And yet . . . here he is, moving and functional, alive in every technical sense.

"Can you . . . feel that?" I find myself asking.

"I'm aware that you're touching me," he replies. "I can *feel* it, logically, if you can call it that."

"Can you sense pain?"

"No. I don't understand my limbs in the same way you do."

"Do you remember what that was like?"

"Yes. I remember everything."

"Except what matters."

"Except what doesn't matter," he corrects me.

I withdraw my hand and let my arm drop back to my side. Zero closes his fingers around my wrist. He pushes it into place against the metal cuff, ignoring my pleading eyes as he snaps it shut again.

"I don't understand," I whisper. "Why do you want this?"

He smiles in amusement, as if someone like him could still understand such a human emotion. "You already know. It's the same answer that Taylor would have given you, that Hideo himself probably once gave you."

"But they had goals because they're *human*, flesh and blood. Taylor wanted control because she's afraid without it. Hideo did it out of love for *you*." I lean forward, straining against my bonds, and grit my teeth at him. "What do you get out of controlling others, besides the satisfaction of doing so?"

"Freedom, of course," he replies. "Now I can do anything. Enter anyone's mind." He nods out toward the dark hall at the world beyond these walls. "I can be everywhere at once and nowhere at all."

And just like that, I understand. It's the exact opposite of what Sasuke had endured at Taylor's hands. When he'd been human, he had been her prisoner, trapped within the confines of this institute for years and subjected to unspeakable horrors, until he'd finally died and had his mind tethered to hers. He'd been fully at her beck and call.

In seizing control of everything, Zero is taking back his freedom and more. It's his revenge against Taylor for all that she had stolen from him.

Taylor's death.

"But there's more to it than that," I go on. "You set Hideo up to kill Taylor, didn't you? You made sure she was with us because you *knew* how Hideo would react to seeing her. You wanted to bring his creation crashing down around him, and you wanted to see Taylor realize the moment she'd lost in her own game." My voice turns more desperate now, angrier, as I make the connections. "You wanted her dead, and you wanted Hideo to do it."

Zero is silent. Something about my words has plucked a string in him. I barrel on before he can continue.

"You wanted to show him how flawed his plan was from the start." My heart trembles as I talk. "You wanted Hideo to realize how he had corrupted the NeuroLink with his algorithm, and the only way you could show him that—the *only* way to get through to the brother you love—was to force him to demonstrate it in front of the entire world." I take a deep breath. "And that's because *Sasuke* wanted you to do it. Because he's still there, somewhere inside you."

I don't know how much of my words reach Zero. Maybe he doesn't care at all. He's nothing more than a web of algorithms controlling a machine, after all, and whatever is still human about him has simply been translated into code.

But Zero tenses at Sasuke's name.

In that moment, I know. Everything Jax and I had assumed is true. Sasuke is still in there. He had, in his own way, tried to stop his brother from destroying himself.

"You're not entirely gone," I whisper.

"You like to solve things, don't you?" Zero says.

"Every locked door has a key," I reply.

Zero turns slightly, as if he'd studied the tattooed words running along my bared clavicle. Behind him, Jax has turned to face us, the new lenses in her hands and ready to be put on my eyes. I don't dare look directly at her. When is she going to make her move?

Zero leans toward me, his presence overpowering. "We're not so different, Emika. Your desire to control and solve is the same as mine. There's nothing you'd like more than to be able to control your world. All the terrible things that have happened to you have been things you couldn't do anything about. Your father's death. Your time at the foster home. Hideo's betrayal of your trust."

Zero makes a casual gesture in the air, and suddenly he conjures a virtual image of my father standing in the room, his familiar smile on his gentle face, his silhouette against the door, outlined in light. He reaches over to pin a bit of cloth on a bustier. I can hear him humming.

The sight threads through me with the precise pain of a needle. Dad glances at me and grins, and all the air rushes from my lungs. Some illogical part of me reaches out, desperate to touch him. *That's him. He's real.*

No. He's not. Zero is rendering him here right in front of me, showing me what life could be like if Dad were still here. He's showing me the inside of the NeuroLink linked directly with his mind, how he will soon be able to control everything I see, everything in the virtual world for everyone.

"Wouldn't you rather have saved your father into a pure data form, to make him live forever?" Zero presses. It's a genuine question, without a hint of malice in it. "Wouldn't you like to see him walking around in your life, just as I walk around in yours? Is this half-life so bad?"

I don't dare admit out loud that he's right. That his words tempt me more than I can say. *Is* it so bad? I imagine Zero as Sasuke, a little boy who could live out the ghost version of his life, grow up and go to school, play games with his brother and laugh with his friends. Fall in love. If Zero wanted, he could make this reality for himself now, creating a virtual version of this life for himself. He could live out a million different lives.

I tear my eyes away from the sight of my father. Tears blur my vision. Zero's manipulating me. If he gets the new lenses on me, he can trap me in this false reality and make me believe anything.

"Go to hell," I whisper with a snarl.

Zero finally, mercifully, leans away from me. He nods once at Jax, who has the new lenses ready for me. "Put her under," he says. "I don't have time to deal with her struggling."

Jax meets my eyes. For a moment, I think she'll do exactly as Zero says.

Then her hand darts to the gun at her belt. In one move, she whips it out, points it at the door, and shoots with barely a glance.

The bullet hits the emergency sensor.

Every light in the building shuts off in unison. The room plunges into blackness—then is washed in crimson red as emergency lights flare on.

The door clicks open at the same time an alarm begins to wail overhead.

Jax swings her gun toward the button on my gurney, right next to my head, and fires. Another perfect hit. My metal cuffs snap open. I almost collapse to the floor.

She points toward Hideo's gurney, firing again. He's freed, crumpling to his hands and knees.

In the scarlet glow, Zero's silhouette is an ominous black hole. Even though he's embedded in a machine, I can sense the surprise coming from him.

Adrenaline born from terror surges through me. I scramble to my feet and sprint toward Hideo.

Zero's head snaps to Jax. "You're with them," he says, his voice low and deadly.

Jax doesn't answer. She just faces him with her steady look and raises her gun again. "No," she replies. "I'm with you."

Then she shoots him.

28

Zero's reflexes are inhumanly fast. His body snaps sideways—Jax's shot misses his neck and instead hits him in the shoulder with the scream of metal tearing through metal.

Jax fires again, but Zero lunges for her at the same time. Her second shot strikes his leg, sending up another shower of sparks. His leg twists oddly, throwing off the grace of his movements.

I reach Hideo. He's struggling to his feet, but his motions are slower as he fights against whatever drug is coursing through his system. I pull his arm over my shoulders and force him upright. We make a run for the door.

Zero turns to stop us, but Jax's hits have broken parts of the suit, making him limp. Still, he's terrifyingly fast. As we reach the door, Zero's metal fingers close around a fistful of my shirt.

Jax is on him in an instant. Under the red lights, her eyes have the savage glint of a killer. She strikes his wrist as hard as she can.

She can't break the metal, but it is enough to loosen his grip and for me to slide through. "This way," she gasps out over the alarm as she shoves the door open and darts out into the hall.

Hideo and I rush after her. Behind us, Zero's suit twists in our direction.

The halls are washed in bloody light. Around the bend comes the pounding of footsteps growing louder and louder.

Jax glances at me. "Everyone in this building is under his control," she whispers. "Get out of the institute. Don't go through the front—there are guards swarming around there. Do you remember the way to the side entrance?"

I retrace the path I'd taken through the building on my first night here, then nod. Beside me, Hideo is regaining some of his strength, but he still leans heavily against me. We're not going to be able to move very quickly.

"Good," she continues. "Get out, then find a way into Zero's mind. When—"

She cuts off. Her stare darts over my shoulder, and I turn to see Zero's dark silhouette behind us.

He flattens one metal hand against the wall. Overhead, all the speakers installed in the ceilings buzz with static, followed by his deep voice.

"You're wasting your time."

Every scarlet light in the building goes out, plunging us into total darkness.

I can't see anything, not even my hands in front of me or Hideo at my side. It's as if we'd been swallowed by a void. At the same time, a round of clicks come from the building's doors, the unmistakable sound of locks being activated.

I can be everywhere, Zero had said. And now, his mind is operating the institute's security system, trapping us in.

From the speakers, Zero's voice envelops us in this impenetrable darkness. "Why are you doing this?" he asks. His question is for Jax.

Jax doesn't answer, but I feel her fingers close around my arm and pull me forward. "The panic room," she tells me. "It's the only place in this building not hooked up to the digital system. Get to the end of this hall and take the first set of stairs. Keep going up until you can't anymore. When you reach the last floor, you'll see two doors at the end of that hall. To their left is a third, embedded flat against the wall. You'll have to open it manually. Lock yourselves in."

The panic room. Tremaine had tried in vain to reach that room before he'd been caught.

I can hear in her voice that Jax isn't coming with us. "But you—"

"Just *do it*. I'm going to hold him off." There's no sound of worry in her words, no sense of fear. She sounds exactly as she did the very first day I met her—cold and confident.

I want to scream at her to come with us, but instead, I feel Hideo's weight leaning heavier against me as she steps away from us. Over her shoulder, she calls at us, "Why are you still here?"

I utter a curse under my breath and do as she says, turning on my grid system.

Instantly, the halls around me glow with a system of lines, showing me a layout of the hall, as if a dim light were still shining in here—

But it's not quite right. Usually, when I use a virtual grid, it can overlay anything, guiding a user through fog or rain or snow. But in here, Zero must have tampered with what the NeuroLink is able to read about the institute, because my grid vanishes into misty patches, its data incomplete. The building probably has all sorts of virtual barriers in place, transforming the halls into illusions.

At least I can also see an outline of Hideo beside me. Jax has her back turned to us, her figure blanketed in green lines, and she's facing Zero, a completely dark silhouette looming in the middle of the hall behind us.

Move. Hideo and I start staggering away. Somewhere in the halls around us pound the footsteps of approaching guards, caught under Zero's spell. If they reach us, we're not going to have Jax's help fending them off.

Behind us comes Jax's voice as she confronts Zero. "Remember when you couldn't leave me behind?" she calls out.

"Get out of my way, Jax." I hear the metallic thud of his suit's footsteps and dare to glance backward.

Jax hoists both her guns, spins them in unison, and crouches down against one side of the hall, ready for Zero to attack. Her pose reminds me of when she had appeared beside me on feet so light she seemed ready to fly.

"It's my turn now," she replies. "And one way or another, this time we're going to leave this place together."

Hideo's weight lifts from my shoulders as he summons the strength to move on his own. His hand finds mine, and in the dark, I take it, squeezing it as tightly as I can. We force ourselves to keep going.

Ahead, the hall is starting to shroud with virtual mist, making it difficult for me to see the grids of the hallway. I slow, sliding my hand against the wall. Through the fog dart glimpses of shadows, figures shuffling left and right, others looking like they're running toward us. Sweat beads on my forehead.

"They're not real," Hideo whispers, his eyes fixed on them in the dark. "The grid's not outlining over them in green."

Sure enough, one of the shadows dissipates into smoke the instant it reaches us. *Not real.* I shut my eyes and keep creeping forward. The steps we've taken scroll through my mind in a list of numbers. Are we ever going to reach the stairwell? Maybe we're not even going in the right direction—

Then my hand hits the groove of a door. I freeze, running my fingers along the metal bar spanning the door's width.

I shove myself against it. We burst into the stairwell, where the grid in my view abruptly reappears in crystal clear lines, highlighting the steps that wind up. In the hall we'd just left behind come the pops of gunshots.

Jax.

I force myself to move as Hideo seizes the banister and leaps up the stairs. His movements still seem exhausted, but at least he's able to keep pace with me. We go up, up, up until we've sprinted three flights and the stairs end. I throw open the stairwell door and stumble into a new hall.

The first thing I see is a pair of figures hurtling toward us. My eyes go straight to the green grids overlaid on their figures. *They're real.*

Guards.

The thought hits me just in time. I drop to a crouch and roll to the other side of the hall, swinging my leg out and catching one of them right at the ankles. He loses his balance and falls forward with a grunt.

The second guard twists around and points a weapon in my direction. I duck, bracing myself—but an instant later he goes flying as Hideo tackles him, ramming him against the wall. The guard throws a fist at Hideo's face, but Hideo is too quick—he dodges, twists the man's arm around his back, and shoves hard.

A sickening crunch, followed by a shriek of pain. The guard

drops his weapon with a clatter. Hideo swipes it up, tucking it at his belt, and rushes to me as I scramble to my feet. Already, the sound of more guards behind us is approaching fast.

The panic room should be at the end of this hall.

We sprint down the gridded corridor. Ahead, it fades again into thick virtual mist, but there's no time to stop and think about it now. We hurtle into the blind spot.

"Almost there," I gasp out. But when I look to my side, Hideo's green figure has also vanished from sight, swallowed in the fog.

I keep my hand running along the wall, feeling for doors. *Hideo,* I whisper, sending it through our Link. He doesn't answer. Had everything connecting us shut down when we stepped into this zone?

A presence near me makes me reach a hand out. "Hideo?" I murmur.

It isn't him. Instead, a steel silhouette emerges from the fog. *Zero.*

Jax. Had he gotten past her? He must have. Had he—the thought jolts through me, too terrible to linger on.

He seizes my arm and hurls me. I go flying across the hall and slam hard into the floor on my back. The impact knocks all the wind out of me. My eyes go wide. I gasp like a fish on land. Above me, Zero comes striding out of the mist, his masked face turned down in my direction.

I scramble backward on my hands and feet, my teeth clenched, edging next to the wall again and hunting desperately for the doors at the end of the corridor.

We're not going to make it.

Zero raises an arm and aims down toward me. I try in vain to roll away.

As I move, another figure materializes beside me. Hideo. He's in a crouch against the floor, and his green-gridded eyes are turned up to Zero, narrowed in rage. His bruised hands are clenched into tight fists. His voice emerges in a growl. "Don't. Touch. Her."

He throws himself at Zero with all his strength. It's enough of a surprise attack to knock Zero backward, and the two of them hurtle to the floor in a crash. "Hurry, Emika!" Hideo shouts.

I hop to my feet and run my hand along the wall. *Come on, come on.*

And then I find it. The shape of the first door. Then, the second. My fingers halt on the groove of a third sliding door. The panic room.

I whirl to look back down the hall. Through the patches of fog emerge Hideo and Zero. Zero has the advantage of brute strength in his metal suit—but Hideo is fast on his feet, nimble where Zero has been slowed down by the injuries Jax has inflicted. Hideo kicks out at Zero's metal chest, sending him back a step. Zero recovers too quickly. He whips a hand out and grabs Hideo's neck, shoving him back against a wall. Then he raises a fist and hurls it into Hideo's stomach.

Hideo lets out a choked cry.

I fumble for the panic room's door handle until my fingers finally close around it. "Hideo!" I scream out as I yank the door open with all my strength. Farther down the hall, more guards are arriving on the scene.

Hideo glances in my direction. He clenches his teeth, pulls his legs up to his chest, and kicks at Zero as hard as he can. Once, twice. The third time, Zero's fingers loosen slightly from around Hideo's neck. It's enough for him to slip free. Hideo hits the ground and runs toward me.

I reach out, seizing his arm as he approaches me, and pull us inside the panic room. I slide the door shut right as Zero gets to the entrance. The last thing I see before I snap the physical hinge across the door, locking us in, is the sight of Zero's shielded face.

Then we're in, the door sealing us behind a thick barrier of steel.

I fall backward onto the floor and scramble away from the door. On the other side comes the sound of pounding—Zero, or his guards, trying to break it down—but we must be behind so many layers that it's hard to hear anything. Inside the room, panels line one wall, showing a series of views of the lab. My breaths come out in wheezing gasps.

Hideo utters a soft groan behind me. I turn to see him slumped against the wall, one hand clutching his side. Only now do I notice the dark red staining his shirt.

I drop to my knees beside him. "Shit," I whisper, touching his arm. He winces as he gingerly moves his hand enough for me to see the wound. Between his trembling, bloodstained fingers is a deep gash, likely made by a blade.

Zero hadn't just hit him in the side with his fist. There must have been a sharp weapon embedded on him, too, and it had ripped open Hideo's flesh.

"Here," I whisper, trying to keep my voice from shaking as I shrug off my jacket and loop it around his waist. Through the wound seeps a frightening pool of blood.

Hideo lets out another clenched moan as I pull the jacket tight against the gash. His breaths are coming in short gasps, and his face is shock white, beaded with sweat. I crouch with him and clutch his bloody hand, overwhelmed by how helpless I feel. Everything is falling apart.

It takes me a second to register what Hideo's whispering. "I'm sorry," he says over and over again. "I'm sorry. I'm so sorry."

My dream. His quiet voice, his hands pulling me close. I squeeze his hand tighter and rest my head against his, cringing at his cold, clammy skin, before looking at him again.

His eyes meet mine. They are so overwhelmingly dark. "I just wanted . . ."

"I know," I choke out, forcing back the tears in my eyes that threaten to spill over. "Concentrate on breathing. Give me time to get into Zero's mind."

Hideo closes his eyes, his lashes resting against his cheeks. I fumble in my pocket for the lenses that Jax had tossed at me. Finally, I pull one of the boxes out and twist off the caps to stare down at the new lenses that will connect me with Zero.

"Link with me once you're in," Hideo whispers as my gaze goes up to him again. He gives me a weak but resolute nod. I nod back. One of the lenses trembles against the tip of my finger.

If this goes wrong, it's all over.

I bring up my hack to hover over my palm again, making sure it's still here and intact in my account. I hesitate a final time. Outside, a *clang* against the door makes the entire room shudder.

Hideo and I exchange a silent stare.

Then I remove my old lenses, and put in the new ones.

A tingle rushes through me. *Quickly now,* I tell myself as I instantly bring up the cube. Before the system can wholly connect me with Zero's mind, I open the cube and let it run.

It bursts into a sphere around me. The panic room vanishes.

I find my virtual self standing in the middle of a black field. It stretches in every direction, a tangible darkness that pushes against the boundaries of my mind, threatening to close in like the deep ocean against a diver. I brace myself against it. Maybe Jax and I had been wrong all along. I'm never going to be able to keep Zero from seizing control.

But the sphere around me holds, pushes back.

At the same time, a single door materializes before me. I know immediately that it is a door leading into Zero's mind.

Zero's mind. It's here. I can step in. A flood of hope rushes through me. I reach out and send a Link to Hideo.

He doesn't respond right away, and for a moment, I fear the worst. *He's already gone.*

Then he accepts it. A familiar wave of his emotions reaches me, and then he's here, standing beside me in this virtual hellscape. In virtual reality, he doesn't look injured, but his movements are slightly jerky, as if he were cutting in and out in the blink of an eye, his real-life pain affecting his connection to the NeuroLink.

"I know this glitch," Hideo says as he steps closer to the door. "One of our engineers had pointed it out, early on, and I'd tasked Kenn with making sure it was patched properly." He narrows his eyes at the mention of his former friend's name.

"Then he lied to you," I finish, and Hideo nods grimly.

For the sake of money, or promises of freedom, Kenn had sold the glitch instead to Taylor.

"Maybe it will all come back to haunt him," Hideo adds. "And this will turn out to be the glitch that saves all of us."

I put a hand against the door's handle. "Let's hope so," I reply.

I push it open. We both step back as the door itself disintegrates into nothing, revealing behind it the first glimpse into the world of Zero's mind—pitch-black, like staring into deep space.

I step forward first. My feet float over an expanse of nothingness beyond the door. Hideo follows me through a second later.

The first change I notice on me in here is that I'm clad from neck to toe in black armor. Hideo is dressed the same. He looks so much like Zero from the neck down, in fact, that I'm unnerved by the sight of him in my peripheral vision.

An invite from Hideo appears in my view. **Play Warcross?** it asks.

I accept it.

The darkness around us ripples. It blurs silver and gray before a virtual world finally materializes, a twisted place formed from Zero's mind corrupting the NeuroLink's Warcross databases of worlds.

Hideo and I find ourselves standing on a stone bridge, staring out at a crumbling city that continues upward and downward forever, surrounding us. Everything is constantly moving—new stairs rise, old stairs break into falling stone, bridges connecting buildings form and shatter, towers morph into shape before collapsing. Dark, glittering marbles hover in the air. I feel an instinctive urge to reach for them, like they're power-ups, while simultaneously knowing they are land mines that need to be avoided.

My armor shifts too, and the equipment I usually have in a Warcross game appears, the familiar pouches and straps hanging from my belt.

Shadowy figures move between the shifting buildings.

Hideo looks at me. "We can't get through this with just the two of us," he says. "We need a team."

A grim smile hovers on the edges of my lips. "We have a team."

29

It's possible that I can't reach Hammie, Asher, and Roshan at all anymore. They've each been Linked with me before—but when I bring up my directory, it looks like a blank slate, and my stomach sinks. Maybe they hadn't come out of the arena without being tethered to Zero's mind.

Then, gradually, it fills in. Lists of names. My connection from inside this panic room is slightly slower from the thick layers of metal surrounding us, but it holds.

I find my teammates, each one glowing a faint green, indicating that they're all online.

Asher is the first to answer. "*Ems,*" he says, his voice sounding like a whisper. An instant later, he accepts my invite and appears on the bridge beside us, his avatar also clad in the same black armor.

Relief floods through me at the sight of him. Even though I know neither of us can feel it, I rush forward and throw my arms around him. He startles at my rapid movement, then laughs once and holds me at arm's length.

"Hey, Captain," I greet him.

He shakes his head at me. "Always my wild card," he replies with a grin.

Soon, Hammie connects, too, followed by Roshan. In spite of everything, they're all here. I greet each of them in turn, while they exchange tense nods with Hideo.

Asher glances down in unease at his armor and takes in the moving, shifting city all around us. "What the hell is this place?" he whispers.

"The inside of Zero's mind," I reply. "We have to find Sasuke, so I can give him this." I bring up the files that Jax had given me, the memories and iterations of him from the library.

Hammie's eyes meet Hideo's for a moment, warily, before settling on me. "The arena," she says urgently. "Everything just stopped—and when we came to, you guys were gone. Everyone in there looks like they've been possessed by a spirit. I guess that's technically true, isn't it?"

Hideo exchanges a look with me. I hadn't even had time to spare a thought for how people outside of the institute might be reacting to Zero's control.

"The entire Tokyo Dome is just a sea of silent people," Roshan adds. His lips are tight with fear, and I wonder if he's thinking of Tremaine, trapped under Zero's control as he idles in his hospital bed. No nurses will be taking care of him if they're just frozen in place. "We fled the arena and made it back to Asher's place, but as we went, we saw subways full of people with blank stares. Roads filled with people standing outside their cars, moving like machines." He shudders at the memory. "We saw an old man in the street who looked like he wasn't affected by the lenses. Maybe someone whose beta lenses didn't get patched, or the odd person who didn't use the NeuroLink. Zero must have ordered the others around him to get him. I saw him mobbed by a swarm of people."

A chill rushes through me at the image. "Then we don't have much time," I answer. "This hack is the only thing protecting us from Zero's mind, but that doesn't mean he won't have other ways to get past it to us. There aren't going to be any rules to this, and no one's going to call a foul. We only get one shot to play the game of our lives."

If Zero manages to catch us, he could seize control of our minds and walk inside them, as surely as we're in his. And with his current power, he could do whatever he wished. Erase parts of it. He could immobilize us, leaving us sitting quietly and staring off into space in the same way he'd done to everyone else. He could keep us like that forever, until we died in the real world. He could swallow us whole, if we're not careful.

I'm ashamed that, even after all this time, I still half expect the Riders to step away and opt out of this. After all, this isn't just some normal Warcross game. Why would anyone want to take that chance with me? Who would put themselves in danger alongside me?

But Asher just whistles at the shifting city. A glint appears in his eyes, the irresistible draw of a challenge pulling at the competitive part of him. He had stared down at me with that look during the Wardraft, when he'd chosen me despite the fact that I was completely untested and unranked.

"Good," he answers. "I wouldn't dream of sitting this one out."

Hammie doesn't even hesitate before she taps her chest twice in the signature Warcross salute. "In," she says.

"In," Roshan echoes, his eyes steady on mine.

Hideo touches my shoulder, then nods at the landscape around us. "He knows we're in here," he says, studying the changing structures. He gestures at the shifting architecture. "See how he's already trying to block obvious paths with obstacles? He must be shielding himself."

Hideo points out a door embedded against one tower's wall, with no stairs leading up to it at all. There are other doors in strange places—underneath stairs, on ceilings, open doors displaying nothing but cement. Doors everywhere. It's dizzying, which is exactly what Zero wants.

But Hideo's hand stops in the direction of one last tower. I can just barely make out a door standing alone on its flat rooftop, the entrance hidden almost entirely by pillars. Dark marbles hover along the edges of the tower, spiraling around it in a silent pattern. A stone staircase runs along the side of the tower, from the very top all the way down to the end of the bridge where we stand.

"There," Hideo says to us. "There is a pathway up to that door, even though he's trying to hide it. It might be our way forward."

"How do you know?" Roshan asks. "Why would Zero even give us a path to anything in the first place?"

Hideo turns to him. "Because," he replies, "that's not Zero. That's Sasuke, calling for us. I can recognize his way of thinking here, designing a way through all of this."

I look back up toward the door. Now I see it. This is a landscape of two minds fighting each other.

"So we go up there?" Asher says. Already, he's trying to break down how we'd do it.

"So we go up there," Hideo confirms.

A clicking sound behind us makes me turn. In the darkness materializes a shape that reminds me of Zero—nothing but black armor from head to toe. A second emerges beside him, followed by a third. There must be a dozen of these security bots coming out of the shadows toward us.

They don't seem to know exactly where we are, but they're facing our general direction. As more gather and they start to move faster, I break into a run toward the tower with the stairs.

"Go!" I yell.

We all bolt in unison down the bridge. As the world around us senses our movement, a thunderous crack sounds from above, and I lift my head to see black clouds forming in between the towers that disappear into the heavens. Lightning forks between them.

One strikes a building ahead of us. It breaks off a boulder of cement from the side of the structure, sending it tumbling down to our bridge. We skid to a halt as the boulder smashes into the middle of our path, blocking us from the tower and scattering debris everywhere.

If Sasuke is the one creating this path for us, then Zero is the one trying to destroy it.

"Stand back," I shout as I pull one of the sticks of dynamite from my belt. I sprint to the boulder, light the dynamite, and toss it at its base. Then I dart as far back as I can get.

The explosion rocks the bridge and I'm thrown facedown. Stone and dust fly in every direction as the boulder disintegrates into pieces. I squint as I hop back onto my feet and run to rejoin my teammates. As I near them, they emerge out of the cloud of dust to the security bots hot on their trail. Two of the bots are closing in fast.

"Move, move!" Roshan shouts at me, waving for me to keep pace with the others as they run along the cleared bridge. He skids to a halt, his leg sweeping a half circle on the ground as he turns to face the oncoming figures.

His forearms come up in a cross. A glowing blue shield bursts out from it. He lunges at the first figure, shoving it back with all his strength.

The bot goes flying at the impact from Roshan's shield, tumbling in a crash of metal until it falls from the edge of the bridge and disappears. Roshan brings his arms apart—the single shield reforms into two, one strapped against each of his forearms. He smashes one shield hard into the second running figure.

The hit is so strong that the figure actually crumples, its chest caving in, as it falls onto its back with a heavy crunch.

Roshan's shields vanish as he brings his arms down and whirls to catch up with us.

As we near the base of the tower's staircase, it shudders. My gaze sweeps from the top of the tower down to the bottom of the stairs. As I look on, a huge chunk of stone breaks off from the stair base and falls, crumbling into pieces. More cracks cut up along the staircase.

We skid to a halt at the broken base. The intact staircase hangs high over our heads, too far up for us to reach. It will be impossible to climb up this way. As we look on, cracks continue to cut along the side of the tower.

Hammie breaks into a smile at the sight. Where others might see a disadvantage, she sees footholds.

"Can you do it?" Asher says to her. Even as he says it, some of the cracks widen while others narrow, and new ones lace across the stone.

Hammie doesn't hesitate. "No problem."

"I'm going with you," I say, undoing the rope at my belt. I toss her one end of it, and she straps it tight around her waist. "Once we reach the staircase, we'll drop the rope down."

"What's this, another showdown between us?" Hammie grins sidelong at me before she launches herself at the tower. Her fingers dig into the first crack on the wall as she pulls herself up. "You know I'll beat you."

"I'll let you beat me ten times over if we can just keep ahead of this breaking wall!" I call after her, before following in her wake, the rope dangling between us, and start climbing.

Below us, Hideo turns to see the security bots pass where I'd cleared the boulder from our path—they break into a run toward the base of the tower. He turns to face them, pulls out the blade hanging from his side, and twirls it once before them. Asher and Roshan brace themselves, too.

I look back up to where Hammie is climbing a foot above me. One of the cracks she's gripping suddenly seals back up like a zipper, nearly slicing off her fingers. She lets go just in time and goes tumbling.

I yank out one of my knives and stab into the groove I'm using, bracing myself hard against the wall. The rope between us pulls taut—it nearly takes me with her, but my knife holds, and Hammie jerks to a stop several feet below me. Instantly, she scrambles for the wall again and finds her footing.

I struggle on. The intact staircase comes into view. I inch my way over, then make a giant leap for it. My upper torso hits the stairs, while my lower half dangles over its edge. I grab until my fingers find a solid crack in the stairs, and I haul myself up. Hammie reaches it right after me.

Down below, Hideo lunges at the nearest bot to reach them, cutting its metallic body in half with a shower of sparks.

Hammie loosens the rope from her waist and tosses it down. She wraps her arms around my waist. "Okay," I shout at them. "Up you go!"

Roshan goes first, followed by Asher. Hammie and I flatten ourselves against the stairs as each of them comes up, pulling themselves onto the staircase. Hideo comes last. He leaps for the rope and barely manages to avoid one of the bots that grabs for his leg. I reach down and take his arm as he makes his way onto the stairs.

We race up the staircase. As we go, the world around us shudders again. Scarlet beacons of light suddenly turn on from the rooftops of the other towers, sweeping across the moving city like prison spotlights. I concentrate on the climb. The steps crack underneath our feet as we go.

Hammie arrives at the top first. The door glows blue around its edges, a startling contrast to its grim surroundings.

She pushes against the glowing door, but it doesn't budge.

"I think we need a key or something," she mutters as she shoves herself against it again. We push along with her, but it doesn't so much as shudder. I look back down at the steps, some of which have crumbled away, and then back at the door. There are two round hovels against either side of it.

Hideo steps away from the door first. "I recognize some of the pieces here." He nods at the dark marbles hovering in the air, and when I look closer, I notice that they glitter a deep scarlet and sapphire.

Immediately, I know what he means. These are from the game that Sasuke had once made up with Hideo, when they'd gone to the park and thrown red- and blue-colored plastic eggs all across the grass and then raced to retrieve them. When Sasuke had been stolen away. Remnants of that memory are now scattered in here, distorted into a nightmare.

I look back at the door's two hovels. They're the slots where the marbles fit, harkening back to how Hideo and Sasuke had once played this game.

"We need to collect them," Hideo says. "One red, one blue."

Hammie looks out at the hovering dark marbles. She nods at the closest one, and before anyone can stop her, she crouches against the steps and takes a flying leap off the side, launching into the air in the blink of an eye.

"Wait—!" Hideo starts to shout.

She seizes the closest one to her, twists in midair, and shoves it into her pocket. As she falls, she shoots out her rope and snags it on a crack in the stairs. She swings in an arc down further on the tower, dangling to a stop below us.

"Got one," she calls up to us.

Every single one of the sweeping red lights suddenly shoots toward us, flooding all of us in a scarlet glow. A deafening horn echoes across the landscape.

This was a trap. The marbles are needed in order to get through the door, but making contact with those same marbles has also alerted Zero to exactly where we are.

"Climb!" Asher shouts down at Hammie, right as we see a whirlwind of security bots cluster at the base of the tower.

Hammie doesn't waste another breath. She starts pulling herself up the rope as quickly as she can. Roshan darts down the steps two at a time toward her, but the bots are moving so fast that I know they'll catch up to them before Hammie can get back to us.

I glance at Hideo and toss him one end of my rope. He catches it. Then I swing down toward Hammie and Roshan. But the bots are swarming up too fast—they'll catch up to them before I can make it. Below me, Roshan has reached Hammie and positioned himself in front of her as she pulls herself up onto the lone island of a step she's on. He narrows his eyes at the approaching bots and crosses his forearms. His shield appears.

The bots clash against it. Roshan winces as he's pushed back, his boots digging hard against the stone steps, trying in vain to keep them from pushing him right off the edge. Hammie hops to her feet and lunges back up the stairs toward us.

Roshan's shield can't sustain the hits anymore. The glowing blue circle shudders as the bots throw themselves once more at it, and then it flickers out. I scream something. They charge forward at him.

"*Hey!*"

My head jerks up at the sound of Asher's voice. He's leaped off the stairs to grab on to another marble. Half of the security bots shift direction toward him now, while the others slow for an instant, giving Roshan just enough time to turn and race up the steps after Hammie.

I dart past them both as they rejoin Hideo at the top. Roshan glances at me. "Where are you going?" he shouts.

I don't answer right away. Instead, I stop beside Asher and crouch down, then pull a stick of dynamite from my utility belt. I fit it against the steps, right before the bots. "Move!" I shout at Asher.

He already sees what I'm doing. As I turn tail, so does he, and we sprint up right as the dynamite goes off behind us.

The explosion knocks us to our knees. Behind us is a gaping hole in the steps, so wide that it stops the bots from following us. They gather at the edge in a crowd—it won't be long before they start leaping across the gap.

"Put them in!" I hear Asher shout. Hammie and Roshan take the two marbles and shove them into the slots on either side of the door.

The bots are climbing and clawing, making their way across the chasm in the stairs. They're racing up toward us.

The door swings open. Hideo grabs my arm. The bots are almost on top of us.

Hammie leaps through the door, followed by Roshan. Hideo

shoves me through the entrance. Beside us, one of the first bots to reach us latches on to Asher's arm, its metal fingers closing around him in a tight grip. He kicks out at the bot's chest—it loosens its hold, and he throws himself inside the door. I turn around just as Hideo barely makes it in, slamming the door shut right as the bots lunge at it.

We collapse against the ground. My heart's racing so fast that I find myself clutching at my chest, as if that would help me breathe.

"Well," Asher gasps out as he meets our eyes. "That was different."

Hideo winces, bracing himself against the door. His face is ghostly pale now, mirroring what he must look like in real life, and I know he's growing weaker from blood loss. The image of his body glitches slightly—flickering in and out before solidifying again.

I hurry to him and touch his arm. We are running out of time, and his wound is our ticking clock. He gives me a slight smile that's closer to a grimace. Then he nods at the new place we've arrived in.

Hammie collapses against Roshan, letting out a long breath. I can feel my hands shaking in my lap. When I look around, I realize that we're all sitting inside a glowing white space, with no walls or ceiling. Where's this?

My thoughts are interrupted by a sharp intake of breath from Asher. I turn to see him clutching his arm, right where the bot had touched him. His eyes are squeezed shut.

"Ash," Hammie says. "You all right?"

Asher doesn't respond. His arm trembles; all the color drains from his face. All of a sudden, he opens his eyes wide—and his irises aren't their usual blue, but an unsettling silver.

The blank, white world around us flickers, replaced for a

moment by a new surrounding. We are suddenly within the interior of a house—banisters of curled iron, potted poinsettias, and broken glass all over the hardwood floor.

I shrink away instinctively. Hammie starts to reach for Asher, but I yank her back.

"Don't touch him," I warn.

"What happened to him?" Roshan says.

Hideo already understands it. "When that security bot touched Asher, Zero found his way in."

Zero had broken past Asher's encryption and gotten into his mind. This must be a world constructed out of his memories.

We look on in horror as the world around us continues to play one of Asher's memories. The boy hurrying down the stairs isn't Asher, but his brother Daniel, unmistakable with his shock of light brown-blond hair and piercing blue eyes. When he reaches the bottom, he shoves Asher in his wheelchair hard enough to send it bumping against the back wall.

"Where the hell are you going now?" Asher says to him. He looks younger, like maybe this happened at least eight or nine years ago.

Daniel doesn't answer him. Instead, he turns to head off into the kitchen. At the sight, Asher's voice shifts into anger. "You know what? Don't tell me. I don't need to know everything about your life when you obviously don't give a shit about mine."

At that, Daniel turns back around. He looks so much like Asher, his eyes alight with the same fire. "You don't need me to care," he snaps. "Don't you get enough attention?"

"Just because you're ignoring the divorce doesn't mean it's not happening."

"And what are you doing? Playing Warcross in your room?"

Asher narrows his eyes, and his expression suddenly turns

cold and hard. "What do you do that's so much better? Maybe you've got some fans, but my local wins are what put food on the table."

This seems to hit Daniel so precisely that Asher hesitates, tightening his lips as if he knew he went too far.

Daniel walks over to Asher, puts one hand on either of the wheelchair's armrests, and leans down to his brother's face. "You're never going to make it," he says. "You're never going to amount to anything in it. You keep throwing yourself into this useless game, like you honestly think they'll choose you as a wild card."

Asher doesn't respond. He just pulls his chair away, forcing Daniel to step away again, and turns his back on his brother.

I want to get out of this place right now—I want to take out these lenses and see the panic room around me instead of this warped mindscape. I don't want to know that, somewhere out there, Asher is just sitting straight in his chair, completely unaware anymore of anything going on around him.

My hand's still on Hammie's shoulder. She looks so tense that she might break.

Hideo gets up. "If you want him back, we need to keep going."

I tear my gaze from Asher's blank one, turn my back, and along with the others, head off again.

30

Before long, we come across another door floating in the empty whiteness of this space. I reach it first, put my hand on the knob, and carefully turn it. Then I enter, followed by the others.

We step out into a bustling, crowded, rain-washed street in Tokyo. I recognize the spot immediately—Shibuya Station, right next to the huge intersection that I'd once overlooked from my hotel window. Beside us is the statue of the dog Hachikō, where people huddle as they wait for friends. All around us swarms a moving crowd.

I blink, thrown off by the change. There are people everywhere—huddled under colorful umbrellas, wearing face masks and hats, draped in coats and boots, shadows over their eyes. Cars splash into puddles as they drive by, and above it all tower bright advertisements showcasing smiling people holding up lotions and creams.

Beside me, Hammie almost seems to relax at the sight. I feel it, too—it's like we're here, instead of inside Zero's mind, walking in an illusion. But Hideo's eyes are narrowed, and he exchanges a quick glance of warning with me.

Roshan frowns at the scene. "This isn't right," he says.

Only after he says it do I realize what's bothering me, too. The scene isn't quite accurate—some of the storefronts aren't supposed to be here, while others are in the wrong order along the street. It's as if Zero—or Sasuke—couldn't remember it correctly.

But what stands out the most is that no one walking around is saying anything at all. All we hear is the shuffling of feet, the rush of cars, and the blare of advertisements. There must be thousands of people here, and no one is saying a word.

I swallow hard. Hideo holds out his arm, telling us to stay close. "We must be nearly there. I remember this," he says, his gaze fixed on the advertisements. "Our mother and father took Sasuke and me here tonight so that we could shop for new boots. That trailer." He nods at a giant screen curving around a two-story coffee shop that now shows a promotion for a new movie. "I was eight when that film came out. Sasuke was six."

Hideo's right. These aren't just the inner workings of Zero's artificial mind anymore. We're inside a distorted memory in Zero's mind, I realize, a twisted fragment of what had once been Sasuke's.

Roshan steps beside me as we stare at the people looking back at us with their sightless faces. Their heads tilt toward us as they draw near. "Security bots," he whispers.

Just like the ones we'd faced earlier—except these are disguised as regular shoppers.

Hideo starts carefully moving us forward. "Don't let any of them touch you."

"Do you know where we're supposed to go?" I ask.

"Yes." He nods toward a department store right next to the coffee shop, where a store worker is handing out coupons to entice potential customers. As we move carefully through the crowd, I see a couple walking hand in hand with two small boys, both of whom have their necks craned up at the movie trailer playing on the screen above them.

My heart twists as I recognize them. It's Hideo and Sasuke.

We pass them, but I can't see their faces. When I look forward again, they're back to walking ahead of us, as if everything had just reset. It's a perpetual, repeating memory.

Hammie bumps into me from behind. I glance back to see her casting suspicious looks at the people walking around her. "Someone just lunged at me," she whispers, quickening her stride. "Zero's on the hunt."

After what happened to Asher, Zero must know the rest of us are in here somewhere. I hold a hand out at Hammie and look her straight in the eye. "Did they touch you?"

"No, I don't think so," she mutters back, even though she's rubbing at her elbow. "She just brushed my sleeve a little, that's all."

My heart seizes. "She brushed your sleeve?" I say—but Hammie looks away from me and focuses on something in the crowd ahead of us. Her eyes widen.

"Hey. *Hey!*" Hammie calls out into the crowd, startling us all, and then suddenly starts pushing her way through the throngs.

"Hammie!" Roshan calls out. But she's already off, heading away from the department store at a slant.

"That's my mom," she says breathlessly, looking over her shoulder at us with a shocked expression. "That's my mom! Right there!" She turns back to point at a woman wearing an air force uniform, with dark skin and dark curls like her own. "What is she doing in here? How does Zero know what she looks like?"

I burst into a run. Hideo does, too—even though we both know it's too late. It's impossible to move as fast as Hammie without accidentally bumping into anyone. More passing people look at us—another person leans sharply in toward Roshan, forcing him to barely duck out of the way in time.

Hammie! I want to shout, but I'm too afraid of drawing more attention.

We finally catch up to her. But she's just standing in the middle of the street now, her stare vacant and unseeing, her posture ramrod straight, her expression completely blank. Above us, the enormous advertisement vanishes, replaced by something that can only be one of Hammie's memories.

It's of two girls, their curly hair hidden behind silk caps. The younger of the two is in bed, laughing uproariously as their father tries in vain to adjust her cap. The older one—Hammie, it looks like—is quieter, sitting at a small, square table across from someone who must be their mother. They're both concentrating on a chess game. I watch as the mom moves her pieces each within the span of seconds, while Hammie scowls and shifts in frustration as she struggles with her own moves.

"Why do you have to go again tomorrow?" Hammie finally mutters as she loses her rook to her mom's bishop.

"Yeah," her younger sister shouts in a singsong voice from the bed as she purposely pulls her cap askew again, making her dad give an affectionate sigh. "Why d'you have to *go*?"

"Stop repeating me, Brooke, I swear," Hammie snaps at her sister, who just giggles in return.

"I'm not gone for long." Their mother leans back in her chair and crosses her arms. Her air force uniform is decorated with several medals. When Hammie finally decides on a good spot to put her queen, her mother nods in approval. "It's just for a few weeks. You girls can even come to the base and see me off, if you want to."

Brooke bursts into protest as their father tugs her silk cap straight again. Hammie looks away from her mom. "You just came back yesterday," she says.

Their father raises a stern eyebrow. "Hammie. Stop making your mamá feel bad. I assigned you plenty of algebra homework to keep you busy for the next week. I can always give you more. Now, that's your last complaint. You understand me?"

Hammie opens her mouth, then shuts it sullenly. "Yes, sir," she mutters.

Their mother smiles at Hammie's face. "It's a good thing," she teases. "Without me around, you can finally win a few chess games. Maybe you'll even put up a fight when we play next time."

Hammie straightens, a little smirk sneaking onto the corners of her mouth, and suddenly she looks exactly like the teammate I know. The spark in her mother's eyes seems to feed her. "Yeah, you'll be sorry. Next game, your king is mine."

"Oh, big talk now." Her mother laughs once, the sound full of warmth. "Listen—each time you play against anyone, pretend you're playing me. All right? That should give you the fire to do your best."

The young Hammie nods at that. "Hell yeah, I will."

"*Hammie*," her dad scolds from the bed. "Language. How many times?" Brooke starts cracking up.

Hammie might be too young to understand it, but I know what her mother's really doing—reminding her that the game connects them, that her mother's presence is there even when she's not.

The scene shifts again to the middle of the night, where Hammie sits by flashlight at the little chess table and plays quietly on her own, her brow furrowed in determination.

Finally, the memory disappears, replaced once again with the endlessly repeating movie trailer.

Hammie stays frozen where she is.

It takes everything in me not to reach out and pull her back with us. I tear my eyes away from her, feeling my heart rip a little as I go. "Come on," I say through gritted teeth, my hand on Roshan's arm. He stumbles a little as we walk by, like he wants to grab her, too, but instead he forces his face forward again.

Hideo marches beside us, twisting and turning his body as he weaves through the crowd. When I glance at him, his expression is stone-cold.

I shouldn't have brought them here. I didn't understand how dangerous navigating Zero's mind would be.

But it's too late to dwell on it.

We finally reach the department store's entrance. The model smiles at us with her blank expression. She holds out a coupon for us to take, but unlike everyone else walking into the store, I hold back and don't dare touch it. Neither does Hideo nor Roshan.

Her smile disappears. Then, suddenly, she raises her voice. It's a warning call.

And everyone near us starts rushing toward us at a frightening pace.

"He's found us," Hideo calls over his shoulder. "Hurry!" He seizes my wrist and pulls me forward. Roshan dashes ahead.

A door at the end of the floor glints, and we make a run for it. People behind us continue to rush forward, still expressionless and wordless.

Hideo reaches the door and shoves it open. We hurry inside. The last thing I see when I look back are the countless determined faces heading toward us. Then I slam the door shut, sealing them out.

I'm trembling all over. Hammie's gone. Asher's gone. And if we don't get to the end of this soon, if we don't restore Zero's mind to Sasuke's, they may never come back.

After the strange, wordless bustle of the Shibuya illusion, this street looks calm and quiet and dim, lit only with streetlights and the occasional stripe of golden yellow light streaming out from homes.

It's the street where Hideo's parents live, but everything looks different at night, and a subtle mist floats around us.

Hideo's breath fogs in the air as he stares at the house. "This is before Dad planted the spruce in the front yard," he says in a soft voice. "The door's a different color, too."

I remember that. When I'd visited his home, the door had been painted a deep red, but in the Memory Hideo had once shown me of his younger self sprinting back home, the door had been blue. That's the color it is here.

Hideo hesitates, as if he were afraid to walk closer. This is a nightmare that he's trapped in, just like how Zero had once used my worst memory against me.

Roshan starts walking toward the house. "Emi," he says quietly, "you and Hideo stay back. I have my shields; it'll be safer for you both that way. No doubt there are security bots here, too."

Hideo shakes his head once and steps in front. "Watch Emi," he replies, then sweeps a hand across the scene. A menu grid appears. "I'm such an integral part of this scene that I'll blend in easily. Zero's not going to find me."

We head up to the house. As we draw near, I can hear the sound of muffled voices in the house, the recognizable hum of Hideo's mother and the lower rumble of his father. Hideo approaches the home, opens the door, and leads us in.

It's a warm, comforting space, as neat and tidy as I remember it—except without the sculptures that Hideo's father would later make in remembrance of Sasuke. In fact, there are still photos of Sasuke on all the walls, portraits of him with Hideo and with his parents. This must be a memory from when he was still back home.

"Hideo-*kun!*"

We turn in unison at the sound of Hideo's mother bustling into the room. She looks startlingly different from how I'd seen her in person—here, she looks like the original sun instead of the shadow, with a straight back and a sharp gleam in her eyes, her smile cheerful and energetic. There's something painful in seeing her this way, before Sasuke disappeared.

Beside me, Hideo makes an instinctive move toward her before he forces himself to stop. His hands bundle into fists at his side. He knows this isn't real.

The floor beneath us shudders for a moment. Roshan braces himself against the wall before exchanging a wary look with Hideo. Already, Hideo's motioning for us to back up.

Hideo's mother pauses with a frown at the sight of her son hesitating. "What's the matter?" she says as I read the translation. She glances back in the kitchen and motions for someone to come out. "Come help your brother."

I blink. When I do, Hideo's mother is gone, as if she'd never been there in the first place. Hideo stares back as the person who emerges from the kitchen isn't Sasuke—but Zero. His black armor glints in the low light as he tilts his head slightly at us. Beneath us, the ground trembles harder.

He looks straight at Roshan, then Hideo, then me. "There you all are," he says, his voice deep and cold.

He shouldn't be able to see us behind our encryption unless he touches us—we're supposed to be invisible to him. But there he is, or some shell of him, or a proxy. Whatever he is, he knows we're here.

"The house," Hideo suddenly murmurs at the same time I realize it. This time, the trap had been the entire house, and all three of us had been exposed the instant we stepped inside.

Zero turns his attention to his brother. Then, he lunges.

Roshan moves even before I can. He brings his forearms up in a cross, and a glowing blue shield arcs protectively before him and Hideo. Zero clashes against it—the force of it splits the shield cleanly in half. Zero seizes Roshan by the neck and slams him against the wall.

Roshan lets out a gasp as he struggles. I lunge toward them to pull Zero off, but Hideo grabs my wrist. "Sasuke," he says in a hoarse, furious shout. "*Stop this.*"

Zero glances back at Hideo. "I know why you're in here. I know what you're looking for." He drops Roshan, who crumples to the ground as he holds his throat.

I rush to his side, but Roshan's hand flies up, warning me to stay away. Already, he's slowing down, his eyes turning blank and emotionless. His hand slowly drops back to his side. As it happens, the world around me flickers briefly with a memory.

It's of Roshan waiting inside a hospital room where Tremaine is resting, hooked up to a bunch of wires. Roshan is leaning his head into his hands, his elbows sinking into the bed. Looped around one of his hands are his prayer beads, and now he's running his thumb across each turquoise sphere unconsciously. His dark curls are a wild mess, the evidence of his fingers raking anxiously through them.

My gaze goes to Tremaine. His wound is as I remember it, his head still wrapped in thick layers of gauze. Nearby in the adjoining waiting room, the other Riders and Demons are finally calling it a night and heading out into the stairwell exit.

This memory is from the evening after I left the hospital, when I went to see Hideo.

The room's quiet, except for the regular beeping pulse from a monitor. When I look closer at Roshan, I notice he's clutching a crumpled piece of paper in one fist. It's a list of hastily scribbled dates, all set for a couple of days from now, one after another—follow-up appointments and an additional surgery and physical therapy. Maybe they're treatment benchmarks for Tremaine to hit, dates when Roshan plans on being here in the room.

At first, I think Tremaine is still unconscious—but then his mouth shifts a little, his lips peeling open in their cracked state. Roshan looks up from his hands to meet Tremaine's gaze from under his heavy bandages. The two stare at each other, then exchange a wry smile. Now I can see how puffy and swollen Roshan's eyes are, and the dark circles underneath them.

"You're still here," Tremaine croaks out.

"Leaving any minute," Roshan replies, even though I can tell he doesn't mean it. "These chairs are the most uncomfortable things I've ever sat on."

"You and your sensitive ass." In spite of everything, Tremaine still has the ability to roll his eyes. "You used to complain about my bed back in the Riders' dorms, too."

"Yeah, it sucked. If there was ever a reason for you to leave the Riders, it was because of that damn bed."

There's a pause. "Where's Kento?" Tremaine finally asks.

At that, Roshan sits back, his prayer beads sliding back down onto his wrist. "Flying to Seoul with two of his teammates," he replies. "He needs to be back in time for a parade in their honor. He sends his best."

Tremaine doesn't follow that statement up with anything other than a cough, which makes him squeeze his eyelids together in pain. After another long silence, Roshan leans his elbows back on the bed. "Emi told you to stay away from that institute's files," he says.

"It wasn't my hacking that exposed me," Tremaine replies. "I stumbled against a stupid plant in that hall, and the vase tipped over and broke. Shit happens."

"Yeah, well, you can only handle a hole in your head so many times before you don't make it through." Roshan furrows his brow and looks down again. He doesn't speak, but I can feel the burn of his anger in his clenched jaw, his hands clasped tightly together.

"What are you thinking?" Tremaine says in a quiet voice.

Roshan shakes his head. "I'm thinking that I'm sorry," he replies.

"Why the hell are *you* sorry?"

"For asking you to help Emi out in the first place. I was worried she'd go off on her own again, keep everything to herself. I shouldn't have put the idea in your head."

Tremaine lets out his breath in a huff. "If you didn't say it, I would've done it anyway. You think a hunter's going to stay away from the chase of a lifetime? Come on, now. Don't give yourself so much credit."

Roshan's eyes are moist again, and he hurriedly rubs a hand once across his face. "You really want to know what I'm thinking? I'm thinking about how everyone else has already left and here I am, still at your bedside like some kind of idiot. The doctors said you've already stabilized; they told me to go home. What am I waiting around for? I don't know."

Tremaine just looks back at him. I can't tell what's flitting through his pale eyes, but when he speaks, he can't meet Roshan's gaze. "Know what I'm really thinking?" he mutters. "I'm thinking about how, if you were the one lying in this bed instead of me, your entire family would be in here. Your brother and his duchess of a wife and their baby. Your sister. Your mother and your father. All your cousins and nephews and nieces, every single last one of them. There wouldn't be any space left. They would have flown in together on a private plane and they would be packed in here, waiting and worrying until you could walk out the door."

He hesitates, as if afraid to go on. "I know you're with Kento now. I know he's better than me in every way. But I'm thinking that, even though there's no one in my family willing to wait around for me, even though you're the only one in here, I couldn't care less, because you might as well be the entire damn world."

He grimaces in the silence afterward, his expression embarrassed. "See, here's the moment after my speech when I'd like to either go right up to you or leave the room in a grand finale, except I'm kind of tied down to this stupid bed, so now it's just awkward. You know what? Forget what I said. It was only—"

Roshan reaches out, takes Tremaine's hand in his, and squeezes it tight. He doesn't say a word for a long moment, but somehow, this contented silence seems like just the right thing to hear.

"You know, I'm not over you," Roshan finally murmurs.

"I'm not either," Tremaine replies. He turns his head slightly, all he can manage, and closes his eyes as Roshan leans down to kiss him.

The memory vanishes, as if everything I'd just seen had

happened in the space of a second. Roshan stays seated against the wall with his eyes staring vacantly forward.

Zero already knows what we're doing and where we're trying to go. He'd even planted this false endpoint here, had used this game against us in order to hunt us down. He knew Hideo would come here, back to their old home.

My head jerks back up to Zero, my eyes narrowed in anger. He just looks at me through his opaque helmet, studying me quietly before turning his attention back to Hideo. To my surprise, though, he doesn't touch Hideo.

Instead, he turns toward me and lunges.

Hideo darts for me. He reaches me before Zero can, clenches his jaw, and crouches before me, ready to attack his brother. Zero halts before Hideo can reach him. Again, he seems to shy away from Hideo, as if making contact with him might have the same poisonous effect as Zero's mind controlling any one of us.

"Touch her, and I'll kill you," Hideo growls.

"You won't kill Sasuke," Zero replies in a cool voice.

"You're not Sasuke."

The ground beneath us cracks more. I lose my balance and fall to my knees. Before my eyes, a huge line divides the entire floor. I try to scramble to my feet and throw myself at Zero, one last-ditch attempt to get to him.

But it's too late. The floor gives way, and all of us fall into darkness.

31

I have no idea where we are. The darkness is all-consuming, and the only thing I can hear is the sound of Hideo's breathing coming from somewhere near me. His breaths are hoarse now, and when he speaks, he sounds weaker.

"Hideo?" I whisper, then say his name louder. "Hideo?"

He doesn't respond right away. For a frightening moment, I think that Zero has somehow gotten to him, too, and that my new theory is completely wrong. Hideo's going to stop speaking. He might already be staring emotionless into space within this darkness.

Or maybe, in real life, he's dying. Bleeding out. We're both trapped inside this panic room with Zero's guards outside our door. At any moment, they could break in and seize us, and I'd feel rough hands grabbing my arms and dragging me to my feet. I'd feel the cold barrel of a real gun pressed to my head.

Then Hideo whispers something. "Emika."

All I can do is whisper back. "I'm here."

He lets out a breath that sounds like relief. "I'm sorry," he murmurs. "I should have known he'd set a trap for us in the one place where he knew I'd take us."

Gradually, the overwhelming darkness around us lightens. At first, I can see only the ground right beneath my own feet. It looks like cracked cement. Then, faint silhouettes around us transform from simple shapes into skeleton trees, and dark walls materialize into soaring buildings. My gaze travels higher and higher as the world comes into view.

It looks like a half-finished city.

Skyscrapers with empty interiors, devoid of light. Streets full of broken pavement. The streets are a ghost version of Tokyo, without the crowds of people I'd seen in the earlier illusion of Shibuya. Neon signs hang unlit from the sides of malls and shops. The buildings have windows, but through the glass, I see only empty rooms with peeling walls. Paintings on the walls are unfinished. When I look more closely at them, I can see that they depict pieces of scenes from Zero's old life. There's a frame that seems like part of their old home, except it looks like a rough sketch with a few daubs of paint on it. There's a portrait of a family, but no faces are filled in.

This is the very center of Zero's mind—a hollowed-out version of Sasuke's memories, a million fragments of pieces with their hearts ripped out.

Zero materializes before us now, his dark figure nearly invisible against the backdrop, his face hidden and impenetrable. As he appears, so do dozens—hundreds—of his security bots, all standing on the ledges of buildings and rooftops and street corners, silently watching us.

"You're wasting your time," Zero says with a sigh. His voice echoes in the space.

"If you're so sure of that, then why are you here to stop us?" I reply.

His head cocks slightly to one side in a mocking gesture, then he ignores me, and turns his attention to Hideo. "Is it ironic," he asks, "to see your creation in the hands of someone else? Did you really think it would always be under your control?"

I can practically see his words hit Hideo clean in the chest. Hideo winces, his eyes still fixed on the armored figure that bears the voice of his brother. "Sasuke, please," he says.

Zero takes a step toward us. The world trembles at his movement. "You're looking for someone who no longer exists."

Hideo stares at him, searching desperately. "You may not be who you once were, but you're still molded from my brother. You know my name, and you know who did this to you. I have to believe that a part of you remembers." His voice turns hoarse. "The park where we used to play. The games you used to make up. Do you still remember the blue scarf I gave you, the one I used to wrap around your neck?"

Zero's posture stiffens, but when he speaks again, his voice doesn't change. "Is that a challenge?"

As he says this, the world trembles again—and then scarlet and sapphire gems appear everywhere, hovering in the air like marbled power-ups, their surfaces reflecting the landscape around them. His bots surrounding us tense, their faces turned in our direction as if ready to attack.

A chill runs through me. Sasuke's hand can be seen here, too—there's no other reason for Zero to bother playing this game with us. But his hold seems to be weakening as Zero's bots continue to grow in number.

A deafening sound roars around us. I look over to Hideo, who has moved into a crouch, too, his hands balled into fists. Under our feet, the floor has transformed into a living thing, a moving block of concrete parts that open and close like jaws, and every time they move, they expose shafts of red light from somewhere within.

It's not real. I remind myself, the way I do every time I step into a Warcross world—but this time, it's not wholly true. We're not just in some random virtual place. We're standing inside the most powerful mind in the world.

There's a second of unbearable silence.

Then, all the bots rush at us with impossible speed.

Every instinct in me rears up. I reach for my last stick of dynamite and hurl it right in front of us. It explodes, throwing back our attackers in a huge arc. But behind them are hundreds more. *Thousands.* They race toward us.

We don't have a chance. But I still loop a quick noose into the rope of my cable launcher and throw it to Hideo—he catches it without so much as glancing at me. He tosses it high up in the air, where the hooked end of the cable launcher lassos around a streetlight, then yanks himself up right as the bots close in on him.

I'm sprinting in the opposite direction. As the first bot nears and makes a lunge for me, I twist out of his coming grasp and sprint for the closest building. I reach it, wedge my boot against the windowsill, and clamber up it until I get to the second-story ledge. There, I manage to pull myself up onto the awning.

Zero's there, waiting for me. He slams his fist into one of the two poles holding the awning up. The pole explodes into tiny pieces. I'm thrown off balance and back to the ground, right as Zero grabs down for my neck.

Hideo's here before I can register him. He lunges out as Zero lands, throwing his own fist at Zero, but Zero dodges easily. He unleashes a scarlet gem against Hideo—light bursts from his hand. Hideo goes flying, hitting his back hard against a wall.

Hideo leaps up, kicking out against his brother's shoulders. It forces Zero to release Hideo's collar. Hideo lands lightly on his feet and rushes again at Zero. There's a rage in his eyes that I remember from his boxing sessions, from the moment he first looked into Taylor's eyes.

I lunge at the closest power-up I can find. It's a neon-yellow sphere. "Hideo!" I shout. He glances over to me for a brief moment. Then I unleash it.

A blinding light swallows the entire space. Even through my closed lids and my outstretched hands, I want to squint against the brightness of it. It washes out everything around us into white.

Zero pauses for a moment. He can't be blinded by something like this, I don't think, but he must be reacting to the overwhelming data wipe—as if everything in his view went temporarily blank.

Then the light vanishes as quickly as it'd appeared. Hideo doesn't waste the chance. He's already dashing at Zero. Zero whips out an arm, seizing his brother, but Hideo takes advantage of the move and instead uses Zero's weight against him—he kneels down and flips Zero over.

Zero's on his feet again in a split second, rolling off his back and leaping up in one fluid motion. He rushes toward Hideo, grabs him by the neck, and pins him against the wall.

"You're a fool for trying," Zero says to him, his deep voice echoing around us and in my mind. He sounds amused, but beneath it all, there's a churning rage—no, something else, something that sounds desperate. "Why don't you go back home? You have all the money in the world now, don't you? Leave this alone and take care of your parents."

Hideo grapples at the metallic hand locked around his neck and says nothing. He just stares hard into the opaque black helmet.

I point one of my knives at him and throw as hard as I can.

The knife slams into his helmet, shattering it.

But Zero just vanishes, reappearing a few feet away from us. He looks completely undisturbed.

"It'll be easier for you this way, you know," he says. "You don't want to hurt your parents, do you? Your poor mother, slow and forgetful? Your father, sickly and frail? You don't want any harm to come to them, do you?"

And I realize that these aren't Zero's words at all. They're Taylor's—I can recognize them solely by the taunting questions. These are things she must have once said to Sasuke, threatening his family to keep him from running away.

Hideo stares back at Zero with a clenched jaw. "You're not going to hurt anyone," he snarls. "Because you're not real."

Somehow, Hideo's not going blank like everyone else had—he's still here, alert and conscious. He slams Zero down against the floor, striking him in the face.

Zero vanishes, reappears again. I sprint for him, only to realize that he can just disappear again and again. How can I reach him and break through his armor to install Sasuke's data into him? It's impossible. I glance desperately over at Hideo as several of Zero's bots reach him. A scream bubbles in my throat.

To my surprise, though, they go around him. They don't touch him at all. It's as if they're leaving Hideo for Zero to deal with himself.

But in my confusion I let one bot get too close to me. I don't react fast enough. His hand shoots out and seizes my wrist.

I gasp. His grip feels so cold, like he's made out of ice. Behind me comes Hideo's shout. *"Emika!"*

I twist around, my teeth clenched, and kick out at his black helmet. My boot smashes straight through the glass. He immediately vaporizes.

I hold my wrist tightly. The ice of his touch lingers, burning straight through me and into my mind, and the edges of my vision blur a bit. I shake my head. The world around me shifts again as I run.

I blink. Where am I? The city had looked like emptied Tokyo, but suddenly I see a layout of intersecting streets that I recognize as New York. I'm passing through Times Square now, except it's not Times Square at all—none of its lights are lit, and no pedestrians crowd its streets. Right beside it is a glimpse of Central Park.

That doesn't make sense at all, I think to myself, as I race toward Zero. Sasuke has probably never been to New York before. The layout of it makes no sense either, as Central Park isn't anywhere near Times Square.

This is *my* home—*my* memories.

I realize with a sickening lurch that Zero's security bots have infiltrated my mind, as surely as he'd done with each of my teammates—that ice-cold grip on my wrist had been him seeping into my mind.

I look wildly around for Hideo, ready to call out for him, but the entire world around me has now transformed into New York City. In Central Park, I see a figure walking. *Hideo. Zero.* I start running toward it.

When I get closer, I stumble to a halt. The figure walking through the park isn't Hideo or Zero at all. It's my father.

"Dad," I whisper. He's here, and I'm home.

I start running toward his figure. It's him, everything about him screams it—his suit perfectly tailored and his hair sleek and elegant from an afternoon concert at Carnegie Hall. He's walking with a young girl in a tulle dress, singing her a concert piece. Even from here, I can hear notes of his humming, off-key and full of life, followed by the accompanying singing of the girl. I can almost smell the bag of sweet roasted peanuts he hands to her, feel the breeze swirling the leaves around them.

Where had I been earlier? Some unfinished illusion of a city. But this? This is obviously real, and here.

There's a warning going off somewhere in me, trying to tell me that this isn't quite right. But I shrug it off as I make my way closer to my dad and myself. It's fall, so of course the leaves are drifting down, and my dad is still alive, so of course he's walking hand in hand with me through the park. The sound of his bright laughter is so familiar that I feel an intense burst of joy. My steps quicken.

They never seem to get any closer, though, no matter how fast I go. I break into a run, but my limbs feel like they're dragging through molasses. The little warning in my mind continues relentlessly. *This happened a long time ago*, I gradually realize— the walk through the park, the sound of Dad's laugh, the smell of roasted peanuts.

This isn't now.

Too late, I start to remember what had happened to the others, the memories that had surrounded them the instant they were touched by Zero's security bots and had their minds infiltrated. This isn't real, and I'd fallen for the same trap. My breaths come in panicked gasps. Already, I can feel myself stalling, my thoughts having trouble grasping on to something. Somewhere in the distance is Hideo's voice, calling for me.

To have come all this way and done all this—just to fail here at the end, when we were so close. To leave this puzzle unfinished, the door locked. My mind churns through other options, but a fog is starting to fill my head, and I can see myself slowing down. Along with it comes a strange sensation of . . . unfeeling.

Was this what Sasuke felt on the final day of his experiment? When he gave up his last breath and his mind, and felt what was human of him scatter to become nothing more than data?

Somewhere before me, a figure approaches. It's Zero, hidden behind his armor, and he stops a foot away from me. He studies me for a moment.

You made it so much harder for yourself, he says.

So. Much. Harder. My mind struggles to process each word. Now I've become part of the algorithm, become one with Zero's mind and the NeuroLink.

Become one with Zero's mind.

Wait. A spark lights the fog creeping into me. I think of what he's been doing to everyone in the world, and what he'd done to Asher, Hammie, and Roshan—he'd merged with the algorithm, with the NeuroLink, and that means that his mind has become one with all of that data. When he shuts down someone else's mind, it's because *his* mind has seeped in and taken control.

But information in the NeuroLink, Hideo had once told me, can go both ways.

During our fight, Zero purposely avoided touching Hideo. Almost as if he were afraid to. Maybe he doesn't want to see what's there—echoes of himself as a child, of their relationship and their happy memories, or of their parents and what has happened to them since his disappearance. He's afraid of absorbing that, just as much as someone might be afraid to click on an attachment for fear of downloading a virus.

The puzzle clicks into place. Zero doesn't know that I have

the older iterations of Sasuke in my account. If his mind invades mine, then he's also going to absorb those files into his data.

I don't have much time—I'm fading quickly, as if I were slowly falling asleep. I have the faint sensation that, in real life, I've slumped to the ground of the panic room, the same thing I'm now doing before Zero in the virtual world. The floor feels cold and metallic beneath me. With the last bit of strength that I can muster, I bring up the files I'd stored away of Sasuke.

The files appear before me, this time not as a cube of data, but as a blue scarf.

Zero stiffens. He can now see everything and anything running through my mind—which means he can see the scarf, too. I manage a small smile. Too late, he's realized what I've downloaded into him.

I take the scarf in my hands. My arms lift slowly before me, like I'm dancing through deep water, and as if in a dream, I reach out toward Zero. I drape the scarf around his neck. And as the last of me wanes, I can feel Sasuke's data merging with Zero's mind, becoming a part of it.

His shielded face is the last thing I see. Even though he has no expression, I can feel his anger through the NeuroLink.

Thief.

No, I reply as my final thought. *I'm a bounty hunter.*

32

Zero freezes, as if he were nothing more than a metallic shell. A strange gasp comes from him, and I realize for the first time that I've never heard him utter a breath before. In that gasp, I don't hear the deep, amused, soulless voice I'm used to hearing from Zero.

I hear a child.

"Ni-chan?"

Brother? The translation appears in my view. Then Hideo's beside me, kneeling down, and I struggle to turn my head so that I can look up at him. Hideo has his eyes locked on Zero.

He heard the gasp, too. A hint of recognition flickers in his eyes.

"Sasuke?" he says.

"You don't look like Hideo."

The voice is coming from a small boy, his dark eyes fixed on

Hideo's form crouched over the now lifeless robot. When had he appeared? Zero is nowhere to be seen now. A bright blue scarf is wrapped tightly around the boy's neck, and as he takes a few steps forward, I see a colorful plastic egg clutched in his little hand.

It's young Sasuke, the first iteration of him, the *real* him.

A shudder runs through Hideo at the sight. He doesn't take his eyes off Sasuke as his brother moves hesitantly forward, his expression suspicious of this young man bent before him.

"Sasuke," Hideo says. A tremor has entered his voice. "Hey. It's me."

Still, Sasuke tilts his head at him, doubtful. He doesn't seem to realize he's a figment of data, a ghost of a memory, and neither does Hideo. In this moment, he is here.

"You don't look like him," Sasuke says again, although he keeps moving closer. "My brother is only a little taller than me, and he was wearing a white jacket."

I remember what Hideo had been wearing that day of the disappearance, and it was indeed a white jacket. Now Hideo wipes a hand across his eyes, a hollow laugh escaping from him. His cheeks are wet.

"You remember what I was wearing?"

"Of course. I remember everything."

"Yes." Another shaking laugh from Hideo, full of heartbreak. "Of course you do."

"If you're my brother, why are you so tall?"

Hideo smiles as the boy finally stops right in front of him. "Because I've been searching for you for a long time, and somewhere in that time, I grew up."

Sasuke blinks at that, as if it triggered some sort of memory in him. Then he's shifting again, and all of a sudden, he's no longer the small boy who had disappeared in the park, but a lankier adolescent, maybe eleven or twelve, the way I'd seen him in some of the recordings. He's still wearing the scarf, but the baby fat in his cheeks has disappeared. He searches Hideo's gaze as he stands there, trying to figure it all out.

"I thought you'd forgotten about me," he says. His voice is at the in-between stage, high and low and cracking, trembling. "I waited for you, but you didn't come get me."

"I'm so sorry, Sasuke-*kun*," Hideo whispers, as if the words themselves were stabbing him.

"I tried going to you, but they locked me away. And now I don't know where I am." His young brow furrows. "I don't remember anymore, Hideo. It's too hard."

My own heart feels like it's crumbling as I watch him. He is a functioning mind, forever frozen in data, but he cannot remember things like a real person can, nor can he think exactly like one. He is a ghost, forever trapped in loops, doomed to exist in a permanent half state.

"We looked everywhere for you," Hideo says. He's crying in earnest now and doesn't bother to wipe his tears away. "I wish . . . I wish you could have known."

Sasuke tilts his head at Hideo in that way I've come to know so well. It's a gesture that had carried over, even with the rest of his humanity stripped away. He reaches out to brush his fingers against his brother's brow. "You have the same eyes," he says. "You're still worried."

Hideo bows his head, a laugh emerging between his tears. Then he's reaching out, too, gathering his little brother in his arms and pulling him into a fierce embrace.

"I'm so sorry I lost you," he whispers. "I'm so sorry for what they did to you." His words break again and again as he weeps. "I'm so sorry I couldn't save you."

Sasuke hugs his brother's neck tight. He doesn't say a word. Maybe he can't, as data. He has reached the limits of what he can do.

Time seems to stand still. Finally, when Sasuke pulls back, he transforms again, this time into his teenage iteration. Even taller, lankier. Dark circles under his eyes. He's no longer wearing the scarf.

But he does recognize his brother. "*Ni-san*," he says as he stands up, looking on at the bowed figure before him. Hideo rises to meet his gaze. "You created the NeuroLink because of me."

"Everything I've ever done was for you," Hideo replies.

If it wasn't for Sasuke's disappearance, the NeuroLink might never have existed. And if it wasn't for the NeuroLink, Sasuke wouldn't be standing here like a ghost from the machine. It is a strange circle.

The young Sasuke disappears again, and finally, in his place, stands the only version of him that I've ever known: Zero, clad in black armor from head to toe, silent and cold. He stands over the broken, soulless robot that Hideo had been fighting.

I tremble at the sight of him. We may have been able to rejoin him with Sasuke, but his decisions are out of my hands and entirely with him. I have no idea what he'll do at this point. Would Sasuke choose to continue what Zero had been relentlessly pursuing? Immortality and control? Maybe he still would, and then all of this would have been pointless.

"What are you going to do?" Hideo says to him in a quiet voice.

Zero doesn't respond right away. He's hesitant now, and in his hesitation, I can see the different versions of his past life merging inside him, filling up part of the well that had been hollowed out of him for so long. He doesn't seem to know what he wants anymore.

"If I don't have a physical form," he finally says, "am I still real?"

As I look on, something strange happens. My father appears before me, with his familiar black outfit and his polished shoes and his sleeve of colorful tattoos. His hair glints in the light.

It's not him, of course. It's the NeuroLink, somehow generating this hallucination before me, using the bits of memories I have left to piece together some semblance of him.

But he looks at me now, stopping before me and giving me that quirky grin I remember. It's as if he were truly here, like he'd never died at all.

"Hi, Emi," he says.

Hi, Dad. My vision hazes with tears, *real* tears, ones I can feel sliding down my face.

His smile softens. "I'm so proud of you."

They're not his real words. They're words simulated by the system, piecing together what it knows of my father to create his ghost. But I don't care. I don't dwell on it. All I focus on is the figure of him standing before me like he never went anywhere at all, his hands tucked casually in his pockets. Maybe, if I walk out of here, he'll come with me, and it will be like he has always been here.

"I promise I'll miss you forever," I whisper.

"I promise I'll miss you forever," he echoes. Maybe it's all the system can do.

He stays a distance from me, and I a distance from him. And before I can say anything more, before I can ask him if he'll stay, he vanishes. Gone in the blink of an eye.

If you had asked me before whether virtual reality could ever cross over into reality, I would have shaken my head and disagreed. It's obvious to me what's real and what isn't, what should and shouldn't be.

But there is a point where the lines start to blur, and I am standing in that place now, struggling to see through the gray. Maybe this is where Taylor had lost her way, too, where she had gone searching for something noble and ended up in the dark.

Real. My father was real, and so was Sasuke, and so is Sasuke now, even though he has no physical form. He's real because of the way Hideo is looking back at him, because he had been loved and grieved, had loved and grieved others.

"You once asked me what I'd wish for, if I could wish for anything," Zero finally says to his brother. "Do you remember that?"

Hideo nods once. "I'd wish you back."

He pauses to glance in my direction before looking at Hideo. "No, you wouldn't," he replies. "The world has already shifted because of the past. It's changed because of it. Make sure it changed for the better."

"Am I ever going to see you again?" Hideo asks him. In his voice is his lost self, the boy who grew up with a silver streak of grief in his hair.

And that's when I realize that, at the end, we'd all wish for the same thing.

Just a little more time.

Sasuke transforms once more. The opaque black helmet shielding him now folds away, plate by plate, to reveal a face—the same face I'd seen when I first joined the Blackcoats. It is like looking at Hideo through a mirror, a vision of what Sasuke might have been. He stares at his brother for a long moment.

I hold my breath, wondering what he'll choose to do now.

He lifts his hand once. Around us, the world crumples, the buildings and sky and park turning into digits and data. Code being wiped.

I let out my breath. My body suddenly feels like my own again, and the ice-cold numbness that had invaded my mind is no longer here.

Sasuke has chosen to dismantle what Zero was building.

Then, finally, he vanishes from sight. Hideo makes a movement forward, as if he could somehow keep his brother here, but Sasuke doesn't reappear. The virtual world around us—the dark sky and the ruined, unfinished city—fades away, too, and a moment later, we're back inside the panic room, alone.

Every inch of my body feels sore and awake, and I wonder if everyone else in the world is slowly waking up now, too, if Hammie and Asher and Roshan are clutching their heads and groaning. Maybe they won't even remember all that had happened. Already, everything feels less like reality and more like just a nightmare.

I suck in a deep breath. My limbs become my own again, and a tingling runs through me as if I'd simply been sleeping on my arms and legs too long. The virtual world has entirely disappeared, leaving me feeling disoriented back in the real world. Near me, Hideo is still leaning against the wall, his face pale and wet with tears.

I crawl to him and touch his face. "Hey," I whisper.

He turns weakly toward me. With all his energy spent, and everything we'd set out to do now done, he seems to sag under an overwhelming weight. His gaze wavers between one state of consciousness and another.

"You're here," he exhales, then closes his eyes in exhausted relief.

"*Hideo*," I say as I hold his face, but he's slipping away, his breathing slowing.

Loud banging from the other side of the door makes me jerk my head in its direction. Through my tears, I see the door to the panic room finally break open, letting in a flood of artificial light.

My hand immediately flies up to shield my eyes. The power in the building has been reconnected.

In swarm figures clothed all in black. At first, I think they're Zero's guards, maybe still under some kind of influence—but then I catch the glint of badges on their sleeves. They're not Zero's guards at all, but the police, freed from the algorithm's hold. There must be dozens of them. Their shouts are deafening. I can't even count how many of their guns are raised, all pointed toward us until we're covered in a sheet of red dots.

"He's hurt!" I hear myself call out, my voice hoarse, tears still streaming down my face. "Be careful—*he's hurt!*"

Police surround his limp figure, and in a blur, I see paramedics step into the space to check Hideo's pulse. Officers force me to my knees and cuff my hands behind my back. I don't protest. All I can do is look on as Hideo's body is laid flat and lifted, disappearing into the blinding light outside the panic room. My limbs feel numb as I get to my feet and am ushered out into the hall. I catch a glimpse of a girl with silver hair in the masses of uniforms, her gray eyes turned in my direction. Then Jax is gone, and I'm not sure if I hallucinated her or not. My gaze sweeps across the scene.

The police are everywhere, their eyes vibrant and alive, their movements and thoughts their own. *My* thoughts are my own. And even though everyone is talking to me, shouting their questions in my face, all I can hear is what's ringing in my mind.

We made it.

I cling to this as I'm led down the hall and out the building. The thought is enough for now, because it is mine.

CHIYODA CITY

———

Tokyo, Japan

33

Fingerprints.

Interrogations.

More news cameras than I've ever seen in my life.

I spend the next couple of weeks in a haze of activity, floating through all of it like I'm living inside another reality. The news—that Hideo had been using the NeuroLink to control minds and wills, alter opinions, and prevent people from doing what they want—has engulfed the world like a storm. News stations broadcast clips of a handcuffed Hideo, still limping from his side injury, being led away by the police. Tabloids print front covers showing Hideo's stoic face as he enters and leaves a courthouse. Thousands of sites display screenshots of mind palettes that the algorithm generated and controlled, of the data that Henka Games had been gathering and the way they had been studying the minds of criminals and non-criminals.

Kenn is arrested, too, along with Mari Nakamura. The Neuro-Link shuts down as authorities investigate every corner of Henka Games. The media has been trying to reach me every day, search-ing for more information to piece together this growing, unwieldy puzzle. But I don't speak to any of them. I only give testimony to the police.

It feels weird to be in a world where the NeuroLink is no longer accessible—that means no overlays, no colorful icons or virtual faces, no symbols hovering over buildings and gold lines drawn on the ground to guide you. Everything is grittier and grayer and more tangible again.

And yet . . .

In spite of everything I'd seen and all I knew about what was wrong with the NeuroLink—I'm sad without it. Hideo had created something that changed all of our lives, often for the better. It was a creation that had probably saved my life. And yet, here I am.

Maybe I should feel like a hero. But I don't. It's always easier to destroy than to create.

● ● ● ● ●

SUMMER HAS ARRIVED in full on the day I finally pull up in front of the Supreme Court of Japan.

It's an imposing structure of rectangular concrete blocks, and for the past few weeks, the grounds in front of its entrances have been jammed with crowds, all eager to catch a glimpse of someone they know. Humidity hangs heavy in the air. When I emerge from the car, the spectators' cameras go wild. I just keep calm, my sun-glasses propped against my face.

There's only one reason why I'm at the courthouse today. It's to hear Jax give her testimony.

Inside, the space is grand and quiet, filled with nothing but the tense buzz of low voices. I sit in silence at the front of the main chamber. It's odd, being in such an orderly place after everything that has happened. There are the Supreme Court justices in their black robes, all fifteen of them, sitting in severe form at the front of the chamber. There are those in the audience, an unusual mix of ambassadors and representatives from almost every government in the world. Then, there's me. A smattering of people from Henka Games. Most prominent among them is Divya Kapoor, the newly appointed CEO of the company. The board has wasted no time putting in new leadership.

I take my seat beside Tremaine. He is still in recovery from his injury, and his head is still wrapped in gauze—but his eyes are as sharp as ever as he nods at me. We don't say a word to each other. There's nothing to say that we don't already know.

As we look on, a girl with short, pale hair is led out in handcuffs to a box at the front of the chamber. Her lips are rosy today instead of their usual dark color, and without a gun at her waist to fiddle with, she can only press her hands repeatedly against each other. She doesn't look in our direction. Instead, her gaze flickers briefly to where Hideo sits with his lawyers near the front of the room.

I look at him, too. He may be in handcuffs today, but he's still dressed in a flawless suit—and if we weren't at the Supreme Court to listen to his criminal case, I would think he was still standing in his headquarters or lifting his glass to toast the entire world, his secrets buried behind his eyes.

But today, he sits quietly. Jax is about to testify against him and reveal everything that the Blackcoats knew about his algorithm that made them target him.

The thought forces me to tear my eyes away from him. I've fought all my life to fix things—but now that we're finally here, now that justice is going to be handed down, I suddenly feel like I haven't fixed anything at all. None of this feels right. Taylor, the one who had caused all of this to happen, is already dead. Jax, who has never known another life, will go to prison for the assassinations she was trained since childhood to carry out. Zero—the last remnant of Sasuke Tanaka, the boy who was stolen—has vanished. I've brought down the NeuroLink, the epicenter of modern society, the cornerstone of my entire youth.

And Hideo, the boy who became the most powerful man in the world for the sake of the brother that was taken from him, who had done all the wrong things for all the right reasons, is sitting here today, ready to face his fate.

The testimony starts. Jax speaks in a measured voice as questions for her start to add up, one after another after another.

Was Dana Taylor your adopted mother? How old were you when she adopted you?

What was your relationship with Sasuke Tanaka?

How often did he speak of Hideo Tanaka?

Even now, she stays calm. I guess after everything she's been through, a trial is almost anticlimactic.

Finally, one of the justices asks her about Hideo.

What did Hideo intend to do with the NeuroLink?

Jax looks directly at him. He looks back at her. It's as if, between them, there is some lingering ghost of Sasuke in the air, the same boy who had upended both of their lives. The words Jax had once shouted desperately at us during our escape in the institute now come back to me in full. I can't tell what emotions go through her now, in this setting, if it's hate or rage or regret.

"Hideo's algorithm was never supposed to control the population," Jax says. Her voice echoes from her place at the front of the chamber.

A murmur ripples through the crowd. I blink, exchanging a look with Tremaine to make sure I hadn't misheard something. But he looks as bewildered as I feel.

"The Blackcoats were the ones who wanted to abuse the NeuroLink," Jax goes on, "to turn it into a machine capable of harming people, of turning them against themselves or others. That was always the goal of the Blackcoats, and Taylor was driven to make sure we followed through with this. You already have heard what she did to me, and to Sasuke Tanaka." She hesitates, then clears her throat. "Hideo Tanaka used the algorithm to search for his lost brother."

I listen in a haze, hardly able to process what I'm hearing. Jax isn't here to make sure Hideo is punished for failing to protect his brother. She's here to protect Hideo with her testimony against the Blackcoats.

"And that was always his intent?" the justices are asking now.

"Yes, Your Honor."

"Never, at any time, did he do anything with the algorithm against the general population with any intent of harm?"

"No, Your Honor."

"Then at what time, specifically, did the algorithm become a malicious tool?"

"When the Blackcoats stole it from Hideo and installed their hacks on his system."

"And can you name everyone in the Blackcoats who was directly responsible for this plan?" one of the justices asks.

Jax nods. And as Tremaine and I listen on in stunned silence, she starts to list names. Every single one.

Taylor.

The technicians at the Innovation Institute who had known about her projects.

The workers who had helped Taylor run her experiments, had taken Jax and Sasuke and stolen their lives from them.

The other Blackcoats scattered around the world—their other hackers, other mercenaries, every single person she had ever worked with under Taylor.

She lists them all out.

My mind whirls. I look toward Jax again. Even though Sasuke isn't here, I can sense his presence in the room, as if the boy who had disappeared has finally, in Jax, found a voice for his story.

After a stunning decision today by the Supreme Court of Japan, Henka Games founder Hideo Tanaka has been acquitted of charges of grand conspiracy and capital murder. He was found guilty of second-degree manslaughter in the death of Dr. Dana Taylor, as well as illegally exploiting his creation, the NeuroLink, in his investigation into his brother's disappearance. Local authorities today raided the Japan Innovation Institute of Technology, where several items of evidence mentioned in testimony appear to be missing, among them an armored suit described in detail by witnesses Emika Chen and Jackson Taylor. The suit has not been recovered.

—THE TOKYO DIGEST

34

Two weeks have passed since Hideo's sentencing.

They felt like an eternity, now that the NeuroLink no longer functions. People wake up and log on to the Internet in the way they used to before Hideo's glasses took over the world. There are no overlays when I want to get directions, no translations for people I can't understand. There's an absence in our lives that's hard to describe. Still, people seem to see the world better now.

As the day starts to fade into twilight, I set out on my electric skateboard to find Asher, Roshan, and Hammie. Without the NeuroLink, I rely on old-fashioned techniques like hoodies and caps and dark glasses. There are a million journalists who want to track me down. If I were smart, I'd take an auto-car.

But I get on my board anyway and head into the city. I feel like I belong out here, facing the rushing wind, my balance honed from years of traveling alone on busy city streets. Around me rises

Tokyo, the *real* Tokyo, trains traveling over bridges and skyscrapers towering into the clouds, temples nestled quietly between roaring neighborhoods. I smile as it all passes me by. My time in Tokyo might be coming to an end, but I don't know where I want to go next. After a few overwhelming months, this place has started to feel like home.

I'm lucky enough not to be stopped by anyone as I reach a garden nestled deep in the middle of a quiet neighborhood in the Mejiro district. There are few people here, and no prying eyes. I hop off my board, swing it over my shoulder, and stare at the simple, elegant entrance against a plain white wall, all of it washed into pinks by the sunset. Then I step inside.

It's a beautifully sculpted space, a large, koi-filled pond surrounded by carefully pruned trees and round rocks, arching bridges and trickling waterfalls. I close my eyes and take a deep breath, letting myself soak in the scent of pine and blossoms.

A voice drifts toward me. I open my eyes and look in its direction.

A small pagoda is at one end of the garden, and waiting beside its pillars are Roshan, Hammie, and Asher, sharing bottles of soda. They wave at me. My smile breaks into a grin, and I head over to them. My footsteps quicken until I reach them, when I stop with a jolting halt.

"Hey," I say to Roshan.

He grins back at me. "Hey."

And then my teammates crush me into a hug.

I lean heavily against them, not saying a word. After everything's that's happened since my life turned upside down, this is the best part of it all.

Minutes later, the four of us sit in a row along the stone ledge of the pagoda that overlooks the koi pond, our legs dangling above the water. The sun has set completely now, washing the sky's orange and gold into softer shades of purple and pink.

"That's it, then," Asher speaks first, breaking the silence. He glances to where he has parked his chair several feet away. "No more Warcross tournaments. No more NeuroLink."

He tries to say it in a liberating way, but then he falters and goes quiet. The rest of us do, too.

"What are you going to do now?" I ask him.

He shrugs. "I figure we're all about to be flooded in movie deals and interviews and documentary requests." He doesn't sound all that excited about it.

Roshan leans back and runs a hand through his dark curls. "It's back to London for me," he says, his voice similarly dejected. "It'll be good to see my fam again, get some quiet time with them, and then try to figure out what I want to do now."

"But Tremaine's joining you, I hear," Hammie adds, nudging him hard enough to throw him off balance.

A small smile grows at the edges of Roshan's lips. He tries to hide it by looking out at the pond. "Nothing's final yet," he says, but all Hammie does is grin harder and poke him in the ribs. He grunts once. We laugh.

Hammie leans over to study the koi swimming by beneath us. "Houston for me," she says. "And back to life before Warcross."

Asher nudges her once. "And?" he adds.

She shoots him a bashful wink. "And frequent visits to LA. No reason."

He smiles at that.

Life before Warcross. I picture the little apartment I'd lived in with Kiera in New York, the daily struggle. Most bounty hunters will be out of a job now, too—no need to hunt down people gambling illegally on Warcross or entering the Dark World. There will always be criminals, but they'll return to operating in the regular Internet. And in real life.

What am *I* going to do now? Go back to New York? How will I settle back into a normal life? I picture myself applying to college now, filling out an application for a job, working in an office. It's a strange, surreal thing to imagine.

"Warcross wasn't who any of us are," I say, mostly to myself.

"No," Roshan agrees. There's a long pause. "It's just something we made."

And he's right, of course. It would've been nothing without them—us—making it matter. Without us, it really was just a game.

"It won't change this," Roshan replies, gesturing at the three of us. "You all know that, right? We're linked forever now."

He lifts up his glass bottle in a toast. Hammie joins him, and then Asher. I lift mine, too.

"To good friends."

"To pulling each other up."

"To sticking together, no matter the apocalypse."

"To our team."

We clink. The sound rings out across the garden, then fades into the sky.

• • • • •

WHEN I GET back to my hotel at night, there's a written message waiting for me on my nightstand. I stare at it for a second before picking it up and holding it up to the light. It's a phone number left by the hotel concierge, plus a message asking me to call.

I check my phone again. In the quiet of the garden and the company of my teammates, I hadn't been looking at it at all. Now

I realize that I've missed a few calls from the same number. I dial it, then walk over to my window and hold it up to my ear.

A woman's voice comes on the other end. "Miss Chen?" she says.

"Who's asking?" I reply.

"I'm Divya Kapoor, the new CEO of Henka Games."

I stand up a little straighter. It's the woman I'd seen at the Supreme Court. "Yes?"

There's a brief, embarrassed pause on the other end. "Miss Chen, on behalf of Henka Games, I would like to apologize to you for everything that has happened. As you know, Hideo's actions were not revealed to everyone in the studio, and I am as shocked as the rest of the world over the allegations. It is because of your help that we have avoided sheer catastrophe. We owe you a great deal."

I listen to her quietly. It wasn't so long ago that I'd walked into Henka Games feeling like a complete outcast. "You called me just to say that Henka Games is sorry?" I say, then immediately wince. I hadn't meant my words to come out so accusatory. Some things never change, I guess.

"There is something else," Divya adds. She hesitates again before going on. "We are in the process of dismantling all that's wrong with the NeuroLink. But we also want to find a way to rebuild it."

To rebuild it.

"There are too many things that rely on the NeuroLink," she continues. "Taking it down entirely is not only an option that the global economy cannot bear—it is also impossible. This is not a technology that is just going to disappear, not even after what had happened. Someone else will make it."

I swallow as I listen to her describe the various things attached to the system. In Tokyo alone, thousands of businesses revolving around the NeuroLink have shuttered. Companies that create and sell virtual goods. Educational services. Universities. That's not even including all the businesses that relied on the Warcross games themselves, which are completely gone without the NeuroLink. But that's not even the heart of what Divya is saying.

Once technology has been made, it cannot be unmade. What Hideo had built is going to keep existing. Someone else will invent new virtual and augmented reality that can do the same things as the original NeuroLink. Maybe even go beyond it. Someone else *will* fill the hole that the NeuroLink left.

The question is who. And what they will do with it.

"We need to rebuild the system, but as you know, we cannot rebuild it to be the same as it always was. It will be done under the supervision of governments and the people, out in the open. It will be done honestly."

"And what does this have to do with me?" I ask.

Divya takes a deep breath. "I'm calling to see if you might be interested in helping us put together a team. We want to target its flaws, cut out the bad, and make something better from it. And you . . . well, you're the reason we found those flaws in the first place."

Rebuild the NeuroLink. Rebuild Warcross.

My entire goal had been to stop Hideo, and that meant stopping the NeuroLink. I'd had my life transformed and turned upside down because of Warcross, and I'd just said my good-byes to my teammates, had braced myself to head back to America without any idea of what I would do next.

But my second thought . . .

Just because the system was flawed doesn't mean it isn't worth existing. Like anything else, it's a tool that depends on those who use it. It has changed millions of lives for the better. And maybe now, with the right minds behind it and the awareness that comes with experience, we can make the NeuroLink into a better version of itself.

Every problem has a solution. But after every solution, there's a new problem to tackle, some new challenge to take on. You don't stop after you solve one thing. You keep going, you find a new way and a new path, try to do better and create better. Tearing something down isn't the end; doing something great, or better, something *right*, is. Or maybe there isn't such a thing as an end goal at all. You accomplish something, and then you shift, ready to accomplish the next. You keep solving one problem after another until you change the world.

Up until now, my life's goals have been limited to stopping what's wrong. Now I'm being handed the chance to participate in another side of fixing things: the chance to create something.

At my long pause, Divya clears her throat. "Well," she says, her voice still reverent and apologetic, "I'll give you some time to think it over. Should you be interested, don't hesitate to reach out to me directly. We're ready to hit the ground running with you. And if you're not, we understand, too. You've done more than anyone ever should."

We exchange a brief farewell. Then she hangs up, and I'm left standing in my room, my phone clutched at my side as I stare out at the nightscape beyond my window.

My phone buzzes again. I look down at the incoming call.

Then I put it on speaker, and a familiar voice fills the air. Once, it was a voice that filled me with terror. Now . . .

"Well," Zero says. "What are you going to say?"

I smile a little. "You were listening in on all of that?"

"I am everywhere online at the same time," he replies. "It's not hard for me to hear a phone conversation."

"I know. You're just going to have to learn some boundaries."

"You're still glad I heard it," he says. "I can tell in your voice."

He sounds almost like he used to—but there is something human in his words now. The part of him made intact by Sasuke's mind.

After the institute was raided by police, and Hideo and I were taken from the panic room, after Zero's suit went missing and all the news broke, rumors began to circulate online that an armored figure occasionally appeared in people's accounts. That someone was leaving cryptic markers wherever he went, signatures with a zero in them. That Jax, when given access to a phone or computer, chats with someone who doesn't exist.

There's nothing to substantiate any of it, of course. Most think it could just be the work of online pranksters and fledgling hackers.

But *I* know. As data, as information breathing between wires and electricity, Zero—Sasuke—lives on.

"Stop analyzing me," I reply.

"I'm not." He pauses. "You know you have my support, if you choose to join her."

"I may need it."

"Well?" This is the Sasuke part of his mind, bright and curious and kind. "What are you going to tell her, then?"

I start to smile. It widens until it turns into a grin. When I open my mouth to respond, my answer is unwavering.

"I'm in."

35

The front entrance of the Tokyo Metropolitan Police Headquarters is crowded with people this morning, just as it has been for weeks. As my car pulls up, people turn and start to gather around, their cameras and attention now pointed at me. I look out at the sea of faces. They're all still here because today is the day that Hideo will be moved from this place to start serving out his time.

Everyone is gathered here, hoping to hear some news. There's been no official announcement yet about his sentence.

Microphones are thrust in my direction as the car door opens, and shouts fill the air. I keep my head down as bodyguards push back the throngs to let me pass. I don't look up again until we've reached the inside of the building. There, I bow my head briefly to an officer and follow him up the elevators.

Someone greets me as I get off. "Chen-*san*," she says, bowing low to me in greeting. I return the gesture. "Please, follow me. We've been expecting you."

She takes me down a hall to an interrogation room with a long glass window. Along the outside wall stand half a dozen police officers, their faces turned sternly forward. It's as if they're guarding someone who is the most dangerous criminal in the world. Maybe they're right—through the window, I can see a familiar figure sitting alone at the table, waiting. It's Hideo.

They bow their heads at the sight of me, then open the door to let me in. When I step inside, he looks up and gives me a small smile that sends a rush of warmth through me.

I hadn't realized I missed him so much.

The room is small and plain. One wall has the glass window I'd seen from the outside, while its opposite wall is an enormous black screen that extends from ceiling to floor. In the center of the room is a single table with two chairs. Hideo is seated in one of those chairs now.

"Hey," I say as I take the seat across from him.

"Hey," he replies.

Everything about this moment should remind me of when I'd faced him at Henka Games as a small-time bounty hunter, anxious and awkward. Hideo looks as polished as ever; I'm opposite him, wondering what he's thinking.

This time, though, a set of silver handcuffs binds Hideo's hands together. His side is still healing, and underneath his fitted shirt, I can see the telltale sign of bandages wrapped around his waist. I'm no longer dressed in my torn jeans and black hoodie— but in a sharp, tailored suit of my own. Hammie had helped me pull my hair up into a high bun. It's the looking-glass version of our first meeting.

There are also other differences that matter. He looks tired, but his eyes are alert, his expression more open than I've ever seen it.

We search the other's gaze. He notices the change in my

appearance, but he doesn't comment on it. Instead, he says, "I didn't think you'd come to see me."

"Why's that?"

He smiles a little, amused and shy. "I thought you were already headed back to the States."

There's something broken in his words that makes me sad. I think of the way he'd turned his face up to me in the panic room, what he'd murmured to me when he thought he was uttering his dying words. I think of his arms around his little brother, his words through his tears. *I'm sorry I couldn't save you.*

Now, after everything we've gone through, he's hesitant to believe that we could ever find our way back to our beginning again. He is ready for his punishment.

I clear my throat and say, "Are you going home today?"

He nods. Hideo may technically have a prison term, but there's no way the police can keep someone of his status in a regular penitentiary, with all of the attention and disruption he would bring. Like other prominent people of the world, he's going to be serving out his sentence under house arrest, with a small army of police around his property and the government keeping a close watch on what he does.

Hideo shakes his head, and for a moment he looks idly toward the glass window, lost in thought. I don't need to say anything to know that he's thinking about his brother. "We were never well matched, were we? There's no version of our story that wouldn't have been doomed from the start."

"If I were to do this all again, Hideo, I'd still have to hunt you down."

"I know."

I'm quiet for a second. "It doesn't mean I don't still have feelings for you."

He turns to study me, and all I can think about is what the world would be like if Taylor had never taken an interest in his brother. If my father had never died young and I hadn't been so desperate for money. How did this chain of events end with me sitting here across from Hideo, our positions of power flipped, the question of *what if* hanging in the air?

"I'm sorry, Emika," he says. "Truly." And the pinch in his eyes, the wince he tries to hide, tells me he's being sincere.

I take a deep breath. "Ms. Kapoor called me. The new CEO of Henka Games. They're going to rebuild the NeuroLink and have invited me on board. I've accepted her offer."

At first, I can't tell how Hideo feels about this news. Surprised? Resigned? Maybe he always guessed that the NeuroLink couldn't die completely, that someone else would eventually take the reins. I don't know how he feels about that someone turning out to be me.

But he just looks at me now. "She's smart to tap you for it. You know as much about it as anyone who has ever worked on developing the system."

"I've been tasked with putting together a team to help rebuild the NeuroLink."

"Have you picked this team yet?"

"I didn't come here today just to see you."

Silence. He lifts a skeptical eyebrow at me.

I nod without a word.

"Emika, I've been sentenced for what I did. You were hunting me yourself."

"It doesn't mean I don't think you still made something remarkable." I lean forward against the table, then glance toward the black screen that sits flush against the entire side of the wall. "Play the footage."

As Hideo looks over at it, the screen turns on.

It is a sequence of videos, news and memories from years past.

There's a snippet from a documentary about an old woman trapped in an unresponsive body who was able to use the NeuroLink to communicate with her family. There's an interview where a journalist travels to a war-torn border, where young refugees are using the glasses to continue their school lessons or talk with separated relatives. There is the inside of a children's hospital that Hideo had once visited, where kids could travel down corridors that looked like fantastical worlds instead of white halls, where their rooms were filled with magical creatures that made them laugh. Alzheimer's patients able to rely on the NeuroLink's recordings of their memories. People trapped in a burning building who could use the NeuroLink's grid to find their way out. The videos are endless.

Hideo watches them without a word. Maybe there will always be a weight on his shoulders, the guilt of what he'd done wrong, the loss of his brother. But he doesn't look away from the videos, and when they finish, he doesn't speak.

"Hideo," I say gently, "you changed the world forever when you created the NeuroLink. And even though no one is perfect, it doesn't mean we don't listen. Become better. There are a million good things left to do, and they can be done responsibly, with thought and respect, without taking away from what's wonderful about the world."

He looks at me. "I don't know if I still deserve a part in all of this," he says.

I shake my head. "It doesn't mean you won't be closely watched. Or carefully guarded. You won't be able to work directly on anything, or write code, or be an official part of the company. There are going to be a lot of rules. I can promise you that." I meet his eyes. "But you know the NeuroLink more intimately than any-one does. Before it was the world's, it was yours. So I still believe there's value in your advice, that we can benefit from your knowl-edge and your help."

The spark in Hideo's eyes now is the one I recognize from his early interviews. It's the creator's gleam, that magical thing that keeps you awake at night, wide-eyed with potential and promise.

"You once said that you were tired of the horror in the world," I say. "Well, so am I. We can still find a way to fight it, the right way. We can find a way to do this together."

Hideo doesn't say anything for a long time. Then, he smiles. It's not his secret smile or a suspicious one. Instead, it's every-thing I could have hoped for. Genuine, honest, full of warmth, like the little boy he'd once been, sitting by lamplight in his father's repair shop and piecing together something that would change everything forever. It's the smile I used to have when my father waved me over and showed me how he stitched delicate pieces of lace, one by one, onto the train of a dress. The same smile from when I stayed hunched over my laptop in the foster home, feeling in control of my life for the very first time.

Maybe we can find a way to move forward, on the same page. We can find a way to be together.

I lean forward into this looking-glass version of our very first meeting. My steady gaze meets his.

"So, I have a job offer for you," I say to him. "Would you like to hear more?"

Emika Chen has accepted the role of CEO for Henka Games. She has pledged the majority of her fortune to a trust dedicated to funding the creations of young women from difficult circumstances. . . . Chen was seen holding hands with Hideo Tanaka as they left a local restaurant early last week, fueling speculation on their relationship.

—*TOKYO LIFESTYLE MAGAZINE*

Acknowledgments

——

If *Warcross* was the easy child, *Wildcard* was the one who always managed to end up in the principal's office. I stayed up many a late night and predawn morning to wrestle this story into shape. It turned into a book I'm deeply proud of, but I could never have done it without the help of an entire team of brilliant people.

Kristin Nelson is always the first person I think of for all my books, but particularly so for *Wildcard* and *Warcross*. I will never forget how enthusiastic and encouraging you were for these books from day one, and given how close Emika's story is to both my heart and my interests, I'll forever be grateful to you. Thank you for believing.

To my incredible editors, the inimitable Kate Meltzer, Jen Besser, and Jen Klonsky—thank you so much for your wisdom and your brilliant feedback, for pulling me through this book's murky waters, and for being such a joy to work with. Anne Heausler, I truly don't know what I'd do without your sharp eye and guiding hand. I dedicate the yacht scene to you!

As ever, Putnam Children's, Puffin, and Penguin Young Readers, you all are a dream team come true. Theresa and Wes, thank you for *Wildcard*'s absolutely stunning cover; Marisa Russell, Shanta Newlin, Erin Berger, Andrea Cruise, Dana Leydig, Summer Ogata, Felicity Vallence, and Venessa Carson—I'm endlessly grateful for everything you do!

Kassie, I can't thank you enough for being at my side and championing this series from the start. I'm so lucky to be able to work with you.

To Tahereh Mafi, one of my favorite people in the world: you were the first to read *Wildcard*, and you gave me encouragement exactly when I needed it. To Sabaa Tahir and to our diabolical pedicure of story woes, where you helped me figure out Zero's entire arc! I will forever associate nail salons with your brilliance. To Amie Kaufman: every time I need a shoulder to lean on, you are always there. And, of course, to Leigh Bardugo, fiercest of her name, who inspired Jax's silver hair and witch-black lipstick. Zero would hack any system for you.

To Primo, story partner and best husband, who has always been the first eyes on this series and who knows more about it than anyone else. To my family and friends, for all your love and support.

Finally, to my readers. You all inspire me daily. Do great things and challenge the world.

TURN THE PAGE FOR A SNEAK PEEK OF

THE
KINGDOM OF BACK

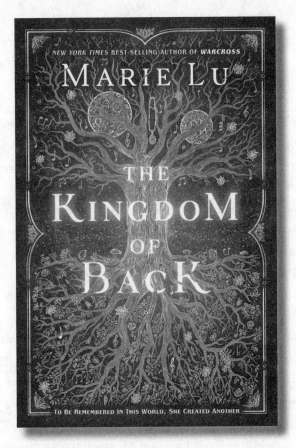

Text copyright © 2020 by Xiwei Lu

I AM GOING TO TELL YOU A STORY YOU ALREADY KNOW. But listen carefully, because within it is one you have never heard before.

The story you know is about a boy named Wolfgang Amadeus Mozart.

You recognize his name. Even if you do not, you know him well, because you have heard his music all your life.

He was here and then gone, a brief, brilliant shard of life, a flash of stardust that ignited the sky. I knew his mind better than anyone else, understood its every winding path and quiet corner as deeply as my own. I remember everything about the way his tiny hand fit into mine, the sweep of his long lashes against his baby cheeks, the expression he would turn on me in the darkness of our shared bedchamber, his wide, fragile eyes glittering, always dreaming of some faraway place. I will tell you how the space in his small chest held so much joy and beauty that, if he wasn't careful, it might all spill out into the streets, drenching the world in too much light. He knew this, and so he held back, made rigid symmetry of the unimaginable so that the world could understand it, and for that his music became all the more sublime.

The story you have never heard is about the sister who composed beside him. In a way, you know her too, for you have also heard her music all your life. She is not the stardust but the steady wick, the one who burns low and quiet. You do not see her by the way she lights up the sky but by the way she steadies herself against the darkness, alone, at night, beside a window while the world sleeps around her. She writes when others do not see. By morning, none would know that her flame had ever been there. Her music is the ghost in the air. You know it because it reminds you of something you cannot quite grasp. You wonder where you have heard it before.

The story you already know is set in a real land, full of real kings and castles and courts. There are long carriage rides and summer concerts and a little boy in a royal coat.

The story you have never heard is set in a dream of fog and stars, faery princelings and queens of the night. It is about the Kingdom of Back, and the girl who found it.

I am the sister, the other Mozart. And her story is mine.

KEEP READING FOR AN EXCERPT FROM MARIE LU'S *NEW YORK TIMES* BESTSELLER

Text copyright © 2011 by Xiwei Lu

DAY

MY MOTHER THINKS I'M DEAD.

Obviously I'm *not* dead, but it's safer for her to think so.

At least twice a month, I see my Wanted poster flashed on the JumboTrons scattered throughout downtown Los Angeles. It looks out of place up there. Most of the pictures on the screens are of happy things: smiling children standing under a bright blue sky, tourists posing before the Golden Gate Ruins, Republic commercials in neon colors. There's also anti-Colonies propaganda. *"The Colonies want our land,"* the ads declare. *"They want what they don't have. Don't let them conquer your homes! Support the cause!"*

Then there's my criminal report. It lights up the Jumbo-Trons in all its multicolored glory:

WANTED BY THE REPUBLIC
FILE NO: 462178-3233 "DAY"

WANTED FOR ASSAULT, ARSON, THEFT,
DESTRUCTION OF MILITARY PROPERTY,
AND HINDERING THE WAR EFFORT
200,000 REPUBLIC NOTES FOR
INFORMATION LEADING TO ARREST

They always have a different photo running alongside the report. One time it was a boy with glasses and a head full of thick copper curls. Another time it was a boy with black eyes and no hair at all. Sometimes I'm black, sometimes white, sometimes olive or brown or yellow or red or whatever else they can think of.

In other words, the Republic has no idea what I look like. They don't seem to know much of *anything* about me, except that I'm young and that when they run my fingerprints they don't find a match in their databases. That's why they hate me, why I'm not the most *dangerous* criminal in the country, but the most *wanted*. I make them look bad.

It's early evening, but it's already pitch-black outside, and the JumboTrons' reflections are visible in the street's puddles. I sit on a crumbling window ledge three stories up, hidden from view behind rusted steel beams. This used to be an apartment complex, but it's fallen into disrepair. Broken lanterns and glass shards litter the floor of this room, and paint is peeling from every wall. In one corner, an old portrait of the Elector Primo lies faceup on the ground. I wonder who used to live here—no one's cracked enough to let their portrait of the Elector sit discarded on the floor like that.

My hair, as usual, is tucked inside an old newsboy cap. My eyes are fixed on the small one-story house across the road. My hands fiddle with the pendant tied around my neck.

Tess leans against the room's other window, watching me closely. I'm restless tonight and, as always, she can sense it.

The plague has hit the Lake sector hard. In the glow of the

JumboTrons, Tess and I can see the soldiers at the end of the street as they inspect each home, their black capes shiny and worn loose in the heat. Each of them wears a gas mask. Sometimes when they emerge, they mark a house by painting a big red X on the front door. No one enters or leaves the home after that—at least, not when anyone's looking.

"Still don't see them?" Tess whispers. Shadows conceal her expression.

In an attempt to distract myself, I'm piecing together a makeshift slingshot out of old PVC pipes. "They haven't eaten dinner. They haven't sat down by the table in hours." I shift and stretch out my bad knee.

"Maybe they're not home?"

I shoot Tess an irritated glance. She's trying to console me, but I'm not in the mood. "A lamp's lit. Look at those candles. Mom would never waste candles if no one was home."

Tess moves closer. "We should leave the city for a couple weeks, yeah?" She tries to keep her voice calm, but the fear is there. "Soon the plague will have blown through, and you can come back to visit. We have more than enough money for two train tickets."

I shake my head. "One night a week, remember? Just let me check up on them one night a week."

"Yeah. You've been coming here *every* night this week."

"I just want to make sure they're okay."

"What if you get sick?"

"I'll take my chances. And you didn't have to come with me. You could've waited for me back in Alta."

Tess shrugs. "*Somebody* has to keep an eye on you." Two years younger than me—although sometimes she sounds old enough to be my caretaker.

We look on in silence as the soldiers draw closer to my family's house. Every time they stop at a home, one soldier pounds on the door while a second stands next to him with his gun drawn. If no one opens the door within ten seconds, the first soldier kicks it in. I can't see them once they rush inside, but I know the drill: a soldier will draw a blood sample from each family member, then plug it into a handheld reader and check for the plague. The whole process takes ten minutes.

I count the houses between where the soldiers are now and where my family lives. I'll have to wait another hour before I know their fate.

A shriek echoes from the other end of the street. My eyes dart toward the sound and my hand whips to the knife sheathed at my belt. Tess sucks in her breath.

It's a plague victim. She must've been deteriorating for months, because her skin is cracked and bleeding everywhere, and I find myself wondering how the soldiers could have missed this one during previous inspections. She stumbles around for a while, disoriented, then charges forward, only to trip and fall to her knees. I glance back toward the soldiers. They see her now. The soldier with the drawn weapon approaches, while the eleven others stay where they are and look on. One plague victim isn't much of a threat. The soldier lifts his gun and aims. A volley of sparks engulfs the infected woman.

She collapses, then goes still. The soldier rejoins his comrades.

I wish we could get our hands on one of the soldiers' guns. A pretty weapon like that doesn't cost much on the market—480 Notes, less than a stove. Like all guns, it has precision, guided by magnets and electric currents, and can accurately shoot a target three blocks away. It's tech stolen from the Colonies, Dad once said, although of course the Republic would never tell you that. Tess and I could buy five of them if we wanted. . . . Over the years we've learned to stockpile the extra money we steal and stash it away for emergencies. But the real problem with having a gun isn't the expense. It's that it's so easy to trace back to you. Each gun has a sensor on it that reports its user's hand shape, thumbprints, and location. If that didn't give me away, nothing would. So I'm left with my homemade weapons, PVC pipe slingshots, and other trinkets.

"They found another one," Tess says. She squints to get a better look.

I look down and see the soldiers spill from another house. One of them shakes a can of spray paint and draws a giant red X on the door. I know that house. The family that lives there once had a little girl my age. My brothers and I played with her when we were younger—freeze tag and street hockey with iron pokers and crumpled paper.

Tess tries to distract me by nodding at the cloth bundle near my feet. "What'd you bring them?"

I smile, then reach down to untie the cloth. "Some of the stuff we saved up this week. It'll make for a nice celebration once they pass the inspection." I dig through the little pile of goodies inside the bundle, then hold up a used pair of goggles. I check them again to make sure there are no cracks in the glass. "For John. An early birthday gift." My older brother turns nineteen later this week. He works fourteen-hour shifts in the neighborhood plant's friction stoves and always comes home rubbing his eyes from the smoke. These goggles were a lucky steal from a military supply shipment.

I put them down and shuffle through the rest of the stuff. It's mostly tins of meat and potato hash I stole from an airship's cafeteria, and an old pair of shoes with intact soles. I wish I could be in the room with all of them when I deliver this stuff. But John's the only one who knows I'm alive, and he's promised not to tell Mom or Eden.

Eden turns ten in two months, which means that in two months he'll have to take the Trial. I failed my own Trial when I was ten. That's why I worry about Eden, because even though he's easily the smartest of us three boys, he thinks a lot like I do. When I finished my Trial, I felt so sure of my answers that I didn't even bother to watch them grade it. But then the admins ushered me into a corner of the Trial stadium with a bunch of other kids. They stamped something on my test and stuffed me onto a train headed downtown. I didn't get to take anything except the pendant I wore around my neck. I didn't even get to say good-bye.

Several different things could happen after you take the Trial.

You get a perfect score—1500 points. No one's *ever* gotten this—well, except for some kid a few years ago who the military made a goddy fuss over. Who knows what happens to someone with a score that high? Probably lots of money and power, yeah?

You score between a 1450 and a 1499. Pat yourself on the back because you'll get instant access to six years of high school and then four at the top universities in the Republic: Drake, Stanford, and Brenan. Then Congress hires you and you make lots of money. Joy and happiness follow. At least according to the Republic.

You get a good score, somewhere between 1250 and 1449 points. You get to continue on to high school, and then you're assigned to a college. Not bad.

You squeak by with a score between 1000 and 1249. Congress bars you from high school. You join the poor, like my family. You'll probably either drown while working the water turbines or get steamed to death in the power plants.

You fail.

It's almost always the slum-sector kids who fail. If you're in this unlucky category, the Republic sends officials to your family's home. They make your parents sign a contract giving the government full custody over you. They say that you've been sent away to the Republic's labor camps and that your family will not see you again. Your parents have to nod and agree. A few even celebrate, because the Republic gives them one thousand Notes as a condolence gift. Money and one less mouth to feed? What a thoughtful government.

Except this is all a lie. An inferior child with bad genes is no use to the country. If you're lucky, Congress will let you die without first sending you to the labs to be examined for imperfections.

Five houses remain. Tess sees the worry in my eyes and puts a hand on my forehead. "One of your headaches coming on?"

"No. I'm okay." I peer in the open window at my mother's house, then catch my first glimpse of a familiar face. Eden walks by, then peeks out the window at the approaching soldiers and points some handmade metal contraption at them. Then he ducks back inside and disappears from view. His curls flash white-blond in the flickering lamplight. Knowing him, he probably built that gadget to measure how far away someone is, or something like that.

"He looks thinner," I mutter.

"He's alive and walking around," Tess replies. "I'd say that's a win."

Minutes later, we see John and my mother wander past the window, deep in conversation. John and I look pretty similar, although he's grown a little stockier from long days at the plant. His hair, like most who live in our sector, hangs down past his shoulders and is tied back into a simple tail. His vest is smudged with red clay. I can tell Mom's scolding him for something or other, probably for letting Eden peek out the window. She bats John's hand away when a bout of her chronic coughing hits her. I let out a breath. So. At least all three of them are healthy enough to walk. Even if one of them is infected, it's early enough that they'll still have a chance to recover.

I can't stop imagining what will happen if the soldiers mark my mother's door. My family will stand frozen in our living room long after the soldiers have left. Then Mom will put on her usual brave face, only to sit up through the night, quietly wiping tears away. In the morning, they'll start receiving small rations of food and water and simply wait to recover. Or die.

My mind wanders to the stash of stolen money that Tess and I have hidden. Twenty-five hundred Notes. Enough to feed us for months . . . but not enough to buy my family vials of plague medicine.

The minutes drag on. I tuck my slingshot away and play a few rounds of Rock, Paper, Scissors with Tess. (I don't know why, but she's crazy good at this game.) I glance several times at my mother's window, but don't see anyone. They must have gathered near the door, ready to open it as soon as they hear a fist against the wood.

And then the time comes. I lean forward on the ledge, so far that Tess grips my arm to make sure I don't topple to the ground. The soldiers pound on the door. My mother opens it immediately, lets the soldiers in, and then closes it. I strain to hear voices, footsteps, anything that might come from my house. The sooner this is all over, the sooner I can sneak my gifts to John.

The silence drags on. Tess whispers, "No news is good news, right?"

"Very funny."

I count off the seconds in my head. One minute passes. Then two, then four, and then finally, ten minutes.

Then fifteen minutes. Twenty minutes.

I look at Tess. She just shrugs. "Maybe their reader's broken," she suggests.

Thirty minutes pass. I don't dare move from my vigil. I'm afraid something will happen so quickly that I'll miss it if I blink. My fingers tap rhythmically against the hilt of my knife.

Forty minutes. Fifty minutes. An hour.

"Something's wrong," I whisper.

Tess purses her lips. "You don't know that."

"Yes I do. What could possibly take this long?"

Tess opens her mouth to reply, but before she can say anything, the soldiers are exiting my house, single file, expressionless. Finally, the last soldier shuts the door behind him and reaches for something tucked at his waist. I suddenly feel dizzy. I know what's coming.

The soldier reaches up and sprays one long, red, diagonal line on our door. Then he sprays another line, making an X.

I curse silently under my breath and start to turn away—

—but then the soldier does something unexpected, something I've never seen before.

He sprays a third, vertical line on my mother's door, cutting the X in half.

HE IS A
LEGEND
SHE IS A
PRODIGY
WHO WILL BE
CHAMPION
?

WWW.LEGENDTHESERIES.COM

WITNESS THE RISE
OF A NEW VILLAIN...